...and give in to her greatest desires?

Praise for *New York Times* bestselling author
CELESTE BRADLEY
and her previous novels and series

ROGUE IN MY ARMS

"Bradley doesn't disappoint with the second in her Runaway Brides trilogy, which is certain to have readers laughing and crying. Her characters leap off the page, especially little Melody, the precocious 'heroine,' and her three fathers. There's passion, adventure, nonstop action, and secrets that make the pages fly by."

—*Romantic Times BOOKreviews*

"When it comes to crafting fairy tale–like, wonderfully escapist historicals, Bradley is unrivaled, and the second addition to her Runaway Brides trilogy cleverly blends madcap adventure and sexy romance." —*Booklist*

DEVIL IN MY BED

"From its unconventional prologue to its superb conclusion, every page of the first in Bradley's Runaway Brides series is perfection and joy. Tinged with humor that never overshadows the poignancy and peopled with remarkable characters (especially the precocious Melody who will steal your heart), this one's a keeper."

—*Romantic Times BOOKreviews*

MORE . . .

"Part romantic comedy, part romantic suspense, and wholly entertaining, *Devil in My Bed* is a delight!"
—*Romance Reviews Today*

"Laughter, tears, drama, suspense, and a heartily deserved happily-ever-after."   —*All About Romance*

DUKE MOST WANTED

"Passionate and utterly memorable. Witty dialogue and fantastic imagery round out a novel that is a must-have for any Celeste Bradley fan."   —*Romance Junkies*

"A marvelous, delightful, emotional conclusion to Bradley's trilogy. Readers have been eagerly waiting to see what happens next, and they've also been anticipating a nonstop, beautifully crafted story, which Bradley delivers in spades."
—*Romantic Times BOOKreviews*

THE DUKE NEXT DOOR

"This spectacular, fast-paced, sexy romance will have you in laughter and tears. With delightful characters seeking love and a title, [this] heartfelt romance will make readers sigh with pleasure." *—Romantic Times BOOKreviews*

"Not only fun and sexy but relentlessly pulls at the heartstrings. Ms. Bradley has set the bar quite high with this one!" *—Romance Readers Connection*

DESPERATELY SEEKING A DUKE

"A humorous romp of marriage mayhem that's a love-and-laughter treat, tinged with heated sensuality and tenderness. [A] winning combination." *—Romantic Times BOOKreviews*

"A tale of lies and treachery where true love overcomes all." *—Romance Junkies*

When She Said I Do

CELESTE BRADLEY

St. Martin's Paperbacks

This is a work of fiction. All of the characters, organizations, and events portrayed in this novel are either products of the author's imagination or are used fictitiously.

WHEN SHE SAID I DO

Copyright © 2013 by Celeste Bradley.

For information address St. Martin's Press, 175 Fifth Avenue, New York, NY 10010.

ISBN: 978-1-250-01612-6

Printed in the United States of America

St. Martin's Paperbacks edition / February 2013

St. Martin's Paperbacks are published by St. Martin's Press, 175 Fifth Avenue, New York, NY 10010.

10 9 8 7 6 5 4 3 2 1

This book is dedicated to my dear friend and partner-in-crime Susan Donovan. The ability to chase down pickpockets in Barcelona is only one of her many superpowers!

Acknowledgments

In order to complete this book, I needed help from many people. From brewers of coffee to deliverers of pizza, from Wikipedia (don't forget to donate!) to TEDTalks, but most especially from the following people: Darbi Gill, Grace Bradley, Hannah Bradley Brazil, Cindy Tharp, Susan Donovan, Monique Patterson & Holly Blanck from St. Martin's Press, and always my dear friend and agent, Irene Goodman.

With such amazing women at my back, how can I do anything but succeed?

Chapter 1

COTSWOLDS, ENGLAND, 1816

Well, isn't this simply lovely?

The icy river water rushed into the carriage, sweeping Miss Calliope Worthington from her seat and crashing her into the tilting ceiling of the contraption before towing her out through the opposite door. Gasping at the shocking chill of the water, she choked on froth and mud and terror.

The river tore one of her shoes from her dangling feet. Callie closed her eyes as she clung desperately to the leather hand loop that had dangled annoyingly over her head for the entire journey from her home in London to this dark, flooded Cotswolds bridge.

The other hand was fisted into the back of the coat of her mother, Iris, who had both arms wrapped around Callie's stout, unconscious father, Archie.

Callie threw back her head and screamed for her brother. *"Dade!"*

At last the grand house loomed up in the dark before them, the fine Cotswolds limestone seeming to glow in the moonlight. No one answered the booming summons as they pounded on the vast oak door. Calliope helped her brother Daedalus ease their father's unconscious body through the unlocked portal and through the dark chill house while Mama followed toting the single small bag they'd managed to recover. No one interrupted their progress through the entrance hall to a small salon.

As Calliope helped her mother clear the dustcovers from a pair of sofas, her heart leaped in relief as her father began to mutter fretfully as he rose to awareness.

Dade turned to her. "Callie, I should go help Morgan with the horses."

The team, elderly and panicked and quite unused to being swept off bridges by icy snowmelt, had managed to entangle themselves thoroughly in their broken harness. Morgan, the Worthingtons' driver and general manservant, had elected to stay behind on the riverbank until the horses had calmed.

Callie helped Dade bundle up against the chill though they had nothing dry but a few musty lap rugs found folded up within the window seat. For herself, she turned a dustcover into something of a toga, and hung her dress to dry by the hearth. Then she bent to make a fire by use of the tinderbox on the mantel.

Once Dade had left and Mama had subsided onto the opposite sofa, gazing worriedly at her husband, Callie had a moment to truly examine her surroundings.

It was a very fine house. Grand even, although one could hardly apply such a word to such terrible house-keeping. Really, some people had no respect for their things.

"Mama—" But Mama had drifted off, soothed by the fire and her husband's even snoring. Calliope brushed a lock of silvering hair from her sleeping mother's brow, then tugged her makeshift canvas wrapper more tightly about herself. Her gown still dripped on the hearth, like her mother's and several items of her father's.

Mama and Papa slept like exhausted children on the paired sofas, now slanted toward the glowing coals heaped in the hearth. If she liked, Calliope could join them in rest, curling up upon a thick albeit dusty rug before the welcome heat.

Or she could satisfy her curiosity as she searched the house for something better for them all.

First, small candlestick in hand, she found the kitchens, situated where most kitchens were—belowstairs in the rear of the fine house. She blinked in surprise at the wealth of hung meat and cheese stored in the vast larder. Baskets of root vegetables sat below the stocked shelves. All things that would keep, to be sure, but why so much in a house where no one had apparently resided for years?

Well, perhaps the owners were on the way even now. Surely they would not begrudge a stranded family a few bites of simple food? Calliope prepared a heaping plate for her mother and another for Dade when he returned with Morgan. Thick slices of salty ham and creamy white cheese kept her own hunger at bay as she carved a bit of cured beef into a pot with water and vegetables to create a soothing broth for her injured father.

She returned to the salon and left the pot of broth to thicken by the fire. She checked Mama's brow but her mother slept deeply and without any sign of fever or chill. She squeezed Papa's hand and he grumbled and pulled away, a lovable grump even in sleep.

After lighting the fine silver candelabra from the chimneypiece and leaving it in the front window to ease Dade's journey "home," Callie could think of nothing more to do. Restlessly, she tightened her coarse wrapper over her still damp shift and took up her little candle.

Soundless in bare feet, she drifted through the first

floor of the house. It was an unworthy thought perhaps, but she reveled in the novel sensation of being completely alone. Her family was large and loving—if sometimes maddening—but she was never, ever, *alone*.

With seven outrageous siblings and two even more outrageous parents all crammed into the comfortable but shabby house in London, Callie could scarcely recall the last time she'd walked in silence and solitude. Surely it had been years.

And now this lovely house lay before her, empty rooms waiting like a box of bonbons to be unwrapped by no one but her! There was a spacious dining room with a long, grand table fit to seat half the House of Lords, two entirely different but pretty parlors, a music room with piano and a looming, cloth-covered shape that could only be a grand harp, and a library that might have been impressive had not the books been coated in a layer of dust too thick to read the titles through.

It was not the vast, endless mausoleum she had first thought. In fact, if one squinted a bit and imagined clean, jewel-toned carpets and polished woodwork, it would be a most cheerful and welcoming hall. She shuddered and brushed a dangling cobweb from her cheek as she pursued her curiosity up the gracefully curving stair and into the upper gallery. Her own home might be furnished in things well past their best years, but it was also, due to her own industry and the ancient housekeeper's tutelage, quite spotless.

Well, except for that odd stain in the parlor, where the twins had spilled something nasty and tried to destroy the evidence by dissolving it with something yet nastier . . .

In the spacious, elegant gallery, silvery light poured through the tall windows along one wall and carved the long room into boxes of light and dark, only slightly blurred by her single flame. Calliope moved into one of the window casements and gazed out at a night turned from stormy nightmare to moonlit dream. She could see the bank of drained clouds moving aside to allow a nearly full moon to spill over her where she stood.

She felt the unwelcome sensation of a string pulled by fate somewhere in the weave of her life. What if they had roused at the inn half an hour earlier this morning? Or had left half an hour later? Either they might have passed over the wooden bridge long before it suffered damage in the flood or they might have simply driven up to it, seen it washed away, and turned safely back.

Yet she must remember to be grateful for the health of her family. It was lucky for them all that Mama had somehow spotted this dark house set back so far from the road.

Callie smiled at the grand space before her and began to run lightly down it in her bare feet, guarding her small candle flame with one hand. Laughing, she curtsied to a very grand old lady in a somber portrait. Some women had no sense of humor. Callie gave the old witch a cheeky salute and spun away, singing just to hear her voice fill the gallery. Just her own voice, alone.

"'O merry maids do come afore, and let thy feet be dancing . . .'"

Ren Porter, recluse and cynic—*and don't forget monster*—had been drunk even before the storm began. He hadn't noticed its arrival and he cared little for its departure, save that he favored his house silent and still.

Draped on a chair before the hearth in his bedchamber— well, perhaps it was bit of a reach to call it "his" bed-chamber. It was merely the latest in a long line. When one room became too fouled by smoke and crumbs and empty bottles, Ren simply moved one door down the seemingly endless hall to clean sheets and clean shirts.

It was his bloody house, wasn't it?

His house, his fire, and his wine cellar, all conveniently provided just when he'd needed it most by an elderly cousin Ren barely remembered.

Feeling unusually mellow due to extreme use of the aforementioned wine cellar, Ren almost tipped his bottle to that cousin, who now doubtless watched the ruination of his fine estate from above—until Ren remembered that he didn't believe in an above. Or a below.

There was plenty of hell to be found, right here on earth.

So instead, he tipped the bottle to the departed storm, for leaving him in peace and silence—

And singing.

Now, Ren had experienced a few fever dreams and many drunken hallucinations, but never had one of these visions included the light lilting voice of an angel echoing through his hallowed hermit halls.

Since the pain in his back and shoulder scarcely allowed any chair to give him comfort, it was no great sacrifice to give in to his curiosity and leave his room in search of that haunting melody. It wouldn't be the first time he tried to chase down an illusion. He'd once spent an entire night chasing a violet dog through the attic, so this hardly seemed odd at all.

The hall was dark but a feeble light shone from an open doorway down the hall. Angel light? Perhaps stealth was in order. Angels didn't much care for monsters.

And he'd never managed to catch that damned dog . . .

Deep within the house, in a grand bedchamber clearly meant for the lady of the house, Callie found a small chest of jewels sitting on an ornate mirrored vanity. She set down her small candleholder so as to reflect in the mirror, doubling her light.

Her dancing had made her warm so she let the canvas wrapper fall to her feet, which freed her hands to run her fingers through the heaped baubles. Playfully she tried them all on, layering strands of rubies, emeralds, and pearls. Her reflection in the mirror was scandalous. Callie grinned.

A slight noise behind her brought a halt to her breathy song. What was that?

Callie frowned at her reflection. It must have been the candle flame guttering, but she almost believed she'd seen a shadow move behind her. That was silliness, of course. The house was empty but for Mama and Papa sleeping downstairs. Perhaps a draft pushing past the shuttered windows had fluttered a bed curtain, just there . . . in the corner of her vision.

Staring so hard she felt her eyes grow hot, she watched the room behind her, too breathless with tension to even turn around. It seemed safer to stay where she was, standing before the vanity, with the mirror to give her the light of two flames instead of just one.

Then a shadow parted from the others and moved toward her. She shivered. "Dade, don't play the fool." Her voice, meant to be sharp, came out a breathless gasp instead. Even as she spoke the words, she knew it wasn't her brother.

Turn. Turn and run. And scream.

She tried. She took one quick step to her right, prepared to spin on her heel and flee to the door. Her body came up against a solid mass and bounced back. Another swift step, this time to the left, only brought the edge of the vanity pressing to her hipbones once more.

Her throat closed in terror as she watched her own

candlelit image in the mirror be dwarfed by the towering darkness behind her. A shade, left alone in the house
to wander in mourning, or in anger.

But no, she had bounced off it as if she'd run full on
into the chest of a human man. According to legend, a
shade would have chilled her, overtaken her, perhaps
even drawn the life from her—but bounced her?

"I—don't—please—"

"Ah, but you do please."

Two hands emerged from the darkness and came
down to cover her shoulders. They were large and heavy,
hot on her bare skin, on the narrow shoulders of her chemise. The weight of them pinned her like a butterfly in a
collection, holding her there, standing before the vanity,
watching her doom come at her in a mirror.

"I name you thief, sweet angel."

Callie started at the deep voice.

"Or are you a wraith, sent to torment me with what I
can never have? Stealing is a crime. Crimes have penal-
ties, do they not?"

Then the hands slid inward, toward her neck, until
her throat disappeared behind them.

I am to die, then.

The ruby necklace slipped its catch, slithering down
almost between her breasts before being caught by one
of the hands. The hand hefted the jewels.

"Warm, for a wraith." The voice from behind her was
husky and rough, although its tones were cultured. It
was also a bit slurred. "Warm enough to heat the stones
whilst they glowed upon your skin."

She shivered as the hand drew the necklace away
from her and deposited it back into the open jewel chest
on the vanity. When she made to twist away, the hand
swiftly returned to hold her still, gentle but implacable,
hot and chilling at once.

The sapphire chain came next. This time the hands held the center stone to let the parted ends slither down beneath her chemise. When the skin-warmed silver hung dangling from her nipples, she realized how erect they were, pressing hard and high from beneath the thin batiste.

A warm exhalation upon the back of her neck told her she was not the only one to have seen. Her face flamed. As the hand holding the sapphire necklace left her to return its prize to the jewel chest, she tried to fold her arms over her chest.

"No." The heavy hands slid smoothly down to her elbows and gently pulled them back, parting her hands and forcing her back to arch. Her breasts jutted obscenely against the tightened chemise, her nipples crowning them like diamond-hard jewels, clearly visible beneath the worn fabric.

"That's better. This is *my* haunting, pretty wraith, and I wish to enjoy every moment of it."

The hands moved slowly back up her arms, eventually allowing her to relax her embarrassing stance, but she dared not try to cross her arms again.

Hot fingers, roughened but gentle, retrieved the earbobs from her lobes. He was only removing what was doubtless his own property, which she'd been very naughty to pilfer, yet as each piece of shimmering glory left her, she felt more and more naked.

"I'm sorry," she began. "I ought not to have—but if you would only let me exp—"

One large hand covered her mouth, wrapping clear across her face. She stiffened in terror, then began to struggle wildly.

One step forward was all it took for her captor to press her so firmly against the vanity that she was immobilized from the hips down. His large body pressed full against her back, flooding her with heat and fear and an intense awareness of being entirely at his mercy. She could see her own eyes, wide with shock in the mirror, then gazed higher to find that the shade had a face after all.

He was half in shadow still, the candlelight blocked by her body, so all that she could see was one eye, one slanting cheekbone, one side of a sculpted jaw. Dark hair fell long and unfettered against that unshaven cheek, shadowing his features until all she could see was that eye, dark and intense and perhaps a little mad.

Handsome. Dangerous. She'd never known a demon could be so beautiful.

Caught by that heated gaze, she didn't move again, nor try to scream around his repressive hand. After a moment, the hand slid from her mouth and wrapped loosely about her throat. She let it, feeling the heat of his palm sink into her flesh, gentled in spite of her fear.

The other hand slid down her arm to remove the diamond bracelet from her wrist. As it reached across her to deposit the jewelry into the case, his muscled arm brushed against her rigid nipples. Callie gasped at the sensations jolting through her at such shocking contact.

Never. Never, ever. She'd never been touched . . . there.

And you never will. Your time has passed, remember? A spinster's life, that's all there is before you.

He froze as well, his arm still crossing her body. Then, slowly, he pulled it back, dragging it intentionally sideways. His fine white sleeve tugged slightly at the paper-thin chemise, rubbing the fabric into delicate flesh so tight it ached.

A sound came out of Callie's throat. Part fear, part shock, part astonished, shivering awakening.

Never, ever.

She began to shiver now, her body caught in tremors beyond her ability to still. His arm dropped away. She closed her eyes tightly.

All he has done is take back his jewels. Perhaps he yet means me no harm.

"A virgin fantasy? Not my usual delusion, but one learns not to argue the point." His tone was soft, odd, as if she weren't even there.

"Seduction, then? Make her want me? Impossible. This is even worse than the damned dog . . ."

Callie's eyes squeezed shut more tightly. He thought she wished to be seduced? Yet what else was a man to think, to find a soaking-wet, half-naked girl in his rooms? Horror laced through her, building in her throat, unable to be released in a scream.

One shoulder of her chemise began to slip down, down . . .

She started, jerking in his grasp. "Shh," he whispered in her ear. "There's nothing to fear, sweet wraith. You are simply too lovely to remain concealed."

One half of Callie's mind was gibbering in panic, running about in tiny circles and waving mad hands in the air. The other half wondered at a man who seemed so determined to be gentle with a woman so entirely in his power.

She felt his arm go around her and then the other tiny sleeve fell halfway down her elbow. A tug on the fabric was all it took to drag the damp, clinging fabric to puddle at her waist, her arms trapped at the elbow by the sleeves. The chill in the room sent another shiver through her that seemed to culminate in her ever-hardening nipples.

She felt rather than heard him drag in a long, deep breath.

"Open your eyes."

Callie hesitated, then did as he commanded her in that

roughened voice. The image in the mirror was a wicked one, indeed. Her shoulders, her torso, her breasts, bare and ivory against the larger darkness of him behind her. The crumpled chemise, pinning her arms, made her look shameless, somehow almost worse than being naked.

She raised her gaze to her own eyes in the mirror, wide and shocked above his big hand covering her mouth . . . *Is that me?*

"You yet have something of mine."

She still wore the long strand of perfect pearls. It draped down between her breasts, gleaming ethereally in the golden glow of the candle.

Her hands fluttered up to take it off, but he caught them like butterflies, trapped carefully in his larger ones. He pressed their tangled fingers between her breasts.

"You could keep it, delicious spirit, if you wish."

The words were broken, as if torn from a throat unused to coaxing anyone for anything.

"A small request, perhaps? No, too many in my mind to choose . . . I could ask for more . . . one for each and every pearl?"

Warm fingers trailed down the strand, brushing lightly on her skin. "There are so many pearls . . . I could keep you for a year or more with such a bounty. Would you return to me each night to earn a pearl? A dying man's wish? I would release you happily in the end, if only you would bring your warmth to my cold evenings and my colder dawns . . ."

Callie felt some of the fear leak away at the loneliness in his deep voice. He did not know what he said, locked into his brandy-soaked fancies. She would explain herself, convince him that she was a real girl, a gently bred one at that, fallen upon his hearth in need of shelter from the storm.

Then, releasing her, his hot hands closed over her

breasts and his hot mouth dove down upon her neck. Her gasp of shock and protest was lost in the deep growl of need reverberating from his throat as he drew her back hard against him.

Then he was gone, torn from her with a violence that spun her hard against the vanity. Unable to catch herself with her arms pinned to her sides, she stumbled and fell to the floor. The strand of pearls caught upon the corner of the marble tabletop and broke as she fell. Iridescent orbs bounced and scattered everywhere.

She scrambled to her hands and knees, frantically tugging her chemise back up, then turned to see two struggling forms in the shadows.

"Dade!"

On her feet once more, she grabbed her candle and held it high. Two heads, one dark and one light—that would be Dade, his hair much more golden than her own! Callie searched for something heavy to swing, ready to enter the fray in defense of her brother.

Then the fight swung closer to her and she saw what had been hidden from her in the mirror. Her assailant's face, twisted and half ruined—dark and demonic!

Callie screamed and lost her grip on the candlestick. The room went entirely dark.

Chapter 2

Quite possibly the most annoying thing about attending a duel was the early-morning hour. Callie yawned behind her glove. Truly, could idiot men not just as easily kill each other in the middle of the afternoon? Say, after a satisfying meal and perhaps a nap?

Callie, being secretly of the opinion that a great number of the world's troubles could be solved by all parties toting themselves off for a relaxing nap, yawned again and glared at her brother. Anger was safe. Much better than thinking about her scandalous moment of madness last night.

Furthermore, Dade was a safer recipient of that glare than the alarming Mr. Porter. Dade wasn't going to glare back, or raise his hand to point to her, or open his mouth and reveal all that had truly happened.

This entire matter would be best forgotten. She hadn't been injured, nor had she injured anyone. It had been an odd mistake, made in a strange dreamlike moment of allowing herself to be someone whom she was most definitely not.

She was very tired from her sleepless night and she

was cold and she wanted to go home. She wished Dade and Mr. Porter would get over their silliness, or at the very least finish up their ridiculous male posturing quickly. *Wave your pistols, fire into the air, declare your selves avenged, or redeemed, or whatever, and let us all simply go home!*

Only it didn't look like silly male posturing. It looked very serious, with Dade stiffly formal in his blue surcoat, his face pale and ill and determined. Mr. Porter, in a hooded cape that hid his frightening face, looked none the less determined in posture and in the way his large hand gripped the pistol at his side. They stood back to back, the sturdy fair-haired young gentleman and the leaning, limping man of shadow.

Callie's belly went ice-cold. This felt horribly wrong. Someone should stop them. Someone should do something! She looked to her parents, but they only stood arm in arm, looking worried and helpless and strangely old.

Archie glared in Mr. Porter's direction. "It is only right that something should be done about the man. 'He is as disproportionate in his manners as in his shape.' "

Iris leaned closer to Callie. "Prospero, you know. *The Tempest,* act five, scene one."

Callie ignored her parents. It didn't do to encourage them. They could go on for hours. She swallowed. "Dade—"

A sharp motion of his hand cut her off. Morgan, acting as second for Dade, began to count off the steps. "One. Two. Three."

Both men moved out, Dade in a slow, purposeful stride, Mr. Porter in an off-center lurching gait.

"Ten."

Twenty paces apart, the two men turned and pointed their pistols simultaneously. Mr. Porter fired at once. The explosion of gunpowder in the silent morning sent birds winging from the trees and Callie's heart into her throat.

The bullet tore into the grass at Dade's feet, sending soil and roots up in a spray to spatter his boots. Dade started, looked down, then looked back up at Mr. Porter, his jaw hardening.

"Do not think that will save you."

Mr. Porter lowered his smoking pistol and tossed it into the grass. "Fire, then."

Dade firmed his grip on his pistol and aimed.

Callie felt sick. Oh, why didn't someone do something?

Mr. Porter began to walk forward, grim determination evident in every lurching step. "Go on. Fire. Don't you think I deserve to die? Isn't that why you gave challenge in the first place?"

He came closer and closer. Each step brought him farther into range. Dade could not miss now, not unless he intended to. One look at her brother's face told Callie that he did not intend to.

Mr. Porter did not intend to stop, either, apparently. He continued his slow lurching walk directly toward the ball about to hurtle from Dade's pistol.

What was he doing? Was he mad? Did he not see that Dade would fire?

Mr. Porter stopped at last when his chest was no more than eighteen inches from the barrel of Dade's pistol.

"I'm waiting." Mr. Porter's rasping voice was clearly audible in Callie's ears. "Fire. Do it. Wrap your finger around the trigger and pull it."

Dade's jaw worked. "You think to daunt me with this game?"

"I play no game. You have a grievance against me. I have none against you. Take your vengeance and be done with it. Let us all bloody well be done with it."

Bloody well be done with it. Callie's thoughts skittered back to the night before. Mr. Porter's strange manner of speaking—as if he thought himself to be soon lying cold in death. Did he want to die?

Yet his hands, his touch, his words, while dark and lonely, had thrilled her with their hunger and need. He wanted to live, she just knew it.

Perhaps he simply doesn't know how.

Bastard. Sudden fury enveloped Callie. To put them all through this, simply because he wanted to give up the fight, to slip beneath the waves of his misery?

And what of Dade? What was he to do now? If he put down his pistol, could he ever forgive himself for the dishonor? If he fired, could he ever forgive himself for taking a life?

But . . . he wouldn't take a life. Would he? On her behalf, on behalf of the family honor, would her honorable misguided brother actually kill Mr. Porter?

With horror she saw Dade exhale, swallow, and blink.

Oh, dear heaven, he would.

Mr. Porter saw it, as well, for he straightened somewhat and lifted his head. And waited.

As if watching a play, Callie could see the future unfolding before her. Mr. Porter's still, bleeding body on the ground. Dade, pale and undone, standing over him, pistol smoking. Mr. Porter, buried here on these grounds, no one in attendance but the vicar. Dade, standing trial, denounced as guilty of murder. Dade, swinging lifelessly from the hangman's rope, his swollen tongue protruding from his mouth.

Callie wasn't precisely sure how she got there. She must have already begun to run across the dewy grass before the moment arrived, because just as Dade's finger began to tighten on the trigger, she slithered to a stop in front of Mr. Porter.

"You can't shoot him!"

Dade jerked the pistol high with a curse. "Bloody hell, Callie!"

Callie planted herself squarely in front of Mr. Porter. In fact, her back pressed right against him—that was how close the pistol had been. "Dade, you mustn't kill him!"

Dade snarled. "I rather think I must."

Mr. Porter exhaled. "Please do."

"Shut it!" Callie ordered Mr. Porter over her shoulder.

"Get out of the way, Callie. This no longer concerns you."

"No longer concerns me?" Callie plunked her hands on her hips. "Well, I like that! Was it not I that Mr. Porter . . . er—"

"Interfered with?" Mr. Porter said helpfully.

"Batten it down!" Callie hissed over her shoulder. To Dade, she held out placating hands. "I didn't want to tell you before but . . ." Blast it, now she was going to have to tell her overprotective, adoring older brother that she'd been a semiwilling participant in her own seduction. She opened her mouth to do just that. It wasn't her fault that entirely different words came out.

"He made me a proposal!"

"He did?"

"I did?"

Luckily, Mr. Porter's low and rasping question reached her ears only. She turned her head to glare at him. She could barely see one shadowed side of his face, the relatively unscarred side. His eye regarded her with surprise and a certain amount of cynical appreciation.

"Yes, you did," she whispered urgently, unable to hide the desperate plea in her voice. "You *must*."

He leaned close. "I only recall a certain proposition regarding pearls." His breath was hot on her ear.

Callie elbowed him sharply. He caught her arm and kept her gaze. "But I have no wish to wed."

"Can it truly be a fate worse than death?" she hissed at him.

"Well, when you put it that way . . ."

Callie shot a glance at the fuming Dade, then turned back to Mr. Porter. "So you agree?"

"Pearls," Mr. Porter reminded her.

She narrowed her eyes, thinking quickly. "Wedding pearls? With the same terms of completion?"

His other arm slid securely—or perhaps it was acquisitively—around her waist. He nodded sharply. "I believe I can live with those terms."

"Then 'tis a bargain." Callie turned back to where Dade was gaping at their tense, whispered exchange. She smiled widely at him from Mr. Porter's possessive embrace.

"Mr. Porter and I are to be married!"

Callie found herself standing in the Amberdell village vicar's austere parlor, overseen by the vicar's austere wife, clutching a minute posy of lily-of-the-valley—the only flowers Mama could find blooming in the vicar's austere garden—being married to a hooded stranger.

She couldn't blame the vicar. He did his austere best to induce Mr. Porter to remove his cape, but Mr. Porter simply ignored him. The vicar dared not press too far upon the area's wealthiest landowner, although Callie saw the man pocket enough gold to weigh down his weskit before agreeing to the ceremony, hood and all.

Iris chose to express her maternal emotions by sighing loudly and waving a long lacy handkerchief as if she bid good-bye to a troop ship. Archie did a great deal of harrumphing and dabbing at his eyes. It seemed to Callie that her parents were tiptoeing right around the matter standing in the middle of the room—hood and all!

I don't even know this man! Someone should really do something to stop this!

Dade would have if he could, she knew. He looked furious and miserable the entire time, and if he didn't relax his fists eventually, his hands were going to freeze that way.

Yet what could he do? What could anyone do?

From beneath the cloak emerged a hand that reached for hers. Callie took a breath, took that hand, and turned to face the vicar.

The vicar was talking. She was sure of it, because the man's mouth was moving and everyone was nodding along. However, all she could hear was the roaring in her ears and the hummingbird beat of her own panicked heart.

I cannot do this. I cannot. Not.

The large warm hand tightened on hers, squeezing nearly to the point of pain. It was precisely what she needed. She clung to that hand, grateful for the heat and solidity of it, as if it were her only tie to certainty. With great concentration, she found her feet still on the earth and the earth still rotating on its axis.

The bizarre ceremony proceeded to its end. After the vicar closed his book, a moment of awkward silence reigned. Archie interrupted it with a double harrumph and Iris blew her nose with a great, goosey honk.

People began to breathe and move again. When Mr. Porter released her hand, Callie was surprised to find that she could stand on her own. Her knees, although weak, were still very much in existence.

I am wed.

In the vicar's office, Dade and Archie witnessed the marriage contract, along with another gentleman who

Callie dimly recalled had come in with his wife just before the vicar began the vows.

Vows. Vows to a stranger.

Callie watched Mr. Porter's hooded form bend to sign the contract, his hand swift, his signature decisive. After a moment, she managed to remember her own name and sign it as well. Yet, it was no longer her name, was it?

Her life, her forever, in this odd recluse's hands.

Well, perhaps not forever. He'd bought himself a wife today, but only a strand of pearls' worth. Callie resigned to stay and live up to Mr. Porter's possibly dastardly demands, but she would hold him to his devil's bargain— when the last pearl was restrung, she would take his name and leave him behind forever!

Oh, dear. *Demands.* Tonight would be her wedding night! She felt faint again. She really would have rather had some time to prepare. Did she even have a decent nightdress among her things? Was it clean? Would— would she need one? Resolving at that moment to dress like a swathed nomad for bed, she lifted her chin and reminded herself of her vow to love, honor, and obey until death did part them.

Or until I earn back those pearls. Whichever comes first.

As if he knew where her thoughts had wandered, Mr. Porter turned and regarded her from the shadow of his hood.

I find those terms acceptable.

Callie looked away. When the papers were all signed and witnessed and sealed with the vicar's seal and Mr. Porter's ring, Callie found herself tightly wrapped in her mother's arms, wafting handkerchief and all.

"Oh, my pet, I don't know what we shall do without you!"

Burn the whole madhouse down, most likely. I give you all a month at the most.

She smiled at Iris and the harrumphing Archie. "You will be fine. Dade will look after you and Orion hardly ever explodes anything anymore."

Iris's dreamy gaze focused on Callie for a single moment. Callie blinked at the sudden canny knowledge she saw in those faded blue eyes.

Iris tapped the tip of Callie's nose with a finger. "Don't tolerate any foolishness from that fellow, my darling—you're a Worthington and don't you forget it!" Then the unaccustomed asperity faded away and Iris began to drift slightly to port. "Such a fine set of shoulders on him, though . . ."

Dade steadied their mother and nodded tersely to Callie. "It's not too late, you know," he murmured. "We can have this whole matter annulled before anyone pours the tea."

Callie shook her head. It was far, far too late. "No."

Archie harrumphed. "Don't be silly, boy! Callie and this fellow are mad for each other. One need only look at them to know that this is a love for the ages!"

Callie felt Mr. Porter before she heard or saw him. She knew the heat of him at her back and let out a breath when his arm twined about her waist from behind. Swallowing hard, she smiled at her father. "Yes, Papa."

It was silly but it would be easier on them all if her parents continued in their self-induced delusion of her love match.

The unknown couple then approached to offer their condol—er, congratulations. The gentleman, a big, brown sort of fellow who sported the clothing of the gentry and the hands of a farmer, stood diffidently awaiting an introduction from Mr. Porter. When the ongoing uncomfortable silence informed them all that none was forthcoming, he bowed to Callie and offered his hand.

"Mrs. Porter, we are very pleased to meet you on this fine day. I am Mr. Henry Nelson and this is my wife, Betrice." The lady was pretty, in a sharp-eyed, watchful sort of way, with delicate features and lovely black hair. Callie liked Nelson at once and decided that while Betrice might seem a bit high-strung, she was a fount of normality compared to Mr. Porter.

Callie curtsied. "Thank you for coming. I—" She stopped, confused. "Did the vicar ask you here to witness?"

Nelson laughed. "No, cousin. It was Lawrence who sent for us."

"Cousin!" Callie's smile widened into something truly welcoming. "Oh, you're family!" She turned her smile onto Betrice. "Oh, if you came so quickly you must live quite close by!"

Betrice nodded, her eyes flicking toward Mr. Porter, who had not relinquished his hold on Callie but neither had he taken the merest notice of his cousins. Callie would have liked to plant her elbow firmly in his belly for being so public with his . . . er . . . affection, but she could hardly let these people, who likely knew everyone in the village, have any worse opinion of her than they surely already did.

Nelson nodded and smiled. "We have the neighboring farmhold, Springdell. Nothing so grand and impressive as the estate of Amberdell Manor, of course."

Callie blinked. "Amberdell?"

Mr. Porter's arm tightened. "Calliope has not yet seen the grounds of Amberdell Manor, but I believe she has a fine appreciation of the house."

Estate. "Yes, the house. I am most . . . er . . . impressed."

He has an estate. Great cannonballs—I have an estate! Her smile widened. "I cannot wait to gain a true appreciation of the grounds," she purred.

Something happened to Mr. Porter. She only knew because he had her pressed to his large, warm side and she was aware of every breath he took—so when she felt his chest spasm and heard a small choked sound in his throat, she was the only one in the room to notice.

Could it have been a rusty chuckle?

Do hermits laugh?

Chapter 3

After the ceremony Callie stood before the entrance of Amberdell Manor, where the aged limestone basked in the last golden light of afternoon, and bid good-bye to everything she knew.

Mama wept, Papa snuffled into his voluminous handkerchief, and Dade glowered. Mr. Porter lurked near the grand door, as if guarding it against intruders. Well, considering the past twenty-four hours, perhaps one could understand his territorialism.

Good-byes went round and then round again. Callie practically had to shove Dade into the vehicle, even as he cast a venomous glare at Mr. Porter over her shoulder.

The carriage carrying Dade and her parents had scarcely rounded the bend and clattered noisily out of sight before Callie began to feel far away from them. She loved them all, entirely and absolutely, but the sweet silence of this remote country estate swept over her like a cool wave in summer. Her primary emotion as she let her aching arm drop was relief.

She'd done it. It was yet difficult for her to believe. After all the years of allowing her own yearnings to be nudged aside by the needs of her parents and her siblings, she had finally acquired a life of her own.

For a time, at any rate. She could not imagine remaining here forever with a stranger. The bargain she must fulfill stabbed at her recent relief and the peace drained from her abruptly.

Mr. Porter had wed her. True, he had only done it to spare himself the bullet in Dade's pistol—but he had done it all the same. He'd made of her a wife and himself a husband. And husbands, she'd been led to believe, had *expectations*.

Well, she would not learn what those would be until she faced him down and demanded he explain his outlandish "terms."

Stalling, she took a moment to rearrange the tiny corkscrews of hair that had escaped their pins and to smooth the front of her spencer. Then, taking a breath, Callie turned back toward the house.

Mr. Porter loomed beneath the portico, rather like the specter of Death in his black hood.

Callie refused to allow the creeping alarm to rise within her. Practicality—that was what was called for to battle such theatrics. If she knew anything after dealing with her mother and her sisters, it was that nothing punctured atmospheric drama like a good dose of common sense.

She tilted her head and smiled at her shiny new husband. "All you lack is a scythe. Shall I fetch you one from the farm stables?"

He gazed at her for a long moment, then grunted noncommittally. Grunting? Really? Callie took a deep breath and firmed her resolve. It was not for nothing that she'd herded her four younger brothers all her life! Lifting her chin, she fixed her smile on with plaster and nails. "Shall we discuss our living arrangements now, sir?"

He said nothing.

Her teeth were beginning to grow dry. Mr. Porter did what he did best, which was to loom, or lurk, or possibly skulk. The blasted hood hid most of his face, as usual.

"Tell me, husband, do you intend to wear that thing for our entire marriage?"

His hand twitched, almost as if he wished to reach for his hood. Would he have lifted it, or tightened it further?

She inhaled. "My brother Orion—he's the third son—had a great attachment to a blanket when he was an infant. I suppose it was not so much a blanket as it was a square of fur cut from an elderly tigerskin rug. It was a prize from my aunt Clemmie's adventuring days. Orion slept with it every night and carried it with him at all times. It was a vile thing, grubby and balding, but it was such a chore to pry it from him that we just let him carry the filthy thing until he tired of it. One day it simply disappeared. We all thought there would a tremendous uproar over it, but Rion never mentioned it again. I used to wonder if it had been part of him for so long that he eventually simply shed it, like a . . . a . . . scab." Um, well, perhaps not the most ladylike topic of conversation on her wedding day. But honestly, it wasn't as though she'd had any practice.

At least it seemed she'd finally gotten his attention. His hood turned to regard her.

"Are you implying that wearing this hood is . . . infantile?" His voice, rough and husky, held a tone of astonishment.

Couldn't have said it better myself. "Oh, not at all!" *Absolutely.* "Why, I'm sure that in the Cotswolds hoods are all the rage." *Nutter.* "I'm sure I'd love to have one of my own. Imagine, er, never having to think of one's hair."

Yes, now she was babbling, but at least she wasn't hiding under a rug, like some people.

"No."

She leaned forward eagerly. "No, what?"

"No, I will not be shedding my hood."

Curiosity made her fingers twitch. If one of her brothers behaved so ridiculously, she'd simply snatch the silly thing off their heads and run for it, giggling. One toss to Attie and the hood would never be seen again, unless it suddenly appeared on the statue in the square.

He seemed to sense her impulse, for he held up his hand, palm out. "You wished to discuss our agreement."

He held up his hand again as she leaned forward eagerly. "Our arrangement shall be thus. I will come to your room every evening. You will do as I command. I will then leave you alone until the next evening. Your days shall be your own, although I desire that you venture no further than the village."

Incensed, Callie crossed her arms. "Command? I hardly th—"

"Hush."

Callie hushed. She didn't precisely remember deciding to hush. She'd never heard such a tone in her life. Except . . .

Once she had accompanied her army-mad brothers to a parade of the troops down Pall Mall. The way the soldiers had moved, as one man, had mesmerized her. Each step was taken in such perfect discipline that it sounded as though a single giant marched past her. They had turned, again as one, so ordered by an officer on a fine and glossy stallion. A single sharp word had redirected the lines and ranks of a hundred men.

Command. Her belly shivered. *Oh . . . my.*

"I . . ." She lowered her voice. "I don't understand."

His hood turned back toward the darkening skies. "My offer this morning was entirely in earnest. You may return to the bosom of your family, someday to be a rich woman, once you have earned back the string of pearls you destroyed." The shadow of the hood turned to regard her once more. "One pearl for each command you obey."

Callie wasn't a fool. She knew that he meant to lie with her. It was his right as her wedded husband. "But . . ." Callie swallowed. "There were hundreds of pearls on that strand." Hundreds of commands. Her belly tightened in alarm. Or something.

"Then I expect you'll wish to begin as soon as possible."

The dry amusement in his tone held a note of ridicule to Callie's ears. Her chin came up. She did not take well to taunting as a rule, but she'd endured enough of it to know that the slightest show of weakness only let oneself in for more.

"Yes, I rather think I shall." She cast an airy glance toward the door. "The evening commences even now. You said 'evening,' did you not? Unless you're suffering an attack of nerves? I shall understand if you need a bit of time."

He stiffened. "You mock me. You should not." He stood and stepped close to her.

Heavens, he was tall. Even slightly bent and lurching, he was a very large man. Powerful. She willed her knees to stop knocking and gazed evenly up into the hollow of his hood. The sun had already set inside that circle of black wool. She saw only the faintest hint of two darkly glinting eyes.

One hand came up to cup her jaw. She flinched at the heat of it on her skin. He held her in place quite without effort. His touch was not rough, but neither was it tender.

"I think . . ." His hand drifted down the side of her neck and slipped over her shoulder. His fingertips dipped

over the edge of her neckline and followed it down . . .
down . . .

Callie couldn't help a startled inhalation. Her
bodice—it was an old gown and none too loose—
trapped his fingers within for an instant. He did not tug
them free, but only dipped farther within once the pressure eased.

Callie's mind flew back to the night before when
she'd stood pinned to the vanity, at the mercy of those
hot, demanding hands . . .

Mr. Porter's thoughts must have followed a similar
path, for his fingers stroked deeply into her bodice, finding her rigid nipple and catching it between his fingers.

Callie jerked and gasped, unable to keep from flinging a panicked glance about the exposed drive. Should
anyone see—But there was no one there. She was alone,
just as she'd so foolishly wished to be.

Mr. Porter stepped closer, shadowing her completely,
making her feel lost in the growing dusk. There was
nothing, no one . . . no one but him, and his searching, teasing fingertips, rolling her nipple possessively
between them.

His voice went low and hot, full of sexual danger.
"I think I shall want you as I first saw you, in nothing
but that little wisp of a chemise, barefoot, your hair tum-
bling down your back . . ."

Her nipple hardened for his exacting touch. She was
dizzy, unsteady in her shock. Her breath left her—no,
she had forgotten to breathe. Alarm roiled in her belly
even as something else hummed a bit lower.

It was his grunt of satisfaction that woke her from the
daze of pleasure/pain.

Men, always thinking they were so blasted superior.

Callie stepped back. Her quick movement removed
his invading hand and he allowed it.

She lifted her chin. "Very well. Chemise, barefoot, hair down. Three pearls."

A sound emanated from him, like the growl of a far-away tiger in the jungle night. "One pearl, one command." His hood turned away from her, as if she no longer existed. "No negotiation."

Callie turned and walked swiftly for the door. She was fleeing and she knew she was fleeing, but hopefully Mr. Porter did not. At the door, she turned back abruptly.

"You forgot something in your bargaining, sir."

"Really. What was that?"

Callie lifted her chin and raised a brow, but made her voice husky and low. "Last night, when we met? I was also . . . *soaking wet.*" At his sharply indrawn breath, she smiled and turned, not fleeing quite so desperately any longer. Served him right.

One pearl. One command. Callie paused as she mounted the stairs. Her hand trembled on the banister.

Hundreds of pearls.

She swallowed but the sudden dryness of her throat didn't ease. Hundreds.

What if she refused? What if she simply locked her door and let his bloody pearls gather dust? Would he demand she earn her food, as well? How long could she hold out?

Actually, she rather thought she could hold out quite a while, though she had never quite attained her sister Ellie's level of gritty resolve. Once when their parents had most uncharacteristically refused Ellie something "for your own good, pet. Monkeys aren't truly as nice as they seem. Rather like rats with hands, I suspect," fourteen-year-old Elektra had starved herself for ten days. On the eleventh, the monkey, a darling but filthy creature, had arrived. It promptly bit Ellie on her opposable digit and was banished imperiously back to the peddler who had procured it.

That night, bandaged hand and all, Ellie had sat down at the dinner table and eaten more than any two brothers together, none the worse for her starvation.

Dade had declared her simply too spoiled to die.

Callie had never been that daughter.

Nonetheless, she was a Worthington, through and through. Worthingtons bowed to no one short of royalty, for their family was as old as the pillars of Stonehenge— that was what Papa always said.

So, if she wasn't to flee and she wasn't to starve, what must she do?

A slow smile crossed her face.

Why, bow to her husband's commands, of course. Because it would not be cowardly, nor spineless—it would be the most perfect revenge imaginable. Worthingtons knew a bit about vengeance!

She would submit to him. She would please him. She would dissolve him into a puddle of satisfied man on his neglected carpet.

And then she would take the pearls—riches enough to give Ellie and Attie each one brilliant Season—and she would leave Mr. Porter in the dust of her carriage wheels without a backward glance.

The girl—Ren thought he ought to call her something else, even in his mind—his *bride* had run from him at last. It had taken her long enough. He didn't know what was wrong with the creature. She seemed most unenlightened regarding her own preservation.

Last night, she'd held still for his drunken caresses. True, she'd screamed bloody murder in the end . . . but by then he'd been thoroughly aroused and knew she was, as well.

Then, this morning, just when he'd thought his reign as monster on earth was at last at an end, she'd stayed her brother's hand. Even his lecherous offer had not deterred her from wedding him in front of her own parents.

Mad little wench.

And just now, standing there defiantly, facing him down with her chin high and her eyes luminous with fight—God, hadn't she looked like the goddess of flaming indignation?—he'd had to go rather further than he'd meant to in order to make her back down.

You forgot something in your bargaining. Unable to hold back a bark of laughter at her parting sally, Ren detoured to the front parlor. Bending painfully, he lighted a candle from the coals of the hearth with the last of the paper spills on the mantel.

The sun had set on their encounter in the drive— had he truly groped his bride whilst standing in front of his house?—and the dim interior had gone quite dark.

As he stiffly climbed the stairs, he forgot to swear as he usually did. He was too busy remembering the feeling of her hot, rigid nipple in his fingers.

It had been so very long, he'd forgotten what the simplest touch could do to that tempting bit of flesh.

He could take her tonight. He had the right, bestowed upon him by the vicar himself. She would await him clothed in nothing but a scrap of batiste. She quite properly loathed him anyway. He had no doubt she would leave the moment she dared call their account settled. No love lost there.

He'd never have another chance for a woman. He hadn't thought he'd ever touch one again. Fate had laid her in his path and he'd tripped right over her.

She owed him. He'd allowed her to save her idiot brother from the gallows, when he'd much rather have been far too dead to care.

She was his to do with as he pleased. Better that she should realize what a monster he was now than later—she did seem a particularly dense female. He could take his last satisfaction and make her hate him in one degraded, bestial night. He could take her hard and fast and sweating and wet—A hot spike of pain shot up his tortured spine. He caught his breath and held very still until the fiery burn cooled and faded away.

Then again, perhaps tonight was not the night.

It didn't take long to prepare for her wedding night. Callie hung the nicer of her two gowns—the ivory muslin had seemed more bridal than the blue—on a peg in the wardrobe, removed everything else except for her chemise, and dug her hairbrush from the small bag of her things that Morgan had managed to dredge from the banks of the river this morning before the wedding.

She sat on the bed and curled her feet beneath her, away from the chilly floor. Someone—Callie suspected it was Dade—had built a fire in the hearth at some time this afternoon. The coals were now glowing beautifully and Callie was grateful of the heat and the small amount of light.

No doubt she would be expected to keep her own fire. There was no one else to light it, or even to fill the coal scuttle so she could do it herself. Fine. She was no weakling.

The Worthingtons had few staff. Only Philpott truly lived in. Philpott, a former theater crony of Mama's, was nominally the "housekeeper" but actually served as cook and Mama's companion. Callie and her sisters did the greater part of the actual housekeeping—which mostly consisted of trying to keep Mama from staining the last good furnishings with her paints. So Callie could light her own fire. She could, if necessary, fetch her own coals.

Tonight, however, she did not have to. Curling up gratefully on the coverlet—no longer dusty, for someone had shaken it out—Callie brushed out her hair and tried very hard not to let fear overwhelm her.

Every wife had a wedding night. Many knew their husbands little if at all. Callie had never dared dream of a great love match like Mama and Papa's. She'd hardly dared dream of marriage at all. She was much too practical to care about such things, really. Mr. Porter was likely no better and no worse than most men.

Hopefully.

Chapter 4

Ren's urge for bestial audacity had worn away by the time he reached the top of the stairs. He couldn't do it.

She was a respectable girl, if a bit odd. It was obvious that she loved her exasperating family, though Ren had already decided that he might happily live the rest of his short life without again laying eyes upon that obnoxious brother of hers.

He wasn't going to force himself on her. He had to seduce her. He had to use every last pearl to arouse her lust so thoroughly that she wouldn't mind consummating their bizarre bargain at some point.

In the dark.

Ren paused on the landing. He ought to bathe. And he hadn't shaved for weeks.

Idiot. Do you really think that's going to make you any less of a monster in her eyes?

Don't you remember her face when she saw you? Have you so soon forgotten her scream of terror?

Ren shook off the thoughts. He meant to either make her want him, to feel the touch of a woman one last time, or to frighten her away so that he might be left in grim peace once more.

Either way made little difference to a man dying a slow but inevitable death.

There was a sound at the door and Callie peered at it, imagining that she could see the turning of the latch. The room was too dim, however, and all she managed to do was to blind herself on Mr. Porter's candle as he entered.

Callie wanted to inch back on the bed—oh, why had she sat upon the bed?—or perhaps dive beneath it. Her wedding night had arrived, hooded in black, the Grim Reaper of Virgins.

Mr. Porter put the candle on the mantel, then turned his back to it and walked toward her. The light cast from behind him turned him into a specter, a creature of shadow and sin. Callie shivered though the room was fully warm.

How could she be here? How could she have come so far in a day? Unimaginably far. From spinster doomed to be caretaker of a careless family mired in a life of chaotic frugality to nearly naked bride of a dark and sinister man and mistress of his great house.

Well, I do like the house.

Callie swallowed down that burst of irreverence. Perhaps it was the hood, or the memory, now rising against her earlier suppression, of a ruined, twisted face of once unearthly beauty. Something told her that her humor would not bear her well through the next few hours.

Hours. Blimey. Would they be hours of wonder or of horror?

One might think, looking at the hooded figure before her, that she had just given her vows to a nightmare. Yet . . .

What harm had this man actually done?

Yes, he'd made a bit free with her the night before—but she had waltzed about his house in the middle of the night in her chemise. One could not precisely call that the act of a virtuous woman!

Furthermore, although Dade had handed the fellow a pistol, Mr. Porter had intentionally shot his bullet into the ground instead of into her beloved brother. Shadowed or not, this man had yet to evidence any desire to do harm to anyone.

So if this night was not to be a horror . . . perhaps it would be . . . a wonder?

Callie had a strong young body that had never felt the touch of a man until yesterday. Personally, she felt it was high time she experienced a little wonder. At the thought, her lips parted on a breath of anticipation.

Mr. Porter stopped short, as if riveted. Nervously, Callie darted her tongue over her lips. Even twisted and limping, he loomed over her.

Callie had always been partial to big men. She liked the sensation of feeling tiny and fragile in comparison.

Right now she felt minuscule.

His hands were big. That she remembered well from last night. Big and hot and gently implacable.

A hot burst of dampness between her thighs might have made Callie blush if she'd been able to drag her mind from the feel of his hot hands on her last night.

She rather thought she'd like to feel them again. Really. Now.

Unbelievably, she found herself sliding down off the bed and taking a step forward.

Heavens. How brazen of me. Oh, look, I'm doing it again.

Two steps brought her within arm's reach of him.

Then even her sensual ambition failed her and she halted. He would likely think her a true wanton now.

Imagine, me—a wanton. A part of Callie was ridiculously pleased at the thought. *And here I thought I was such a shriveled old maid.*

Oh, wait a moment. I'm married.

The wave of justified lust that swept through her made her draw a swift breath. Mr. Porter's eyes were on her. She could almost feel his riveted gaze upon her uplifted bosom.

Yes, Mr. Porter. You can have these if you like.

She felt bold, brash . . . and very, very naughty. When Mr. Porter held up a single pearl between his large fingers, Callie felt just a little bit like a woman of ill repute, selling herself to a mysterious stranger. Heaven help her, but it made her blood flow all the hotter.

"Open your mouth."

She obeyed instantly. After regarding her for a moment, he placed the pearl on her tongue.

"Don't speak." A husky note of humor wove through his deep voice. "And don't swallow."

Oh, my. Callie let her lips close over the pearl and rolled the smooth orb over her tongue. Effectively gagged by the gem, she wondered what else this strange man had in store for her.

"Put your hands behind your back."

Callie hesitantly placed her hands palm to palm behind her back and laced her fingers together. Now she stood as if bound. Oh, clever fellow. Her compliance was the only restraint he needed to prove his command over her. His dominance. And conversely, her submission.

The thought made her knees get a bit wobbly. *I think I might be more than a little wanton. I think I might be a great deal wanton.*

Mr. Porter stepped closer to her. His voice was little more than a husky whisper in her ear. "Close your eyes."

Yes. Her own instant compliance caused a deep throbbing down somewhere low and delicious. Bound, gagged, and blind—it was a heady rush of fear, lust, and more than a little naughty thrill. Her admiration for her own boldness grew by the moment.

I never knew I had such wickedness in me.

However, the true question was . . . how had Mr. Porter known?

This was most definitely something she ought to think about.

Later.

In this heated, breathless moment of waiting, all she could think about was the moment his hot hands would touch her tingling skin.

The first thing she felt was the warmth of his breath as he bent close to her. "Little Miss Calliope Worthington— do you know what you unleash in me?"

It seemed more a personal thought than a direct question, so Callie felt a bit sorry for interrupting but accuracy was important to her. "Porter," she breathed, after tucking the pearl into her cheek.

"Hmm?" He didn't seem to be listening.

Callie cleared her throat. "Calliope Worthington . . . Porter."

She felt his stillness. It seemed to last an hour, but it was likely only a breath or two. Then a low, rusty murmur breathed over her neck. "So you are. Now, shut up while I prove it to you."

The possessive intent in those words stole Callie's breath completely. She'd given herself over to this man, now standing bound, blindfolded, and gagged—well, sort of—before him.

Ren could scarcely believe his senses. The girl was . . . well, she certainly wasn't fleeing him.

Even now she stood before him, her eyes closed, her lips holding the pearl, and her hands quite willingly clasped behind her back.

She looked so sweetly erotic that Ren had trouble looking away long enough to remove his hood and leave it close to the door. He kept his back to the candle, just in case she peeked, and approached his bride uncovered at last.

So willing. Could it be true? Perhaps she was screaming on the inside, biting back her revulsion . . .

Ren reached for her with one damnedly tentative hand. She started slightly when his fingertips brushed her neck, but she didn't draw back. Emboldened, Ren allowed his touch to trail down her throat, down to the hollow. She swallowed, he felt it, but unbelievably, she did not seem panicked in the slightest.

Curious, he shifted direction and laid his open palm over her heart, just covering the top of her breast. Her pulse pounded, healthy and strong and, yes, excited or perhaps frightened, but not shaken or panicked.

Her skin . . .

He'd been aware of the heat of her last night, of the soft roundness of her bottom pressing into his groin, of the weight of her breasts in his hands for that brief instant, but now he found himself mesmerized by the simple fine-grained perfection of her lovely skin. He ran curious fingers up over her shoulder and down her upper arm. She was like warm satin, or perhaps sweet cream, whipped to firmness. Though his lust throbbed like a long-aching wound, Ren found himself perfectly willing to do no more than touch his deliciously submissive bride.

His lips quirked at the thought that if he asked no more of her this night, he would have lost only one pearl . . . and he rather thought he could make the other two hundred and twenty-odd pearls last.

If he played his hand well, he could keep this appealing creature at his side for nearly a year.

He had to be sure. "Pretty Calliope. You seem rather . . . resigned to your fate tonight. Might I even suggest . . . willing?"

Callie didn't bother to hide her shiver of anticipation. Willing. Well, yes. Or one might say eager. Enthused. Ardent.

Once she had overheard Dade and Lysander discussing how long it had been since they'd had a lover. Upon Lysander's admittance that it had been more than a year, his brother had been nearly dumbstruck with pity. "How have you survived for so long?"

That was how Callie felt at this moment. She'd been living her life, filling her days, and never allowing herself to think about the fact that for her, it had been so much more than a year.

It had been always.

It had been *never*.

How had she survived so long?

She felt as though she strained toward Mr. Porter like a hound on a leash. She wanted so much to feel, to touch, to be touched. She felt absolutely parched for love. And if Mr. Porter didn't hurry it up, she was going to expire completely for the lack of it!

At the touch of his fingertips on her neck, Callie shivered and nearly wept with joy. Whether for good or ill, she would be bedded tonight, well and proper. The great mystery, the empty places, the great and gloomy lack in her life would be fulfilled at last.

Then all rational thought was swept away.

Hands. Hands all over her, like shocking hot brands searing her skin, making it tingle and burn and live.

Hands wide and rough and powerful, sliding all over her body, up under her chemise, dipping and scorching and teasing. She felt encompassed. She felt owned. She felt invaded and yet also protected. No harm would come to her whilst she dwelled in those hands. He was not tender . . . yet she could feel the care in those hands. He knew his strength and he did not use it on her.

A man with hands like those had touched a woman before. Many women? She scarcely cared. All the better to prepare him for this night, for this time with her, time that just might turn out to be a wonder after all.

Hot seeking hands covered her bare hips, gripped them, tugged slightly, rocking her in a motion she didn't know yet recognized in some primal corner of her soul. *Yes. Hold me there. Hold me tight while you . . .*

But he didn't. His hands slid down, stroking and cupping her buttocks, squeezing slightly, lifting and parting them. She was exposed. She shivered, because although her eyes were closed and she was blind, he was not.

"Be still," he commanded.

She stilled. All the lust she could ever wish to hear was contained in his voice, husky, aching. Did he know he gave himself away to her like that? This man she'd never truly seen, was seeing her . . . yet he was not as hidden from her as he might like to believe. When one couldn't see another's face, one listened more closely to their voice, was more sensitive to their touch. This man . . . though his voice shook with lust and need and stark, agonizing loneliness, his touch caressed and protected.

He didn't love her. He scarcely knew her. This could have meant terror and intimidation for her . . . yet his need exposed him to her closed eyes as if he stood in full sun.

I see you, Mr. Porter.

"Remove this." He'd stepped away from her, taking his hot hands with him.

She shivered, feeling suddenly colder. Since she wore nothing but the chemise, it was clear that he meant her to be entirely naked before him. Callie hesitated. Yet, what did it matter if he wished to see what he had already touched? Keeping her eyes closed most obediently, she reached for the hem of the chemise and lifted it over her head.

Chills swept her as her nipples hardened further in the cool air and her nerves, stimulated by his touch, sent gooseflesh rising all over her body.

Suddenly the front of her felt warmer. He'd stepped closer. He moved so soundlessly, though he limped so badly.

"Are you afraid?"

No. Yes. Then, nevertheless, *no.* She shook her head.

"I will not harm you."

She nodded.

"Put your hands behind your back once more."

She obeyed. He moved behind her. Warm palms came down upon her shoulders, then slid down her arms to her elbows. He pulled them back, as he had the night before, making her back arch and her breasts thrust forward, high and pointed.

Was she facing the mirror this time? She rather thought so, for he remained behind her, yet she could hear his breath deepen. He gazed at her for a long time.

Then he released her arms. Slowly, she let her posture relax a bit, though she kept her bosom high . . . for his pleasure?

I like that he wants to look at me.

She ought to have felt shamefully exposed, yet what was the use of shame? Her husband liked to look at her. Surely that was rather the point of marriage? All within was sanctioned, permissible.

Enjoyable?

So far.

"Kneel."

Jolted, she hesitated. Then, slowly, she bent her knees until she could drop more or less gracefully to them, keeping her hands behind her back.

She was closer to the fire now and she felt the warmth ease the tight sensitivity of her aroused skin.

His large hand came to rest upon her head. Slowly, his fingers moved through her hair, stroking and combing, digging great fistfuls and then letting the strands slide free.

"You do not resist."

Callie hesitated, not sure if he wished a response. Slowly she shook her head no.

"How far does your obedience go, I wonder?"

She remained quiet. There was something in his voice now . . . a curiosity and a . . . threat? Suddenly she knew he wished to find her limit. She lifted her chin. *I'm rather interested in finding that out myself.*

Yes, she was interested in finding out what this man knew about her body that she did not. What did he know about the longings of her skin and her nipples and the hot wet place between her thighs? More than she did, certainly.

So she waited for him to press further in his curiosity. She supposed she would know when he'd discovered the line of "too far." At the moment, she felt liberated by her willingness to experiment. Liberated by the wedding ceremony and the fact that her family was on its way back to London. Liberated by the knowledge that she could do anything she pleased here in this fine house, in this fine room, with this man, and then someday soon she could leave it behind her.

This was her only chance to feel this. And she wished to miss not a single thing.

Chapter 5

When Mr. Porter commanded Callie to get on all fours, she did it fluidly, instantly, pleased with her own shocking willingness, pleased at his roughened voice, aware that her breasts swung and her bottom rose in the air and pleased that she knew he liked what he saw.

He moved behind her then and knelt. His clothed knee slid between her bare calves and she was forced to spread her knees apart. His other knee joined the first. She knelt wide, exposed, interested and a bit shy about it, but not yet alarmed.

He wrapped big hands around her hips, like before. Yes, that was what she'd wanted. He pulled her back against his body for a moment, providing her mind with all sorts of images for later consideration.

Then his hands slid back, over her bottom and down. His hot palm covered her dampest place. She felt the urge to press down upon that hand, but it moved on too quickly. As he brought his fingers drifting back from there, he stroked a fingertip over her anus.

Callie jerked in response, and heat flooded her face,

shattering her bemused serenity with hot embarrassment. What? *There?*

My goodness.

Then his hands slid up once more, over her hips, moving up her sides, dipping beneath to pass quickly over her breasts, then rising up her arms and shoulders, and digging once more into her hair. This time he wrapped his fists in her long hair, pulling her back against him, pulling on the reins of her tangled hair.

"I wonder . . . so willing . . ."

Then, suddenly, his arms wrapped about her waist and she felt herself lifted up off the carpet. In less than a second, he had her flat on her back before the fire. She almost opened her eyes in surprise, but he covered them with his hand quickly.

"Keep them closed."

He slid his hands over her once more, his touch less detached, more urgent.

Callie felt him watching her face, waiting for her to respond, to cringe away. So instead she lay open and relaxed, allowing his touch as he ran his hard rough palms over her belly, her thighs, her breasts and shoulders. He parted her thighs and looked at her. She turned her face away slightly, but she did not resist, although it was possible she blushed, and not just from the heat of the coals.

Ren pushed his bride until he thought he could bear no more and still she did not stiffen in resistance, she did not push his hands away, she did not fight him in the slightest.

One had to admire the purity of her determination. She truly wished to return to her family as soon as possible. Surely she must be relieved by the fact that he'd made sure she need not look upon him.

Was it someone else she pictured behind her closed

lids? That would explain her dreamy compliance. He could hardly resent it if it were so. A man like him had no right to this tender sweet flesh.

The thought made him take his hands to her again, sweeping them over her, taking every inch of her into his memory for longer, colder nights ahead.

A man such as he with a woman such as she . . .

He'd thought her pretty in the dark last night. He'd thought her pleasing in the light of day. Now, spread out before him like a feast for his starved, aching eyes, she looked like a long-limbed ivory goddess, with her tawny curls spilling over the carpet and her long amber lashes lying on faintly freckled cheeks.

What would it be like to have a woman like this love him—willingly, without payment, without coercion, without her eyes closed?

He would never know.

"Good night, Mrs. Porter."

Callie could not have been more astonished when she felt Mr. Porter leave her side, heard his footsteps stride away, heard her bedchamber door shut behind him . . . heard the silence of her chamber echoing in her ears.

She opened her eyes. He'd left her, trembling, thighs damp with unfulfilled longing, staring after him with fury and frustration.

He'd treated her like the untried virgin that she was.

Bastard.

Far southeast of the Cotswolds, a man sat in a London gambling hell, toying idly with a deck of cards. Afternoon sunlight slanted into the room through high rounded windows, turning the carpet from nighttime plush to daytime shabby and causing dust motes to glint and dance in the air.

Another man entered, just as tall and dignified as the first, if a bit less relaxed.

The first gentleman looked up. "You again."

The second gentleman drew out a chair and sat. Permission was neither asked nor granted. "He has married."

The first gentleman lifted a brow, arched over a silvery gray eye. "Married? I had no idea there was an engagement."

The second gentleman, whose blue eyes warmed a room rather than chilled it, leaned back in his chair and shook his head. "No engagement. Met her, compromised her, dueled her brother, and then married her, in less than twenty-four hours."

"Impulsive bloke."

The second gentleman ran a hand through none-too-tidy black hair. His brow furrowed with worry. "No, he isn't. Ever. He maintains a very low profile, is rarely seen about, and keeps no society whatsoever."

"And this makes you suspicious."

The second gentleman shot the first gentleman a wary look. "Of her? Entirely. Of him? Well . . ."

The moment of hesitation lasted a bit too long. "You swore he would cause no further problems." The gentleman with the chilling eyes sent his cards out onto the crimson felt of the table in a perfect fan. Then he stood. "I don't like alarming developments. We shall have to see about this strange departure from the norm. And this mysterious bride."

The second gentleman moved as if to protest, then drew a long breath instead. "It is, of course, your call."

The first gentleman began to walk away, then turned to look back over one broad shoulder. "How generous of you to state the obvious."

The second gentleman shook his head. "Supercilious aristocrat," he muttered under his breath.

"And you're a chimney sweep with delusions of standing." The first gentleman did not turn again. "Go home, Simon. This is my club now. My men. My cards. My game."

"Dalton, this girl may not be a playing piece in the game. Sometimes a girl is just a girl."

"Perhaps. And perhaps not."

"What will you do, then?"

Dalton's jaw tightened. "You of all people ask me that? You know perfectly well that we exist outside the boundaries of law. We exist so that the dear people of Britannia need not sully their hands with the dirty business of national security. You cannot tell me that you never ordered an assassination when you held my post."

Simon looked down at his hands.

Dalton sighed. "I hardly ride about England ordering the deaths of young women, Simon. But we do all this so no one else has to."

Simon nodded. "I know. Right now I'm ever so glad that it is you and not I."

Dalton gave a resigned snort. "Thank you."

Simon turned, draping an elbow over the back of the chair. "Oh, by the way, Dalton, Milady wanted me to tell you to tell your lady that she will take another kitten in any case."

Dalton, his dignified exit now in ruins, shrugged and nodded. "I'll let her know. I suppose we're all dining together again tonight?"

Simon waved a surrendering hand. "I go where I'm told, most happily."

Dalton pursed his lips. "Hmm." However, he didn't argue the statement. He, also, tended toward the slavish adoration of his bride. "Tonight, then."

Simon nodded crisply. "Try not to murder any little girls before then."

On the other side of the city, in a rambling, shabby house whose last shred of elegance hailed from another era—rather, several eras ago—a great deal of clamor and upset rang through the extensive network of halls.

Atalanta Worthington, last and smallest of the Worthington offspring, crawled beneath the easel that held her mother's latest rendering of *Shakespeare with Piglet* and tried to inspire her physical body into invisibility while the argument raged above her head.

It wasn't that she was banned from such "open forums" as her father called them. In fact, she'd been included since she was old enough to perform the thumbs-up or-down gesture of the Roman audience, which Lycurgus, or some such fellow, declared the original form of democracy. Archie Worthington was a great proponent of democracy. Even infancy had not excused little Attie from performing her family duty by voting.

It was only that family discussions seemed to be so much more intriguingly fervent when Attie wasn't present. So she sat with her bent knees tucked up beneath her skirts and willed herself to look like a potted plant.

With ears.

"I should never have allowed it! *You* should never have allowed it!"

That was Dade. He looked very fine, striding back and forth over the paint-spattered sitting room carpet with a scowl on his face. In Attie's opinion, Dade was the best-looking of her many brothers, although Castor and Pollux claimed that they, being identical twins, were twice as handsome as the rest.

"I can't believe she married without me there! I am her sister!"

Attie scowled at lovely Elektra. Ellie made it sound as if she were Callie's *only* sister! Ellie was just jealous that Callie wed before her. Everyone in the family had assumed that Ellie would be the first, because she was the prettiest and because she was so hell-bent on the notion.

Attie liked the term "hell-bent." She was allowed to use all sorts of words that made other people—people not Worthingtons—gaze at her with startled alarm. She knew all the proper Latin terms for the human body, at least the female one. Mama—who preferred to be called "Iris" by her children, though none of them complied—had declared it perfectly obvious that a person ought to know their own parts. "'Tis your carriage, Atalanta. You ought to know how to drive it."

Cas and Poll, never ones to let Ellie flail about in theatrics for long, decided to pester Dade about the duel itself.

"So you never pulled your own trigger?"

"Not even a little bit?"

"Not very brotherly of you."

"Not at all. One would think—"

"—That you didn't care a whit—"

"For your own sister's well-being!"

"The fellow could be a madman!"

"He sounds like a madman to me."

"Living in that dank, dark house—"

"God knows what he's up to in there!"

"Enough!" Dade spun about to face the twins, his hands clenched in fists until his knuckles went white. "Callie made up her own mind, as she always does!"

Cas grunted, nodding. Poll smiled angelically. "We know. We just wanted to make sure you did."

Iris raised a languid hand. As usual, a paint-smeared handkerchief trailed from the wristband of her sleeve. "Daedalus, darling! Just because he was a rather unusual fellow—one does wonder at the lack of candles, to be sure—is no reason to assume he isn't perfectly wonderful in his own way."

Archie nodded sagely. "True, true. The greatest minds of history were all a bit eccentric, in their way. I myself have been called 'odd' on occasion!" Archie smiled at that bit of nonsense.

Attie laid her cheek sideways upon her knees and contemplated her father with great fondness and no illusions. Papa was as mad as a hatter. Everyone knew it except for him. But he was an affectionate sort of papa, the kind who remembered that she was very fond of butterscotch drops and books about ancient queens and bloodthirsty chess matches that lasted for days.

Dade shook his head as if shaking off his parents' delusions. "I cannot believe she knew what she was doing."

"She knew precisely what she was doing. The only logical conclusion is that she acted to save you."

That was Orion. Attie wiggled a bit in anticipation. Rion, who was in reality a genius, not just someone who thought he was a genius, like Papa, hardly ever spoke up in family discussions. In fact, unless he was lecturing on one of his scientific papers to the Babcock Scholars, he rarely spoke at all.

Dade turned to Rion in surprise. "Save me? From what?"

Rion put down the massive tome he was reading and pushed his spectacles up his nose to better regard Dade through them. Attie suspected that he didn't really need his vision corrected. It was only that he was so very attractive—in a darkly sinister way—that he felt he would not be taken seriously if he didn't wear the useless bits of wire and glass.

"Save you from yourself, of course." Rion shook his head at Dade's obtuseness. "The result of your ill-considered heroics would have been your own hanging on the charge of murder."

Attie's eyes widened. Oh. Oh, no. Callie would do it, too. Callie put everyone else first. She always had. The whole family knew it and accepted it as simply being Callie's lot.

Elektra smoothed her skirts primly. "I would like to know what Callie thought she was up to in the first place. I mean, we're not truly swallowing this oops-I-accidently-ruined-myself story, are we?"

All heads swung toward her. Attie shrank down into her shoulders. Ellie could be a right cow sometimes.

At her family's scowls, Elektra raised her chin. "Well, what was she doing wandering around a strange house in her shift, I ask you?"

Iris relaxed and waved a dismissive hand. "Oh, that! I imagine she was communing with the souls of the past and forgot she was in her underthings. That can happen, you know."

Ellie grimaced. "To some of us more than others," she muttered.

Archie took his wife's hand and smiled. "And didn't you look like a drunken sailor's dream?"

Dade glared at their mooning parents. "She wasn't communing with the spirits! She'd almost drowned, Ellie. Her things were drying by the fire and her *chaperones* fell asleep."

Iris nodded helpfully. "Oh, yes. Archie and I drank our brandies and went straight out. I suppose the brandy didn't help Callie at all."

"I knew it." Ellie narrowed her eyes. "She was in her cups! Drunk and consorting with strange men!"

Cas and Poll shook their heads.

"Drunk and consorting, yes—"

"But with a single strange man—"

"Not a platoon or anything."

"Not that we know of, anyway."

They turned as one to look at Dade.

"Was there a platoon?"

"You didn't say. Details, man—"

"Details!"

Another time, Attie would have giggled at the way the twins made Dade twitch. Now, however, she simply scowled and worried about Callie.

If Ellie was right—which thought alone was alarming—and Callie had gotten herself in trouble with a stranger, why, that stranger could be any sort of rotter! Dade certainly seemed to think so, and he'd actually met the man.

Mr. Porter, who had formerly inhabited a rather swash-buckling fantasy form in Attie's imagination, shrank and deformed into a monstrous hulk, a creature who assaulted innocent drunken maidens wandering about in their un-mentionables!

"I've given you all the details!" Dade was nearly shouting now.

"Temper, temper, son," Archie said mildly. "The lads were simply trying to help."

"There's nothing they can do. There's nothing any of us can do to save her now."

"That's not strictly true." That was Orion again. Attie craned her neck to see her third-eldest brother.

Orion was leaning back in his chair, staring at the ceiling. The other Worthingtons assumed a respectful silence, even the twins, for this was Orion's thinking pose. Many outstanding and dangerous moments had come from such a pose. Not all had involved fire, flood, or famine, either, despite the rumors.

Orion went on distractedly, as if he were speaking to himself. "The marriage will likely have been consummated by now, so annulment will be of no use . . ."

"Callie refused, anyway," muttered Dade.

Orion blinked. "So, logically, there are two more possible solutions. Divorce—"

Ellie started. "No! Absolutely not! If there is a divorce in the family, I will never make a decent match!" When most of the brothers scowled at her, Ellie shrank a little. "Well, neither will Attie! And Callie would never want that!"

Orion hadn't so much as glanced Ellie's way during the interruption. "Or the last possibility—" He sat up and gazed benignly at them all. "Widowhood."

"Ooh." Iris brightened. "I could wear black. I look positively ethereal in black! And Callie would make a lovely widow, wouldn't she, dearest?"

Archie beamed. "Stunning!"

The twins stood as one.

"So, we're all in—"

"For a spot of murder?"

"What shall it be? Poison?"

"Too girlish. Not enough blood."

"True, true. I see your point."

"A carriage accident?"

"Hmm. Might harm the horses."

"We can't have that. No, indeed—"

"There will be no murder!" Dade stood in the center of the room and pointed them all out in turn, one sibling for each word. He didn't see Attie, who had been still as a stone during the twins' dialogue.

Poison.

Heavens to Betsy . . . what an interesting idea.

Chapter 6

Callie woke early. Outside the tall windows of her bed-chamber, the Cotswolds countryside was still dark, as the spring days had not lengthened enough to match her sleep patterns. Curling into a tight ball beneath the heavy coverlet, she tucked her clasped hands beneath her chin and breathed into the silent darkness.

Married.

Married to a strange man.

A flash of the night before crossed her thoughts and half-embarrassed, half-aroused heat washed over her body. A very, very strange man.

Callie had lived among strange people all her life. Her mother, Iris, who was no slouch in the realm of eccentricity, had two sisters, both odder than herself. Auntie Poppy cleaned everything she touched thrice. Every time she touched it. Auntie Clementine was prone to collecting small yapping dogs, which she sometimes carried in the drooping bodices of her gowns. Poppy expressed great disgust every time Clemmie kissed them on the mouth.

Therefore, strange was not so strange, not for Callie.

However, nowhere in the crowded, cheerful penury that passed for existence in the Worthington household did dwell such darkness as flowed through every corner of this luxurious manor.

Realizing that there was no point in hiding away from her abrupt change in destiny—for cowering in bed changed nothing and never would—Callie threw back the covers and swung her feet to the icy floor. Was her husband a miser, to keep the place so cold? Or perhaps a spartan, who did not feel the chill the way she did?

Well, that simply wouldn't do. She'd always hated being cold.

Questions about Mr. Porter filled her mind: questions about his present, his past, and his intentions. She would prefer that answers took their place, answers that were not to be had in the safety of her bedchamber.

With a bit of luck, she managed to find a single glowing coal in the hearth with which to light her candle. She roamed the room, lighting every wax stub she could find. Light turned her bedchamber from a black cavern to a surprisingly graceful room. The lady's chamber, obvious by the look of the pretty spindled chairs and the delicately inlaid vanity. The room where she'd met her . . . husband.

The jewel casket was gone from its place on the vanity. Callie turned away, refusing to dwell on that fateful night and its alarming revelations.

Shaking her head at the crockery pitcher sitting dry and useless on her washstand, she dressed without bathing. Pinning her hair up in a tight bun, donning the more workaday gown of the two salvaged from the river—for clearly she was going to have to do for herself in this servantless hall—she prepared herself for her new life.

The richly carved oak door of her bedchamber had kept out her destiny for the night. Taking the largest of her candlesticks, she put her hand on the latch and pressed. Time to face her future.

Nearly an hour later, she had to conclude that her future had gone out for the day. Mr. Porter was nowhere to be found, not even in the farthest reaches of the manor. He must have left before the dawn that now stretched rosy fingers across the eastern sky.

Odd. He hadn't seemed the out-and-about sort.

Frustrated that her hard-won bravery had come to nothing and relieved, as well, she decided that the first order of her solitary day would be to supply her own needs. Water could be had in the kitchens. And food. She'd seen that the larder was fully equipped on her first pass of exploration that fateful night.

On closer inspection, she noted the signs of past random rummaging through the hung meats and cheeses. Frowning, she couldn't decide if such disregard for conventional household help was admirable or pathetic. Apparently Mr. Porter was prone to feeding himself rough-hewn chunks of this and that. In response, she carved herself thin, delicate slices. She also left a tray of them, attractively arranged, for Mr. Porter's next foray.

Humming, she carried her meal into the baking kitchen. Great ovens covered nearly the whole of one wall, ready to cook for dozens of staff and household and visitors. In the growing light through the large glazed windows, they looked dusty and desolate to Callie— simply crying out to be used, to be required, to be needed.

Well, then, so be it. Stuffing the wood box of one of the giant beasts took most of the logs she found outside in the kitchen yard. Lighting it was no problem, for the wood was old and very dry. Soon the roaring flames warmed the kitchen, turning the sad, desolate room into a cheery haven.

Eggs were to be had in the henhouse that resided out beyond a long-neglected kitchen garden, where it appeared that someone was lackadaisically tending a sparse flock. To be sure the eggs were recently laid, Callie sank her finds in a bowl of water. The ones that floated she discarded. The ones remaining, she beat into a rich batter with butter found in the larder and flour and sugar from the vast cavern of a pantry. Without a yeast starter, she could not make bread.

"Let them eat cake," she murmured to herself with a smile. Soon the kitchen wing was redolent with the sugary, light smell of sweets baking within.

While the cake baked, she heated several pails of water on top of the stove. She found the copper bathing tubs stacked in a storeroom not far away and managed to wrest the smallest one down the hall. Grinning at the horrendous screeching sound of metal on the stone floor, she did her best to be as loud as possible in the matter. Something needed to fill this hollow shell of a house.

By the time she'd wrangled the thing into the overly warm kitchen, she was rather warm herself. Pushing her falling hair back with one damp wrist, she promised herself the soak of a lifetime. All she lacked was some sweet-smelling soap or bath salts.

Soap eluded her search. It must be kept somewhere else in the house, someplace that made sense to the staff of thirty that ought to be here. Asking thin air worked not at all.

Terrible place. No staff, no occupants. Not even a decent ghost about!

Callie satisfied herself with filling a small bowl with a handful of salt and dried herbs. Rosemary and mint scrubbed as well as anything. Just in case, she peered carefully up and down the hall of the kitchen wing before she stripped off her dress and underthings.

Gasping at the heat as she slid into the water, she exhaled in a moan of exquisite pleasure as she sank up to her chin.

Although she adored being clean, bathing was always a challenge in the Worthington household. One did with lukewarm water so as not to tax the elderly staff. Baths were usually brief due to constant interruptions by her sisters and sometimes canceled altogether due to abrupt spikes in the usual level of chaos. Callie would be called out dripping and fuming to put out fires—sometimes literal fires, in fact. Orion's recent experiments tended toward the combustible and Atalanta's fascination with flame had kept them all on edge in her early years.

So was it any wonder that she now soaked until her skin turned red and her fingers pruned? The cakes cooling on their racks filled the air with sweetness and the herbs in her bath lent a spicy undertone. The quiet reverberated in her ears until she dunked her head to escape the exquisite disturbance it caused in her chest. Silence such as she had only dreamed of, peace so deep she felt as if she were the only survivor of the human race—should it not be pleasurable? Yet she found it unsettling. It seemed a tense sort of silence, as if the entire house held its breath, waiting . . . waiting for what?

Rising from the water, she shook off that silly fancy as she shook back her dripping hair. Using the coarse cleanser she'd created, she lifted one leg onto the side of the tub and began to bathe.

The scrubbing salt did a marvelous job and the herbs left a delicious tingle on her skin. The only disadvantage to her solitary luxury was that she had no housemaid or sister to scrub her back. Twisting, she reached as far as possible but there was still that one spot between her shoulder blades—

A large male hand, with muscled forearm exposed by

a rolled-up sleeve, reached past her to delve into the bowl of salt and herbs. Callie squeaked in alarm, quickly curling up around her nudity, then froze as that hand began to move in slow gentle circles over her back, smoothing the gritty scrub into her skin.

Swallowing the sudden dryness in her mouth, she cleared her throat. "Mr. Porter, I am quite capable of—"

"Hold out your hand."

She obeyed unthinkingly, her thoughts still consumed by the large warm hand moving over her naked skin. Into her wet palm dropped a single pearl. Ah. The terms. Callie slowly closed her hand over the pearl, then closed her eyes and dropped her chin to her chest. Permission granted.

Although only a small portion of her back had needed assistance, Mr. Porter now used both hands to stroke the salt scrub over her entire back, from her shoulders down to where the water met the middle of her back. In the silence, the single drops of water falling from his hands sounded through the room like the ringing of a bell. Callie tried to breathe evenly, but her nakedness and this strange man—her husband!—looming over her made her heart beat at a panicked speed. Her breathing soon matched it.

Behind her closed lids, she could not help but replay last night's erotic scene. Naked in the candlelight, the dark sinister shape of him looming over her, the feeling of his large hands on her chilled skin . . .

Her nipples turned to diamonds, and without realizing it, she began to lean into his touch. His hands slid to cup her shoulders, then stroked slowly down her arms. Callie let her head fall to one side, inviting him onward.

Cleansed of salt by the water, his hot palms slid back up her arms to travel over her shoulders to her neck. For several long moments, his fingers moved in delicious massaging circles over the tension there, tension that had lived there since she turned sixteen and took on the running of Worthington House. Surprisingly, her eyes dampened in gratitude for that small attention and she let out a long, sighing breath as her body surrendered to his touch.

How wonderful. When had she last felt tended, cosseted? As a child perhaps? Sometime before Castor and Pollux were born, surely. Twins were bound to upset any family, and her brothers, darling wicked charmers that they were, had continued to cause havoc ever since.

Havoc that now had nothing to do with her. The distance from her family regained a little of its glory at that thought. This manor in the Cotswolds was a place of quiet and possibly even serenity—

All thoughts of serenity abruptly vanished when Mr. Porter's hot hands slid down to cover her breasts.

Ren's eyes closed in pleasure at the feel of her full breasts in his hands. God, she was sweet, so soft and silken. He was charmed by the tiny damp curls behind her ears, by the delicate point of her shoulder, by the line of her spine as it led his gaze to the deliciously curved buttocks beneath the water—water that, without soap, hid not a single womanly thing.

But mostly, he was fascinated by her delicious breasts.

He'd always thought he had a preference for short brunettes with large eyes, not tawny-haired busty goddesses. Apparently he was more flexible in his preferences than he'd thought.

When he'd been tantalized out of hiding and into the kitchens by the mouthwatering scent of baking, he'd not been prepared for the astounding tub of sweets that awaited his gaze.

Calliope. His wife.

His wife, naked and soaking wet, her pale skin shimmering like polished opal in the daylight that poured into the kitchen. Long pale legs extended into the air as elegant hands rubbed them pink with vigor. Her hair, neither blond nor quite brown, ran in wet rivers down a lean, graceful naked back.

And, oh, yes, best of all—firm, full breasts, sweetly rounded, wet and glistening, capped in tender points as pink as rosebuds.

Now, her rigid nipples pressed into his palms, begging for his attention. Could that be? Did she enjoy his touch? It seemed an outrageous notion, yet bent close over her as he was, he could hear the uneven pace of her breathing. He lifted her breasts above the level of the water just to watch the ruby tips crinkle further in the cooler air.

As if watching someone else's hands, he saw his fingertips wrap gently around her erect nipples. He tenderly squeezed. She inhaled sharply. Her back arched. He softly twisted. Her hands fisted on the rolled copper edge of the tub. He plucked delicately, pulling the sweet pink tips longer and harder yet. Then he combined all three motions until her breath came fast and her thighs began to scissor together beneath the surface of the water.

It seemed it had not solely been a drunken delusion that first night. In defiance of her serene performance the night before, it seemed his pretty virginal wife did enjoy his touch.

She let out a small, broken cry of pleasure. The pearl, forgotten, slipped from her hand to sink to the bottom of the tub. When her head dropped back to roll upon his thigh, her eyes closed and her pink lips parted in quick, panting breaths. Ren could see the flush of arousal on her cheeks and down her throat and chest. His own aching lust rose like a dormant volcano kept too long beneath the fractured earth.

His want was sudden, as fierce and molten as lava breaking free. His mouth went dry and his head pounded with a rhythm matching the throbbing in his groin. To take her, to plunge hard into her sweet wet heat, to drive himself deep while he ravaged her mouth with his, swallowing her cries—

It was only with the most powerful restraint he had ever forced upon himself that he kept from stripping off his clothes and joining her there in the bath, from slipping down beneath her, lifting her astride him to impale her beneath the water, to fucking her hard and fast until he burst inside her and the bathwater ran across the floor from the great waves he created with his lust.

That would be a lovely way to treat a virgin. Rape her in the kitchen.

His lust rose in argument. She was his wife. A man could do as he liked with his own wife.

Sorry, mate. That is not how we conduct matters here. Be on your way.

Ren's lust retreated, sullenly and with many a threatening glare, but it retreated. He allowed his pretty wife's luscious breasts to slip out of his shaking hands. Her confused, breathy sigh cut directly through him. Then, drawing deeply upon every last scrap of his gentlemanly restraint, he stood and turned his back on her.

"Enjoy the remainder of your bath, Calliope. I shall see you tonight."

Her swallow was quite audible. "Tonight? But—"

She clearly thought this interlude had bought her a reprieve. "Tonight." No reprieve. It was all he could manage to wait that long to touch her again.

Gentlemen did not assault their wives. They did not pull them naked and dripping from the bath to bend

them over kitchen worktables and take them vigorously
from behind.

Bounder. Cad.

Beast.

God, how he wanted to take her vigorously from
behind.

Callie slid down in the chilling water, covering her
breasts with her hands and listening to Mr. Porter's uneven stride fade away down the stone-paved hallway.
Then, remembering, she scrabbled on the floor of the
tub for the pearl.

Tonight.

He wanted more? More than having her naked and
wet, writhing shamelessly for his pleasure?

Of course he wants more. And so do you.

Parts of her did. Parts of her yearned for a great deal
more.

Callie knew a little something about sexual congress.
All the Worthington spawn did. They'd had open access
to literature from around the world. She'd known the
basic mechanics of intercourse since she'd turned twelve
and her mother handed her a heavily bound medical text
with an airy wave and a "Don't mind the illustrations,
darling. All those drawings were done from cadavers."

Callie had barely been able to look at the book after
that. Still, her curiosity had compelled her to warily
peek between the pages and glean enough facts to make
her blush and shut the book with a gasp. Outrageous!
Whose bright notion was *that* ridiculous scenario?

Now, with her nipples tingling hot and hard from Mr.
Porter's . . . er, interference . . . the scenario seemed not
quite so ridiculous. In fact, her body hummed with a
hunger she'd never felt so intensely before. Her feminine
parts throbbed with a sweet ache that made her squeeze

her thighs together tightly and shudder at the jolt of pleasure that resulted.

Mr. Porter wanted to do much more to her, she knew. By the way his hands had slid so reluctantly from her breasts, by his heavy, almost angry stride as he'd left her . . . oh, yes. More was definitely in store.

Licking her lips, tasting the salt and herbs, Callie rolled the pearl across her open palm and pondered the notion that when she returned to her home in a few months, she might return a very different woman than when she'd left.

And she pondered the earthshaking realization that she might just be rather comfortable with that outcome.

Leaning back in the lukewarm water, Callie allowed that astonishing thought to settle and take root in her mind. Closing her eyes, she also allowed her hand to settle between her thighs. What fascinating texts might Mr. Porter have read? Perhaps it was her newly heightened erotic senses, or perhaps she was simply losing her mind, but the thought of doing such a thing outside the privacy of the bedchamber—why, the thought of doing such a thing at all!—sent a hot jolt of excitement through the center of her belly.

I won't. How silly. I would never.

I wager I could be safely done before anyone knew.

Anyone. You mean him.

Yes, I mean him.

He is nowhere near. Unless . . . unless he's watching from the hall.

I won't.

Even as she told herself that, her hand began to stroke softly.

I have become more than wanton. I am decadent. When her fingertips slipped between her labia, she let her head fall back onto the high slope of the copper tub with a liquid moan. She stroked herself and thought of him . . . of his hard, hot hands and the way his breath caught when he touched her . . .

My husband. My mystery lover. A man I have never truly seen.

She thought of a way he could take her while retaining his mystery—as a stallion takes a mare. The image of that, of her on her hands and knees, naked before him, exposed—of being mounted like a wild creature—of rocking hard and fast into him, of him plunging into her again and again until their wild cries turned to animal howls . . .

Chapter 7

Once Callie had dressed and wrangled the heavy copper tub from the kitchen, she was relieved to feel her former exasperation welling up once more. She tracked Mr. Porter down in his study.

"We . . . you need servants."

He'd turned quickly away when she'd entered and pulled his cowl over his face. "No."

If Callie had a sovereign for every time she'd planted her fists on her hips in the last two days, she wouldn't need Mr. Blasted Porter's Blasted Pearls. She'd practically worn sore spots on each side!

Still, there they went, white-knuckled with frustration, digging into her hips again. *I could count to ten. Perhaps one hundred.*

I could turn and walk away, stop trying to talk to the blasted man, stop trying to reach him—

Worthingtons do not quit. Ever.

"Who had the raising of you?"

Ren turned from his pretense of gazing out the window at nothing, glad that he'd remembered to keep his hood on while still in the house. "Whatever are you talking about?"

"I mean, were you raised in a house, by human parents, or perhaps in a cave, by a bear?"

It sounded so very like something his mother would have said that Ren almost laughed aloud. Startled out of the urge by the urge itself, he turned back to the window. "I had human parents once, though perhaps they would not claim me if they could have lived to see me now."

She gave an unsympathetic snort. "Not if they could see how you treat your things. It seems a bear has been loosed in the hall. Perhaps not one bear, but several. There are rooms upon rooms that look as though rather impolite beasts have been making free with them!"

Impolite beast. An accurate enough description. "I have a hundred rooms. I shall scarcely run out in my brief remaining time."

She went silent at that, as she always did when he brought up his imminent demise. Now she was likely ashamed for baiting a dying man. He turned, regretting his bluntness.

She didn't look ashamed. She looked perplexed, annoyed, frustrated, and most of all, delicious. He could still feel her breasts heavy in his palms. He fisted them to keep the sensation safe within.

Mostly annoyed. He felt a pang of wariness. There was a gleam in her eye that reminded him of a certain industrious and exacting governess he'd had as a boy.

Impulsively, he offered her appeasement. "Human parents, but not for long. They passed away when I was but eighteen, within a year of each other. She died of influenza. He simply couldn't live without her, I suspect."

Ren didn't like to think about the way his father had slipped away from him, his gaze always heavenward as if his own son weren't enough to keep him tethered to the earth. *Don't you want to stay around to see how I turn out, Papa?*

Now he might as well take comfort in the fact that no one in the family had been put to the burden of that—at least no one but a distant cousin like Henry.

Callie refused to give in to sympathy. What happened to one as a child deferred blame from the child, but not from the adult. "Perhaps you like living in a dusty, dank tomb, but I'm rather fond of the scent of lemon polish and a roast in the oven."

"You'll be back to that life soon enough."

It was as if he simply didn't care. How could someone not care if walking through a room threw up a cloud of decades-old best-not-dwell-on-it?

He doesn't see it. He doesn't see anything past his own private horrors, whatever they are.

He doesn't see me.

Oh, look. Now her arms were folded over her chest and her toe was tapping. Even Cas and Poll knew enough to flee before her tapping toe. Lysander, back before the war when he'd been the sort to make jests, had dubbed it the Toe of Doom.

However, poor ignorant Mr. Porter ignored the evil toe and went on being insufferable. Callie almost pitied the man. Almost.

"Are you quite sure you won't reconsider? Just a cook . . . and a few housemaids, of course. A laundress. Perhaps a stable boy. A housekeeper to run matters. And it wouldn't hurt to do something with the grounds . . ."

He turned to gaze at her from the depths of his hood. She couldn't see his eyes but she glared at him anyway. His eyes were in there somewhere. How far off could she be?

"No."

The toe-tapping increased in speed. "I'm afraid I

can't hear you. It must be the muffling effect of all that wool. Say again?"

He stepped forward slowly until he loomed over her and she could feel the warmth of him on her skin. Despite her suddenly hammering pulse, she managed to keep her gaze fixed on his "eyes."

Worthingtons had great fortitude.

Said fortitude took a blow when he leaned close into her and bent his hooded head next to hers.

"No." It was only a murmur, husky and deep. It rang through her like a bell. Her heart skipped, her knees weakened, and there was something wrong with her vision . . .

She managed to draw a breath. "Go? Is that what you said? Go hire a full staff, this very day? Well, I did have a relaxing day of lying about planned, but if you insist—"

"Calliope."

Her name became something molten and mind-bending when he murmured it into her ear like that.

She fought the breathlessness. "Calliope was a muse, you know. The muse of epic poetry—as if the world needs any more of that!" Blathering again. Better than fainting into his arms . . . well, better for her pride, anyway. She tried not to think about being in his arms. Lust played bloody hell with pride. "I'd much rather have been named after the muse of music, or even the muse of dance—although Terpsichore would be a burdensome sort of name, wouldn't it?"

He raised his head and loomed at her for a long moment. "Do you ever stop talking?"

She never spoke a word when he put a pearl upon her tongue, but she wasn't about to remind him of that at this moment. Too late, she realized he'd already remembered it all on his own.

His hand came up to cup her cheek and his thumb traced the outline of her lips. His touch was fire to her heightened—and might a girl mention "unsatisfied"?—senses.

She couldn't help it. She licked her lips. Her tongue touched the tip of his thumb. He went entirely still, as if he were a man caught in the Arctic ice. His hand tightened on her face—not rough, but urgent.

"Why do you not draw away from me?"

His raw-edged whisper was no attempt at intimidation, but a query torn from somewhere deep inside him. Callie thought back to the moment she'd glimpsed his ruined face in the night.

The face of a god, torn in half and replaced with that of a demon. What else had been ripped apart when he'd received those scars? Where? When? How?

Before she could ask her questions, she ought to answer his. "Why should I fear you? You have not been unkind to me."

Ren felt as though she were speaking another language, to another man, about another topic. Her words jangled meaninglessly in circles in his thoughts then became clear. Yet he could not believe them. Not unkind?

"You have a strange definition of kindness, if you believe me thus."

She lifted her chin. "I did not say you were kind. I said you were not unkind. There is a difference, in anyone's dictionary."

Not unkind. Ren decided he would accept that, since it was vastly preferable to the way most people seemed to define him. The words made him feel . . . almost . . . like a man.

"And what about you, talkative muse? Are you kind?"

She blinked long amber lashes slowly. He found

himself distracted by the peculiar hints of gold and brown flecks in her mostly green eyes. Like a semiprecious stone he'd once found on his travels. Just a raw chunk of rock, until one held it to the light. It sat somewhere in this house even now. He'd meant to have it polished and set, one of the many things he'd never do now. Jasper, it was called.

"I am very responsible," she said with a slight wrinkle between her light brown brows. "I take care of my family—at least, I keep them from toppling over the edge of disaster . . . mostly, at any rate."

Then her expression turned tragic. "I don't know if I'm kind! I try to be good, and dutiful, and I've never truly harmed anyone . . . but that isn't the same thing, is it? That's—that's merely 'not unkind' again, isn't it?" She looked absolutely devastated—the goddess of distress.

He laughed out loud. He ought not to have—especially in the face of her anguish. He'd considered being condemned as "not unkind" as very nearly a compliment, yet this girl behaved as though she'd just discovered herself an inadvertent murderess!

He brought his other hand up to cradle her face, a part of him yet marveling that she did not shrink from his touch. The other part simply marveled at her. "Mrs. Porter, in the last two days you have rescued your parents from a watery death, myself from pistol point, and your brother from the noose. In your spare time, you baked me a cake. I believe you can promote yourself from 'not unkind' to 'kind' forthwith."

She was gazing at him with a stunned expression. If he hadn't known his hood was well in place he would have thought she saw him.

"You laughed."

He shook his head. "I did. I apologize. It was rude of me."

She blinked. "You laughed—and I can hear a smile in your voice right now."

Ren tilted his head. Hear his smile? He had smiled, he realized. Who was this girl, to see through layers of wool and years of isolation so easily?

"And you tried to ease my distress . . ." Her eyes narrowed. "You know what that means."

He hadn't a clue. He was much too distracted by the sweet planes of her face beneath his touch. He still cradled her cheeks in his palms. His fingertips dipped between the strands of hair at her temples. Her silken, wavy, wayward hair . . . he could touch it for days and never tire of it. And yet she behaved as if nothing unusual occurred, now nattering on again about something—

"I fear I must inform you, Mr. Porter, that you must also rise from your former status."

He blinked, pulling his mind back from the fantasy of her hair trailing over his chest and belly as she kissed her way down—

"What?"

She raised an accusatory brow and poked him in the chest with her forefinger. "I've found you out, Mr. Porter."

Wait. Found him out? God, what had she heard about him? Or worse, what had she found in the house?

He dropped his hands as if scalded and took a step back from her. "I—"

She folded her arms. "You, Mr. Porter, are not the monster you like to seem."

Oh, but he was. And she, poor thing, had no idea.

He took a deep breath, struggling to attain his former imperviousness. "The answer, Mrs. Porter, is still no."

She only smiled. "Fine. Perhaps you ought to take a stroll about the grounds. It would do you no end of good, a bit of fresh air—and I won't have you underfoot."

With that mystifying statement, she turned on her heel and left him with brisk strides that fluttered her skirts behind her.

Ren had settled back into his own dreary—er, blissful—silence and had finally managed to banish from his mind the way that his bride's luxurious breasts sat high and full when she crossed her arms beneath them and stood just that way, chin up, eyes bright, hip cocked while one foot tapped out a vexed rhythm . . .

He still hadn't the slightest idea what had vexed her, but he'd enjoyed the sight of her high color and the way her bosom had jiggled in time with her peevish foot . . .

A rude clang and clatter assaulted his ears. Ripped from his pleasantly lascivious thoughts, he found the mistress of those thoughts had dumped a great armload of things—cleaning sorts of things—broom and buckets and mop sorts of things—

She dusted her hands and grinned at him. "Let's get to it, then, shall we?"

Frankly, Ren had never really considered himself a coward before. But a woman with her hands full of cleaning implements and that peculiar hell-bent look in her eye—

He ran like a rabbit, fleeing the room, and when she began to expand her efforts, he fled the house entire.

As he lurched down the lane, his cloak flapping in the breeze, unsure of his destination except that it be elsewhere, Ren realized that the little vixen had done it.

He was taking a walk.

Vengeance aside, Callie rather enjoyed a good spring cleaning. And while she had no helping hands, neither need she bear distraction! All in all, she thoroughly enjoyed sweeping the carpet, pulling a reluctant shine from wood long unpolished, scrubbing down the hearth and hauling the ashes from the grand fireplace. Windows, freed of years of coal dust and lampblack, let the gorgeous spring light pour in, setting the entire chamber on fire.

Still, she wasn't completely satisfied. Only the inside of the glass was clean. The outside needed a good stiff brush and a bucket of vinegar. She peered down at the mossy cobbles far below the second-story sill and bit her lip.

She would also require a ladder.

Ren walked until he thought he might have made a clean getaway. Then he walked a bit more, just to be sure. Then, surprisingly, he rather felt like continuing his tour of the estate. The day was very fine, cold but clear and with a spicy green smell in the air—the smell of new growing things and freshly turned soil, and, somewhere, there were flowers blooming.

He breathed it in deep, filling his lungs with clean air and his eyes with the aching beauty of the Cotswold countryside.

And it was his.

What an astonishing thought.

Yet, why was it astonishing? He'd taken hold of his inheritance more than three years past. He'd hired a carriage to bring him here. He must have ridden this very lane—yet he had no real memory of it. He'd arrived on the doorstep, seen his few crates unloaded, and then sent the driver away. Henry and Betrice had suggested a woman to come and cook for him, but he'd asked them to arrange a simple regular deposit of foodstuffs instead. And then he'd gone to ground, like a wounded fox taking refuge in its den.

He topped a small rise and paused, enjoying the burn of exercise in his thighs and the cold, fresh air in his lungs. Before him spread a low, rolling vista of fields separated by rock walls of the same honey-gold stone as Amberdell. They poured over the slopes in irregular lines, following the curve of the land more than any sort of human design. If not for the near-perfect furrows plowed into them, one might almost imagine the fields as naturally grown scales covering the back of a great slumbering dragon. Ren almost smiled at the whimsy of that thought, but then he felt the pull of the scar tissue down his cheek and his smile died almost unborn.

More than three? And not once had he taken a turn around his own estate?

He wasn't much of a master, was he?

Then again, what would be the point? He was failing more every day. Every month his body stiffened and bent as the pain grew. If he cared to count and recount his physical impediments, he knew he'd see a similar decline all over. Rather than ponder that grim inevitability, he chose to drink and brood his few remaining days away.

Drink, and brood . . .

And possibly, spend a bit of time in bed.

Not yet, unfortunately. Soon.

Soon he would have his bride so under the spell of her own unsatisfied desires that she would gladly suffer his hideousness hovering over her. Or behind her.

Or beneath her . . .

It was a fine day to stand on a hillock and think about buxom Calliope, pink and perspiring, riding his cock with the same great energy and determination that she now expended scrubbing down his study.

He wondered if she were finished yet. Almost without conscious will, his feet turned back toward home. He wondered if perhaps, grimy from her work, she might take another bath in the kitchens . . .

*   *   *

The ladder Callie found in the garden shed was old and
splintery. For a moment, she questioned whether it was
safe or not, but then decided that she felt more stubborn
than apprehensive and forged on. She leaned the ladder
on the side of the house and wedged the two feet down
between the cobbles. It seemed sturdy enough when she
started to climb, so she carefully continued, one rung at
a time, testing each as she went.

The ladder was just tall enough to allow her to clean
each pane if she stretched just a bit. It wasn't often that
she longed for more height! Quite a novel experience,
really.

One suite of rooms today, start to finish, inside and
out. She smiled to think what Mr. Porter would think of
his masculine retreat, now fit for a lord—albeit a stubborn, undeserving one!

Bending carefully, she dipped her brush into the
bucket of vinegar solution sitting balanced on the outer
sill, then stretched to her toes to reach the topmost corner pane.

Blast it. She was just inches too short.

She glared up at the offending pane. Start to finish—
except for one last pane of glass. There was no help for
it. She would have to climb down, resituate the ladder,
and climb up again.

Or . . .

It wasn't a terribly dangerous idea to step off the ladder onto the sill. Besides, the stone sill was sturdier than
some old rickety ladder! And the formerly shy and retir-
ing windowpane came easily into her reach. A quick
scrub and there! All done, start to finish!

Crash.

"Oh!" The sound from below her seemed to shake her

entire body. The slippery brush flew from her grasp as she grabbed for the window frame in her surprise. She watched the scrub brush fall down, down, down . . .

To clatter on the cobbles next to the shattered remains of the old ladder.

Callie would be the first to admit to the usage of some very bad words at that moment. She was quite glad Dade couldn't hear her.

Well, she could always open the window itself—

In her mind, she clearly relived the moment when she'd automatically thrown the window latch as she'd shut the window.

Start to finish, blast it.

A few more choice words were in order. Thank heaven her vocabulary had them to spare. Five brothers, after all. For a long moment, she leaned her forehead against the cool dripping glass and waited for her breathing to tame her wild heartbeat.

Think, you idiot! Think it through!

Well, being short a ladder meant there was no possibility of climbing down. The latch on the window meant that there was no possibility of climbing in. For a moment she entertained the possibility of climbing up—

No. No higher. She couldn't even conceive of releasing her tenuous hold on the stone embrasure on either side of her.

Break the glass and lift the latch.

Yes. Good idea. The heavy wooden brush would have done a dandy job of that. Blast it.

Tentatively, she let go of the stone rim and raised her hand over the windowpane. Her open palm did nothing but cause the old, thick glass to resonate like a drum.

She would cut herself badly anyway. Perhaps her elbow?

One awkward half twist later and she was done for. Her boot soles skidded on the wet, slippery stone beneath her feet and then she was falling—

The screaming part was entirely involuntary. So was the mad grasping for any handhold. She found one in the deep ridge that time and wind and rain had worn into the stone sill where the window frame met the embrasure. Her descent halted with a jerk that tore at her fingers.

"Help!" There was no point, of course. There was no one in the damned house! "HELP!"

She hung by her hands. Her feet kicked in the air, scrabbling for purchase in the tight seams between the great stones. Her gown got in her way and she cursed it, longing to be a man for one single moment.

No one. No one for miles.

From the hilltop to the southeast of the house, Ren found a rather stunning view of Amberdell Manor glowing like a castle of gold in the slanting light of late afternoon. He made a throne of a large, sun-warmed boulder and took a moment to contemplate his empire. Not bad, really.

For a monster. Except that today, he didn't feel quite as monstrous as usual. For Ren, late of day usually meant stiffness and pain, and often opening a fresh bottle in which to drown it.

Not this time. He'd walked perhaps five miles, up and down hills, awkwardly clambering over dry-stone walls and stomping through tiny tributaries without bothering to jump them. He was exhausted, sweating, and his boots were unpleasantly damp.

He was, however, not stiff. The pain was still there, lacing up his spine, spreading down from his shoulder, yet even that felt different. Looser, somehow—less crippling. He found himself looking forward to a hearty meal and possibly even some sleep later that night. Yes, there would be wine, but he found himself more interested in seeing his bride in her chemise—or in nothing but bathwater, or feeding her bits of cake—than in drowning his senses with spirits.

With an eagerness he found dryly amusing, he straightened from his gargoyle-esque crouch and headed toward the great house.

Headed toward home.

Callie could not hang on. The stone sill fought her grip, warding off her desperate hands with slippery bird dung and gravity. Her own weight dragged her from safety and she regretted every bite of the morning's cake. Her wails and curses never stopped, but not because she thought anyone could hear her. She simply couldn't bear to die without at least sending up a protest.

She was a Worthington, after all.

With great regret, she felt her fingers losing their last bit of leverage on the sill. The unforgiving stone, obviously having plotted against her from the first, now paid her the final insult of abrading her skin from armpit to palm as she fought against her slide to death.

"Great George's Baaaaaaaaaalls!"

Callie's impact shook her from toe to crown, addling her brain in her head and smacking the very air from her lungs. She lay still, not breathing, not quite conscious, not really very interested in becoming so—because really, what was the use when she was just going to die slowly. Pity the window hadn't been on a higher floor. She'd be at peace now if it were, all shining and heavenly, not lying shattered on the cobbles.

Except she didn't feel shattered. Not really. Her bum hurt and her head ached and the lack of air was painful and shocking—and she rather thought she'd bitten her tongue, for her mouth was filled with the metallic taste of blood—yet it wasn't truly as bad as—

Her lungs filled again in a hoarse, gasping whoosh.

When the girl on top of him sucked in a whooping lungful at last, Ren closed his eyes in gratitude. She lived.

That was important. He couldn't recall precisely why at the moment, but somewhere in his mind, he felt relief at that knowledge.

The other things he felt didn't really bear thinking about. There was that terrible wrench in his back and shoulder. There was the feeling that his brains were leaking out the back of his head onto the cobbles of the yard.

On a brighter note, there was the sensation of a warm, full breast spilling out of his palm, swelling upward with every hoarse breath she took. A gentleman would shift his grip.

Ren figured he deserved it, payment for services rendered.

What had the silly creature been doing, hanging out of the window like that? Was she entirely mad?

"What the hell were you doing hanging out of the window like that? Are you entirely mad?"

He was shouting, he realized. It made his head throb rather powerfully, but he truly couldn't help it. Just the thought of that moment when he'd rounded the corner of the house to see her slipping over the edge—

"You bloody little fool!"

She lay sprawled across him, her back to his front, coughing and wheezing her lungs back into submission while he lay wrapped around her, gripping her parts with all his might and shouting in her ear.

It was ludicrous. It was laughable.

He wasn't bloody laughing!

He'd thought his heart would stop forever when he saw her falling, fluttering through the air, and he couldn't make it, couldn't make his battered body move fast enough, reaching desperately, flinging himself between her and the stones that were about to shatter her, break her, ruin her even as he was ruined . . .

"You mind-boggling, addlepated, moronic, bloody *nightmare* of a female!"

The wheezing gasps turned to choking sobs. Oh, hell. He ought not to have shouted at her. Poor frightened—

Bloody hell. The mad little terror was laughing!

Ren nearly pushed her off him right then and there. Then he realized his hood was somewhere else. As in, not on his head, not fallen about his shoulders, not anywhere . . .

He couldn't let her see him.

His hand left her warm, soft breast—really too bad about that—and covered her eyes. For some reason, that set her off even more. She wasn't just laughing now. She was howling, arching in his arms and outright screeching with laughter.

Ren sat up awkwardly, lifting her into his lap while keeping her eyes covered. He felt a foolish smile tug at the scar tissue of his face. She was a complete madwoman. The fact that she was still alive and whole was bloody miraculous. He felt a surge of the same absurd relief, somewhat counteracted by his fury with her.

Looking around him, it wasn't hard to re-create the scene. An old ladder lay splintered on the cobbles. Next to it lay a brush and a dented bucket. He looked up. Filthy water still dripped from the sill high above.

"What were you thinking? That ladder must be decades older than you!"

She lay in his grasp, giggling limply, not even trying

to push aside his covering hand from her eyes. "Perfectly sturdy ladder . . ."

"Obviously not, if it collapsed beneath you."

She drew in a deep breath. "Didn't collapse—goodness, breathing is wonderful, isn't it?—it just fell away. I wasn't anywhere near it."

"That's ridiculous."

"Not if someone pushed it."

So now she was not only mad, she was irrationally suspicious? "There is no one within a mile of this house, but for you and I—and it certainly wasn't I!"

"No . . . no, of course it wasn't you . . ."

Bloody hell. "It was not I!"

"I know that . . . I do. I don't suspect you at all. Not even a little bit . . . really."

She didn't sound terribly sure. Ren fumed and glared up at the offending window ledge. And then down at the guilty ladder.

And then realized that it was, actually, entirely, completely his fault.

The lady of Amberdell Manor had nearly died washing her own windows.

This *was* his doing, his fault for refusing her request for household staff. His fault for expecting a nice, sane—well, not sane, perhaps, but not mad in the same manner as he—young woman to live like a hermit in a cave.

He'd nearly killed her and they'd only been married for two days.

Chapter 8

All in all, Attie found that murder was not terribly difficult. Take a jar of crystallized ginger from the shelf of the spice market stall, drop it into the bottom of her basket, then purchase the small bag of cinnamon bark with a coin and wide innocent eyes.

The spice merchant scarcely looked at her and most certainly didn't notice the way the handle of the basket suddenly cut deeper into the crook of a little girl's elbow. Attie spared a moment to wonder if perhaps all unsolved murders were committed by children. Really, sometimes it was most convenient to be invisible.

Once at home, she dashed inside through the kitchen, depositing Philpott's order of cinnamon upon the vast worktable and disappearing down the hall before the old woman even turned around.

Clasping her basket, Attie wove her way down the hall with the ease of a lifetime of maneuvering around the piles of clutter—which had always been there and how did people live in those horribly empty houses?—and ducking past doorways to rooms occupied by siblings, all the while sidestepping the worst of the creaks in the floorboards as she leaped and ducked and sidled through the narrow bits.

It was a vast, jumbled, nonsensical maze. Attie knew precisely where everything was and loved every square inch of it.

At her own door at last, she locked herself into her small chamber—no one wanted to sleep with her due to her tendency to thrash, kick, and talk loudly in her sleep, a standard she'd established at the wise age of three—placed the very large jar of ginger in the center of the carpet, then crawled beneath her bed to find the box of Philpott's medicine she'd stolen from the housekeeper's room the day before.

Philpott was well-known for her primary health complaint, which wasn't so much an illness as a tendency to decline servings of anything that had once grown from the ground. Lifting the lid on the pasteboard box, Attie gazed down upon the rows of folded paper packets with great satisfaction.

Philpott took one a day with her evening tea. If a single one did service as a mild purgative, surely one hundred of them should kill a man?

Attie, upon counting out her treasure, was disappointed to realize that the box contained a mere ninety-five packets. Scrunching her face into an expression of stormy disapproval, she proceeded to empty each slender packet into her washbasin. A small pile of crystalline powder accumulated in the center. Attie began to fear that her brilliant plan to restore her family might come to naught.

Still, she was a Worthington, and Worthingtons were nothing if not persevering. She gamely carried on, stripping open packet after packet until she sat surrounded by a snowstorm of shredded apothecary paper and had a pile of purgative roughly resembling a handful of sand.

Next she dumped the tall jar of crystallized ginger into the washbasin. Brown, sugar-coated chunks tumbled down to be mixed with eager, vengeful hands.

Then, back into the jar and the metal clamp done up properly again. Attie cast a critical eye upon her project and decided that her reputation as an evil mastermind was not unfounded in fact. The medication had coated the nuggets and mingled most convincingly with the sugar crystals there.

Carefully cleaning her hands and the washbasin as well—she was not foolish enough to leave evidence behind!—she tossed every tiny scrap of apothecary packet onto the coals of her bedchamber hearth. Then, after decorating the jar with a bit of ribbon and a note wishing the newlyweds well—most carefully not written in her own cramped penmanship but in a grand looping style that Attie imagined an empty-headed lady of the *ton* might use—she wrapped it carefully in parcel paper and buried it in the bottom of her basket once again.

This afternoon would do to post it. It should arrive within a day, and then Mr. Porter would eat it and he would die. Attie smiled. She had no worry that Callie might be injured, for Callie despised candied ginger.

In her bedchamber, Callie set down the tray she'd carried up from the kitchens. It held a pitcher of hot water and a pitcher of cold, more of her herbal salt, and a plate of thick slices of beef and creamy white cheese. She was quite ridiculously attached to the cheese. It must be something the local dairymen made, for she'd never had it before. She would miss it when she left.

Her fire was lighted tonight. She'd hauled up a full scuttle of coal earlier in the day, when she'd filled the one for Mr. Porter's study. She would have done the same for his bedchamber, if she could have discerned which of the several disordered rooms he was currently using.

Well, he was welcome to sleep in his damned study . . .

She paused as she spread a freshly shaken canvas dust-cover on the carpet before the fire. Would he wish to sleep in here, with her?

Pensively she removed her gown and her underthings. Before she hung her gown up on its peg, she took a pearl out of the pocket.

One for the bath today.

Crossing to the vanity, she deposited the pearl with the other in the little shell bowl there. Two round orbs shimmered in the faint light of her candle across the room.

This is going to take forever.

The thought was perhaps not quite as upsetting as it had been yesterday.

Taking a few things from the vanity, she knelt upon the pad of folded canvas. First she pinned up her hair, planning to brush it after until all the house dust and other detritus of her busy day were gone.

Her hair was an unassuming shade of light brown, less interesting than Elektra's shimmering blond or even Atalanta's rich amber curls. Not curly, not straight—simply badly behaved.

She didn't mind being the nondescript Worthington daughter most of the time, for she was far too busy for comparisons or envy—and she was well enough, in her way. Certainly she didn't consider herself plain, simply a bit lackluster.

Yet I am the one with a very fine house.

Complete with a very strange husband inside it.

No matter. She soaked her washcloth in the salted, herbed warm water she had mingled in her washbowl and began to remove the remains of her mad, outrageous

day from her skin. She was no silly child, to feel slighted
by the Fates because her life did not resemble some sort
of fairy story. She was far too practical to long for grand
fantasies of love-everlasting, or some such nonsense.
As husbands went, the mysterious Mr. Porter was no
fantasy.

On the other hand, he wasn't cruel in the slightest.
Yes, he'd raged at her about the blasted ladder, yet she'd
not been frightened by his noise. He'd been upset, of
course. If she'd been married for more than two days,
she might even think he'd been concerned for her.

She scoffed at herself as she ran the cloth over her
arms and torso, luxuriating in the warmth of the glowing coals radiating on her bare skin. Mr. Porter had been
no more concerned for her than he would have been for
anyone who had nearly been injured. She paused, halt-
ing in the act of washing her neck. Didn't that very fact
make him a good man?

Ren had also taken some time to prepare himself. There
was nothing he could do about his ruined face and broken form, but there was no reason to subject his bride to
an unwashed monster.

If anything, he ought to try to polish up a bit.

Yes, be a pretty monster. That will help.

He wished he could stop thinking about her. All day,
his thoughts had never been more than a moment away
from her. From the way she'd felt in his arms when he'd
snatched her from Death's very jaws. His heart had
pounded from the danger . . . and much more.

It was as though he'd awoken in that moment, truly
awoken to the feel of her skin, the weight of her breasts,
the sweet warmth of her breath as she sighed at his
touch.

He felt quite wild with it, as if something he'd tried to

pen up, to forget, had been unleashed. It was untamed and it was hungry.

All the more reason for care, for control. He dared not let her see him, not his face and not his dark, inner core where the man he'd once been had left a man-shaped hole not properly filled by the bitter angry urges of the beast. Any hint of that pain-born being would only ensure her departure at the earliest. She would leave any-way, as soon as she could. Even half the pearls would bring in a tidy bit of coin, so there was no guarantee that he would have an entire year with her.

You're lucky to have had one night. Every moment she allows you to touch her is one more than you have any right to expect.

In his most recent room, wrestling himself into an-other loose-fitting shirt that was decades out of fashion, Ren caught sight of himself in a small mirror hung over the washstand. He thought he'd removed them all.

Stepping closer, he gazed at himself in the glass. *Yes, look hard. See what she saw when she screamed in ter-ror. See what she will see if she ever dares to open her eyes.*

He put one hand up to block the most damaged side of his face from his view. When he did this, he could get a glimpse of the visage that had greeted him the first twenty-five years of his life. It was like catching sight of a stranger he'd once known well. An older, worn, sallow version of that stranger. A crescent-shaped scar the size of a guinea marred his brow, and narrow white lines cut into his overgrown beard, but it was still a familiar sight.

He'd been called handsome, before. He'd certainly never had difficulty catching a girl's eye, being always ready with a smile and a flirtatious word. He'd walked with confidence in a dangerous world, as sure of his superiority as he'd been of his immortality. He'd belonged in that world, as surely as Miss Calliope Worthington . . . Porter . . . belonged in her ridiculous family.

Brotherhood, camaraderie, a sense of being part of something larger and more important—more than enough reward, he'd thought then.

Until one of his brethren betrayed him into enemy hands, sold like an unbroken horse to a disreputable trader, without a care of the consequences to him. He'd believed in that mad band of misfit patriots—believed with a faith built of the same stone as his loyalty to them.

He moved his hand, to show the other half of his face. Consequences.

The worst scar ran from his forehead down over the corner of his eye and down his cheek to his jaw. It pulled his eyelid down as if his flesh were melting and twisted his mouth into an ugly grimace. There were more scars, stretching back from his cheekbone and tracing through his hair, to the place where his skull had been cracked with a rock, a final act of mercy leaving him for dead.

Incompetent bastards. When one set out to kill a man, one ought to have the decency to see it through. Beaten, brained, and stabbed, and they still hadn't managed to finish the job.

They'd driven a pike right through him, into his chest and out through his back. The rest of his injuries from that dark night that he could not recall were minor in comparison, but left his face and body a map of scars—a map that had led him here, to hide his monstrous self away while he waited for the end that a London physician had assured him would come mercifully soon.

He hadn't cared. Why would he want to live in the world? To frighten children and make pretty girls scream at the sight of him? To make the local villagers twitch their fingers against the evil eye when they were forced by necessity to make deliveries to his cellar and his larder?

His hand dropped to his side and he gazed at his entire face.

Good morning, Mrs. Porter. How did you sleep last night, bedded in with your lurching Caliban of a husband?

One swift step brought him close enough to send his fist into the mirror, smashing the glass and cracking the elderly wooden frame into three pieces. As he placed his hand on the latch of his bride's chamber door, Ren noticed his bleeding knuckles.

More scars for his collection.

"Keep washing." The deep voice came from the doorway behind Callie, sending a jolt of surprise through her. She sensed him moving across the room toward her but kept her gaze on the small blue and gold flames darting through the coals of the fire.

"Keep washing."

Slowly she bent to wet her cloth, then raised her arms to wring it, letting the rivulets flow down them to trickle over her body. The drops of hot water struck her chilled skin and she shivered at the contrast.

Then she ran the cloth over her arms to her shoulders and the back of her neck. A large warm hand covered hers there, taking the cloth from her.

"Allow me."

The gracious phrase did not have the ring of a request.

Command.

For the second time that day, he bathed her. The warm cloth moved over her back, around to her belly, over her breasts, between her legs. Callie writhed slightly at his thoroughness. Why was this so much more intimate, more invasive, than his shocking exploration of her body last night?

Perhaps it was the tender care he took, or the way he swept her hair off the nape of her neck with one hand while he washed it with the other, or the way his warm exhalation tickled her ear when he reached around her from behind and she heard his breath catch as he slid both wet hands over her skin.

The night wrapped hushed about them. The house hovered silently over them like a protective shell, shutting out the world and its noise and bother, leaving only the soft *shush* of the washcloth on her skin and the crystalline *pings* of the water dripping back into the washbowl and the breathless thundering of Callie's heartbeat in her ears.

It was arousal, yes, most definitely, but it was so much more—it was the way he spread her fingers to wash carefully between, as if she were a tiny child, and the way he cupped her chin in his warm fingers as he turned her cheek toward him to remove a smudge she'd missed.

When he put down the washcloth and picked up her hairbrush, Callie felt her throat close at the considerate, careful strokes of the bristles through her tangled hair.

She relaxed into the brush, sitting silent and naked with the fire warming her skin in front and Mr. Porter's large presence warming her from behind. He kept on, stroke after stroke, long after her hair was shining and tangle-free.

She'd not known she needed such a thing until it was given to her. She'd not realized how the long years of nurturing others had kindled a deep and silent ache to be cosseted and cared for.

He had known. Mr. Porter must surely understand the arid lack of such in her life, or he would not handle her thus.

The poor man.

The poor, kind, *good* man.

"I like it when you are naked. I like it even better when you are naked and wet."

Perhaps "good" wasn't precisely the right description.

Yet Callie felt not even the slightest shiver of fear. He had saved her life today. The ladder . . . well, he clearly didn't believe her, but once she'd worked the shaking out of her knees, she'd realized she could hardly think him guilty of endangering her and in the same breath thank heaven he'd been there to catch her!

Quite frankly, if he gave her the slightest encouragement to accost him, she would have him down on the carpet in a heartbeat, showing him exactly how much his thoughtfulness meant to her.

Slowly, now. Mustn't frighten the wary wild thing away.

If she waited, patiently—well, stubbornly, anyway—and pretended a passivity she didn't feel, he would show himself to her.

Oh, not the hood. She had no hope of that anytime soon. No, he revealed himself with the way he touched her. The sensation of being touched with such longing and deep, aching need was most exhilarating. Especially now that she knew that not only would he not harm her, but that he would go to great lengths to protect her.

So when he held out the shimmering little symbol of their bargain, she took the pearl upon her tongue and closed her eyes.

He stood and, taking her hand, brought her to stand up before him. The heat radiating from his body surrounded her, soothing and burning at the same moment.

"You belong to me, Mrs. Porter. For this little while, you are mine. I have bought you."

Callie nodded, lowering her head in submission. The

rough emphasis in his voice when he said the word "mine" . . . a streak of hot fire went through her at his intensity. It was a heady combination, this mingled excitement and trust, anticipation and faith. What might have been frightening became intense and stimulating. What might have shrunken her soul with fear became glowing and empowering. To be wanted the way this man wanted her . . . she'd never thought to know such a thing!

She wondered if she would want him the same when she had him in her grasp at last. She heard the rustle of fabric and knew that he had removed his hood. His face . . .

One really shouldn't care about superficial things like that . . . yet, didn't she revel in his lust for her body? Didn't she want to be wanted? Surely he wanted to be wanted, as well?

Oh. Oh, my. It was as though the key to him fell into her hands as she stood compliant at his command. He wanted her to want him . . . so he thought to make her want him so intensely, to taunt her body so wild with lust, that she wouldn't care about his damaged face and form.

The sharp bite of sympathy went through her. Not pity. He was too powerful and intimidating to truly stir her pity. Yet, to be so sure one was unworthy of love . . . to think that manipulation and extortion was the only way . . . it was just bloody heartbreaking, that's what it was!

She felt him lean in even closer. The crisp, clean scent of him was quite astonishing. Her rigid nipples brushed the silk of his dressing gown.

They stood so close they were almost one.

He leaned closer yet . . . and softly kissed her neck.

The exquisite tenderness of it quite took Callie's

breath away. Oddly, her eyes stung behind her closed lids as he trailed a line of small, warm kisses down her throat and then up the other side of her neck to her jaw.

She turned her head instinctively, seeking to meet his lips with her own. She felt him draw back.

"Be very still."

Yes, he liked her to remain still. She would obey. She would be as still as a hunting cat in the dusk.

He kissed her cheek, then her temple, where his breath stirred the tiny hairs at her brow. He kissed below her ear and then traveled back, tilting her head down to kiss the back of her neck, moving around her slowly, working his mouth, now softer and warmer, now hot and wet, around the back of her neck and out along the ridge of one shoulder.

Then he came to stand in front of her again. This time when he kissed her throat, she lifted her chin and leaned slightly into his kiss. She couldn't help herself. How was she supposed to feel when from the darkness came soft, tender lips and hot, tracing tongue and gently nibbling teeth? He was fair to driving her mad and he'd not yet shifted below her collarbone!

And then he did, dipping down her sternum until his lips pressed directly between her breasts.

Oh, yes. Yes, please. Please . . .

Then his mouth, seeking slowly, found her nipple at last.

Where before she'd experienced the demanding intensity of his hands, it had in no way prepared her for his mouth.

Fierce. Urgent.

Oh, Sweet Charlotte's Arse! Oh, the *heat*! The swirling tongue and the way his teeth brushed gently across her hardening nipple, the way he sucked her in, deeper. A cry escaped her lips, wordless and wild. She could feel his need as he fed upon her . . .

A hot throb of wetness erupted between her thighs and her knees wobbled.

His response was to wrap both his big hands about her rib cage and pull her up, arching her back to bring her breasts to his seeking hot volcanic mouth.

She rose to stand on tiptoe, with no fear of falling whilst in his hot urgent grasp. Her head fell back in complete submission while he sucked first one nipple, then the other—sucked, licked, nibbled, sucked again, harder as she felt her nipples swell and spring forward as if begging for more. She would have begged as well, had not the pearl in her mouth kept her silent.

Ren could not get enough. He slid his hands down her smooth back to grasp her bottom hard. Lifting her, he sat her upon the vanity to more easily avail himself of those lush, white mounds. He moved between her widened knees in order to feast upon her.

His bride tasted of salt and rosemary, of sweet creamy virgin and wicked temptress. Inflamed, he squeezed her bottom hard, making her gasp and wiggle in his gasp. God, he wanted to devour her, to consume her, to engulf her until there was nothing left of him.

Bending, he dropped his mouth down to the soft pale curve of her belly, to the saucy flare of each hip, to the peach-and-cream perfection of her open thighs. There was no stopping.

Almost kneeling before her now, he kissed his way up from each knee, her skin getting warmer as he moved higher, warm and damp and then the sweet-salt taste of her desire upon her inner thighs.

No, he dared not. If he plunged his starving tongue into that sugared, tangy delicacy, he would not stop until he'd ravaged her body in every imaginable way. Twice.

Dizzy lust almost overwhelmed him at the thought.

No. He was too hot, too wild tonight. Control . . . he'd meant to exert control.

So, with agonizing restraint, he planted one fervent, promising kiss upon the short damp curls of her mound, and then he took a single agonizing step back.

Oh, no. Not again.

Chapter 9

Callie couldn't believe it. Again Mr. Porter brought her to such a damp and throbbing arousal and again he meant to leave her like this?

I am going to make him pay for this somehow. Gone were her sympathetic leanings. She was near tears of sheer frustration.

Mr. Porter, I'm going to make you moan and ache and writhe . . . and then I'm going to step back and let you sit cold and empty and alone!

The door closed. Callie opened her eyes. The first thing she noticed was that he'd knocked the little shell bowl from the vanity in his want. Her pearls were spilled across the floor. Two pearls. She opened her mouth and removed the third.

When exactly did he plan to consummate their bizarre bargain? Perhaps upon the tenth pearl? The twentieth? A celebration of the first hundred?

Oh, blast, what a terrifying thought.

Ren strode down the hall, cursing himself and her and then, abruptly, rejoicing in the memory of the taste of her sweet flesh.

Bloody hell, he'd never wanted someone so, not even his fiancée, Lisbeth.

Odd. He'd dwelled upon the pain of Lisbeth's rejection for so long . . . and yet in this moment, he could not quite put a hand upon that formerly ready pain.

He'd been so enamored of Lisbeth's doe eyes and shy smile . . . although she'd not been shy at all, he realized now. He'd been too young and stupid to know then that he was being hunted most professionally. She'd laughed at his poor jests and beamed up at him with those large soulful eyes, and when he really thought about it, she'd never really said much about herself, never really said much of anything, except how wonderful/brave/interesting he was.

Nothing like his bride. Irritating Calliope wouldn't shut up. All she did was talk about that bloody family of hers.

Except when he put a pearl in her mouth. Then she became something else, something soft and malleable in his hands. At that moment she wasn't his outrageous, outspoken, unconventional bride, she was . . . she was whatever he wished her to be.

Every man's dream, no doubt. And he'd created this creature. He'd designed it.

He was beginning to hate it.

How could he have been so witless? If a man wanted nothing more than willingness, he could pay for it—although Ren couldn't bear the thought of a whore's reluctant exercises whilst hiding her revulsion.

But Calliope's willingness was based on something strange and wrong. He'd extorted this from her, taking advantage of the impossible position her family had put her in. That he had put her in, damn it.

This twisted perversion of passion wasn't good for her. He only hoped he hadn't ruined her forever.

Perhaps the only way to break her from this strange enchantment was to shock her out of it? She was so compliant . . . what would it take to make her push him away?

Suddenly, bitterly, perversely, he felt the need to discover that limit. She would leave him someday soon anyway.

Why not discover what would really drive her away from Amberdell?

The next morning, Callie had scarcely reached the bottom of the stair when the knocker on the great door startled her into flinching.

Goodness, she'd nearly forgotten there were other people in the world!

The parcel she was given at the door was a gift, a great jar of crystallized ginger. "Oh, dear," Callie murmured. There was no signature on the card, although the handwriting seemed familiar.

"I despise candied ginger," Mr. Porter said dismissively. "You may have it."

Callie gazed at the giant jar with dismay. "I can't say I care for it, either," she murmured to no one, for Mr. Porter, who had only emerged for a moment when the unaccustomed sound of voices in the hall had roused his interest, was already gone. Of course, the insufferable lout had waited until the post boy had left, taking Callie's last penny with him.

Now the silence of the house descended once more and Callie fought an unbearable urge to flee the place.

Eyeing the ginger with her nose wrinkled, she let out a breath. "There must be two pounds of it in there, at least. A shameful waste."

Her gaze slid to the brilliant spring day visible through the open door. Another waste, that lovely day . . .

Worthingtons were never wasteful.

An hour later, Callie had on her spencer and her best bonnet and her feet under her. It had been quite fun, tying up portions of the gifted ginger into pretty little muslin packets and tying them with odd bits of ribbon from her workbasket. They made a cheery pile in the basket she carried over her arm and an even better excuse to visit the village and introduce herself there.

It was more than a mile to the village. The day was crisp and sweet-smelling and the lane stretched out before and behind her. The great house was long out of sight and the village not yet near. Callie was entirely alone. No clamoring family. No brooding bridegroom.

A short laugh of delight burst from her lips. To test the surety of such an unheard-of moment, she picked up her skirts and did a twirl in the middle of the lane.

Heaven. It was as if she were the only person in the entire world!

She dipped a deep, ironic curtsy to no one at all.

Go on, fellow, grab your girl.
Take her hand and let her whirl!
If she comes back, then dance you on.
If she don't, then hell, she's gone!
Take the next one, she might do.
If she won't, then take you two!

Callie was none too sure of the words of the bawdy country dance but once upon a rainy evening, Cas and Poll had entertained them all performing such dances. Poll had looked most fetching in Callie's old dress, although Ellie had later complained that he'd distorted her best bonnet by shoving it down on his big fat head.

Now Callie spun and dipped and curtsied to her happy solitude, laughingly mangling the bawdy song until she had to stop, gasping and grinning in the sunlight.

"Idiot," she admonished herself fondly. When she'd caught her breath, she spared a moment to pin her hair back up properly and to brush some of the dust from her hem.

Then, very lady-of-the-manor, she made her way sedately down the lane. The only remaining sign of her silliness was a small, beribboned packet fallen deep in the high grass on the bank.

Slowly, at a pace guaranteed not to catch up to a strolling pedestrian, a horse's giant black hooves clopped down the lane. When they reached the bright bauble left behind, they stopped.

Ren gazed down at the pretty parcel, but in his mind all he could see was the woman, skirts picked up high to reveal sweetly turned ankles and calves and the occasional maddening glimpse of ivory thigh, dancing and laughing in the light of day.

Callie's high spirits did not last past the first glimpse of the village of Amberdell. It was a pretty enough place—the quintessential English spot, just prosperous enough to be proud, but not a center of industry. The nexus of activity was of course the high street, with its handful of essential shops and a smithy.

It wasn't the village itself that drained Callie's good cheer as much as it was the way everyone in the village seemed to turn and gaze at her in the selfsame instant. Callie became abruptly aware of herself in a way she'd never quite felt before. It was as if she were being examined beneath a convex glass, the way Orion would magnify plants and insects for study. In London, the Worthingtons were considered eccentric, but that was genially tolerated due to their long acquaintance with, well . . . everyone. Callie was accustomed to a rather blithe disregard for opinion, bolstered by old family connections and the simple fact that in her family, she was considered quite unremarkable.

Now, she realized, as the new lady of Amberdell Manor, the finest estate in the area, she was anything but unremarkable. Although the lingering stares felt like an icy wind upon her skin, Callie pasted on a friendly smile and strode on into the belly of the bea—the center of town.

Her first encounter, aside from the suspicious gazes and behind-the-hand whispers, was with the proprietress of a shop signified by gold figured lettering as MDM. LONGETT, DRESSMAKER.

Callie had no intention of ordering a gown, really. She had several at home, waiting to be shipped here. She'd simply ducked into the nearest recognizable refuge. She could not afford a bootlace, much less a new frock.

This sanctuary revealed itself to be a trap. Callie found herself in a shop absolutely filled with titillated gazes. A full dozen persons of the female persuasion occupied the room.

She felt like a mouse suddenly introduced to a boxful of cats.

A woman in a dressmaker's pinafore whom Callie assumed to be Madame Longett surged forward with a frozen smile. She was rather stout and plain and ruddy faced. Not at all like the exotic presentation on the front window. Still, Callie smiled back.

"Hello. I am—"

"Mrs. Porter!" Teeth still clenched in the unconvincing grin of greeting, Madame wrung Callie's hand. "How . . . um, charming to meet you . . . er, at last . . ."

At last. Callie had been in the area precisely four days. Apparently that—and an admittedly short courtship, and

wedding a man who was never seen without a hood—
was all that was needed to cause a storm of gossip and
speculation.

Yes. Well. Rather.

Callie tried to smooth matters over by pretending that
she'd come especially to see Madame herself. "I'm in
dire need of your help, Madame. I've just come from
London and I find I've nothing suitable for the country."

Callie had simply meant that she was in need of some
practical walking dresses, which she wasn't, really, but
even as the watching eyes narrowed in resentment she
heard the words falling from her lips.

"—like she's trading silks for flour sacking."

The hostile murmur sounded quite clearly in the awkward silence. Gasps and horrified giggles were the group
response.

Callie raised her chin and valiantly forged ahead. "A
muslin, I think, for the warmest days. Have you anything
in a stripe?" She'd find a way to pay for it somehow.

It was no good.

"Naw, we ignorant country folk haven't progressed to
stripes yet." Again, the snide murmurer had the room in
repressed stitches.

Madame was obviously torn between alienating her
usual custom and obtaining the patronage of the new
lady of the manor. Her eyes conveyed desperate pleas to
Callie.

Come back later.

Or possibly, *Come back never.*

You have a basket of gifts on your arm. Use them.

As what, defensive projectiles?

She had a fine right arm, for a girl, Dade claimed.
Callie pictured the invisible murmurer with a face full of
lumpy ginger. The absurdity allowed her to turn to the
wolves—er, ladies—with a cheerful smile. Reaching

into her basket, she pressed a packet into each reluctant hand.

"Just a small token of greeting, so nice to meet you all, do hope you'll call . . ."

It wasn't working. Blasted country imperviousness! In desperation, Callie heard herself uttering dangerous words.

"We're hosting a ball soon, you must say you'll come—"

What? No. Oh, Sweet Charlotte's Arse, what am I doing?

"Such a fine, large house, I can't wait to fill it with guests—"

There was no hope for it. Her mouth, apparently, belonged to someone rather more impetuous than she.

"Oh, soon, I should think. Mr. Porter is most eager to greet the village at last—" *Not impetuous. Suicidal.*

Somehow, Callie escaped the dressmaker's having promised a ball and, without really knowing how, having ordered half a dozen muslin gowns in the "latest style," whatever that was.

Callie practically ran from the village, blindly thrusting packets of ginger into the hands of everyone she encountered, stammering, "So nice to meet—really must come—what a lovely day—"

Once out of sight, she sat on a grassy hillock near the lane and buried her face in her hands. *I panicked, I plead insanity, I don't know what came over me . . .*

What were the chances Mr. Porter would merely chuckle indulgently and pat her on the head and say, oh, where's the harm in a little gathering, just the nearest and dearest . . .

Entire village. I invited the entire village to a ball.

I invited the blacksmith to a ball.

And quite possibly his dog, as well.

Oh, no, sorry. That was his mule.

Hysteria bubbled up inside her, carrying with it the thought that this, indeed, might convince Mr. Porter that she ought to be sent home at once . . .

Panic subsided like boiling water doused in oil.

Mr. Porter didn't like strangers. Mr. Porter was going to be furious with her.

Callie's lips began to turn up in a slow, evil smile. If she'd had a mirror near, she'd have been surprised at the resemblance to her youngest sibling.

Except that even Attie wouldn't dare go this far.

In the dressmaker's, the women of the village were still in full riot, carrying on about the ball. Betrice stepped out from the group and watched Callie's back as she rushed down the lane.

A ball. It was brilliant, really. Betrice wondered how Callie meant to pull it off in a mere week, but she supposed with Lawrence's resources, one could have whatever one wanted.

She gave a sigh as she contemplated the blue silk she'd been fingering before Callie had entered. It was far too dear, though it would look fine on her and Henry never begrudged her anything—but a blue silk gown wasn't worth doing without sugar or the fragrant cinnamon that Henry so loved. Betrice's mother had raised her to put her husband's desires first in all things.

Betrice let the silk slip from her fingers and resolutely turned her back on it.

Such a beautiful blue . . .

She left the chattering shop behind her with relief. Too much temptation by far.

Callie was still in sight in the High Street. Betrice found herself abruptly turning the other way, though she had no business there.

With her head turned, her gaze still on Callie, pondering the capricious nature of fate, she didn't see the giant man before her until she nearly bounced off his chest.

Vast hands wrapped about her upper arms, catching her when she stumbled in surprise. "That's it, now, Mrs. Nelson."

At the deep voice Betrice looked up in recognition. "Unwin!"

She hadn't seen him for ages, although he likely delivered Springdell's supplies on a regular basis. Betrice was not one to mind the tradesman's entrance, leaving that to Springdell's cook.

Now, she gazed up into a face she knew as well as anyone's in the village. Wide and coarse now, his features had once seemed manly and rough to her, like her romantic imagination's pirate or highwayman. A passing fancy, a silly girl's fascination with the forbidden, that was all.

He'd always wanted her, although she had ever been out of his reach. She, the only child of a very prosperous farmer, and Unwin just the old grocer's boy. She'd tried out her budding flirtation skills upon him when they were not much more than children, and she'd felt his eyes following her ever since.

Now his gaze had followed where hers had been fixed. He scowled, his thick features darkening in anger.

"Should've been you, up in the fancy house. She isn't as fine as you, nor as pretty."

Betrice looked down, adjusting her gloves. "Mrs. Porter is from a very old family. I'm sure she'll make a fine mistress of Amberdell Manor."

Could she be blamed for the slight hint of bitterness in her tone? Not by Unwin. He was a bully, really the closest thing the village had to a true ruffian. To Unwin, she could never sink low enough to be unworthy, or improper.

Something of a relief, really.

"Mr. Porter was the next in line. There was no help for it. Mr. Nelson would perhaps be a better master, as far as the village is concerned, but he cannot take what he has no right to, can he?"

"Porter is ill, some say. Some say he's dyin' even."

"I'm sure I cannot say."

"Well, he ought to die, that's what. Him dead, there'd be no one standin' between you and Amberdell Manor!"

Betrice shook her head. "I can wait for Mr. Porter to take his natural time of life. He is a sad man and full of despair . . . but if he should have a son . . ." She sighed. "Well, the future will be what it will be, I suppose."

She turned to give Unwin a quick, sad smile. "You ought not to worry about me. Mr. Nelson keeps me in bread and shelter. The finer things . . . well, perhaps someday." His sympathy was a balm, but she wouldn't like to be seen in long conversation with him. "Now, I must load up my pony cart and be on my way. Give my greetings to your family, Unwin."

As she left town, traveling a good bit faster than Callie was, she could feel Unwin's eyes upon her, like always.

It was nice to know she hadn't yet lost her looks.

Chapter 10

Callie smiled, happy to have found a friendly face at last.

Hadn't it been kind of Betrice to stop her cart and invite Callie to Springdell for tea? Callie longed for tea, having unearthed none in the Amberdell kitchen as yet.

Betrice showed her into a large and comfortable parlor. To Callie's newly enriched eye, the room showed the wear and tear of years. Compared to the richly appointed manor, it was apparent that Betrice and Henry lived in genteel poverty.

Of course, compared to the negligent chaos in the Worthington household, this home was a haven of serenity!

Callie wondered if it bothered Henry to live so close to the riches that were almost his. However, when he bustled into the parlor a few minutes later, his open face and welcoming smile dispelled that unworthy thought.

"Calliope! My dear, how are you today? You look well—doesn't she look well, Betty? Yes, you look very well, indeed!"

Callie laughed aloud at his boisterous greeting and

returned his bearlike hug with real affection. Henry's outgoing nature did a lot to explain Betrice's reserve—she likely had no choice!

After she'd been seated and served and regaled with Henry's latest adventure digging out a vitally important spring that had been clogged with a recent rockfall—this story being accompanied by illustrative hand motions and relevant sounds—Callie had a moment to reflect upon the couple when Henry's foreman appeared to discuss another farming crisis and Betrice rose to pour the man a cup of tea.

When she returned, Callie cast a glance about the room. "I had not the chance to inquire . . . do you and Mr. Nelson have children?"

"Not as yet." Betrice smiled wistfully. "I hope we will have children. My Henry is such a paternal sort of man, don't you think? I daresay he'd like half a dozen children about the place."

Callie forced a smile and nodded. Mr. Porter wasn't the slightest bit paternal . . . was he?

Paternal? He's barely even human half the time.

He was a protective sort, but when Callie thought about her own sweet grumpy papa, testy when disturbed from his scholarly pursuits, yet always so indulgent and approving—even of Cas and Poll's semilegal adventures.

Papa never roared.

Mr. Porter had a tendency to do just that. Snarling, certainly. Callie felt as though she were describing a not very well trained pet.

Papa, Papa, take off your hood!

No, perhaps not the most paternal sort . . .

Callie sipped her own very nice tea and thought about the vast, cold emptiness of Amberdell Manor. Rich and tasteful, indeed, but so very silent and sad.

When Henry returned to the table, Callie was determined to learn more about her new home and her new husband, as well.

"Lawrence?" Henry pulled a contemplative face. "No, we were not acquainted as children. I knew of him, of course. I always envied him, living a glamorous life in London, going to fine schools, traveling the world . . ." At Callie's blank expression, Henry paused his expansive speech.

Callie swallowed the sip of tea that had just gone a bit bitter on her tongue. "Traveling the world?"

Betrice poured more tea into Callie's china cup. "Yes, of course. Haven't you noticed all the exotic treasures at Amberdell Manor?"

Callie stirred her tea, though she'd added nothing to it. "Yes. I simply thought . . . well, he did inherit the place." She cleared her throat and forced a smile. "So these travels—they must have been . . . *before*."

Henry squinted and wrinkled his bulbous nose. "Before what?"

Betrice planted a subtle elbow in her husband's side. Callie only saw it because she was a proud practitioner of that particular tradition with the males of her former household. With Castor and Pollux she often wished her elbow were encased in armor. With spikes.

"Harrumph! Oh, yes, well . . . that would definitely have been . . . before. He used to write to our cousin a great deal . . . before." He chuckled in memory. "Rather racy, those letters!"

Betrice did not seem amused. "Cousin John would call for Henry every time a letter arrived," she said to Callie. "He and Henry would go over every detail, debating what Lawrence might mean by a certain phrase or innuendo. Old John actually suspected Lawrence to be a *spy*." She said it with a ladylike hint of disdain.

"Silly notion." Henry waved a large hand. "I thought

him simply a mad adventurist, perhaps planning to write it all down one day as a published memoir. I believe it was the chief source of entertainment for both of us for years."

Where were those letters? Could she read them? Callie desperately wanted to pry. She shouldn't. Oh, well, why not? "Has he ever told you what happened to him?"

Betrice shook her head. Henry, however, took on a stuffed expression that Callie recognized. When seen on the face of a man such a look meant that he knew something, desperately wanted to share the aforementioned something, but rather thought he ought not to.

Very well, then. Callie did her best imitation of her sister Elektra and let out a long, sad sigh and turned deeply troubled eyes upon Henry. The big man's eyes practically crossed in his effort to keep his secret.

Hmm. Add a little Atalanta? Callie let her lower lip tremble ever so slightly.

"I feel terrible asking such things. I know I should wait until Mr. Porter sees fit to tell me . . . it isn't as though he knows me . . . or even l-l-loves me . . ." To her surprise, actual tears began to swim in her eyes. Goodness. She'd watched Ellie use such tactics on Papa since her sister learned to talk. As Henry began to spill out words so quickly Callie could scarcely keep up, she noticed Betrice eyeing her with something like respect.

Ah. A fellow fighter in the war of the feminine. She turned her attention back to Henry, who was still urging her not to weep.

"It's not as though I know very much, not much at all, really, considering he's my very own cousin—but our cousin's solicitor had to search for Lawrence for a very long time before he was found. There was a time when it was discussed that he be declared dead and that I be named heir. Then a man came—"

"Sir Simon," Betrice supplied helpfully.

"Yes, Sir Simon came and he met with the solicitor and when he left, the solicitor would speak no more of the case, not even to me, which seemed very odd. To tell the truth, the man seemed to be almost . . . well, frightened."

Callie drew her brows together. "Frightened? Whatever of?"

Henry leaned forward. "Well, it was that fellow, that Sir Simon Raines, that was his name. He knew that Lawrence wasn't dead, that's what. And if he knew that, then he might also know where he's been and why he's so . . . well, yes, that's only idle curiosity, I suppose. The sort that killed the cat, I'd wager." Henry nodded vigorously. "That fellow, he's the one that found Lawrence and sent him here to us, I'm convinced of it."

"But found him where?"

Henry shrugged, his big shoulders moving like boulders. Callie turned her gaze upon Betrice, who only smiled and shook her head.

"It isn't only you who wonders," Betrice said. "Lawrence is a popular topic in the village. Now, you are, as well."

Callie blinked. "I? Why, I'm nothing at all."

Henry found himself called away again at that moment. He left graciously enough, but Callie could tell he'd become uncomfortable with the conversation.

Excellent. Betrice was much more forthcoming.

Callie struggled with the proper opening. "Marriage is certainly an adventure, don't you think?"

Betrice looked slightly perplexed. "It is the only adventure, is it not, if one is unlucky enough to be female?"

Her statement carried a hint of flat bitterness that made Callie's fingers twitch with curiosity. There was clearly a great deal going on beneath Betrice's serene manner.

"Well, yes . . . I suppose so. I rather think most marriages begin a bit more conventionally—although I wouldn't mind so much if only I could persuade him to remove his hood."

Betrice stared at her. "Have you never seen his face?"

"Oh, of course I have! Well, once anyway. Just for a fraction of a second." She turned to look at Betrice. "Have you?"

Betrice shook her head slowly. "No. Henry has, or did once, when Lawrence first returned. He found him quite terribly drunk and picked him up and put him to bed in one of the chambers . . . but when I asked Henry wouldn't speak of it. He only told me to wait until Lawrence learned to trust us."

Wise and tolerant, but annoying and entirely not useful.

"So . . . how is that little matter of trust coming along?"

Now it was Betrice's turn to look embarrassed. "I've always tried to be gracious . . . but I cannot help the fact that he frightens me a little."

Callie's eyes widened. "Frightened? But he's . . . he's . . ." She pursed her lips, unable to define her own reasons for trusting Mr. Porter. "He saved my life just yesterday."

Betrice blinked. "Saved your life? Was your life truly in danger?"

Callie, like all Worthingtons, relished a good tale. "Oh, yes. I was cleaning windows, you see."

Betrice frowned. "But you're the lady of the manor. Why in the world would you . . . Oh, well . . . I suppose it must be difficult to acquire staff."

Callie waved a hand, uninterested in that less amusing domestic sidetrack. "I was cleaning the glass in the study, because I could scarcely tell the time of day through it! So there I was, hanging from the sill by my hands when my fingers began to sli—"

Betrice gasped. Callie turned to see her new friend had gone entirely ashen. "What is it?" Callie thought back. "Oh, pooh. I forgot to tell the part about the sabotaged ladder—"

Betrice's hand went to her throat in shock. "*Sabotage?* You believe . . . you believe someone intentionally tried to harm you?"

Callie blinked. Somehow her adventure, while dire enough at the time, had taken on the glow of a good narrative once resolved. It took her slightly aback to see how the simple retelling of it seemed to bring Betrice to a state of shock. She frowned slightly. "You are a very sensitive girl, aren't you?"

Betrice blinked. "I . . . I mean . . . what?"

Callie sighed. This was always happening when Worthingtons encountered outsiders. Her own family would have seized upon the excitement and drama of the fall and rescue, with Mama caroling joy at the romance of the groom dashing to save his falling bride at the last possible moment.

Betrice was behaving almost as if . . . as if the entire matter had been *real*.

But it had been. Callie could've died. Something icy went through her belly at that realization. "I might have died," she repeated to herself quietly.

Betrice had her hands pressed to her face, only her wide stricken eyes showing.

Callie wasn't pleased with this new, grim, sharp-edged view of the world. She lifted her china teacup and shot a determined smile at her friend. "Betrice, really. Everything came out just fine. No harm done and the matter persuaded Mr. Porter that a bit of staff about the place would be beneficial." She patted the stricken Betrice on the hand. "So stop gazing at me as if you'd sighted the ghost of me." Really, Betrice did tend toward the overly sensitive sometimes. Why, she'd had nothing to do with it, so there was no reason to sit there looking so devastated.

"Oh! I haven't yet told you of the mad thing I somewhat accidently did!"

Now this really was a strange story. At the end of it, Betrice simply stared at her. "You spontaneously invited the entire village to a ball?"

Callie grimaced at Betrice. "I know. I don't truly know how it happened. I just wanted them to . . . you should have seen the way they looked at me."

"I daresay it isn't you at all." Betrice set down the tray on the pretty carved stand next to Callie. "I'm afraid when the heir to Amberdell Manor was found, the local folk thought that they'd been saved. A new squire in the manor should have meant an influx of custom. A new staff should have been hired, maids and footmen and gardeners, a stable full of grooms and stable boys . . . they were most disappointed, as you could assume."

Callie nodded. It made sense. "And then there's the . . . ah . . ."

Betrice shot Callie an unreadable glance. "Yes. The hooded recluse persona. Not the openhanded squire they had hopes of. Quite a lethal combination for village disharmony, I'm afraid. You really shouldn't have braved it alone. You could have handed out gold sovereigns instead of ginger and you still wouldn't have stood a chance."

"But what should I do? Now they all think I'm mad, too, like as not."

"Perhaps you should go back to London—"

Callie looked up in surprise. Betrice was carefully not looking at her.

"But I—"

"If I had any family left, anyone at all," Betrice said with quiet ferocity, "I wouldn't let them out of my sight."

Callie subsided in pity. Poor Betrice. With only Henry at her side, she must be terribly lonely.

Betrice poured the tea and handed Callie her refilled cup before she'd even realized it was empty. Callie spared a sigh of envy for Betrice's effortless hostess skills.

"You ought to have been lady of the manor," she said with a rueful smile. "You appear to have been born to it."

Betrice's tea slopped over the rim of the cup, just a bit. She shook her head violently. "No, I should have hated it. I'm all right here, with the staff I've had all my life and the villagers I've known forever. But I—I'm no good at all with new people."

Callie blinked. She'd thought Betrice reserved, but could it be that her new friend was really quite shy? "You're good with me and I'm new."

Betrice shot her a small smile. "You're family. That's different."

The chill caused by Callie's rather horrible morning began to thaw at once. *Family.*

Imagine, finding family all the way out here in the Cotswolds. It was like being handed another sister!

Then she narrowed her eyes at Betrice. "You're not by any chance an evil mastermind, are you?"

Betrice blinked in frank shock. "Wh-what?"

Callie shook her head and wrinkled her nose. "Sorry. Never mind."

Betrice wasn't a Worthington. Just a nice ordinary-variety sister.

When Callie left Springdell behind and made her way back to Amberdell Manor with a lighter heart and a swinging stride, her smile had nearly regained full brightness. Two new cousins! Lovely people. Generous, as well, for at the thought of her walking, they'd promised her the loan of a mount and a lady's saddle until she sorted out transportation at Amberdell.

Her smile faded slightly as her thoughts wandered to the prospect of indeed hostessing a ball. Yet . . . why not?

If the village resented Mr. Porter for his reclusive ways, what better way to show them all that they needn't fear him? If they came to meet him, all of them, it would dispel the mystery and a grand night of food and dance should dispel the resentment, as well.

And if everything came from the village—if Callie ordered from the butcher and the grocer, and perhaps Betrice would lend her very excellent cook. And wasn't there a school for unfortunate girls nearby? Callie could ask the girls to come and serve and perhaps pick out a likely lass or two to take on housemaid positions—ones with strong nerves and cheerful dispositions—then Mr. Porter needn't fall back into his lonely ways when Callie left . . .

By the time she'd reached the bridge over the river, Callie was half convinced that she'd planned the ball all along for Mr. Porter's benefit.

If only she could convince him not to hide behind his hood—

Suddenly she gasped and clutched her spencer to her chest. Oh, heavens, she was brilliant!

She would throw Mr. Porter and the village a grand masque.

Chapter 11

Scarcely a quarter of an hour after Callie had left Springdell, Betrice answered an urgent pounding upon her front
door.

It was Teager, a carpenter and general man of work
from the village.

His usually genial round face was tight with worry.
"Please, missus, you got to come. There's a sickness in
the village!"

Betrice's first instinct was to pull on her cloak and fly
away to the village to render aid, as she had always done,
as her mother had done before her as the wife of the
steward of Amberdell—the closest thing the village had
to a lady of Amberdell.

Her mother had filled those shoes all of Betrice's life,
had instilled in her daughter the urge to tend the village,
and all unknowing, had filled Betrice's head full of aspi-
ration.

Now that dream lay in the dust of the lane, trampled
by the unknowing strides of Calliope Worthington.

Betrice turned expressionlessly to Teager. "I think
perhaps you ought to call upon the lady of the manor."

Teager shook his head vehemently. "We need you, Missus Nelson. No one will allow that one into their homes!"

Betrice blinked in surprise. "But whyever not?" Surely a few social gaffes in a dressmaker's shop wouldn't cause such an aversion!

"Because it were her what brought the sickness!"

Callie frankly dawdled on her way back to Amberdell. The late-afternoon light painted the stunning country-side with a golden brush. Even the dusty gravel of the lane seemed to glow. Could it truly be that more wild-flowers had bloomed since she'd walked the lane this morning?

After her lifetime in London proper—although of course she had journeyed out of it on occasion—Callie felt as though she drank the beauty in through her very skin. She paused on the same bridge where she had al-most washed away just a few nights ago. Now the river chuckled amiably below her, shimmering with fiery glints that made her eyes water.

London was gray stone and soot and noise, and yes, art and culture and science . . . but peace? Not in the Worthington household. Not outside it, in the bustling streets. Not even in the parks, which on fine days were filled with people, horses, dogs, and children.

Never alone. Callie thought if two words could de-scribe her existence before this, it would be those. Now, she spent so much time alone . . . what in the world should she do with herself?

She'd known what to do once. There had been a time before Attie's birth when her brothers had been away at school and she spent her time avoiding Elektra's girlish prattle by keeping her nose in a book, or by . . . by drawing.

She closed her eyes against the river's shimmer and let her eyelids turn the reflections into a rosy peaceful glow. Once upon twelve years or so ago, she had spent hours of every day drawing and painting intricate botanical studies. She'd loved it so, for it combined the two things she found most stimulating—art and science together. Not for her those hazy, dreamy watercolor landscapes, sentimental and inaccurate—yet not the single-minded study of botany, either, turning the very symbol of life itself into dry, scholarly facts.

Then Attie's birth had turned difficult and Mama had nearly died. She'd remained in her sickbed for many months, and had little strength for nearly three years afterward. Callie had cared for Attie and Mama both, and been happy to do so. Attie was her darling and Mama perhaps the only person on earth who truly understood Callie's innermost soul. Young Elektra had been appalled when she learned Callie meant to pass on her Season, but funds had ever been short and who would care for everyone while Callie wasted her time talking to boring people and spinning in circles on a dance floor?

Still, she did plan on finding a husband. Eventually Mama had recovered and Attie, once so tiny and frail and constantly ill, had become a robust and ingenious toddler who had progressed directly from screaming animal sounds to complete sentences. Dade had come home from the war unhurt and ready to take some of the burden from her shoulders. Callie had felt the world open up around her, although she'd never thought of herself as being caged before.

Then Lysander had fallen in the Siege of Burgos. The news of his death—confused and untrue, of course—had sent Callie's parents into deep mourning. Then he'd been found, fevered and raving in a soldiers' hospital. Callie had instantly disposed of her renewed plans for a Season and set herself to healing her dear, broken brother.

Time and rest and loving care had eventually healed his body, but it had been a very long time before Lysander spoke to any of them—at least, spoke anything resembling calm and rational sense. The family was perhaps not so swift to recover.

First mourning his death, then worrying over him, had done something to Mama. She'd drifted away from them, losing herself in her paintings. Papa had hidden from Lysander's ravings in his Shakespearean studies, composing endless versions of the same paper extolling the possibility that Shakespeare had in fact been a woman. His evidence was slim and his scholarly community scornful, so the days grew into weeks into months into years while Papa polished and researched.

Callie found herself dealing with Mama's responsibilities, while Dade took on Papa's. Their dear, sensitive, but injured parents became two more children in a house full of them.

But she and Dade were not Mama and Papa, and their siblings knew it. The house became a place of abrasive conflict and constant, noisy unrest. The bonds of love were strong, but the hands steering the course were untried and sometimes hesitant. Dade did his best to understand Lysander and to keep the twins' antics within legal limits. Orion became analytical and cold, scorning the theatrics of Elektra and the dark shadows of Lysander. Attie spun from one sibling to another, now drawing Lysander out with a brutal game of chess, now piquing Orion's temporary interest with her intellect, then joining Cas and Poll for a spot of sibling terrorism, or allowing Elektra to spoil and pet her like a doll, then finding herself ignored by her glamorous sister.

Callie tried to help, providing a steadying influence, but Attie, out of all of them, had the least illusions about her family. She'd never known the early days of serenity and joy and, yes, occasional madness but always something to laugh about later. Callie felt sorry for her sister, just about to slip into womanhood without ever really having a childhood, at least not the sort of childhood Callie and the others had enjoyed.

Guilt stung her eyes and chilled her belly, but Callie did not allow herself to dwell upon her abandonment of them. She'd had no choice. The loss of Dade would have ruined them all forever! And this arrangement wasn't everlasting. She would return home someday soon. The pearls would help so much, and someday she might find herself a rich widow.

That part of the plan felt unpleasant and hollow now. She could not longer pretend to be blithe about the fact of Mr. Porter's limited time on this earth. The poor man.

Perhaps, when he'd become more accustomed to her presence and did not flee the house every time she picked up a broom, she could find a way to do more for his comfort.

Something plopped into the river and Callie opened her eyes. The frogs were out once more, popping from their muddy winter homes. Soon the warming evenings would be filled with their peeping song.

After their brief rest, her eyes drank in the beauty anew. It was all so glorious, from the greening trees to the burgeoning tiny lives to the brilliant color of the wildflowers. Like her awakening body, warming and pulsing with life.

And right now, Callie had nothing better to do than to enjoy it all.

Gazing down at the riverbank, she smiled. Cowslip flowers peeked yellow eyes up at her. As common as grass, yet Callie had always loved the cheery little blooms clustered at the top of their bobbing stem. Cowslips meant the winter was gone and better times were ahead.

Come to think of it, she had a bit of paper in her basket, meant to leave as lists and orders in the village—and she always had a pencil in her reticule . . .

Penny Longett, the Amberdell dressmaker, was a woman of small talent and great determination. She'd had a brief career in the London shops as a modiste; well, to be perfectly frank, she had worked for a well-known modiste, at any rate. She had traded on that slightly embroidered reputation when she'd moved into the country with her husband years ago. He had died soon after, but he'd left her with enough coin to open a shop and she'd done all right in her way.

There weren't many true dressmakers in any nearby towns or villages, so she had a bit of custom from the surrounding areas and not a great deal of competition.

However, with no lady in the manor and with even Mrs. Nelson, dear girl that she was, inclined to pinch her pennies until they squealed . . . well, it was all a widow could do to survive in such times. She hadn't counted on the way women in the country did for themselves, trimming their own bonnets and refashioning their gowns every year for a new look at a fraction of the price of new!

So when a strange little man rode up in an extraordinary little pony cart, entered her shop and offered her a thick wad of banknotes to abandon her post for a long holiday in Brighton . . . well, Penny had kissed him upon the top of his balding little head and dropped her shop keys into his palm without a tremor of guilt. It would all keep until she came back . . . if she ever came back!

He was following her again.

A hunter upon the scent.

More like a hound after its mistress.

It wasn't as if he had anything better to do. Amberdell Manor was losing its brooding appeal, room by room, as Hurricane Calliope swept through it. How was a bloke supposed to lurk properly in rooms full of light and flowers and the smell of beeswax polish?

Positively irritating.

When he had first come to Amberdell Manor, it had been shut up for more than a year already, silent and dark. Ren had never thought to look beneath the dustcovers in most of the rooms. It turned out he had a very fine house, indeed.

She was doing something else today. At first he'd thought she was headed back from the village again, but she'd turned aside at the bridge and was following the riverbed, picking her way down the bank, turning her head from side to side. Had she dropped something? If she were looking for some of her lost possessions, she might wish to look downriver instead of up.

Suddenly she exclaimed and bent to pluck something from the ground.

She was picking flowers. Again.

Ren didn't think the house needed any more.

Yet Callie didn't seem to want a bouquet. Instead, she stepped closer to the river and carefully washed whatever it was she had found. Then she crossed to a higher bank and seated herself in a patch of sunlight. Her basket apparently contained a sheaf of papers and a pencil.

She was drawing.

Bemused, Ren continued watching from the rise behind her, allowing his mount to drop his head and graze the hillside. There his bride sat, upon the damp ground, her stack of paper on her knee and her pencil in action. She made a pretty picture, a shapely girl sitting on a grassy bank on a sunny day. He only regretted being too far away to see what it was that fascinated her so.

Chapter 12

It took Callie several tries to recapture her onetime ease with the pencil. Drawing was nothing like writing. She most flagrantly used up sheet after sheet, covering them on both sides with tiny beginnings of a leaf, or a petal, or a root system.

Then, suddenly, she had it again. The pencil seemed directly connected to her eyes, with no awkward hand in between. Each stroke pulled detail from the carefully arranged specimen before her. Not just the shapes, mind you. Botanical drawing wasn't simply a pretty picture. The illustrations had to represent, truly, every scientific aspect of the plant.

Yet Callie also wanted to capture the way the tiny yellow flowers made her feel. She wanted someone looking at the drawing to understand her joy at the burgeoning spring about her, and in her discovery of a perfect example of this common little sprout, this harbinger of warmer rain and longer days. Spring wildflowers seemed brave to her, chancing a bloom that might yet be struck down by frost. She loved the summer flowers, as well, with their lush abundance and fragrant blooms, often bent heavy with bees drinking their fill of the nectar within.

She adored even the seed pods formed in late summer and bursting in fall, flinging out hope for the next season, assurance that even if this plant did not survive the cold weight of snow, there would be blooms in the years to come.

She would have to come back after the seeds set . . .

Her fingers moved faster and faster, her mind already filling in the colors of the petals, deeper in the center, and the way the underside of the fuzzy leaves gleamed a silvery tint.

Ren watched her for over an hour. He had dismounted and crept closer, stretched out on his belly like a boy watching ants. The front of his coat and trousers became damp in the grass, but his back baked warm in the sun, the dark wool drawing it in, relaxing the muscles of his aching back and shoulders.

He nearly fell asleep in the sun, like a lizard on a rock, listening to birdsong and the burbling of the river and the crunch, crunch of his horse cropping grass behind him.

She was singing again, absently, in tune but without much thought, simply repeating a few phrases of that country dance tune she'd sung in the lane as she pared away at her pencil with a tiny penknife. Sometimes, when she seemed to be concentrating particularly hard, her bonnet bent low over the paper, she would simply hum the melody. Then it blended with the birdsong and left him with the drowsy impression that he'd been hearing her accompany the birdsong all his life.

Except for the last few years. He'd not heard a single note from a bird since waking from the deep unconsciousness of coma. He'd not noticed, not precisely, yet he'd missed it all the same.

Where had the birds gone?

The birds are where they've always been. Where did you go?

I was locked in my own mind, following the spiral of pain and anger.

That swirl of loss and agony seemed to have slowed, allowing him to dismount that unbroken steed and set foot on the earth and the sun-warmed grass once more, just for a moment.

However, he was beginning to ache in this unfamiliar position and clouds had risen to cover the sun. Callie nearly lost her stack of drawings to a sudden gust of wind and Ren spent several moments admiring her lithe form as she chased down the errant leaves.

The disturbance seemed to bring a halt to her enthusiasm for the moment and he watched her pack up her basket and shake out her skirt. He allowed her to get ahead of him, for he feared it would take some time to pry his aching bones from the ground and remount his horse.

The breeze blew a sheet of paper past him and he caught it reflexively. It was a simple practice sheet, covered with unconnected leaves and petals and wiry lines he realized were roots. Even in the quick sketchy manner he could see the skill.

A good cook, a superb housekeeper, and a talented artist. And yes, a rather attractive person, especially naked in the candlelight.

How such a girl could have sprouted from the madness of the Worthington soil he could not imagine.

Well, he would send her home rich enough to bring her ease, and when he died she would easily find another husband with the fortune her widowhood would bring her. No longer would she be wasted tending that ungrateful mob.

As he peeled his reluctant limbs from the damp ground, he scowled at the thought of that other husband. The bastard had better treat her properly.

Ren arrived back at the house to find Callie's spritely pace had returned her long before he'd walked his aching bones home on his bored horse. He'd pushed himself to properly stable the gelding, but now he stood in the front hall, leaning on the newel post and wishing he'd remembered that he was a dying man, not a spry youth who could lie about in a meadow and pay no price for it.

With his eyes closed, he realized that the scents of flowers still filled his senses. Flowers and . . . beeswax. And drifting up from the kitchens came a hint that she was doing something delicious to ham and potatoes.

Before she came, the house smelled of dust and tobacco and, during some of his worst weeks, him. Before, it had smelled of solitude and despair.

Now, Ren stood in the hall of his fine house and drew in deep breaths of life . . . and woman . . . and home.

Any woman could have improved this place. I could have hired a housekeeper and been living like this all along.

He opened his eyes and let his gaze follow along the wall until he found the source of the fresh flower scent. His lips twitched. She had taken a priceless Ming dynasty vase and stuffed it full of nondescript weeds. It was like dressing a charwoman in satin and putting her on a throne.

Yet the motley bouquet smelled spicy and lively, bringing spring inside the house in a way he'd never before experienced. So, not just any woman, then. Only

Calliope would choose flowers for their scent and not their blooms.

On the two-hundred-year-old commode that had lived in the homes of kings, next to the vase, there also lay a stack of drawings and a tiny stub of pencil . . . and a fist-sized chunk of Cotswold limestone, just the right size to keep paper from blowing in the wind.

Ren smiled slightly, ignoring the pull of scar tissue in his cheek.

No, there was only one Calliope.

His smile faded. It was truly going to hurt when she left him behind. The house would go stale once again, reeking of dust and tobacco.

He ran a hand through his hair, dislodging a bit of grass there. He crumpled it in his fist with a snarl. Rage rose within him—rage at himself for allowing that damned family to take refuge in his house and at her, for bringing life and laughter and flowers, and then bloody taking them away again!

When Callie had prepared a simple potato hash with onions and ham for her supper, she automatically filled a plate for Mr. Porter, as well. Then she gazed perplexedly at it. Would he join her? He'd certainly been nowhere to be seen all day. Would he find it in the larder eventually? It seemed a shame to let the steaming treat chill and congeal.

With a small smile, she put both plates on a tray and picked it up and, with a candle in her other hand, made her way through the dark house to Mr. Porter's study. She tapped on the door with the back of one hand, juggling the tray and candle. No answer.

She pressed the latch and opened the door. "Mr. Porter?"

But the somber, masculine room was dark and cold, not even an ember in the hearth. The man wasn't even home.

"Fine," Callie muttered. "Enjoy whatever the mice leave you in the morning." She plunked his plate down on his desk and stomped out of the room.

Really! She cooked and cleaned and played willing virgin every night—the man could at least have the courtesy to come home for supper!

Callie stopped halfway up the stair, halfway through a truly satisfying grouse. Sweet heaven, she sounded like someone's wife!

She looked up the steps into the shadowy floor above. "I am someone's wife." In that moment, the entire matter seemed entirely surreal. Any moment, one of her family was surely going to pop out and laugh about the good trick they'd played on her.

But the house remained dark and silent and entirely Worthington-free. Which was what she wanted. Truly.

Suddenly very weary from her busy day, she trudged up the rest of the stairs while chewing thoughtfully on her bottom lip.

I am alone. I wanted to be alone. I used to ache for just an hour of solitude.

At that moment, she couldn't for the life of her remember why.

When she got to her room, she entered listlessly and set her candle and tray with her own supper on the vanity. She leaned a half-turn away from it and put her hands behind her back to undo the buttons of her gown.

Her candle went out.

The room was plunged into total darkness. Callie's small gasp was drowned out by the sound of something moving toward her, fast. Before she could inhale to scream, she felt a hard arm go about her waist and was lifted from her feet.

The darkness whirled around her, then she found herself on her feet with her back pressed to the chill plaster of the wall.

He was on her like a starving beast. Big hands dug into her hair, pulling it from its pins, dragging it down over her shoulders, then sliding down her shoulders to wrench at the tiny buttons behind her even as his hot mouth descended upon her bare neck. As he ground his body into hers, he growled with lust and need.

It was terrifying. It was wild and animal.

Callie found she liked it very much. Her heart pounded. Her breath caught. She stood completely still and allowed every second. She could have stopped him if she wished. Five brothers, after all.

He had trouble with her buttons, so he flipped her, pushing her bosom against the wall while he stripped her gown open down the back.

She could feel the hardness of him behind her, feel the heat from his body, feel the urgency of his desire in the urgent roughness of his big hands on her skin.

Oh, yes. Mr. Porter was beginning to lose control.

Callie was glad the darkness hid her satisfied smirk.

Then he took both shoulders of her gown in his hands and pulled it down to her waist in a single hard motion, trapping her elbows tightly at her sides and baring her breasts to the chill plaster of the wall.

She'd wanted to break through to him . . . but now she feared she would be the one to break.

Ren could scarcely think for the hot blood coursing through his veins. His cock was so rigid it was painful to be trapped against her soft bottom . . . fantastically, outrageously exquisitely painful. He could not resist the urge to thrust harder against her yielding flesh. Her response was to gasp softly . . . but though she held no pearl in her mouth, she gave him no protest.

She didn't know. She thought him a man. She thought she wanted him but she'd never seen him, not really. He was a broken, ruined thing, a creature that should be kneeling at the feet of a vibrant healthy beauty such as hers.

She thought she knew him . . . when she'd never even seen him in the light of day.

This darkness now, this suited him. For all that he craved to see her he felt freer in this blackness than he'd ever felt even in the safety of his hood.

Coward.

I never claimed not to be.

Now, he had to make her desire so overwhelming that she would come to him, willing. Eager. Ardent.

He finally gave himself permission to have a taste of her . . . he bent, inhaling the sweet, flowery scent of her soap and the sweet, earthy musk of her arousal, to press his mouth to the skin of her shoulder. He felt her go very still. He thought she might even be holding her breath but he refused to be charmed by her sweet willingness. His fury and his lust burned through him, firing his blood, overwhelming his thoughts and his second thoughts and even the ache of a day of unaccustomed activity.

He took her shoulders into his hands again, roughly turning her to face him so that he could bend to taste, to consume, more and more of her.

Her neck, her throat, the sweet hollow at the base where her pulse throbbed against the tip of his tongue.

Down . . . down . . . the tops of her breasts, lush and full. He devoured them, sucking her flesh into his greedy, starving mouth. He almost forgot his plan then, as he bent over the sweet luxury of her breasts, the silken skin, the strawberry roughness of her nipples. He circled them with his tongue, ignoring her gasp . . . no, absorbing her gasp, storing it away in the vast empty bank of memory, right next to the overflowing storage of fantasy.

He sucked each nipple into his mouth in turn, sucking hard, taking ownership of them with his lips, tongue, and teeth. She writhed in his grasp now, gasping and whimpering at the pleasure/pain he gave her.

She didn't protest, she didn't push him away, only stoking his lust with her broken whimpers, even as he let his teeth graze over her sensitive flesh. Her submission excited him, frustrated him, enraged him—would she never allow him to see within her? Would she never show him her true revulsion?

His hand seemed to travel down her torso all on its own. Her undone gown gaped open, fallen and folded about her waist—he thrust one seeking hand down inside, even as he fisted the other in her hair, tilting her head back the better to devour her neck and throat with his mouth.

Oh, that wayward hand, slipping down past her satiny belly, diving questing fingers into the silky curls of her pubic mound . . . Her thighs were tightly pressed together. He spared a thought to wonder if she was trying to refuse him, until he realized that she was scissoring the damp plump flesh of her inner thighs together to find some instinctive relief from her arousal.

His hand dove between, a thief in the dark, stealing into that sweet, hot heaven that was far, far too good for the likes of him.

Callie nearly screamed in passionate release at his merest touch. Oh, yes, finally . . .

Mr. Porter's hand was a wild ride upon a half-tamed horse. His fingers slipped into her, around her, through her. Hot and wet, coaxing and demanding, invasive and inviting, he broke her down into a panting, mewling wanton creature, her hands trapped, forgotten, still submitting, still willing.

Yet it eluded her. She didn't know what precisely she sought. She knew the names, climax, fulfillment, orgasm. She'd explored her own body's pleasure points . . . she was thirty years old, after all. Yet never, ever had her own touch done this to her!

She opened her thighs wider, without even being urged, her hips thrusting out to aid him in his quest. More, please, more . . . so close, she knew not to what . . . lust trembling on the precipice, needing one more step to fling herself over the edge. His long finger stroked deep within her, withdrawing, thrusting, invading, owning, violating, satisfying . . .

She orgasmed, hard and suddenly, writhing between his pinioning hands and the cold plaster of the wall. Wild, anguished, broken moans poured from her, but the sound was so far away she was scarcely aware. Hot waves, icy shivers, ripples of undulating pleasure stole her breath and her words and her thoughts, leaving her bucking and gasping at his mercy. Rippling outward from her center, they faded at last, dropping her down, down, gently down, until she realized that she stood shivering, half naked and sweating, trapped between a wall and a man she had never truly seen.

This is mad. This is too strange, too wicked.
This is wonderful.

All those years of loneliness and deprivation, years of lack and longing, swept away by this man and his hot mouth and his clever, clever hands.

Callie's knees gave way. She slithered down the wall. He came with her, supporting her graceless, unselfconscious fall until they were both on their knees, facing each other.

Callie's arms were still trapped by her gown twisted about her waist, or she would have flung them about him and wept upon his shoulder. As it was, she could only drop her forehead upon his sternum and press herself, breast to chest, into her savior. "Thank you," she gasped. "Oh, thank you so much."

Ren, who had been lost in his own lustful haze, driven there by her quivering, eager flesh and her wildly arousing moans, and was darkly contemplating rolling her down upon the carpet and fucking her until he'd spent himself at least three times, was brought abruptly back to reality by her words.

She thanked him . . . for what? For pushing her up against a wall, ripping her clothing off, and stealing her first orgasm for himself? For debasing a fine and respectable young woman with his dark urges? For tricking and trapping her, for compromising and then virtually kidnapping her from her life and her family, for offering her a sullied bargain of jewels for sexual favors?

Who the hell was Calliope Worthington, that she would thank a man for that?

So Ren found himself wrapping his arms carefully about his shuddering bride, too stunned by her gratitude to either push her away or to ravage her, or fulfill any other of his beastly intentions. Instead he simply held her close until her tremors eased and she lay still and limp against him.

When Callie caught her breath at last, she realized that she could still feel Mr. Porter's towering erection pressing into her hip. What should she do? It only seemed polite to offer some similar relief—sweet heaven, what a relief!—but she didn't have the words or knowledge to do so. Then she became aware of the tenderness of his embrace. He held her as carefully as if he thought she might flee him, lightly as one would capture a living bird.

In all her life she could not recall such an embrace, so protective yet at the same time almost tentative. It made her want more. Suddenly, wildly, she ached to feel more such things—the tight longing embrace after parting, the easy affection of intimate laughter, the harsh wild embrace of lust unleashed . . . There was so much more to be had with a man . . . with this man . . .

And by heaven, Callie wanted it all!

Chapter 13

The following morning, Callie awoke in fine mood, indeed. She stretched sensuously in her big bed, shared by no sister, and contemplated her first true orgasm.

It would be a bit embarrassing, but she wished she could tell Mama. Mama would be so happy for her, like when Callie had gotten her courses. There had been cake with sugar icing and the gift of a lovely, lace-edged handkerchief, the kind a woman carried, by her plate that evening. The boys had pestered to know what the occasion was, but Mama had only smiled. Elektra had known, had been jade-green with envy, Callie recalled with satisfaction.

Callie buried her smile in her pillow. *Oh, Ellie, if you only knew.*

And yet, she and Mr. Porter had not yet consummated their union. She'd truly expected him to, right there on the floor. She'd felt it in his hands and his mouth and the way he pressed his erection against her.

More was in store. Callie's smile widened wickedly.

She was terribly interested in that erection. She'd seen illustrations, of course, and one couldn't live with six men without stumbling across the odd penis. In fact, she'd changed her younger brothers' nappies as a young girl.

However, that did not at all explain what she'd felt against her last evening. Mr. Porter seemed very large. One assumed that nature would provide, but Callie dearly wished she had one or two of those manuals at hand today to compare. Surely her imagination had been fired by her lust.

Surely.

Then Callie recalled that she had a much more pressing problem.

She'd invited the entire village to a ball—and she had nothing to wear!

This time when Callie entered the village, hardly anyone seemed to take note of her presence at all. She found out why when she entered the dressmaking establishment of Madame Longett.

Everything looked much the same, but suddenly an elfin little man popped up from nowhere, his face wreathed in a smile. "Hello, dear lady! How may I be of service?"

It was not for Callie to comment upon the strangeness of finding this smartly turned out little man where she'd so recently encountered the somewhat frowsy Madame Longett.

It was possible that he'd been there all along . . . although by the gaggle of astonished women she'd seen lingering on the walk outside, she doubted it.

Still, he beamed at her in a most friendly fashion and that alone was such a relief that she nearly wept upon his elegant shoulder.

His beaming smile had not lost a single candlepower. "Have you need of my assistance, madam?"

Callie smiled helplessly back. "I ordered a few dresses yesterday . . . well, then I decided to throw a ball to celebrate my marriage . . . well, not decided exactly . . . it just sort of erupted out . . . do you know, I felt exactly like a volcano . . ."

She was acting like a gibbering idiot and this nice little man simply smiled encouragingly, as if she were making all the sense in the world. At his mild approval, she felt her nerves calm a bit. She smiled and shook her head ruefully. "My apologies, Mr. . . ."

He bowed. "Button, madam. I have stepped in whilst the fine Madame Longett is taking her holiday. I should be happy to make you anything you desire. I assure you, my skills will not disappoint."

She had a feeling he wouldn't disappoint. One didn't live with Elektra Worthington without picking up a notion or two about fashion, and Callie was certain that the dapper Mr. Button was the most fashionable person she had ever encountered. She had a feeling that he was having a bit of joke on her . . . and yet she didn't mind. If it was a jest, it was sure to be a kindly one and she would likely benefit from it and look back upon it with rueful approval.

She knew this because that was precisely what she did to her own family . . . and a bit like what she was planning to do to Mr. Porter, now that she thought on it.

Straightening, she nodded crisply. "I require a ball gown and I only have a few days. I have very little of my own at the moment. I know my family intends to send my things on, I thought they would have done so by now, but without me there to direct matters . . . well, things tend to slide a bit."

Mr. Button beamed at her as if she'd hung the moon and then for an encore decided the stars were too few. "I imagine your family misses you terribly. Such a lovely smile you have, madam. It has surely brightened the halls of your family home all the days of your life."

Thinking of her occasional screeching fits of frustration, usually brought on by Cas or Poll, or Attie, or Cas *and* Poll *and* Attie, Callie blushed. "I imagine they are toddling on without me well enough." *They are surely sinking like a barge made of stone.* "Mr. Button, I realize it isn't possible to have a proper gown made up in only a week's time—"

"Ah, but impossible is my forte, madam. I eat it for breakfast and hang it out to dry by noon." He winked.

She laughed at his absurdity, yet his madness was very convincing somehow. She certainly couldn't be any worse off than she was already. "It would be lovely to leave the matter in your hands, sir. I've never thrown a ball before and I hardly know what to do as it is—"

He held up a hand, palm flat to her. "My dearest Mrs. Porter, say no more. I know precisely how to throw a ball. Tell me, do you have thoughts upon a style? A theme, hmm? Spring is quite lovely in the Cotswolds. A pagan rite, perhaps? Or classical, with you gowned as Persephone, Goddess of Spring?"

"A masque," she said firmly. "And I dare not make it too elaborate, for I've invited the entire village, and I'm not certain but it is possible there will be livestock attending, as well."

She'd got him there. He paused, mouth open, doubtless ready to extol upon his skills once more, but she could see the shiny brass clockworks inside his mind turning as he regarded her in blinking startlement. "Well, it isn't as though I'd meant to invite the blasted mule!"

For a long moment, she worried that he might in fact faint. Then he finally drew a breath.

"Invitations," he blurted, a bit desperately. "Yes, invitations are quite the thing. When one has an invitation in hand, a reference to the event, so to speak, with clear instructions as to attire and er, er . . . attendees . . ."

"Yes. Invitations. I suppose I could write them out tonight." But tonight she would be naked and anyway her calligraphy hand was hideous. She was much more inclined to a crabbed, scholarly style.

The miraculous Mr. Button merely waved a graceful hand. "No, madam, I insist. I shall see to the matter myself. Er, is there anyone . . . else? The village of course, and what a marvelous notion, a lovely opportunity for everyone to greet you and congratulate you upon your very fine match." He dismissed the population of the village as if penning the invitations would take no more than a moment of his time. "You mentioned your family? Do they reside nearby . . . close enough to attend?"

"Family. Oh, dear." *A recipe for a nightmare, that is.* "I love my family but . . . my husband . . . it was rather difficult to . . . er, no. No, I don't think my family could possibly make it here for the ball. They reside in London, you see. I'm sure it is too much of a journey after they have only just arrived back home." Reasonable and relieving. The idea of Mama trailing scarves and Papa spouting Shakespeare and Cas and Poll quite possibly unleashing the four horsemen of the apocalypse on this, her first ever ball . . . no. It was for the best.

Ellie might murder her later, at least until she heard about the attending beasties. Then it would be Attie who would be furious to have missed it.

Mr. Button was indeed a wonder. After only an hour, Callie left, quite bemused, toting a parcel of exquisite underthings to replace those lost in the river, her measurements most swiftly and respectfully taken. She'd never been measured by a man before. Then again, Mr. Button was an entirely different sort of fellow, wasn't he?

Furthermore, she left with the promise of two gowns within the next few days and a gown of silk by the day of the ball, which hardly seemed possible, and yet whilst standing within the spell of Mr. Button's confidence, it had seemed most entirely feasible.

What a strange little man. She absolutely adored him.

And it was nice to have found another friend.

She wondered how he'd known her name.

Mr. and Mrs. Lawrence Porter

Beg your attendance
On the evening of Thursday next
For a Masque
To be held in honor of their recent marriage.

When one was about to spring a surprise ball upon a hermitesque gentleman, one ought not to approach said fellow empty-handed. Mr. Porter had a sweet tooth. The answer?

Pies. Callie's pies were known far and wide as portions of juicy heaven wrapped in cloud crusts. They made men shudder with pleasure and vow to slay dragons for her. Or in the case of her brothers, lured them into doing Callie's more unpleasant chores.

A girl needed something in her arsenal other than her winning personality.

The pies she wanted to bake required more apples than the number sitting in their basket in the pantry. It would require a trip into the cellar to find them . . . and Callie was none too fond of cellars.

It wasn't that she was frightened of the dark. Exploring in the dark had gotten her into this mess, hadn't it?

And it wasn't that she was precisely frightened, either. Just . . . cautious. Very, very cautious. Cellars were dark and chill and usually old and . . . well, they simply made her skin creep!

"Oh, for a lowly housemaid. Or a manservant. Or a highly intelligent dog." She thought about that for a moment, then shook her head. "Oh, dear. That wouldn't work, would it? I must have green apples and dogs cannot see colors. How would he ever know which ones to put in the basket?"

With a sigh, she took up a lantern from a hook near the door, lighted it from the fire in the stove with a burning twig, and left the house. Cellar entrances were generally found near the kitchens, so it only took a few minutes of poking through the overgrown weeds to spot the trail worn by generations. She followed it, hiking her skirts over one arm as she strode through the warming day, swinging her basket in her other hand. Such a shame to have to leave the brilliance of this beautiful spring morning to go . . . down there.

She half hoped she wouldn't be able to find the entrance, but after a moment the trail led her to a short, wide plank door built into the side of the house. Faded and flaking, it looked as though no one had opened it in Callie's lifetime, although that couldn't possibly be the case. Taking a deep breath, almost as if she were going underwater, she pulled the simple ring latch to open the door.

It stuck a bit, scraping over the frost-heaved cobbles of the step before it. The screeching sound of wood on stone sent a cold chill up her spine. Callie had an unpleasant thought of being trapped within.

"Oh, no," she scolded the door. "That won't do at all."

Looking about her, she spied a chunk of firewood lying cast off in the high grass. It was just the right size to wedge firmly into the doorway to keep the sagging plank door wide open. Satisfied, Callie picked up her lantern and carefully picked her way down ancient cut-stone steps spiraling into the bowels of the house.

"Unfortunate word, bowels," she muttered to herself. "Puts one in mind of an giant's digestive tract."

It didn't help that the architecture of the cellar was a maze of rooms like half barrels, the stone carefully fitted by long-ago hands to hold up the vast house above.

She stopped halfway down the stairs. "Oh, I wish I hadn't thought about that." Now it seemed as if she felt the very weight of the house itself above her. She raised her lantern high. Before her was a room that on closer inspection seemed perfectly solid. In fact, it was surprisingly dry and clean, empty but for a head-high stack of empty crates in the far corner from the staircase. Other than a few spiderwebs, there was nothing objectionable in sight.

"You're such a ninny, Calliope Worthington . . . er, Porter. Look at this place! Verily indestructible! Probably built by the same blokes who built the pyramids of Egypt, in their spare time, of course. It will stand long after you're dead." Her bravado faltered. "I wish I hadn't said dead."

Her voice didn't echo in the network of arched caverns before her. It, too, seemed to sink beneath the weight of the house above.

"Apples. Find the blasted apples. Find the blasted apples and then get back out into the sunlight." She held up the lantern once more and began to make her way deeper into the warren. "It's a beautiful day. I needn't go back indoors for hours. Pick some flowers for the dining room. There must be more vases somewhere. And there will be mushrooms in the woods. I can make a sauce that will bring Himself drooling from the smell of my cooking."

She randomly went left at a joining, but the next vault into which it led was only a wine cellar, filled with vast racks of dusty bottles. Wine was nice but she hadn't a clue what might be good, what might be precious, and what might be decades-old vinegar.

Reversing her path, she took a meandering tunnel that at last led her to another vaulted room, this one satisfyingly full of stacked bushel baskets of all sorts of edibles. She filled her basket with brilliant green apples, very pleased to find the proper sort for pie. There were some of last year's pears as well, a little withered but perfectly suitable for stewing in a sugar syrup on another day. She was much cheered by a gracious plenty of other things from the previous autumn. Piled high about the room were bushels and crates of pumpkins, potatoes, carrots, and onions, the colors glowing like the treasures in Ali Baba's cave. At least Mr. Porter didn't intend to die by starvation any time soon.

Feeling better about the cellar in general, Callie had to roll her eyes at her own earlier fears. "A right ninny, indeed."

Yet as she made her way back to the exit, she saw no beckoning light from the open door. She was going the right way, she was sure of it. Yes, there was the gloomy entrance to the wine cellar. Yes, here were the stacked, empty crates. She turned in the room, holding the lantern high. Yes, there were the stairs up to the doorway to sunlight and fresh air.

A doorway that was now most obviously closed.

Now, most women wouldn't be all that alarmed by a simple closed door, especially on a brisk spring day full of sweet fresh breezes.

Most women didn't have five brothers.

Nerves twanging, Callie climbed the steps and put a tentative hand on the latch. It twisted easily enough, but when she pushed on the door, nothing happened. She pushed harder, juggling her basket and the lantern to one hand and throwing all her strength into a one-shouldered shove.

The old planks creaked in protest, but the door didn't budge.

"Bloody hell," Callie breathed. If she weren't nearly a hundred miles from London, she would swear she could hear Cas and Poll snickering on the other side of that door!

But that was madness. It couldn't be a prank. Who would do such a thing? Who even knew she was here? It certainly wasn't Mr. Porter. To even consider that possibility, one would also have to concede the faint possibility that Mr. Porter had a smidgen of a sense of humor, albeit a most juvenile one—and that was patently ridiculous.

Yet Callie knew a prank when she was the victim of one. A surge of anger had her pounding on the door, but she knew no one would come. The prankster would hardly help her, and Mr. Porter was somewhere in the great house, far from her muffled noise. She would have to be her own rescuer, as usual.

"Well, then." Putting her basket and lantern carefully out of the way on the step below hers, she briskly dusted her hands in preparation.

She hammered, she shoved, she yelled, and she pushed. Finally, she resorted to throwing herself bodily against the planks, gasping curses at the top of her lungs. Well, five brothers, after all.

As she flung herself particularly violently at the planks one more time, she felt her shoe slide on the gritty stone step. Her balance shifted precariously and her foot kicked out sideways, knocking her basket of edibles over and endangering the lantern.

Apples be damned. Callie grabbed for her only source of light.

"Got you!"

Immediately after which, Callie forgot how to breathe. Bent nearly double over the rickety railing, the rescued lantern swinging from her fist, she had a perfectly marvelous view of the writhing mass of glossy black snakes as they slithered from their winter nest in the curve of the stairs, disturbed by apples falling from above.

"Sweet flaming hell," Callie whispered, hoping with all her heart that snakes couldn't climb stairs.

And then the railing snapped.

Chapter 14

Where the hell was she?

Gone for a jaunt across the countryside without his knowing? Rambling about the rooms of the manor, digging through some obscure closet?

Dangling by one hand from some great height? Again?

There was no help for it. Ren had to enlist the help of the men of Amberdell, whom he scarcely knew. There was one, the fellow who delivered the goods for his larder, a brutish bloke by the name of Unwin. Unsavory perhaps, but he evidenced no fear or curiosity toward Ren.

Unwin was nowhere to be found. Ren was forced to approach his second choice, Teager, the carpenter who had repaired a section of the stables for Ren's horse.

Teager agreed to help, politely not trying to peer into Ren's hood, although the men he enlisted to search were perhaps not so self-restrained.

Ren turned away from them, riding on the outside of the group, deflecting their curious stares.

Fury fought with worry. Damned woman, forcing him into this mortifying position!

Where the bloody hell was she?

Callie perched high on the teetering stack of crates, the lantern clutched in her hands and her gaze locked on the snakes.

She'd tried counting them, but they would keep moving. Somewhere between ten and thirty, she thought. Perhaps two dozen snakes, between her and the door to . . . well, nowhere.

She'd tried twice to make her way back to the stairs. It had taken every scrap of courage she could muster to climb down to the enemy-occupied floor. Yet every time she'd taken a step, she was sure the snakes' heads turned her way. Quailing, she'd clambered back up the pile of crates, just as she had done when she'd landed on her hands and knees on the stone floor. Her palms were scraped raw and stinging and her knees ached abominably and the chill of the cellar was seeping right into her bones, but really, all that was nothing compared to her terror of the snakes.

She knew she was being silly. She knew, or rather, she'd been told repeatedly by the scientifically observant Orion, that snakes were more frightened of her than she was of them.

"Horse apples," she muttered. "Rion, you are full of horse apples!"

These were not ordinary snakes. These were demon snakes, sent from some snake hell to enact revenge upon her for all the creatures captured, kept, and/or dissected by her curious brothers. Yes, and Attie as well, although Callie blamed Cas and Poll for her baby sister's diabolical bent.

Although, to be fair, it had been Orion who had put the snake eggs in Callie's bed when the family had gone on holiday in the country. True, he'd only been twelve years old on that trip, and true, the hatched snakes had been tiny green things, no bigger than a pencil. But it hadn't been until she was fully asleep that her investigative brother had slipped the eggs into her bed to keep them warm, because, as he quite logically explained afterward, if he put them in his bed, Lysander would have rolled over onto them.

The hatchlings, quite logically, decided to find the warmest place about—this was according to Orion, for Callie had no actual conversation with the snakes themselves—which happened to be none other than Callie's . . . um . . . nethers.

She'd woken at the wriggling between her thighs and had shrieked the roof of the inn down, rousing every single guest and servant to rush to her aid where they found her climbing her bedpost like a bell rope in her panic. Naked.

She'd been so sure there were more snakes in her nightdress that she'd stripped it from her without a thought.

A handful of tiny green snakes had left her so afraid that she'd shamelessly exposed herself in front of strangers.

Two dozen yard-long black shapes now writhed on the floor below her. They were as black as night and as thick as sausages. Fascinated by their slithering explorations, Callie could not look away.

She rather thought she'd happily parade herself before an entire garrison if only said garrison would pool their combined might and break down the bloody cellar door!

Yet for all the maddened panic boiling up within her,

she didn't shriek. She didn't make a sound. She didn't dare. If the snakes had been attracted by her nearly silent footsteps, what might they do if she disturbed them with her shouting?

There was nothing to do but wait. She was high and safe, with her one salvaged apple and her trusty lantern. Determined to be courageous in her captivity, Callie took the apple from her pocket and polished it on her skirt.

Unfortunately, the apple had a worm.

Even more regrettably, the lantern was almost out of oil.

It seemed to Callie that a hundred years had passed in the dark. Then, a scrape assaulted her ears and light jangled her wide-open eyes.

"Eh, missus? You in 'ere?"

"Yes!" Oh, the snakes! "Shh!"

But the man had already turned away to call out to someone behind him. Callie blinked desperately to accustom her eyes. She'd been staring into the black for days, or possibly only hours—the longest hours of her life. Still perched high on the teetering crates, she sat with her lantern clutched in her hands, though it was cold and dead.

Her bones were frozen in place, she just knew it. She'd spend the rest of her life just like this, bent and immobile, her hands clutching air. Her family would have to push her about in a barrow. Cas and Poll would probably push her down the stairs.

As her life in the barrow welled up in her mind's eye, tears welled up in her real eyes. She stopped them at once, for a dark form blocked the rectangle of dim blue light beaming through the small door.

Evening? Must be . . .

Ren ducked through the cellar door and trotted

quickly down the stairs, his gaze locked on the ridiculous tableau before him. Raising his lantern high, he took in the sight of his bride perched atop a dangerous stack of boxes like a rumpled dirty doll on a shelf. The floor was littered with apples. He refused to acknowledge the depth of his relief.

"Be careful," she whispered hoarsely, her eyes wide and frightened. "They're everywhere!"

I married the only woman in the world terrified of apples. It's a bloody good thing she's pretty.

Ren handed his lantern off to the village man who'd found her. "Hold this, will you . . . ah?"

"Teager, sir."

"Yes, thank you, Teager."

It was only a bit of a reach to her. Ren wrapped his hands about her waist and lifted her down. Just before he let her feet touch the floor, she wrapped her arms tightly about his neck and would drop no farther. The lantern banged into his spine.

"No! They'll get me!"

The novel sensation of being clung to aside—she was a soft, pliant burden that made his thoughts go a bit sideways—Ren feared that physically wresting her grip from his neck would paint quite a picture for Teager and the other men now clattering down the cellar stairs. So he held her off the floor until he had taken her several steps up the stairs. Then he lowered her to sit upon the stone.

"Here, let me take this." Crouching before her, he carefully pried her icy fingers from the empty lantern.

She released it, then wrapped her arms about her midriff. She was cold, but Ren wanted to understand why he'd been forced to rally a motley crew of strangers from the village and surrounding farms to search his estate for the past seven hours. Straightening, he re-

moved his own surcoat and wrapped her in it, pulling
her clenched hands through the sleeves as though he
dressed a small child.

"Now, what happened down here?"

She swallowed and licked her dry lips. He tried not to
be distracted by the flick of pink tongue.

I want that tongue.

"Th-the door shut on m-me."

"Aye, that was like to be the wind, missus." That was
Teager, who hovered over Ren's left shoulder.

"N-no, I blocked it open, w-with a bit of wood."

Ren looked over his shoulder at Teager, who had been
the first at the door. Teager spread his hands in a silent
shrug, unwilling to put the lie to a lady.

"Then I c-couldn't open it." She looked at Ren with
suspicion. "Someone blocked it!"

Teager shifted behind Ren. "Well, it do stick a bit,
right enough. Naught but a good shove wouldn't open it
for ye."

She raised her gaze to the village man. "I sh-shoved!"

Ren pulled her attention back by the simple expedient
of turning her by her chin until her gaze met his. "But
why did you not call out? We've been searching all day,
dozens of us. Someone would have heard you."

She shrank again, curling about herself. "I didn't
want the snakes to hear me."

Someone behind Ren muffled a snort of laughter.
"Snakes don't 'ave ears."

Ren pulled her chin up again. "There are no snakes
here."

She must have been warming up, for a bit of spirit
rose in her haunted eyes and she twitched her chin from
his grip. "There were. A great many. I counted them, or
I tried to . . . they move, you know. All over the floor, a

river of snakes . . ." Her shivering intensified. "They *could* hear me. Every step I took—I couldn't g-get to the stairs—"

Ren straightened and gazed down at his wife with disappointment and growing fury. It was a ridiculous story, obviously meant to cover her embarrassment over shutting herself in the cellar like a helpless child. He'd been forced to face strangers, pounding on their doors in his damned hood, his gut roiling, feeling like a beggar, enduring their wary stares all day—

"Well, you've certainly received more than your share of attention lately."

Her head came up in surprise at the anger in his tone. "Or did you not know that half the village was made ill after you gave them that damned ginger?"

"Ill? No, it couldn't have been the ginger—that was a gift from—oh no, the card—"

He narrowed his eyes. "So now you think someone was trying to poison you instead?"

She bit her lip, blinking at him with eyes wide and tearful. Ren refused to play along.

"Take yourself off to the house and clean up, for pity's sake. You look like an urchin."

He turned his back on her and faced Teager. "Is there someone in the village who can fix the bloody door?"

"Yes, sir." Teager's gaze went behind Ren, following Mrs. Porter up the stairs. It was refreshing, really, not being the one watched.

"Good. And if you lot wouldn't mind, get those damned crates out of here."

"Certainly, sir. The grocer can sure make use of 'em." Teager frowned slightly. "Will she be all right, sir?"

"She'll be fine," Ren said shortly, then turned to stride up the narrow stairs. "I'm the one she'll be the bloody death of."

Ren turned away from the controlled chaos in the cellar and stalked back to the house. The path through the kitchens was deserted, as was the front hall. The girl had evidently not lingered, which was all to the good. He didn't really want to face her again in his current anger.

Callie prepared for bed as Mr. Porter preferred, yet the usual shiver of anticipation was missing tonight. She'd thought that after last night's exultant connection, there would be some hint of something in his manner toward her. Nothing seemed to be working. No matter how she tried, she could not seem to reach through Mr. Porter's harsh exterior shell.

There was something good and true inside him, she just knew it. Like this house, though he'd been left alone too long, it was not too late to recover the strength and goodness within. Tears of weariness, body and soul, stung behind her eyes. Perhaps it was too late. Perhaps she was just a silly girl locked in a devil's bargain with a man who was just what he seemed . . . irretrievably lost.

She sat upon the coverlet, tucking her icy feet beneath her on the mattress. As she brushed her hair down the way Mr. Porter liked it her shoulders slumped.

She was so very tired. Her back ached from the tension of her bizarre perch all day. Her nerves were quite shot—once she nearly leaped a mile when she heard a sudden hissing. It was only a bit of steam escaping the coals, yet she'd felt her belly shudder with fright at the simplest and most ordinary of sounds.

Fear of snakes . . . it looks as though I'm still going to have to work on that one.

The brush dropped from her fingers as she stared glassily into the coals. She wished he would come soon.

The faster she gained her pearls the sooner she could go home, and far away from him . . . and his bloody cellar.

Striding into his study, Ren tossed back his hood and passed a hand across his damp brow. He'd tramped more miles of his estate today than in the past years altogether! Forced outside into the day, yet. What could she have been thinking to cause such mayhem? As a ploy for attention, it had most certainly succeeded—except her eyes when he'd found her had not been triumphant or even pleased. She had only seemed profoundly exhausted, as if held in a state of true terror for some eternal time.

Apples. A snort of amusement escaped him unaware. Good God.

Was she mad, or simply maddening? He truly couldn't tell. Part willing vixen, part runaway bride—

Truth or lie? What part of her was the true woman and what part a game she played? He didn't know. Moreover, he wondered if she even knew.

The oddest part, the part that he only reluctantly allowed himself to consider even now, was that he'd been sincerely worried about her today. Which was only responsible, of course. She was his legal wife.

Yet that didn't explain the subtle but deep strand of black terror that had run through this bizarre day. He'd been afraid, not just for her, but for himself in some strange way. He'd feared . . .

The loss of her.

He sat abruptly. Oh, hell. He wasn't getting attached, was he? When she was such a wild, exasperating mess of a creature? When she'd plainly stated her desire to leave as soon as he allowed it?

Another thought occurred to him. Had today's display been a calculated attempt to force his hand? To make of herself such an unbearable burden that he would gladly throw her back to her family? Games . . . rules . . . boundaries . . . he feared he was the only one who did not know how to play.

His hands, draped over his knees, closed about nothing. He looked down to see his knuckles whitening at the very thought of letting her go.

You are in for it now. Because she is leaving. Every day, every night she grows closer to completing her side of the bargain.

When she had, would he be able to complete his?

"Sir?" The gruff voice of the village man, Teager, came from the doorway. Ren remained turned away.

"Yes, what is it?"

"Sir, the missus said there were snakes—"

"The missus says a great many things," Ren snapped, his bitterness rising without reason.

"Er, yes, sir, only—when we moved them crates out, sir, we found this."

Reluctant but resigned, Ren flipped his hood back over his face and turned to see that Teager held out one work-roughened hand, as if making an offering. Across his callused palm lay something wrapped in cloth. Ren took it from the man and turned toward the window to undo the folds in what appeared to be a large rough-hemmed square of linen—a workingman's handkerchief.

The parcel unwrapped to reveal a coiled pile of something papery and parchment-thin. It rustled dryly at his curious touch. The unmistakable pattern, raised and outlined in whitish lines—scales. "A snakeskin."

"A right champion one, too, sir. Biggest I ever seen."

Ren picked up one end of the pile and let the length drop. A yard of snake at the very least. Perhaps a bit longer.

And you told her to shut up and take a bath.

Bloody hell.

"If the missus were down there all day with just one o' them, she's lucky to come out alive."

Ren turned to Teager. "What?"

Teager nodded. "That's asp, sir. Dead poisonous. Not mean so much as nervous like. Keep to themselves, but ye wouldn't be wantin' to rile up a whole nest of 'em."

A river of snakes, running across the floor.

Ren stared at the unmistakable length of reptilian evidence. "I . . . think I've been a bit of an ass."

Teager shuffled his feet. "Sir, I hope ye don't mind a bit o' advice—ye bein' newlywed and all—"

"Advice?" Ren sighed. "Teager, I need a bloody book of instructions."

Teager snorted. "'Tisn't just the fine ladies what need that book, sir. I been married near twenty years and, well, I must say, sir . . . there ain't no way back outa callin' a woman a liar."

"Did I do that?"

Didn't you?

I suppose I did. "No way back, hmm? So what do you suggest? I'm afraid I haven't a clue."

Teager considered the ceiling for a moment. "It's a tough one, it is. Beggin' forgiveness works . . ."

Ren inhaled.

". . . sometimes."

His breath left him in a whoosh. "I fear I'm not the begging sort, anyway."

Teager squinted at him. "Then why'd ye get wed?"

Ren rotated his head on his neck, easing the tightness that grew by the moment. "As soon as I know the answer to that, I'll let you know."

Teager screwed up his fleshy face in thought. "She's a pretty thing and she seems kindly enough. I don't think the bad ginger was her fault. She sure seemed surprised.

If a woman'll ever forgive ye, it'll be now, at the beginning. Afore the shine wears off, so t'speak."

Ren could have laughed, but it might have come out as a howl. "Shine . . . has not been part of this particular picture, I fear." She was the one who shone. He was all in shadow.

Teager seemed manfully determined to aid him, however. "Women like posies and confections and such. Pretty words . . ." He gazed at Ren in consideration. "If a bloke can manage that. Even the shyest mare'll come round for a sugar lump."

It wasn't a bad suggestion, yet Ren hadn't the faintest idea how to implement it. What would tempt Calliope? What did she want more than anything?

To leave you and your mausoleum in the dust of her carriage wheels, the sooner the better, you loathsome ass.

Chapter 15

Ren entered his bride's bedchamber with his candle stub lighted as usual but his soul filled with misgivings. He ought to apologize for his disbelief.

Disbelief? Are you sure it wasn't a little more full-blown than that? Say . . . scorn?

Teager was right. She deserved to have her honor respected as surely as any man. The fact that she'd not exaggerated the size of the snakes now made him wonder if all her mad stories—including the ones concerning the Worthington clan—were, in fact, completely truthful. If so, her family was verging on criminally insane!

Says the man in the hood.

She was not standing before the fire as she usually was. Ren took a turn about the room, and finally discovered her when he pushed back the bed curtains and found her sprawled limply upon the coverlet. His foot touched something on the floor. He bent to pick up her hairbrush and blinked at it. She was aggressively tidy. Not for Calliope was the careless tossing aside of her things!

He tilted his head as he considered her. From the

strange angle at which she lay, it looked as though she had simply fallen over sideways from a seated position. Her hair hung over her face so he brushed a finger across her brow to clear the straying locks away.

She did not stir. A little alarmed, he held the candle close to her face, but she was reassuringly apple-cheeked as usual. So this was Calliope at rest. His fingertip traveled to her cheek, touching the shadow of weariness lurking beneath her eye. Then down, to the corner of her pert mouth. Her lips were slightly parted, plumping softly with each breathy exhalation. Those lips that did not lie. It was shocking to think it. A woman who kept faith in even the tiniest of facts.

The more he came to know this glowing, vibrant creature, the more convinced he became that he did not deserve to stand at her side. It was more than his former distance. Last night he'd lost control. Now he had truly begun to worry that he might undo her somehow, that he might bring her down into his dark and twisted homeland—where dwelled mewling slimy beings and demons and him.

She wasn't an angel. She was far too gloriously real for that. She was odd and free-spoken and askew from the rest of Society—although it seemed she might be one of the most normal people in her bizarre family.

No, she was not a perfect being . . . yet her oddness became part of her appeal and her surprising insights kept him interested in spite of his attempts at withdrawal. Pretty Calliope engaged him fully, bringing him sights and sounds and scents and thoughts and dreams that he'd quite given up on. It was almost cruel, her deep joy in life. She would not let him be.

He ought to be longing for his former peace and solitude. He ought to resent her noise and her clatter and her constant disturbance.

The tip of his thumb traveled around the perimeter of those pink lips, more softly than a feather's touch.

He was quite pathetic. *I am sitting here, wishing she would wake up—eager to hear the next outrageous words uttered by that pretty mouth.*

I like her. I hate how much I like her. The man who wins her when I'm gone will count himself lucky to be there, never knowing quite what to expect, never quite sure what she'll say next.

What if that man didn't appreciate her? What if he looked at her and merely saw a rather pretty woman, with a good figure and rather too much to say? What if he called her annoying and urged her to keep her thoughts to herself? What if he used that lovely body and returned no pleasure for the gift? What if he ignored her? What if he struck her?

I wouldn't do that.

Shut up. You're gone. You were beaten out of me, seeping out of me as I lay dying on the dockside. You don't get a say in this.

I could love her.

You don't exist.

I exist here now in this moment. I exist for her. She feels me inside, whether you feel me or not.

Giving up on his half-mad self-argument, Ren rose and went to the other side of the bed to turn down the covers. Sweeping his hands across the linens, he warmed them. Then he returned to her, picking her up as easily as if she were a child. He had become stronger in the last few days. His body drank of her life and vitality. She gave him strength and blood-pumping anxiety and heart-sinking terror, all at the same time.

He tucked her into the covers, pulling her limbs out straight and comfortable. She instantly turned upon her side, curling into a cramped ball. He smiled ruefully.

Obstinate even in sleep. Yet, her hands and feet were so icy. He didn't like leaving her this way, chilled and alone. What if she woke in the night, frightened of dream snakes . . . or real ones, in her memory?

I might stay with her, just to keep her warm. Just to soothe away the midnight terrors. I might stay.

You are *a midnight terror.*

Then I shall leave before light.

With mingled daring and longing, he undressed, tossing his things over the spindly chair at her vanity. At last he was naked. If she woke just then, she would see him in all his damaged, pain-racked deformity, his scars, his twisted back, his ruined face.

Abruptly he was too weary to care. All he wanted was to climb into bed with his wife, curl around her and warm her until he fell asleep upon her shining hair.

He lifted the covers and did just that.

Just this once.

Betrice paced her bedchamber, glaring at her sleeping husband in their large bed. If she lived in the manor, she would have her own lady's chamber. Henry would visit her and then he would leave her be, in a luxurious suite, surrounded by her lovely things, and not make her listen to his snoring all night long. She strode to the bed and picked up her pillow, gripping it with fingers white with strain. She paced slowly around the bed, until she stood gazing down upon Henry's face. One moment with the pillow, could she suffocate him before he even woke? He was ever a deep sleeper.

Then she snatched the pillow back to her bosom, with a small cry. She was terrible! What an awful, treacherous thought! Henry was a good man. She was terribly fond of him . . . most of the time. He'd never raised a hand to her, he'd never denied her anything, often going

without something he liked so that she could have a new
gown or order a new pair of kid slippers. He'd given up
his tobacco for an entire winter just so she could go to
London to shop for a gown, when she knew perfectly
well that a pipe by the fire on a winter's evening was one
of his favorite pleasures.

He was a good man . . . a good man who should have
been master of Amberdell Manor—who deserved to be
master of Amberdell!

Callie opened her eyes. Her room was as dark as the cellar. She heard a noise—

"Shh." A hard warm arm came about her, tugging her
into a circle of heat and skin and man. "All is well. Sleep."

Callie's surprise was not enough to keep her exhausted eyes open. Her lids fluttered shut upon her, mid-
thought. *I think he's na—*

Naked. Callie's eyes flew open.

What? Naked?

She ran a hand across her body, feeling the thin fabric
of her shift. She wasn't naked.

If not her, then who?

The morning light came streaming in through opened
drapes. She clearly recalled closing them against the
chill last night. She pushed herself to a sitting position.
Her bedchamber was bright and warm and a most astonishing pot of tea steamed under a towel next to a cup on
her side table. *I have tea.*

She blinked. The tea remained where it sat, the fat
little pot jolly in the beams of sunlight pouring into the
room.

Then Callie's eyes fell upon the mussed bed. The
other side of the bed.

Naked.

Had that been true? It could not have been true.

Then she saw it, loitering in the dent someone's—his!—head had made in the pillow. A single gleaming pearl, nesting there, all round and shining and impossible.

Callie reached a hand to the teapot, pouring black hot tea and gulping deeply, scalding her tongue. She sucked air into her mouth as she regarded the new pearl in wonder. Then a slow smile crept across her face.

Then she spotted the basket on the side table—a basket full to the brim with green apples.

Snakes or no, Mr. Porter had given her a gift!

That afternoon, after a flurry of pie-baking with the lovely apples, Callie set up her drawing area in the library. There were tall, lovely windows with marvelous views, and just the scent of old books made her feel at home.

First she set the carefully cleaned cowslip plant upon a small stack of books, holding the petals in midair so she could see them in their natural state. A proper botanical artist would have a little stand made, where a plant could be clipped onto a glass vase. It would stay fresh for more than a day like that.

Carefully, she dried the roots, pressing them softly with a clean cloth until the plant could be laid down upon a blotting sheet. Callie preferred to work fresh, what with all the bounty currently blooming all around her. If she wished, she could press this plant and continue to work on drawings for a year or more, yet it was the live plant that drew one's gaze in the wild. That life was up to her to convey, the life and the death, too, for the final portion of the drawing would be the seedpod, which would not be formed until later in the summer or even possibly the autumn. She would simply leave a portion of each drawing empty, a ghost space that would someday be filled.

The cowslip lay playful and bright in the shaft of light coming in the large window. She would have to work quickly. Now she was very glad she'd spent so much time sketching in the wild. Her fingers felt nimble and it was only moments before she was imparting the petals, pistils, and stamens with concise, delicate strokes of her pencil. The drawing went so well she decided to get the entire plant in one go.

Drawing came easily enough. She used a small magnifier she'd found in the library. The cunning little thing was no more than a round lens held by a small bone handle, but in good light she was able to see the tiny hairs upon the plant's stem and even the way the veins in the leaf were three different shades of yellow-green.

Her drawing complete at last, Callie studied it for a long moment. This was always the difficult part. How she wished she could preserve it somehow before she possibly spoiled it with the paints. Still, she could clearly see the colors in her mind's eye, the way she would tip the petals with just a touch of orange, to bring out the sweet lemon-yellow of the inner construction.

With her tongue pressed to her top teeth in concentration, she bent to make the first wash of green upon the stem. Her gaze flicked back and forth between the drawing and the plant. Yes, it was an excellent version of the stem color . . . she only needed to wash a narrow line of yellow-green into the junctions for the leaves and stem . . .

Ren leaned one shoulder on the frame of the library door and watched his bride bend over her work, looking ever so slightly mad with her brow scrunched and her tongue poking out of the corner of her mouth. She looked intense and ridiculous . . . and adorable.

He wanted to enter the library, pull her away from her efforts, and put a pearl upon that tongue . . . no, he wanted that tongue in motion, chattering away about some mad childhood adventure of hers while he took down her hair and unbuttoned her gown.

He did nothing. He wouldn't dream of disturbing her, or of robbing himself of a moment of this delightful view of her. She had a pencil thrust into her wound hair. It poked above her brow rather like a unicorn horn. Indeed, she was as rare a creature, his mad Calliope.

She scratched her nose thoughtlessly, leaving a streak of green pigment there. Ren rubbed a hand over his covered mouth, forcing back a rusty chuckle. How he wished he were an artist, as well, to capture her ludicrous charm. He would simply have to remember it instead. Always.

In the silence there was nothing but the faint stirring sound of her brush in water and the ticking of the clock on the mantel. Ren eyed the polished wood of the mantel and all the shelves in the room. His books had never looked so fine. The ticking soothed him—a long-silent heart, beating again.

At last she sat up, tilting her head comically as she frowned at the paper. Then she pursed her lips and blew across it to dry the color washes. Ren imagined he could feel her cool breath upon his naked skin, as if her lips were pursed for him . . .

She was fair to making him mad with lust for the simple act of drying a sheet of paper!

He forced his gaze away. Her stunted little weed looked a bit worse for wear. Callie noticed it drooping at the same moment and plucked it from its roost, dropping it back into a beaker of water with her eyes full of concern.

I should like to be that plant, looked after with such care.

Bloody hell, he was jealous of a plant.

What had she done to him? More importantly, what would she do to him when she left?

Since her concentration seemed well and truly broken,

Ren cleared his throat. "You've left pencil shavings on my carpet." His tone was meant to be teasing. He feared it came out gruff and accusatory.

She didn't even glance at him. "Our carpet," she corrected him absently.

Ren halted even as he was about to enter the room. *Our carpet.* Two of the oddest words to ever bring light to a man's dark corners.

Carefully keeping his tone mild this time, he gestured toward the painting. "May I see?"

She nodded, although she didn't look happy about it. "It's only the first one. I should like to try again, I think, although I will have to collect a new specimen."

Ah, more woodland strolling. Ren couldn't deny the appeal of another day of watching Callie clambering over fence stiles. Such a charming view when she hiked her skirts.

Then Ren realized what he was gazing at with some surprise. He'd studied enough botany to know a good representation when he saw one, and her painting was entirely accurate. Yet, she'd somehow managed to do something else with it, something that made him think of strolling through spring meadows, and hearing birdsong and feeling the warm sun on the back of his neck.

You would have to take off your hood first for that one.

He nodded. "I like it."

"Truly?" She glanced up at him.

Ren realized that she always did, although there was no possibility that she could see his face. Most people whom he was forced to deal with either stared searchingly into the shadow of his hood or kept their gaze elsewhere, like somewhere over his left shoulder, or hovering around his knees. Callie looked *at* him, looked through the hood as if for her, the cloth was not even there.

". . . something is missing, I think."

He caught up on the conversation with an effort. "I don't think there's anything missing."

She frowned and stuck her paintbrush into her hair, causing a mad counterpoint to her unicorn horn pencil adornment. Ren didn't laugh. He made sure of it.

"I think the yellow is off." She sighed. "I wish I had my own paints. I scrounged these from the nursery."

I have a nursery? Ren resolved to get her better paints on the next coach from London.

"Well, I'm glad to see you so recovered from your ordeal yesterday."

She glanced at him, then blushed. He tilted his head. "What is it?"

She fiddled with her little weed. "This morning . . . there was a pearl."

Ren kept his tone offhand. "Yes. Did you mind?"

She shook her head quickly. "No, not at all. It's just that . . . well, I think I woke once . . . were you . . . ?"

"Was I what?" Damn, she was going to say it. She was going to writhe and blush and ask him if he'd slept naked wrapped around her and then he was going to have to kiss her . . .

"Nothing." She lifted her chin. "How are we going to find out who locked me in?"

He drew back. "I believe we know what happened."

She brightened. "Oh, excellent. Who was it? What are you going to do about them?" Her brows drew together. "I don't think you should punish them too harshly. It was only a prank—"

"You locked yourself in and then panicked because the door stuck just a bit."

Oh! Callie couldn't believe it. Mr. Porter had the nerve to stand there and—

She whirled, pacing to the fireplace and back. "It

stuns me that you persist in denying that something is going on here! First the ladder . . ."

"You were very careless to endanger yourself with that ancient ladder."

". . . and now with the cellar door. I told you how I braced it with the log!"

"I'm sure that while you sat in the dark you wished you'd thought of that . . ."

"Oh!" She stalked back to the fireplace again. "You unbearable lout!"

Offended, Ren folded his arms. "Now you're just being silly. I admit I didn't realize I had such a serpent problem, but they have been cleared out and you'll see no more of them. Perhaps if you'd used a bit more forethought when venturing into the cellar—"

The peculiar noise she made, something between a shriek and a growl, was drowned out by the ringing sound of a sword being drawn. Ren realized she was arming herself with one of the ornamental sabers that were mounted, crossed, over the mantel.

She swung about, pointing the sword at him. "You insist on calling me a liar or labeling me a fool! *En garde!*"

Chapter 16

At the sight of his dainty bride wielding a sword, Ren laughed out loud. Then he heard the whistle of steel in the air and the top button of his weskit flew away, landing with a pinging sound on the floor halfway across the room.

"What?"

His dainty bride returned to a quite proper fencing stance. One delicate eyebrow rose. "Arm yourself, sir, or lose every button you own."

She tossed him the other sword. He caught it automatically, shaking his head. "You realize that now I will be compelled to tie you up and lock you in the attic, like all the other mad wives of legend."

Her smile was equal parts sweetness and poison, like treacle syrup laced with cyanide. "You, sir, shall be too busy crawling about the floor looking for your buttons."

Ping.

"Bloody hell." This time it was from the arm of his surcoat.

He went *en garde*. The battle was on. She was rather good, he realized, as she blocked and parried and almost managed to rob him of another button. "You've been trained."

"My aunt Clemmie trained us all," she said nonchalantly. "Dade is better than I, but not by much. He had no one to practice with. You see, being older than his brothers gave him such an unfair advantage."

"But no unfairness in your being female?"

Swing. Block. *Clash, clang*—oh, bloody hell!—*ping*.

"At first he quite bullied me, I admit. I didn't give him a truly fair fight until I realized that while he had the reach on me, I was just a hair . . . quicker."

She flew past him. *Ping*.

Ren felt good with a sword in his hand again. He was an accomplished swordsman . . . or at least, he had been. Now he feared his spritely bride was about to debutton him most ignominiously. Perhaps a distraction?

When next she whirled by him, he twitched his saber. *Ping, ping, ping*.

Three tiny buttons disappeared from the back of her dress.

"Oh!" She glared at him. "You rat!"

Now that she was distracted by her damaged gown, Ren managed to get in past her defenses once more. *Rip*.

The seam of her tiny cap sleeve parted. The left side of her bodice began to slither most interestingly downward. "My gown!"

She flew at him, fury redoubled. His weskit hung open now, and his sleeve dropped down over his wrist, entirely parted at the shoulder.

"Brat!" He gave her bottom a sound swat with the flat of his sword as she danced past him.

She repaid him by turning his cravat into a handkerchief. Ren's eyes narrowed. She'd been going for the hood!

Damn it. She was going to get past his defenses. He could not manage a full frontal assault with his shoulder damaged and she wasn't holding back in the slightest. Indeed, she seemed to be relishing it.

He needed to tire her out, or make her careless, distract her . . . he grinned beneath his shadowed covering.

Whish. The other sleeve of her gown parted. With no buttons to hold the bodice high, she was now fighting half exposed, her left hand clutching her shredded gown to her bare bosom.

She looked like a goddess on the run. He wanted her so fiercely he could scarcely take a step for the ache in his groin. She noted his arousal, her glance widening as she understood just how the stakes were rising.

"Calliope," he growled. "Drop your sword . . . or drop your gown."

She regarded him with a cocked head for a moment, then boldly released the bodice of her gown, letting it fall. It slipped down, past her waist, leaving her standing topless, wielding a sword, wearing only a sheer pair of pantalets.

She looked like a pirate's dream.

Ren's coat fell off in three pieces. Damn. She'd distracted him with all that luminous ivory flesh. God, didn't she look delicious against the setting sun, naked in his library—surely he'd suffered some sort of fever dream. Surely he did not have this nimble creature, eyes flashing, sword swishing through the air . . . oh, hell. *Quick!*

He disarmed her with a twist of his wrist and some bloody good luck, though he would never admit it. It was quite validating, the way her sword spun away to imbed its point into the opposite wall. Startled, her eyes wide, she held out both hands. "I surrender, Mr. Porter. That was well . . ."

Snick. Whish.

The ties of her pantalets were no more. Her undergarment fell to the floor to tangle about her ankles. She gasped and stumbled back, falling on her bottom on the carpet.

Ren advanced upon her. She tried to scramble away. He went down upon one knee, planting it upon her ruined pantalets, pinning her in place, with the fabric tight about her ankles. Looming over her, he put the point of the sword just below her chin.

"Say it."

She gazed at him through wide eyes. "I . . . I surrender."

He lifted the sword away, then used his wrists to part her knees wide. Then wider still. "Say it."

Her breath began to come fast. She lay back upon the floor. "I surrender," she said softly.

"Close your eyes and reach your hands above your head."

She did so, crossing her wrists and immediately becoming his maddest, wettest fantasy come to light.

He traced the cold flat of his blade down between her breasts so gently there wasn't even the hint of a mark left behind. "Do you grant the field?"

She inhaled sharply, her breath a shiver, her breasts quivering. The cold steel touched her belly. She sucked another shuddering breath. "I grant the field," she whispered.

Ren laid the sword aside and covered her labia with his hands. "This field. Is it mine?"

Callie lay trembling, her eyes closed, her hands clasped tight above her head, her ankles tethered by his weight. She felt open, helpless, conquered. "Oh, yes."

There came the familiar rustle of his hood being removed. Then his mouth—hot, seeking, unerring—

She cried aloud at the pleasure. It was mad, wicked, outrageous to taste her there . . . she'd never known. Never . . .

In an instant she was his, aroused, swollen with lust, damp with it, and he took it. He spared her nothing. Lips, tongue, teeth, nibbling, licking, oh, sweet heaven, licking and teasing and delving deep to taste the inside of her . . .

She cried out recklessly, in total abandon, spread before him on the carpet like a madman's drunken feast. There was no end to his mouth, it was everywhere, she could not bear it.

"Screaming will not aid you," he growled into her wet, throbbing flesh. "Although you should feel free to try."

She screamed. She howled, she begged, not knowing what she begged for . . .

He thrust a large finger deep into her and she came apart, shuddering as great wicked waves of pleasure stole her breath. He thrust his finger again and again as he used his mouth on her like a well-wrought weapon. She gave way before him, laying down arms, surrendering completely. She writhed, she bucked, she undulated at his every motion, yet it was not enough for him. He took her again and again with his mouth. He made her rise and come again and yet again, relentless, turning her into a shivering, sweat-soaked shell of a being, with nothing to say but hoarse moans and helpless whimpers.

After her third orgasm, she lay limp and exhausted. Her mind slipped sideways. Her only coherent thought, *Will he take me now? Will he make me his at last?*

He did not. Instead, he withdrew his wet hand from her and gently urged her parted knees together. She rolled to her side, gasping and dizzy. She wasn't truly aware of him walking away from her. She merely felt chilled and abruptly alone. She opened her eyes.

On the carpet a few inches from her nose lay a single pearl.

And there were hundreds to go . . .

I shall not survive this.

Ren left the library at a near-run, lurching down the hall to the stairs. He leaned on the newel post for a long moment, fighting back the impulse to take his wife hard and fast on the carpet, plowing her in the library like a couple of randy servants. Calliope. She was delicious, so sweet and abandoned and willing, and he was a bastard, making a twisted game out of her first adventures in lovemaking.

Yet, he wanted her so badly that the thought simply pounded through him like his own pulse. He ached for her, ached for release, ached to be touched, to be held, to be . . . to be loved. The answer should have been to fill her with such lust that she'd be willing to tolerate him, but now he wanted more. He wanted her. He wanted her to want him. Not for pearls and not for wealth, not even for pity.

If only he were still a man.

As he was, he might be able to make her cry out at his touch. He might be able to ignite her body, but there was more . . . so much more . . . to sweet Calliope than simply her lovely body.

Damn it to hell, he wanted it all.

He ran a shaking hand over his face. His beard scratched at his palm. He'd scraped her skin with it, as well. Her thighs had been afire with the abrasiveness of his beard. He'd only grown it out of indifference. What did it matter if he shaved, when no one saw him without the hood?

Now he had a reason to return to a smooth face. It wasn't as though the beard did much to hide the scars anyway. Surely it only made him look wilder and less human.

When he'd stood in the doorway of the library he'd realized that he liked her. Could it . . . would it ever be possible for her to like him?

Yet, why should she? What had he ever done to deserve her good favor?

It was a strange and chilling realization, to understand how restricted he'd become, how selfish. His thoughts scarcely ever left his own doom.

Callie baked him cake and washed windows and wrapped up bloody ginger for the village, disastrous though it might be for them. Callie took care of her ridiculous parents and her outrageous siblings and now she took care of him.

The gears of giving were rusty with disuse, but Ren resolved to think about what he might do for Callie, not simply to make her like him, but because it was high time someone did!

Callie spent the first part of the next morning repairing her damaged gown. Sitting in the sun-drenched window seat of the library, she painstakingly stitched up the torn sleeves and replaced the buttons. The search for those had cost her many minutes of crawling about the carpet.

She'd done that already once, when he'd startled her in her room the other night. By all rights, she ought to have been furious at the damage, but even as she bent over her sewing, she could not keep a small smile of remembered pleasure from tracing her lips. What a ridiculously wicked night it had been. At the thought of cold steel on her skin she shivered.

I'd certainly like to do that again sometime.

It wasn't the sword fight or the way he'd sliced her gown from her—although that had been exciting indeed, like something from a very naughty pirate story!—it was him, Mr. Porter, and the way he made her feel when his hot hands shook with longing and his voice dropped low with need.

I wonder if it is possible to love someone you've never seen?

The sunlight made her feel sleepy and the thoughts of pleasure and sewing and wonder began to mingle in her mind.

There was more to the act, she knew it. Which meant he'd fled her again, just when she'd been quite willing to welcome him into her body to slake his own desire. He'd given her so much bliss, she was beginning to feel a bit guilty about having the lion's share of the fun.

Yet, was she truly ready? She had no sentimental attachment to her virginity, other than the need to remain respectable for the sake of her family. What could be more respectable than to consummate her marriage with her husband? Yet in so many ways, Mr. Porter was still a stranger to her. How could she give herself to someone when he would not even show her his face?

She leaned her head against the window glass, her hands dropping to her lap, her sewing nearly forgotten as she gazed dreamily out at the vivid landscape. Who was he? How had he come to be the way he was? What sort of man was he? He wasn't unkind . . . yet neither was he precisely kind. He lived in this fine house, yet he did nothing to improve it. He had the eye and ear of the village, yet he did nothing to benefit his people. His family awaited his attention, yet he barely spoke to them. Could that be a good man?

Yes, he'd rescued her, risking himself to keep her from breaking on the cobbles of the yard, yet he'd been perfectly willing to die at Dade's hand. Perhaps it hadn't been a risk of anything he hadn't been willing to lose.

Mr. Porter was indeed a puzzle.

A dark flutter at the edge of her vision caught her attention. She turned her head to catch it, idly sharpening her empty gaze a little. What she saw so jolted her that she sat upright and pressed one hand upon the glass. There, at the end of the lawn, between two shady trees, stood a man.

Callie had explored that area only a few days ago, so she knew the true size of those trees and that they seemed much smaller at a distance. The man, therefore, must be a giant.

Callie held very still, wishing she hadn't moved so abruptly, hoping he hadn't caught the motion, hoping that he couldn't see her in her pale gown, sitting in the sun . . . it was worth wishing for at any rate. The man's features were hidden beneath his shapeless hat . . . she cast a glance about the library over her shoulder, wondering if there might be a telescopic viewer somewhere about.

When she turned back to the window, the figure was gone. Though she strained her eyes searching the shadows, there was nothing where he'd stood but two majestic trees.

Tap, tap.

Callie's heart thudded in her chest, but it was only the front door knocker. When she answered, she found that Betrice and Henry had sent over the mare they'd promised to loan her. The pretty red-coated creature danced at the end of the groom's lead, already wearing a lady's sidesaddle and bridle, ready for a ride.

The groom promised to prepare a stall for her in Mr. Porter's stables so that all Callie would have to do was to unsaddle her and shut her in after her ride.

Hesitantly, Callie agreed. She knew how to ride, of course, but there was a bit of difference between posting sedately down Rotten Row in London with her brothers at her side and spending all day on horseback in the countryside.

Sally was the name of the horse. "Hello, Sally. You have very nice . . . ears. Very delicate and, ah, pointy," Callie told her. Perhaps it was silly to compliment an animal, but Callie had learned long ago that being nice never did any harm.

The aforementioned ears swiveled forward at her voice and Callie felt herself quite thoroughly inspected by the creature.

Female, not heavy, and not particularly strong. No problem.

Callie lifted her chin. "Do not underestimate me, Sally. I raised four younger brothers. *Worthington* boys, yet. I can handle *you*."

Perhaps it was her imagination, but she thought she saw a little of the smugness fade from Sally's limpid brown eye.

The groom had left to see to his duties in the stable, so Callie tethered Sally to the iron circle imbedded into the post out front and ran lightly back into the house to fetch her drawing supplies. With Sally, it would only take minutes to ride into the village to consult with Mr. Button about the ball. That would leave the rest of the day free to explore the valley and add to her collected specimens!

She donned her spencer quickly and changed into her walking boots. With no proper riding habit, she would make a silly show riding in her gown, but there was nothing to be done about it. At least the saddle was not astride!

Chapter 17

Calliope left the house so swiftly that it was all Ren could do to saddle his own horse and gallop down the lane after her. Henry's groom simply nodded respectfully when Ren rode by him in a rush, as if hooded madmen were an everyday occurrence. Ren spared a thought to wonder if Henry would lend him the fellow. Calliope was quite correct. They truly did need a staff about the place.

Once into the rhythm of the ride—once upon a time he could stay in the saddle for hours, even days if required—inevitably his thoughts turned back to his night with her . . . sword fighting in the library . . . Calliope on the floor before him, conquered and helpless . . . her shameless cries of lust and longing . . .

It wasn't long before he spotted Calliope on Henry's new filly, far before him. She slowed as she turned into the village lane, so Ren pulled the reins just past the bridge. It was just in time. Riding astride with an erection was ill-advised. He would linger out of sight until she finished her business in Amberdell.

He felt oddly alive . . . alive and lusty and prone to daydreaming about hot, wet, sweet places. And yards of

pale ivory legs. And creamy breasts topped with rasp-
berry nipples.

And long, honey-mead hair spilling across his chest.
And a gamine grin. And teasing hazel eyes that looked
directly at him . . .

He shifted restlessly on his mount, making the gelding sidle and snort. God, now he was infecting his horse
with his agitation.

Would she never finish her business in Amberdell?

He cast an impatient gaze about the area. She could
not have passed him, could she? No, he was being rid—

A chill went through him. There, on the crest of a
small hill, as still as the great limestone boulders that had
hidden him, there was the silhouette of a man—a giant.

Ren had known a giant once . . . a killer, the most
dangerous man Ren had ever encountered. Once they
had been on the same side, and Ren had even felt a wary
camaraderie with the fellow.

But he had been betrayed and had turned his back on
that man and all his kind.

Surely that man was still safely in London, where he
could do no harm to Ren and what he held as his. Surely.

Yet, there were not so many giants in the world.
When the man turned away, disappearing over the crest
of the hill, Ren nudged his gelding into a trot, heading
for the mound of boulders. He simply had to be sure.

As she neared the village, Callie dismounted. Leading
Sally would perhaps lessen the impact of her incorrect
riding attire. Oh, where were her clothes?

Dade, I am going to eviscerate you.

There was a horse post outside the smithy. Callie left
Sally there, where the smith's young son stared ador-
ingly at the bay filly. "She's a right one!"

With her borrowed mount in caring hands, Callie

knew she could take her time in the village . . . whether she liked it or not. Still, there was business to be done. First, she posted a letter home, relating a great deal about the house and village and nothing at all about Mr. Porter—and nagging, er, reminding her family to send her things on.

When she entered the post office, dead silence fell upon the half-dozen people within. They parted before her, mostly women and a few elder men—for of course the able-bodied men would be doing something farmish on such a fine spring day—and allowed her passage directly to the postmistress.

Callie smiled and handed over her letter, trying for some harmless commentary on the fine weather.

"Naught but too dry, it is, missus."

Callie translated the woman's thick Gloucestershire as, "Good weather is bad in the spring when we need the rain."

Her smile faltering slightly, Callie nodded. "Yes, I suppose that's true. I was only admiring the wildflowers."

The woman slid her eyes to the others waiting behind Callie. Someone grunted. "Weeds."

"Yes, well . . . Good day."

She fled.

Outside, she felt resentful gazes following her like vengeful wasps. It was only a few steps past the church and school, yet to Callie it felt like miles. In truth, the entire village wasn't much more than a collection of smithy, church, shops, and, down closer to the river, a mill. Callie had yet to see the place on market day, when everyone from the surrounding farms would come in to trade, but on a day like this the village almost seemed oppressive, as if occupied by nothing but pessimists and naysayers.

If ever a place needed a ball, it was this one.

At last Callie entered Mr. Button's shop—or rather, Madame Longett's shop where Mr. Button seemed to have taken over. She was dismayed to find herself at the end of a long queue of customers. There was no parting of the seas for her this time. Even in the country, fashion was a deadly serious matter.

However, Mr. Button spotted her at once and waved an assistant over to take his place serving a stout matron who seemed to be dithering over a selection of lace. Callie was distracted by the highly ornamental fellow. Goodness, he was the most beautiful young man she had ever seen! Elektra would be beside herself.

"His name is Cabot," Mr. Button said nearly in her ear. "Shut your mouth, dear, you're a married woman."

Callie gurgled, blinked, and then remembered her terribly urgent business that had caused this morning's unpleasant venture into Amberdell. She turned to Mr. Button, grasping at his hand.

"Mr. Button, I think someone is trying to kill me!"

She found herself tucked away in Madame Longett's frowsy sitting room, with a cup of strong tea in her hand and Mr. Button's full and undivided attention.

"Have you informed your husband of these attempts?"

Callie shrugged. "Yes. He thinks I am either mad or childish." She shuddered. "As if I would make up a thing like those snakes! That is why I came to you. I just wanted someone to . . . to tell me that I'm not mad."

Mr. Button sat back in his chair and gazed at her with his head tilted. "Is there even the slightest exaggeration in what you have told me?"

Callie closed her eyes in resignation. "You don't believe me, either."

Mr. Button tapped her sharply on the wrist. She opened her eyes in surprise to see him frowning at her.

"Don't be an infant," he admonished tartly. "I believe you, my dear. I am simply after all the facts. Tell me about this man beneath the trees again. Was he truly as large as you say?"

Callie picked at the tassel on her reticule. "In fact, he was a bit bigger. I didn't wish to sound, well . . . mad."

"You would know him if you saw him again?"

She wrinkled her brow at him. "It would be effortless. He was quite the largest man I have ever seen."

"Hmm." His puckish face looked, just for an instant, ever so slightly . . . lethal. Much the way that Mr. Porter sometimes did, when he seemed to stand at the edge of what normal people called sanity. Callie felt a flicker of alarm. She kept encountering all these dangerous people . . .

Then the little dressmaker smiled and the ridiculous notion fled her mind. He patted her hand gently and gazed approvingly at her. "You must come to me at once if anything else should happen. Do you understand?"

Callie felt better immediately. Nothing had truly changed. Her situation was still very strange, indeed. However, a sympathetic ear could be as good as a helping hand sometimes. Sometimes a girl just needed someone to listen.

As she made her way out through the women flocking into the shop, she noticed Betrice near the door and made her way across.

Betrice greeted her easily, if a bit reservedly. Callie could hardly blame her, with all the eyes of the shop upon them.

"Are you shopping for the ball?"

Betrice nodded. "I received my invitation this morning. Goodness, you certainly have lovely penmanship."

Callie slid her gaze to the heavenly Cabot, who quirked a single perfect brow at her from his post behind the counter. "Er . . . I'm so glad you'll be coming. Is Henry excited, as well?"

Betrice looked down, folding her gloves together. "Henry will enjoy visiting with the other farmers, of course. I very much doubt he shall dance."

Callie laughed. "If Mr. Porter can dance, I'm sure Henry will find it within him to do so." Oh, dear. She'd spoken loudly enough to be heard over the hubbub— right when the hubbub hit one of those inexplicable silences. From all around the shop, wide gazes pinned her like a bug in a collection. She swallowed and tried to keep her smile even. Then the whispers erupted anew, louder than ever.

Even Betrice was staring at her. "Lawrence will be attending? Dancing? In front of the entire village?"

I have no earthly idea. "Of course he will!" *Perhaps I shall run away to Jamaica.* "It is his ball, after all." *Dear God, I'm rhyming.* "I daresay he will dance with all the ladies!" *Someone stop me, please.*

Cabot appeared at her elbow. "Excuse the interruption, madam, but I have a question about the sprigged day gown you ordered. Which of these ribbons would you prefer for the trim?"

Across his large, elegant palm lay two ribbons of nearly identical tints of pale green. Callie stared down at them in blind panic. With a spastic wave of one hand, she apparently selected the one which Cabot most approved, for he bestowed a breathtaking smile upon her and bowed himself away.

When Callie turned back to Betrice, she was surprised to find her friend had disappeared into the crowd. Surprised but honestly relieved. When she got back to the manor, she was going to have a very stern talk with her runaway mouth!

It wasn't until she had made her escape and was

safely halfway back to the smithy that Callie realized that she hadn't ordered a sprigged day gown with pale green trim. *Bless you, Cabot!*

Cabot entered the sitting room where his master sat idly stirring a cup of tea with a spoon. Since Cabot knew perfectly well that Button never took sugar, he maintained a respectful silence during his master's "deep think."

Eventually, Button ceased stirring and took a sip. Then he put the cup down on its saucer with a clink. "Yes, I believe steps must indeed be taken before matters get entirely out of hand."

"Yes, sir."

"When one takes on such an assignment, one must be prepared to deal with the unexpected."

"Yes, sir."

"It is not as though I could leave the poor thing dangling out alone, like the last leaf on the autumn tree!"

"Most well put, sir."

"Reinforcements, that is what is needed here!" He rubbed his hands together. "Cabot, fetch me the—"

A tray appeared at his elbow, supplied with pen, ink, and a stack of already penned invitations to the Porter masque. Button gazed at it with delight. "How would I do without you, dear boy?"

"Brilliantly, sir. As always."

Betrice turned a corner into the churchyard and stopped her headlong rush. With one hand pressed to her aching midriff, she leaned back against the sun-warmed wall of the church and closed her stinging eyes.

Damn. Damn, damn, damn.

Betrice was a lady, she would never say damn in a churchyard, even in her mind, were she not driven to it!

I daresay he will dance with all the ladies!

Callie, damned bloody Callie! For the past few years Betrice had truly believed that she might at last become the lady of Amberdell Manor. Everyone in the village had thought so, had indeed treated her as de facto mistress of the hall. She looked after them, and listened to them, and settled their piddling disputes, and carried soup to their ailing children and—she brought her gloved fist down to smack against the stone behind her—arranged the flowers every Sunday in this very church!

But it seemed that poor, half-mad, dying Lawrence wasn't quite as ill or insane as everyone had been so certain.

Callie had seemed so confident, so bloody damned *giddy* about him—like a girl in love, knowing her man would do absolutely anything she asked, even live.

"You've hurt your hand."

Betrice straightened with a start, opening her eyes to find Unwin standing before her, his thick features dark with concern. She gazed down at her hand, realizing that she was cradling the throbbing thing in her other hand. Her glove was torn down one side and blood had beaded on the scraped flesh below.

Apparently she had struck the wall more than once.

Her eyes filled with tears of frustration and fury. She let them come. Unwin would understand. Unwin wouldn't think less of her for her rage. He knew a bit about rage himself.

Callie gleefully left the village in her dust, riding Sally away at a careful gallop. Sally, who had more than a hint of Thoroughbred in her veins, would have liked to have made it a full run. It was only with difficulty that Callie kept the filly to an easy pace. She merely wanted some distance from Amberdell. She didn't wish to end up in Scotland.

A wide path ran alongside the river, likely from the passage of horse-drawn barges. It made for a lovely bridle path and Callie enjoyed her ride very much. When she felt the tension of the village fall far behind her and Sally had become bored with pulling at the bit, they slowed to a prancing walk.

Callie let her hands ease, flexing her fingers. It had been a long while since she'd ridden regularly, what with her duties running the household. Not that riding had ever been terribly entertaining to her. The Worthington mounts were ever so slightly . . . elderly. Every one had survived through successive young riders and were stolid and slow-paced, immune to encouragement and unimpressed by anything short of cannon fire.

So she was entirely unprepared when Sally let out a shrieking neigh and leaped powerfully sideways, then bounded high. Callie felt herself lift entirely out of the saddle, then come back down to find that Sally was elsewhere.

Oh, ow. Not a brilliant last thought, but all she really had time for before she flew the great distance from Sally's Thoroughbred back to the hard-packed earth of the path. *This will hurt.*

It did.

Ren drew his hood down so that not even an errant breeze might reveal him and rode his horse slowly down the village High Street. He felt the furtive stares scurry across him like mice, and just as unwelcome.

When he'd returned to his post just past the bridge after his efforts to find the giant had been to no avail, he'd become impatient when Calliope did not appear after half an hour. He'd missed her, he was sure of it.

He'd felt compelled to check. Now, with his shoulders twitching from the weight of all that resentful curiosity, he wished he'd gone directly home. She wasn't here. Her bay filly was nowhere to be seen. She'd made swift with her business apparently, for which he could hardly blame her. Did they treat her so grimly here? Surely not. Calliope's cheerful manner and open friendliness must find purchase even with these surly country folk.

Or did it? She had been here thrice in less than a week, and each time she seemed to leave as quickly as possible. No idle gossip with the ladies, no invitations to a cup of tea, no kindly overtures to the new lady of the manor?

Apparently not. He remembered the ginger fiasco . . . and his own churlish treatment of her after discovering her in the cellar, even in front of the village men.

His gut went cold at the thought of her certain unhappiness since she'd wed him. He must appear a madman to her, bent on only lust and the occasional scolding. She'd been torn from her insane but loving family, that outrageous mob, only to find herself completely isolated from even making new friends by her husband's reputation for darkness and deviltry. It must be some sort of special Calliope hell. Handmade by him and delivered to her bound by a broken strand of pearls.

With a muffled curse, he turned his mount and spurred it into a gallop, right down the village street, causing village curs to scurry and pedestrians to dodge out of the way.

Back to his bloody manor, may it do him no good whatsoever. She would only come home and drive him mad with mingled longing and exasperation. No place on earth was safe from the flavor of Calliope, that taste of uncompromising sweetness, with just a tantalizing hint of rosemary and salt.

Chapter 18

Callie lay upon her back in the middle of the path and contemplated the gathering clouds in the afternoon sky. When had the sun disappeared?

Her head ached. Had she landed upon it? She didn't think she'd gone unconscious but perhaps a bit . . . discombobulated. Slowly she pushed herself up with her hands until she was sitting up, rather like a child's dolly. For a long moment she gazed fuzzily down at her skirts until she realized that they were rucked up to her knees. She pushed them down with clumsy hands.

Yes. Definite discombobulation.

Sally. Looking around her, turning her head carefully on her neck, revealed no horse. The filly was gone, probably back home to her barn. That was good. When a horse came back without a rider, people became concerned. People like Mr. Porter. And . . . and Betrice. And her husband. Callie stared blankly at her filthy scraped palms for a long moment until it came to her. Henry.

Mr. Porter and Betrice and Henry would see the silly

Sally coming home with no one in her saddle and they would immediately set out to rescue silly Callie.

Someone would come.

Being rescued was a good thing, of course. Irritating, but good. Still, there was no good reason to wait here like this, sitting in the dirt like a discarded plaything.

Getting to her hands and knees went well. She was feeling clearer by the moment. She now very clearly felt the throbbing in her head. And, when she tried to stand, she very clearly felt the nauseating pain in her ankle.

Hobbling carefully, she made it to the edge of the path to rest upon a fallen log there. Much more dignified, to be discovered reclining sedately upon a stump than to be sprawled in an ungainly way in the path.

The breeze picked up, swirling about her and creating little eddies of leaves in the path. She shivered. When had it gotten so chill?

She gazed up at the hidden sun for a long moment, half shielding her eyes with one hand while she thought. It had been late morning when she'd left the village. Now it was well into the afternoon. She'd only ridden for a quarter of an hour or so downriver from the bridge—albeit at Sally's long-legged racer's gait—so . . .

She must have remained discombobulated for quite a while, first of all. An hour? More?

Time for someone to begin searching for her. Time enough, in fact, for someone to find her?

She could sit here and wait, although she wore only her woolen spencer and her gown was damp from lying on the ground and the breeze was becoming good and stiff now. The clouds were darkening, as well, becoming quite black to the northeast. Recalling the storm that had nearly washed out the bridge on her first night here,

Callie knew she would not like to be lost in it, alone and hindered by her injury.

Mr. Porter would come.

Wouldn't he?

The thing was . . . well, she simply didn't know if he would come for her or not. He'd been so angry about the ladder, and the cellar, and the ginger . . . at what point would he simply decide to disregard her?

Since she had been gone for hours before, to the village and visiting with Betrice and rambling through the wildflowers, he might very well simply be expecting her to appear back at the manor in her own time.

Letting out a long, sad breath, Callie came to the conclusion that she was well and truly on her own.

Alone.

Perhaps not quite as enjoyable a state as she'd originally supposed.

Ren looked up from his study fire to frown at the breeze rattling at the window glass. He'd been enjoying his first real brood in a while, dwelling upon the stares and glares of the villagers and of how he hadn't had to deal with such aggravation before Miss Calliope Worthington had waltzed half naked into his life.

She was taking her bloody time about coming back from her ride. The house was too damned quiet without her bustling and sweeping and singing silly rude songs just under her breath so he could only hear half the words . . .

There were no delicious cooking smells today. The weeds she insisted on sticking into his antiquities were wilting. The house was growing colder, almost as if it didn't think she was coming back—

A shattered ladder. A jar of poisoned ginger. A

mysteriously jammed cellar door and a nest of asps. A dark silhouette on a hilltop.

An explosion of icy fear suddenly froze his gut.

I believe.

Ren rode his gelding into the wind for nearly an hour, searching the areas where Callie had gone drawing in the past. There was no sign of her, not so much as a pencil shaving.

She might have ridden quite far on Henry's restive bay filly without realizing it. Amberdell estate was bounded on one side by the river but on the other three there were only a few ancient stone cairns to mark the lands. She could have wandered into a different county by now!

Ren pulled his mount to a halt at the top of yet another hill and stared hard in every direction. Impatiently he pulled his hood down, letting it fall like a cowl about his neck as he strained his eyes in the fading light. It was not yet sunset, but the black clouds boiling up from the northeast had turned day into evening. Ren could not spot the filly's bright coat, nor Callie's pale muslin gown nor her nut-brown spencer.

The filly had seemed well broken to Ren, if a bit youthfully excessive. Surely Henry would never send over a dangerous mount for a lady!

But Callie had lived in London all her life. Posting paths did not pose the same dangers as country riding . . . and there was the giant stranger to consider. If Callie had somehow come off her horse, the creature would surely have returned by now—

Returned to Springdell, not Amberdell.

Ren cursed, even as he towed his mount in a half circle and spurred him to a full canter. Springdell was nearly three miles away, but the big gelding's stride made short work of the distance. In less than half an hour Ren pulled his blowing mount to a halt in Henry's barnyard. Ren tossed his reins to a staring groom, only then realizing that his hood was down. Indifferent to the man's gaping curiosity, Ren only pulled it back up when he saw Henry's wife Betrice running from the house, her skirts picked up and urgent concern on her face.

"Is she all right?"

Ren's heart fell. "I thought she might be here."

Betrice shook her head. "No, I haven't seen her since this morning, in the village. Sally came in just now, her reins broken and no sign of Callie." She pressed both hands to her face. "Oh, if something happened to her—I shouldn't have told Henry to give her the filly. I just thought Callie would like her, she's such a pretty beast—"

Ren realized that he didn't know Betrice at all, though they'd been neighbors for three years. She seemed sincerely worried over Callie.

"Where did the horse come in from?"

Betrice pointed. "Over the west pasture, from the direction of the river."

Ren shook his head. "I've already checked near the bridge. There's no sign of her."

Betrice clasped her hands under her chin, too dismayed to worry over the wisps of her hair becoming dislodged in the building wind. "Henry rode out that way just a few minutes ago to look for her. I was just coming out to send Jakes to fetch you from Amberdell. You may take him with you now."

Ren nodded, mounting his horse once more. The groom led out a fit farm beast to ride, already saddled. When Ren reined his mount about, he saw a strangely significant look pass between Betrice and the fellow, Jakes. Then Betrice turned back to Ren. "Should I go to Amberdell, just in case she returns there?"

Ren nodded shortly. It was a good suggestion. "My thanks."

Riding out with Jakes keeping well up with him, Ren spared a thought from his growing worry to wonder why he'd avoided conversation with Betrice for so long. She seemed an extremely good woman.

Callie had made a pact with herself. For every ten steps, she could rest for a count of ten. Ten walking. Ten resting. She kept to the river path, retracing Sally's steps, for one could not get lost when following a river. That way all her attention could be spent on counting to ten, again and again.

At least the effort of lurching along, using a stout branch for an ill-fitting crutch beneath her shoulder, kept her somewhat warm. It wasn't so bad until the wind picked up, sending icy drafts up beneath her thin skirts and making her hands stiff with cold.

Ten walking. Ten resting.

Every now and then she varied her routine by thinking up ten ways to enact vengeance upon Mr. Porter for his neglect. Stinging ants in his drawers. Asps in his bedsheets. Poisoned ginger.

Having seven imaginative siblings gave Callie a great wealth of vengeance to call upon. Unseamed trousers. Burrs under the saddle.

Changing the locks of Amberdell.

Making him moan and cry out and shiver on the carpet. That was Callie's favorite. She was bloody tired of always being the one to fall to pieces in a soaring orgasm every night. All right, then, not really. She adored it. But it was about bloody time that Mr. Porter had a taste of what it was like to be truly powerless with lust!

She probably ought to do that one before the stinging ants. They had a tendency to cause swelling—and not the good kind!

Ten. Ten.

She was becoming colder and she didn't think she'd come very far at all. Sally had been cantering for such a long while . . . miles? Surely not . . . yet a horse could cover a great deal of ground at a run and she'd let Sally run herself for a good long time . . . a horse could run at perhaps twenty miles an hour? So, for perhaps a quarter of an hour . . . which was twenty-five minutes, no, wait, that was a quarter of one hundred . . . and an hour was sixty minutes . . .

Her head hurt and it was difficult to make the numbers stay still in her mind. They danced and pranced together, their shoes clad in tiny spikes that sent tiny lightning bolts across her vision . . .

Ten. Ten.

"I want [step] to sit before a fire [step]," she said out loud. "I want [step] a hot bath [step]." The crotch of the stick dug painfully into her armpit. "I want pillows!" Step. "I want tea!" Step.

I want my mum.

Fat tears of self-pity began to roll down her cheeks. She let them. It was high time she gave in to a good howl! Bloody Mr. Porter and his bloody dusty house and his bloody rude villagers and his bloody cold Cotswolds!

Well, but . . . she loved the Cotswolds. She'd have to think of something else to hate.

Sally. She hated bloody Sally. And right then she even hated Betrice and Henry, for loaning her that idiot horse. Except she wasn't an idiot horse. She was a very nice horse.

*Something made her spook, I just know it. The same
something that knocked down the ladder, and locked
the cellar door.*

Not the ginger, though. Best not think about the
damned ginger.

Well, she had plenty of time to contemplate the puzzle, what with the miles and the math and Sally's long,
high-bred legs. And the fact that, apparently, Mr. Porter
hadn't even missed her.

Ren never did spot Henry riding toward the river. By the
time he took his gelding down the grassy riverbank to
the old barge towing path, he'd forgotten all about his
cousin. Before him, dug deep into the damp earth of the
path, were hoofmarks. One set, rather dainty, with fine,
well-smithed shoe marks, set far apart.

"That'll be Sally," grunted Jakes.

The other, large, unshod, the hoofmarks of a farm
beast. Like a hundred other plow horses in the valley,
except for a rather large crack in the right fore.

"That's a horse what'll come up lame," commented
Jakes with a concerned scowl. "Poor beastie."

The larger horse's hoofmarks covered Sally's. Both
sets led off upriver, up the path. Ren set his gelding at
an easy canter, keeping his eyes on the ground, but it
wasn't hard to follow the dug-in marks of two horses at
a run.

At a chase?

The plow horse's track was deep, indicating a heavy
horse and a heavy rider.

A giant silhouette on the top of the hill.

Not really the giant's style, riding a farm plug—
although it might be for reasons of cover. Could someone from his past be taking a strange sort of vengeance
on his bride? But why?

Ren spurred his mount faster, feeling the urgency grow. *I have a bad feeling . . .*

When the first icy raindrops fell on the back of Callie's bent neck, she stopped and glared at the sky. "Now you're just being vile."

Then the drops became harder, water turned to ice high in the air.

"Oh!" Callie lurched to the side of the path, dragging her stick, then crawling on all fours—*which is bloody difficult in a muslin day gown so where the devil are my proper clothes, Dade?*—up the grassy bank and into the dubious shelter of a small willow tree. With dismay, Callie settled into a shivering crouch and glared at the view filled with bouncing white hail the size of hazelnuts.

She watched them plopping into the river, splashing large like stones, turning the surface of the water into a roiling mess. Then, as she gazed outward, she saw him.

The dark shape of a man, standing on the opposite bank. Callie shrank back beneath the little tree, crawling nearly behind it, unable to take her shocked gaze from the figure in her view.

A giant, dressed in dark clothing, wearing a shapeless hat, staring directly at her, unmoving, oblivious to the hail battering him without mercy.

Chapter 19

Ren, riding hard through the hail and the stinging rain that came down in its aftermath, almost missed it. There, across the path, a line drawn as if with a stick, scored right through the tracks of the filly and of the plow horse. Reining the gelding to a squealing halt, Ren twisted his mount about on the narrow path and trotted back to the mark. Jakes followed a few minutes later, remaining respectfully back from the evidence.

Ren dismounted and knelt to inspect it. The mark was strange but the ones preceding it were stranger. A series of small depressions, single footprints? No, they were opposed by a hole, dug into the trail by a stick? A small woman with a cane? Or a crutch.

She is injured.

His belly tight with worry for her, he followed the odd line to the edge of the path, and then followed the scuff marks through the soaking grass on the riverbank. Someone had scrambled up the bank.

The trail of crushed grass led to a small willow tree halfway up the slope. Its infant withies barely swept the tall grass. Through the dangling branches Ren saw a flash of something pale. A shapely pile of muddy muslin.

He found her within, curled up on the far side of the trunk, her gown and spencer and face daubed in mud.

"Calliope?"

She opened her eyes. "Oh, it's you." She sat up a bit. "I didn't think you were coming after all."

"I'm sorry. I had a late start."

She blinked at him. "Were you brooding again?" she asked indifferently.

Guilty as charged. He nodded, bemused. "I fear so."

"I knew it." She shivered. "Such a bloody waste of time, brooding."

He was beginning to see her point. He reached for her hands. They were like ice. He drew her up into his arms and easily lifted her.

"I want a bath," she declared flatly.

"Yes, you do. You look as though you had a fight with a mud monster."

"I did it deliberately."

"Why ever for? It made you nearly impossible to see."

"Exactly." Her gaze was fixed at a point across the river, but when Ren looked there was no one there.

Ren rode at high speed back to Amberdell with Calliope in his arms. He left Jakes in the yard with the horses and carried her straight up to her room. He found Betrice there, pouring a steaming pail of water into the smallest copper tub.

"I had a farmhand carry it up here. I hope you don't mind. Oh, goodness, Callie—quickly, into the tub!"

"I have her, Betrice. But thank you."

Betrice gaped at Ren for a long moment. Then she seemed to fade a bit, shrinking into the background as she had always seemed to before. "Of course, Lawrence."

She left, closing the door behind her. Ren stood Calliope on one foot and swiftly began undoing her wet spencer. The damp wool fought him for a moment. She slapped weakly at his hands.

"No, you'll stretch the fit. I haven't another."

Ren paused. She didn't? As he eased her arms free of the clinging wet short coat, he tried to remember what she'd worn for the past week.

There was a pale blue gown and then a sort of white one. Ivory, the ladies called it. Which, he realized, was the filthy ruin she now wore.

"Were you traveling with nothing at all when you came here?"

She blinked at him. "We lost almost everything in the river that first night."

"I didn't know."

"You didn't ask."

I believe I'm going to lose this one, too. "Do you not have more things at home?"

She sighed wearily. "One would think, wouldn't one?"

He'd not even noticed her doing without. "Then you must order some new items at once. There is a dressmaker in the village." He lifted her gown over her head.

"There is something so satisfying . . ."—her voice was muffled. Then she popped out again—"about post factum permission."

He frowned. "Meaning you have already done so."

She stood shivering in her damp chemise. "You have no idea the bill that is coming your way. Mr. Button is quite persuasive."

Hmm. He could certainly afford a few trifling gowns. He bent, swept her into his arms, and deposited her into the steaming tub, chemise and all.

"Eek!"

He frowned. "Too hot?"

"Mmph. Ah, no."

Her fair skin was already turning pink, but she seemed to savor the heat. He pulled on the floating hem of her chemise and tugged it over her head, leaving her entirely naked.

"Nothing else?" He frowned. "No pantalets?"

She kept her eyes closed. Was she blushing? Then Ren had a blood-heating memory of slicing her pantalets off with his sword. Ah, well. Yes.

Then he realized something. "You never wear a corset, do you?"

She turned her face away. "Mama says they aren't healthy."

"Well, I agree. Your figure needs no improvement."

Startled, she drew back. "That is the first time you've ever paid me a compliment." She blinked. "In fact, I believe this is the longest conversation we've ever had . . . that didn't end in a sword fight, at any rate."

He poured a pitcher of steaming water over her head. She gasped and sputtered. "Don't worry, I daresay I'll fall back into a brooding silence soon."

She pushed back the hair streaming into her face and scowled. "Death is silent," she threatened.

He almost kissed her. He didn't mean to. She simply looked so delicious and bedraggled and she still had a smear of mud on one cheek and her skin was blotchy from the heat and her breasts floated so temptingly in the sudsy bathwater.

He *wanted* to kiss her. He bent to do just that, then remembered that he still wore his hood. Hoods played bloody hell with kissing, that was the truth. In addition, hideous scars probably didn't do much for it, either.

She was busy scrubbing at her hands and arms and

neck with the sponge Betrice had found somewhere. "Soap! I've missed proper soap!"

Ren blinked. "I like that salt you use."

She rolled her eyes. "I've been here for a week and the only soap I could find was that harsh lye stuff I used on the floors. I wanted proper bath soap."

Ren conceded that it might be easier to bathe with soap—and she'd only needed to ask him—but he was going to miss the scent of rosemary on her skin. Perhaps he could find rosemary soap in London . . . for what purpose? She would likely be gone before he could find it.

Reminded, Ren rose to his feet and began to roll down his sleeves. "I shall leave you to your bath, then, since you seem to be feeling better. There must be some bread and cheese in the larder. I'll leave it outside your door."

She frowned up at him, gazing, as always, right through his hood. "What about tonight?"

He tilted his head. "I assumed you would be too tired . . . and your ankle . . ."

"Oh, bother that." She waved a soapy hand, spattering gobs of suds on his muddy boots. "I've been through much worse than this. Once Lysander tried to win a race by putting Chinese rockets on the back of his pony cart. My mount took exception and dumped me into the Serpentine in Hyde Park in the middle of February. I went right through the ice.

"The Serpentine isn't very deep, you know," she informed him seriously. "I simply pushed off the bottom and popped right back up through the hole. Dade got me out by using Lysander as a rope. Mama never even knew a thing."

She smiled. "Dade set Lysander straight, though. My younger brother had to sit upon a cushion for a week!"

"He beat him?"

"No, of course not! He took all the springs out of the pony cart! Orion helped him. He's so good at everything mechanical."

"And malevolent," Ren murmured. "But you don't mean that you still wish to . . ."

She nodded briskly. "Oh, yes. That is our contract, is it not?"

She wanted the pearl. Of course. The faster she earned back the pearls, the sooner she could leave him in her memory, to be just another adventure like the pony carts and Chinese rockets.

He wanted her.

She wanted to go.

She could simply leave. She must know that. There was very little he could do to stop her. Although some husbands would simply bring their straying wives home by force, Ren would never imprison her here. The pearls were meaningless to him, just a twisted bargain made by a man with nothing left to lose.

Abruptly he wanted her to go. He wanted her to leave now before he became any more attached to her body and her voice and her wide hazel eyes and her clearly mad way of looking at things . . .

Disregarding his shirt and his weskit, he plunged his arms into the tub and scooped her out. He deposited her on the carpet before the roaring coals Betrice had built up. Then he blew out the candles and stood before his bride. She curled her injured ankle almost beneath her, sitting with her legs tucked up next to her and her back straight, looking at him, with only the glow of the burning coals to light them. He dug into his soaked weskit pocket and held up a pearl. "You understand what I request of you?"

"Yes." She gazed at him for a long moment, her expression somber. "Do you?"

Then, she closed her eyes, put her hands loosely

behind her, and opened her mouth. He placed the pearl upon her tongue, letting his fingertip trail over her lips when she closed them. Would he never know her kiss? Would he be able to let her go if he did?

Quickly, he stripped off his wet clothing, leaving his hood on the filthy pile. He took a moment to wipe the last of the mud from his arms and neck, then he stood before her, naked as he had never been before.

He stepped closer. His erection jutted before him, hardening and thickening at the thought of her sweet innocent mouth upon him. She would see what a bastard he was. Now, she would see the beast in truth.

"Open your mouth."

Her jaw dropped. Her eyes were still closed so when he pressed the head of his cock to her parted lips, she frowned in confusion.

Her hands came unclasped from behind her back and she began to reach upward.

"No," he commanded. "Just your mouth."

Callie realized what it was now. Shock trembled through her belly although she was careful not to show it. Yet, he had put his mouth on her, had he not?

Her tongue darted nervously to her lips, and in doing so ran feather light around the blunt tip of . . . it.

She heard him gasp. It was a vulnerable sound, a sound of need and desire and lack of control.

Ooh, yes. An excellent development.

Callie flicked her tongue again, this time more slowly, more exploratively. He twitched and she could hear his breath come faster, although he didn't make the same sound again.

I want to make him do that again.

The pearl still lay upon her tongue, so she used it on him, rolling it over that now-wet tip, using her tongue to massage it in a great circle round the end.

There it was. That sound again.

Mr. Porter, you are mine now.

He'd made her whimper and scream and cry out non-sense that echoed through this empty house.

Worthingtons knew a bit about vengeance.

Callie opened her mouth and took him in. The blunt tip ended in a sort of ridge. With her lips now wrapped around his rod just past that ridge, she ran her pearl-tipped tongue around and around it.

If she was not mistaken, the man had begun to trem-ble, just a bit. The pearl was getting in the way now, so Callie discreetly let it fall from her lips and focused en-tirely on taking the thick length of him into her mouth. When he'd pressed to the back of her throat and there was still more, she withdrew slowly, thinking it was time to assess the situation.

"Oh, God!"

Callie stopped in surprise at the guttural exclama-tion. That was the good part? Slowly she slid him into her mouth again, then drew back, trying to re-create the moment entirely.

He only groaned this time. Something was missing. Again, but this time she accidentally sealed her lips about him and suction was created as she withdrew him from the depth of her throat.

One big hand came to fist in her hair and she heard him breathing hard and fast.

Aha.

Poor Mr. Porter. He was in for it now.

Callie dove upon his rod, licking and sucking and sliding up and down it, all in a rush. He cursed breath-lessly, then drove his other hand into her hair and stead-ied her pace.

Her mouth full of man, Callie allowed it while she thought it over. He wanted a slow sliding pace? With suction. He wanted to go deeper into her throat, but it took a while before Callie caught the trick of that. His breathless gasp rewarded her and he moaned her name.

"Callie."

He'd never called her that before.

Suddenly this act didn't seem to be so much about vengeance as it did about pleasure. She wanted to please him, as he had pleased her the night before. She wanted him to feel that brilliant explosion of delight, that languorous blissful slide afterward.

So she gentled her mouth. She took him in as far as she could. When she could go no farther, she lifted her hands to wrap around the base of him, warming the length of him, covering him, and yes, owning him.

He allowed it, too lost in her mouth to demand obedience. Encouraged by this lack of attention, Callie opened her hands and spread them wide. She dared not open her eyes . . . not because he commanded it, but because she didn't know who she would see, the angel or the demon.

All she wanted was the man.

So she spread her fingers out to fan on either side of his rod, questing through the patch of hair, like her own, but wiry. Then upward, over a flat stomach, hard and lean, down, along muscled thighs sprinkled with crisp hair, bravely back upward and back, to feel his buttocks hard and muscled as he flexed them, thrusting into her mouth. She sucked him, using her hands on his firm buttocks to press him deeper. He groaned, forgetting his protest, and she had him in her power once more.

She deeply enjoyed the sensation of her hands on his buttocks and lingered there a moment longer, digging her fingers into that hard manly flesh, so different from her own soft round bottom. Then, unwilling to lose this chance to explore, she slid her hands up his flexing back.

He was lean all the way up, although she'd known that from the fit of his somber clothing.

She liked it. It excited her to touch him, to steal this invasion while she sucked him senseless. She liked owning him this way. Her labia dampened and she squirmed her thighs tighter together, pressing them to relieve the throb of wanting. It was big. Too big to fit in her mouth and her throat. Callie wasn't sure but wasn't her vagina smaller than her mouth and her throat?

Yet even that alarming thought was arousing. She wanted him big. She wanted him to fill her completely,

Then her questing fingers found a thick ridge of scar on his back, curving like a crescent across one shoulder blade and almost to his armpit.

Her other hand found another, a lumpy, starburst shape, round and radiating smaller scars.

Trying not to lose her pace, she allowed her hands to slide back to the front of him. She could not reach all the way to his shoulders, but yes, there above the hard plates of his chest, an answering scar to the starburst, another angry round ridge of flesh.

Something had gone clear through him.

Then Callie felt his rod surge in her mouth. Quickly she slid her hands back down to encompass him, holding him while she sucked faster. He must be close. He was making the same sort of wild nonsense sounds she had.

Then he orgasmed and she felt her mouth fill with salty, tangy liquid.

Goodness!

Her eyes flew open, her surprised gaze lifting up to his face.

His head was thrown back as a guttural cry was torn from his lips. It was no good. She couldn't see his face at all, only the ridges and bumps of the scars, lacing over that shoulder and more over his chest and ribs.

Ooh, the poor man. What had happened to him?

Then he dug his fingers in her hair and thrust his cock deeper, shuddering, pumping more of that salty substance into her throat.

She swallowed reflexively, with him still deep within her, and he released his breath in a great groan as he shuddered. In ecstasy? It certainly seemed like it.

Callie shut her eyes quickly, feeling as though she had stolen something from him. Did he think his body ugly with his scars? Damaged or not, he seemed rather magnificent to her. She treasured the image of his tall muscled body thrumming with tension and pleasure as she held him captive in her mouth.

When his fists eased free of her hair and he slid his rod from her mouth, she let her hands fall away and sat back, working her weary jaw and savoring the strange taste of him on her tongue.

Remembering his command, she put her hands behind her back once more but there was no help for the lost pearl, discarded somewhere on the carpet. She would find it later.

For now, she fought the urge to smile, instead keeping her expression the mild, obedient one that she knew drove him mad with frustration. She had just sucked him to a great groaning orgasm. She could still hear him panting, and if she wasn't mistaken, he stumbled a bit.

"That . . . that will be all tonight, Mrs. Porter."

As Callie listened to her husband flee her bedchamber, a smile quirked her lips.

Just you wait, Mr. Porter.

Chapter 20

Betrice entered the front hall of Springdell and began to unbutton her damp coat. Now she would have to block it carefully in the kitchen, checking it often to assure it did not shrink badly in the heat from the oven.

Someday Callie would have a lady's maid to do such things for her—if Lawrence ever overcame his ridiculous aversion to staff.

She had to hand it to Callie, though. The house, while still vastly undermaintained, looked genuinely comfortable now, at least in the living areas occupied by the two of them. Callie had scoured the place down to the floorboards. It quite literally shone.

It was annoying, really, how Callie made it very difficult to truly hate her. It would have been so much easier if the new lady of Amberdell had turned out to be some spoiled, supercilious creature.

Betrice felt quite ill thinking about what might have happened earlier that day. At the very least, that empty-headed filly could have killed Callie!

She shook off her unhappy thoughts and pasted on a smile for Henry's sake. Still carrying her wet coat—for who was there to take it from her?—she sought out her husband in his study.

"Good evening, dear. I suppose Jakes informed you that Mrs. Porter made it home safely?"

Henry sat in his favorite chair, gazing into the fire. He didn't look up at her with his usual bland but welcoming smile.

"Betrice."

She went still. Betrice, not Betty—which she loathed. "Yes? I really must go press this coat before it—"

"Betrice, when Lawrence came seeking information about his wife, you told him that Sally had only just returned."

Damn Jakes.

Betrice blinked innocently. "I don't think so. I don't really remember what I said. I was in such a state of worry."

Henry turned to look at her then. She nearly flinched from the flat disappointment she saw there.

"Betrice, that horse had been home and stabled for several hours. I was under the distinct impression that she had been courteously returned. An impression you imparted to me."

She shone a wide gaze at him. "I thought Sally had been dropped off at the stables without any of us realizing it."

Henry's eyes were cold now, like ice in winter. "Betrice, I will ask you this just once. You will answer truthfully."

She tilted her head, blinking back tears. "Of course, Henry. I always do."

"Did you cause harm to Lawrence's wife today?"

Sweet relief poured through her. She smiled pleasantly. "Of course not, Henry dear. What a silly question."

She saw the doubt creep in past the anger and knew

she had him again. Leaning forward, she dropped a kiss on his balding head. "Enjoy your pipe, darling."

As she left the study, she breathed out a long sigh of relief. Thank goodness Henry had phrased that question just that way!

Ren paced his bedchamber. It was a new one, the one he'd been meant to have all along, the master's chamber adjoining Calliope's.

Outside the sun was near to rising. Though his body ached he could not rest.

She had nearly come to serious harm yesterday. It seemed that someone in Amberdell wanted his wife gone.

Gone . . . or dead.

Why? She had scarcely been there a week. She had been there but a day before the first attempt. Even a Worthington could hardly make an enemy so quickly . . . unless it was possibly Dade Worthington. Yet Callie had challenged no one, had confronted no one. She had wed him in the village in the vicar's parlor and in less than twenty-four hours someone had tried to prompt her to fall off a window ledge!

Unless it was not about Calliope at all . . . which was the thought he'd been trying very hard not to think all along. It was the very reason why he'd not been willing to listen the first few times she'd told him her suspicions.

A man with a past had to expect that past to follow him, like a hound upon his trail.

The giant . . .

Ren had once belonged to something he'd thought was wonderful. A band of brothers, comrades-in-arms. A club, as rich and delicious a secret as any boyhood club could be. Yet he'd not been a boy, but a man, in service to the Crown.

Yet even the Crown would disavow this club if it were

asked. Thieves, spies, saboteurs . . . and assassins, like the giant.

One lived in that club or one died in that club. One never left that club. Yet Ren had. He'd considered his debt paid in full . . . but there were those perhaps who did not think his life payment enough.

He *had* died for that club. Beaten to death on a slimy dock, left bleeding out his duty and his loyalty to the last. If it hadn't been for a ship full of wounded soldiers unloading nearby, with staff already trained in medical procedures, he would not have made his way back to life.

He'd been unconscious for weeks. Months. When he'd woken, he'd been half crazed with pain, so broken he could scarcely function, scarcely walk, scarcely talk. Yet he'd crawled from that private nursing bed and donned the fresh set of clothing left optimistically near his bedside, and he'd simply walked out.

They'd found him eventually . . . or he'd found them. Driven by half-mad thoughts of vengeance, or longing for what he had lost—he still wasn't entirely sure—he'd aimed his broken, fevered body at them like a weapon, determined to make every one of them face what they had done with their betrayal.

For he had been betrayed, turned in to the enemy by one of those selfsame comrades for a bag of coin and a Napoleonic pat upon the head.

The enemy had begun picking off the betrayed one by one, attacking, murdering . . . even as he had been murdered.

Now his supposed brothers were back, sending their most dangerous man against a pretty, odd, warmhearted young woman who had never heard of them or their mission!

No, it wasn't about Calliope at all. This was all meant for him.

What could be their aim? To silence him? What need had they now for his silence? The Peninsular War was won, with Napoleon losing more ground every day.

Calliope . . . Callie . . .

He paused in his pacing, leaning one hand on the mantel and gazing into the red eyes of his coal fire. She'd dealt him a killing blow last night. When she'd devoured him, taken him into her warm, wet mouth and made him cry out her name . . . it ought to have been an act of dominance, of humiliation.

Instead it had been quite nearly sacred—a benediction, a blessing, a gift.

He'd been too lost in her sweet, hot cock-sucking to realize it at the time, but she had put her hands upon him, sliding them over his hot skin like cool balm, soothing and stroking even as she sucked and tantalized him. For all that he'd plunged deep into her mouth, he felt as though he were the one invaded, assaulted, deflowered.

She'd done something to him. She'd ensnared him, ensorcelled him with her giving mouth. He was not the same man he'd been a week ago.

Yet he was not the same man he'd been three years ago, either. He was someone new—someone with all the youthful arrogance gone, yet with his eager romantic heart still struggling to beat. He was a man with all his bitterness and despair gone, yet with scars— honorable battle scars. She was a gift, a lesson in humility and generosity. As lessons went, he'd not got off too badly.

The sun began to peek out over the easternmost hilltop. Ren snapped his mind back, away from the way she'd run her small questing hands all over his naked, broken body, and focused his mind upon today's mission.

He meant to find the giant.

Callie had been ordered to sit today and frankly she didn't mind. She'd thought she might work on her drawings, but her specimens had faded and she hadn't brought any fresh home from yesterday's venture.

The day outside was gray and chill, making the window seat unappealing.

Reading didn't tempt her, for her head still ached. Sewing seemed pointless, for the ivory gown was far too ruined to rescue. The blue she was wearing was all she had, but she had hopes that Mr. Button would keep his promise of others within days.

In the meantime, she found herself in the unique state of . . . well, boredom.

Boredom was a dangerous state for a Worthington. Things tended to explode, or at least catch fire. Or flood.

In one corner of the library stood a dainty Chinese cupboard. It was just a small red-lacquered box, really, set high on outrageously carved legs finished in gold leaf. In the somber room it fairly glowed, drawing Callie's restless gaze.

She hobbled closer, bending to admire the inlaid ivory pictures on the doors. The intricate designs looked like nonsense at first, but as she peered more closely, she realized that the figures were people . . . oh, no . . . animals? Yes, definitely people, but with the heads of animals. There were tangles of them, leading round and round in a sort of square spiral . . .

Callie's eyes widened. Oh. Animal-headed people who were . . . er . . . fornicating.

Straightening, she crossed her arms and gazed dubiously at the cupboard. Really? And she'd thought Mr.

Porter such a respectable sort of man. She knew he had an erotic side, of course, but she'd no idea he had a *whimsical* erotic side.

The cupboard was positively exuberant with naughty-boy enjoyment. Callie knew it when she saw it. Five brothers, after all.

She bent to examine the pictures again, following the pattern of tiny orgies with one fingertip . . . just in case, well, there was something *new*.

It wasn't as though she'd never seen erotica before. Her mother had a lovely collection of illustrations from an ancient Indian sexual text. One learned where one could.

The pressure of her seeking fingertips released something inside the latch and the little bowed door swung open into her hand.

Oh, well, don't mind if I do.

Callie went awkwardly to her knees to peer inside. One by one she lifted out an assortment of tiny objects.

First she pulled out a folded packet of silk. She unfolded it to find nothing within, then realized that the swath was a long sort of shawl, as fine as spiderweb, dyed in the most brilliant pattern of Turkish blue and emerald green. It was as vibrant and lovely as a peacock's feather. Callie longed for it with all her girlish heart, but she carefully folded it up and set it aside. She found another small cubical box. Nested inside was a stunning ring of exquisite sapphire. The stone was easily the size of Callie's own thumbprint. The jewel was surrounded by smaller green stones that must be emeralds. Though Callie had never seen them before. . . . except among the jewels in the casket in her room.

This ring, however, was no antique treasure. It was cut and mounted in an ostentatious height, very much the style of a ring recently presented by the Duke of

York to his mistress and much gossiped about in the tattle sheets.

It had to have been created some time in the last five years or so. Ellie would know. She kept on top of all the latest trends among the wealthy and titled—just in case she ever became one, Callie supposed. If anyone could rise so far, it would be Elektra Worthington.

The ring and the exotic silk shawl had doubtless been intended for the same lady . . . one with a taste for the vivid and ostentatious.

Mr. Porter had been in love. With someone who quite obviously didn't remain long enough to receive the ring Callie now clenched in her hand. A ring from the last five years. Scars that were four years old.

Gifts refused and rejected? Mr. Porter summarily dismissed from some shallow woman's favor?

Had he loved her?

Did he love her still?

Rage rose within Callie at the imagined rejection he'd suffered, at the unfeeling female who had looked at his suffering and his scars and then looked away.

She was being ridiculous, creating stories about matters of which she knew nothing. Perhaps the lady was still waiting for Mr. Porter, languishing somewhere, while he refused, stubborn man, to show her his ruined face and beg for her love. Now her ire rose against Mr. Porter himself!

Callie looked down at the treasures in her hands and laughed out loud at herself. She was becoming as fanciful and romantic as Mama.

Firmly setting aside the ring and, a little more slowly, the shawl, Callie reached back into the opening.

Next she extracted a letter in an envelope of the finest rag linen paper with a waxen seal in a design that made

Callie's eyes pop. She set it aside, trying to remember that prying wasn't nice.

She dipped her hand farther inside. The compartment was narrow but deep, like a long loaf of bread. Toward the back of the shelf she found a small inlaid wooden box, flat and oblong. The box was richly made but simple. Its only decoration was a carved emblem on the lid that rather alarmingly resembled the waxen seal of the letter.

Callie raised the lid slowly, unable to resist the sensation that she was committing some petty act of spying.

A medal, gleaming golden and rich, lying on a velvet bed. An ornate Latin inscription ran the edge of it, around the cast profile of none other than—

Callie's gaze slid to the letter. She picked it up, weighing the hefty paper in her hand. It was addressed to "R." That was all. Just "R."

Mr. Lawrence Porter was in possession of a letter that was written to someone else. By Callie's easily rationalized Worthington reasoning, that meant she had as much right to read it as he did.

The seal was broken anyway, lifted whole off the paper of the envelope beneath the flap.

Callie peeked. Then frowning, she pulled the entire letter from its envelope and opened the folded missive.

My dearest Ren,

I've sent you the damn medal anyway, even though I know you'll loathe it. In addition I've entered your name in the Rolls of Knighthood, regardless of your protest.

Bloody hell, Ren, when are you going to get off your high horse and forgive us all? I'd command it but I know you'd just disobey me and then I'd have to hang you for treason, you stubborn bastard.

I hope you like the Chinese cabinet. Even though I know you won't. Once upon a time, you would have laughed out loud.

Come back to Us soon. Our patience wears thin. Damned thin. Geo

Then beneath, scrawled large in a careless hand, were three letters that stole Callie's breath clean away.

"H.R.H."

His Royal Highness.

Geo. George. Prince George. The Prince Regent.

I'm reading Royal Post.

Callie's hand began to shake and the letter began to flutter obligingly. *I'm fluttering Royal Post.*

Now I'm stuffing the Royal Letter back into the Royal Envelope and locking it back into the Royal Deviant Cupboard. Callie slammed the little perverted door and stepped back from the cupboard as if it were on fire.

Then it struck her. Lawrence. *Ren.*

"Ren." Callie breathed the name aloud. Mr. Porter suddenly became someone warmer, easier, more understandable. More *Ren.*

Are you sure it isn't just the affectionately exasperated letter from the Prince Regent?

Callie's knees weakened and she sank to the carpet to sit tailor-fashion, gazing perplexedly at the cavorting ivory figures as she absently rubbed her ankle.

A medal. A knighthood. A friend named George.

Who are you, Mr. Porter?

And when do I get to meet Ren?

Chapter 21

Callie hesitated before answering the knocker that morning. As she hobbled through the front hall, it occurred to her that the giant might simply walk in.

Or it could be Betrice, coming by to see how she was feeling. Whichever, Callie refused to take on her husband's hermitlike attitudes. She flung the door open with a welcoming smile—a smile that widened when she spied the small, puckish fellow upon her doorstep.

"Mr. Button!"

He waved a handful of wildflowers at her in an elegantly ridiculous bow. "For you, madam."

Callie took them with a laugh. "How did you know I like wildflowers?"

He lifted a brow. "Cabot is privy to absolutely everything known to any village maiden—they simply won't leave him alone!"

Callie took a moment to muse upon the male perfection of Cabot—a tribute most deserved!—before grabbing Button by the arm and dragging him into a spontaneous hug. "Oh, Mr. Button, I'm so glad you're here!"

It took two cups of tea and a raid upon the larder before he'd managed to squeeze every detail of her adventure from her. They sat in companionable silence over cake and cheese in the kitchen while he savored his tea and contemplated her tale.

"And you have no notion of what made the horse bolt?"

Callie shook her head, then noticed the way the little man was stirring his tea, the tea in which he took no sugar or milk. "Why do you ask? What is it you know?"

Mr. Button sighed. "It is Cabot again. The dairymaid at Springdell, who is stepping out with the groom, Jakes . . . she told him that Jakes told her that the filly had a cut across the top of her haunch. A . . . a slice, actually. The sort of crease a . . . well, that a bullet might make, if aimed just a mite too high."

Callie felt her belly go cold. "Or too low . . . and a bit to the right . . ."

"Or the silly thing might have run into a thornbush!" Mr. Button leaned close and patted her on the hand. "Just in case, I do think you should stay close to your husband. These things never seem to happen when he's with you."

Callie leaned away from him. "I should say not!"

Button smiled proudly at her. "Look at you, bristling like a furious kitten. Does he know he has such a valiant defender?"

Callie deflated grumpily. "No. He thinks I hate him. I've tried in every way to show him that I won't reject him . . . I wouldn't, either, no matter how scarred he might be! I wouldn't be like that—that woman!"

She told him of her discovery of the scarf and the ring and the medal . . . although she kept the letter from the Prince Regent to herself. Truly, he wouldn't believe her anyway!

Then she remembered something. "Oh, no!" She turned to Mr. Button in a panic. "I've arranged for my gown—but what of Mr. Porter! I simply assumed he had something to wear—but it is a masque! What sort of man keeps a selection of costumes in his wardrobe?"

Mr. Button blinked. "I have several available at all times . . . but then, I am in a rather specialized line of work."

She spread her hands. "Precisely my point! Oh, what shall I do? The ball is tomorrow and I haven't—I haven't even told him—"

Mr. Button's eyes widened. "Oh, goodness, don't do *that*. It is so much easier to apologize after the fact!"

She nodded. "Yes, well, that was my thinking, but if he must be fitted with a mask and— Oh, what have I done?"

Mr. Button took her hands in his. "My dear, don't fret. Truly, I have already thought of everything. All I shall need is a suit of his clothing to copy."

"But what of fittings and—"

"No fittings necessary."

Callie frowned. "But how—" Then she sniffled back her panic and laughed damply. "Because you are skilled beyond the understanding of mortal woman."

He twinkled at her. "How marvelous to be so well understood!" He went on tiptoe and pressed a kiss to her forehead. "Furthermore, I shall offer my services as valet for the evening! I still know how to dress a gentleman, I believe. Goodness, you should have seen Cabot before I got hold of him." He shuddered. "Really, the most poisonous weskits!"

Callie mused upon the thought of Cabot in a poisonous

weskit . . . then out of a poisonous weskit . . . then in nothing at all—

Mr. Button's fingers snapped sharply in front of her nose. "Now, now, dear—like I try to tell the village maids, there is no use pining for what one cannot have! Furthermore, you're married!" He took her hand and dragged her from the kitchen.

Callie grumbled. "I might be wed, but I still have a pulse!" She stumbled along behind him, up the stairs and into her bedchamber. Her ankle twinged a bit, but really, it was much better than she'd expected. She'd be quite able to dance tomorrow!

Mr. Button spun her into her room with a laugh. "I shall have more things for you tomorrow, but I believe this will come in very handily . . . perhaps tonight?"

Callie halted in her mad, giddy spin, frozen by the shimmering thing of beauty draped over her bed. "Oh, Button!" Stepping forward hesitantly, she reached out one hand to stroke disbelieving fingers over sheer, rose-pink silk. She picked it up—it weighed no more than a spiderweb—and held it before her. Turning to the mirror she saw that it covered no more than a spiderweb, as well!

"Oh, Button." She blushed, thinking of what she would look like in it, of the way the neckline—heavens, it was nearly a waistline!—would show off her breasts right down to her nipples.

Mr. Porter had seen her naked—but he had never seen her *more* than naked! She laughed out loud and spun a bit, making the shimmering skirt flare out around her. "Oh, Button, you are a naughty fellow."

Button smiled indulgently. "A man might forgive a woman anything, wearing that gown . . . well, perhaps we should call it a negligee . . . a boudoir gown."

Callie shook her head in wonder. "I only fear it shall

be rags on the floor when Mr. Porter has had his way with it."

Button folded his hands in saintly approval. "That is its sole purpose in being. Just a little something for a bride to wear at home."

Callie stroked wondering fingers down the clinging fabric. "Happy honeymoon to me."

When Ren returned from his search, he found the house quiet. At first he thought Calliope must be resting, but she was not in her room. When he'd searched her usual haunts, the kitchen, the library, even his own study, he was beginning to worry until he saw candlelight shining from beneath the door into the dining room.

He pushed open the door to find the table set, the room warm from a flagrant overuse of coal in the fireplace, and one end of the dining table set for two. It was a very long table. Ren was not entirely sure he'd ever really seen this room without the dustcovers. He had a very grand dining room.

Then he rounded the table and saw her. She sat in one of two chairs by the fire, clearly waiting for him . . . until she'd dozed off. With great relief, he moved to wake her—then his mouth went dry.

She was wearing something new. Not the simple blue and not the ruined ivory, either. This was a confection of deep pink, a color that reminded him of the inside of a conch shell . . . or, quite frankly, of the inside of Calliope.

He wondered dimly if that were intentional, for the gown seemed designed to inflame him.

It was doing a bang-up job of it.

She wore that hot, sexual invitation of a gown and yet sat most demurely, with her ankles crossed and her hands folded in her lap. Her hair was piled on top of her head in a messy, just-rolled-in-the-hay style. His fingers itched to take it down. Her head tilted into one of the wings of the chair and her lips were parted sweetly. Except that anything a woman did while wearing a gown like that was not sweet, it was suggestive in the extreme.

Ren could see her bosom, even to the upper aureole of her nipples. He could see her skin shimmer beneath the sheer fabric, just enough to understand quite thoroughly that she wore not a thing beneath it. The gown was obscene. Ren liked it very much.

He cleared his throat . . . because if he touched her he would take her.

She lifted her head and blinked at him sleepily.

"Was I asleep?"

Ren nodded. "Were you expecting me for supper? I didn't know."

She glanced over her shoulder at the set table. "Oh, yes, well . . . I wanted it to be a surprise."

"You succeeded in surprising me."

She stood and shook out her skirts. She seemed to not even realize the extreme vulgarity of her gown. Her poise made it less so, yet, perhaps, more so as well. It was if by behaving normally, she made him the one who was stealing glimpses of luminous ivory flesh, and not the other way around.

Clever. And very alluring.

When she turned and passed before the fire, Ren got a bit dizzy. It was just a flash, just a moment . . . when the gown became all but invisible and her entire luscious body became outlined in fire. It was maddening. He nearly swallowed his tongue. He'd seen her naked before . . . although the treat of it had not become mundane in the least, it did not throw him sideways like this play of silk and light on skin. Where had she obtained such a gown?

"Mr. Button brought it over, as an advance on my order. Do you like it?"

Mr. Button was either a genius or an instrument of evil. Possibly both. Nearly blind with lust, Ren followed Calliope to the table and obediently seated her in her chair. He then seated himself, without ever taking his gaze from her plump pale bosom. In the corner of his vision he noted a covered silver dish on the table. Calliope leaned forward to lift the cover. One pink, rigid nipple slipped free of its home. Ren forgot how to breathe. Then she leaned back and the little culprit disappeared again. It was with an effort that Ren managed to tear his eyes away to look at the dish. It was a simple supper, a cold concoction. It was laid out in simple rings of ham, cheese, fruit—apples!—and small leafy things that Ren did not recognize. It was quite beautiful. A work of art in food. He glanced sharply at her. "Did you do this?"

She nodded serenely. "Oh, yes. Most of it is from our larder, but the greens—"

"You were supposed to be resting! What of your ankle?"

She dimpled at his scolding tone. "Much better, thank you for asking. And I did not leave the house. Mr. Button kindly braved the cellar for me. The greens I gathered the day before yesterday. I had them in water in the larder, keeping cool."

He blinked down at the platter. "We're eating your specimens?"

She laughed. "Please, don't worry. I shall be able to gather more when I'm better."

Gingerly Ren reached out to take a leaf. He nibbled at the tip, tasting lemony and sharp, but quite nice actually.

"That is sorrel," she told him. "When we get a proper staff, I'll have it put into the garden if you like."

She wanted to hire a gardener. She wanted to put in a garden.

The moment struck Ren with the force of a blow. He was sitting at the supper table with his wife, discussing servants and gardens and . . . and the future.

He felt his breath coming fast.

The future was not a thing he'd dared think about before. He'd not dared dream of, not since he'd waked in the dark room in a strange place and realized what he had lost. A future . . . the weight of that took his breath, made his heart pound, sent shocking spikes of sensation up and down his spine. A future meant things he'd lost faith in, things like hope. Things like love. Risky things all to dangle before a dying man.

He wanted to flee. He wanted to howl. He wanted . . . he wanted to live.

Abruptly, he pushed back from the table and stood. "What are you about, Calliope?"

She looked down at her plate. "I thought you might like to call me Callie . . . again." Her voice was soft, tentative. Hopeful.

He could not bear it. He could not allow her to hope, could not allow himself to hope.

"I told you . . . I told you I am dying. You know that."

She raised her hazel eyes to meet his gaze. "I know you believe that. I know why you believe that . . . but I'm not sure I do."

He backed away from her. "Do you think this is just some mad fantasy of mine? Do you think I created this fable of death to amuse myself?"

"No, I think some idiot doctor told you you were in very poor health. I think some idiot doctor dwelled a bit too much on that and not enough on the future. I think some idiot doctor decided that he had all the answers and foretold your ruin."

Ren flung out a hand. "Stop it! You don't know what you speak of! I was beaten, broken, stabbed—left for dead! Do you think a man can simply come back from that? That he can go back to being the man he was before?"

"No, I don't. I do think a man can go *on* from that. He can become another man, a changed man. The man he is now."

She lifted her chin. "Once, a long time ago, my father took a very bad fall. True, he should not have been clambering about the balcony of the Globe Theater, but he wished to research a scene from Juliet's perspective and the balcony was necessary. He slipped and fell to the ground below. We thought he would die. A doctor told him he would certainly never walk again. My mother nursed him. I nursed him, even though I was but a child. He still feels pain, and in bad weather he likes to lie abed and smoke a bit of opium, but he does walk . . . and dance and occasionally play Othello to Mama's Desdemona." She folded her arms. "So that's what I think of doctors and their portents of doom."

Ren wrapped his hands about the back of his chair and gripped it until his knuckles turned white. "A death sentence cannot be commuted simply because you wish it!"

She regarded him somberly. "No . . . but perhaps it can . . . if *you* wish it."

He stared at her. "Don't be ridiculous. Of course I do not wish to die!"

"Really?" She raised a mocking brow in challenge. "Because I have seen little evidence that you wish to live!"

He stared at her, dumbstruck by her cruelty, her obliviousness—didn't she realize what he would give to stay with her, to grow old in her arms, to die aged and wrinkled and happily hers—

With a roar he flung the chair down and strode from the room. His gut roiling, his mind on fire, he bolted up the stairs and strode to his room. At his door he paused, struck by a realization. He'd bolted up the stairs. The stairs that little more than a week ago, he'd only been able to climb stiffly and with great care.

In the past week he'd walked for miles, ridden for hours, made love to a beautiful woman night after night.

His back . . . yes, it ached, from his day in the saddle. His shoulder pained him a great deal . . . but he could move it—and had been able to since the day he'd caught Calliope in her fall. Somehow, that old scar tissue that had ratcheted his shoulder down tight had loosened or broken, that day. It had hurt, he recalled, quite a bit, but he'd been so distracted by her sweet body and her soft voice and the way he'd looked forward to sunset like an addict to his pipe . . .

What had she done to him?

Yet, had it all been her? He'd been hiding out here in this house for years, drinking and brooding and waiting for his death. Wouldn't any man feel poorly after such a bout of self-pity?

It was an odd notion, but perhaps the last few years that he thought he had spent dying, had he perhaps spent them healing?

Death was inevitable, the physician had told him. Yet, was not every man's death inevitable? Did not Ren, in fact, yet live?

Could it be so? Could he be healed?

Could he seize life again? Could he have that life with Calliope?

With a growl he flung open the door to his bedchamber. In another moment he was pounding down the stairs once more.

Chapter 22

Calliope sat quietly in her chair at the table, her face sad, her eyes downcast—a disappointed goddess of temptation. When Ren entered she looked up in surprise.

Without speaking, he flung out his arm and a great shower of pearls scattered over the table, rolling down the great cherrywood expanse of it, bouncing into the plate of food and flowers, spilling into her rose silken lap. She gasped and caught a few pearls in their flight, then turned wide eyes to him.

"I want the entire night," he rasped. He came to stand before her. "I want it all."

She smiled up at him with that single taunting brow raised. "Well, I want to see you . . . all of you."

Appalled, he took a sharp step back. "You have seen me. You found me quite horrible, if you recall."

"Of no consequence." She waved a careless hand. "And unfair. I'd had a long and trying day . . . and you were assaulting me, *if you recall*."

He looked down. She had a point. But to do this . . .

Callie waited, her heart pounding, her hands shaking with tension. She dared not let it show. She would only frighten him if he knew what this meant to her. So she kept her fierce desire under wraps and only gazed at him coolly.

"Well? Those are my terms." She held up a single pearl between forefinger and thumb. "One command, one pearl. No negotiation."

Ren could not do it. He couldn't watch her smile fade and the light in her eyes go out, and even if she could bear to stay in the same room as him, like Henry, she would never look at him again . . .

Yet he was tired. So bloody tired. Tired of hiding in the shadows of this house, in this hood, so bloody tired of hanging on to the past and the loathing and betrayal. This girl, with her sweet mischievous smile and her stubborn, valiant heart . . . perhaps this girl would not reject him.

Callie waited. This man, this wonderful, good, heroic, dismal, hopeless, injured man . . . how could he believe she could reject him? How could she possibly resist such a man?

She stood, her position bringing her next to him, almost upon him. If he could not do it, she would help him. Always. She held the pearl up for him to see, then tucked it into his weskit pocket. Then, trying hard to seem confident, but in reality with shaking hands and tremulous heart, she slid her hands up his chest, over his weskit, up to where the edge of the cowl nearly covered his cravat. Her fingers touched the hem, yet he had not protested nor moved a muscle. He was, she suspected, not even breathing.

The feeling was mutual.

First, she slid her fingers beneath, following the cravat knot up to his collar, up past it to his throat . . . on to his jaw—

He had shaved! Gone was that tangle of neglected beard! Her fingers twitched at the urge to touch his cheek.

Gone was the bristly brush of his beard scraping upon her skin. Instead there would only be smooth-shaven cheek upon her flesh. His mouth would be all tantalizing heat and his lips would be teasing and his teeth would be softly nipping and his cheek would be so smooth against her thighs . . .

She lifted the cowl just a bit. She'd wanted for so long to see his mouth. She loved his mouth on her, loved the way his lips felt warm and firm.

It was a beautiful mouth, even tugged slightly awry by his scars. She could understand why it had felt so good on her. His mouth was made for kissing.

She went up on her toes and kissed him, her first kiss . . . their first kiss.

She felt him take a sharp breath, felt him shudder, as if some fierce inner tension had released itself, the snapping of a taut bowstring of fear.

He at last began to kiss her back softly. Oh, it was lovely. Her lips parted in her eagerness. His tongue flicked out, dampening the seam of her mouth, dipping, teasing . . . that tongue that had driven her wild, that he had used on her body more than once . . . she slid her own naïve tongue to meet his, dipping it between his perfect lips.

The kiss deepened. His hands came up to thrust urgent fingers into her hair. She slid her arms about his neck. The rumpled cowl remained just above the tip of his nose, but at that moment she needed nothing more than the lips she'd so longed for . . .

Ren wrapped her in his arms and kissed her with everything he had, every hope, every fear, as every

distant clanging of imminent doom fell away. She was
here. Now. And now was all that mattered. Not the
past. Not the future. For all his sudden fierce dreams of
her, of them, it turned out that the best thing about Callie was losing himself in now.

She kissed him back, as fiercely and ardently as he did
her. She rose up on her tiptoes and pressed her sweet body
into him and clung as tightly as any man could wish.

Yet he knew it was a stolen moment. She kissed him
now . . . but she had not yet seen the worst. It was not
right to make her think that he was someone she would
ever want to kiss again.

He set her back down on her feet. He took two steps
back then, slowly, he pulled the hood up and away.

And waited.

Callie looked at him. She saw what she had seen that
fateful night. She saw what she had seen that made her
cry out in fear and shock.

Yet this was no dark demon in the night. This was
Ren. Yes, Ren. Hero. Recluse. Caring man. Indifferent
master. Tantalizing lover.

He'd been stunning once. She could see it now. His
features were square but noble. His dark auburn hair
thick and curling. His eyes . . . the angels themselves
must envy eyes of such a summer-sky blue! They were
riveting, stealing one's attention even from the sad, terrible scars.

It must have been a blow for a handsome young man
to lose that gift of beauty. Yet she might not have ever
grown to know that handsome lad.

Then the other side, the poor, shattered, betrayed
side. She lifted her hand and let it rest upon his slashed
cheek. "You must have been terribly frightened when
you were attacked."

He remained very still beneath her touch. "I don't remember. I only recall being angry, angry that I would not continue breathing, continue being."

She smiled softly, though her eyes were damp. "Yet here you are, with me, right now, breathing and being."

"Yes," he breathed. "I am. Here. With you."

Her fingertips passed over his brow, slipping into his hair, tracing the scars along his scalp that left those wild, white stripes in his dark curls.

"Did I ever mention that I don't care for handsome men?"

She surprised a short laugh from him. "No, I don't believe our conversation ever touched upon your taste in men."

"Handsome men do tend to be such knobs." She grimaced slightly. "Dade is humble because I keep him so, but my other brothers spend their good looks on flirtation and fickleness. I've spent my life surrounded by handsome men. I am so far unimpressed."

She gazed unflinchingly at his face, a fingertip following the crease where his torn cheek tugged at the corner of his mouth. "I suppose it isn't kind to lump all handsome men in one bonfire, but really, they can be so thoughtless and arrogant . . . and all because of gifts that were given them, not earned."

He said nothing for a long moment. "I used to be that man, I think."

She lifted her other hand, touching the mostly unscarred side of his face. "Yes, I imagine you were. I likely would have hated you."

He frowned slightly. "I don't think I was quite that bad."

She shook her head. "No, I've quite got it into my mind now. You were a shallow, self-absorbed town clown. A dandy, even."

He caught at one of her hands, and kissed her knuckles.

"Bite your tongue. I was a hardworking sp—fellow. I had responsibilities."

She smirked. "Yes, I know. All those favors for the Crown." He stared at her. "What—how did—"

She laughed and twined her arms about his neck. "I snooped. You said I could spend my days as I liked. I'd like to meet George someday. Mama speaks of him with great fondness."

He stared down at her, stunned by her ease, not yet ready to truly believe. "Your mother knows the Prince Regent?"

She tucked her head under his chin. "Darling, the Worthingtons know everyone."

She called him "darling."

She'd seen him. She'd touched him. And now she called forth pet names?

He believed.

"Callie . . ."

"Mm. Yes, Ren?"

"The night begins now."

He bent and swept her easily into his arms. This time he didn't bolt up the stairs. He took them slowly, gazing into those shining hazel eyes . . . eyes that had always seen him, hooded or not.

When he paused before her bedchamber door, she put out a hand.

"No. This is a new beginning. I want another room."

He frowned at her. She lifted a hand to stroke his face.

His scarred face. Unbelievable.

"Let's try your room, shall we?"

Ren hesitated, but couldn't think of anything particularly revolting left lying about that room. He'd only recently taken possession.

When he pushed open the door he halted in shock.

Callie laughed aloud.

His room had still been half wrapped in dustcovers when he'd left this morning. Now it had clearly seen the hands of Calliope. Every surface gleamed and glowed and smelled of beeswax.

"For the master of the manor," Callie said lightly. "'Tis only fitting."

"But how could you know that I . . ."

She shrugged. "I am most determined, but just in case." She reached beneath his pillow and pulled out a sprig of rosemary.

"I made sure you would think of me all night long."

He shook his head in amazement. "The stunning thing is that you don't know that I already think of you all night long."

She smiled and dipped him a little curtsy from the circle of his arms. "Why, thank you, Sir Lawre—"

He held up a hand. "Ren. I like the sound of it on your lips. I thought Ren was dead . . . but I think he was only sleeping, until you woke him."

Callie smiled. "I've heard that I am impossible to ignore."

He laughed and swept her in a big circle that had her rose-pink skirts fluttering like silken sails.

She let her head fall back and she laughed.

They landed on the bed. Callie reached up to run her fingers through his wild hair. "You look like a lion with all those dark red curls. We shall have to do something about this."

He buried his face in her bosom. "I am already a changed man. How much more do you want?"

She cradled his jaw in her small hands. "Why, Mr. Porter, don't you realize? I want it all."

He kissed her, kissed her until he'd climbed on top of

her and had tangled his fists in her hair, until they were both breathless, until she writhed under him, until he had to stop, too dizzy with wanting to do anything but pant into her neck. "I knew it," she breathed into his ear. "You are a most passionate man, Ren."

He went still. "I have starved for so long . . . until last night. I am still so hungry. I don't know if I can be . . . be the way you need me to be, for your first time."

She twined his hair about her fingers for a moment. He imagined her thoughts like vining tendrils, seeking and twining and grasping with little spirals of cleverness.

"I think you will be precisely what I need, the first time and every time. You have already taught me so much."

He closed his eyes for a moment. "I am ashamed of that demeaning bargain."

She made a doubtful noise. "I don't know that you should feel so demeaned by it. In the end, I treated you very nicely."

He laughed, he couldn't help it. "You're right. I promise to no longer feel demeaned."

She tickled his ear with her fingertip. "Are you feeling in more control now? I would like to kiss you again."

Ren's heart soared at her words. He, who'd thought that he would never be kissed again. He rolled her over in a great bear hug, until she rested atop him. Her mussed hair hung in sweet tendrils about her face and her bosom fell right out of the decadent dress.

Ren decided to show his appreciation for such fine craftsmanship and sucked a pink nipple into his mouth. Soon she was gasping and squirming in his grip. His erection took the brunt of the punishment, but it was such sweet delicious pain, feeling Calliope writhing atop him, grinding her hot, damp center down upon his trapped cock.

Then she dipped her head down and caught him up in kissing her once more. Her sweet mouth, untutored but so very interested in education, nearly cost him the night. He held her shoulders in his hands and lifted her away while he caught his breath.

Callie took advantage of this opportunity to divest him of some of his clothing. She tugged at his surcoat sleeves, pulling the thing off in seconds. Then his weskit was unbuttoned and wrested from him. At his shirt, Ren hesitated. "My face is not the only thing that is scarred."

She grinned down at him. "I know. I peek, you know. You're quite the swashbuckler, aren't you? Did someone run you through with a sword?"

Ren sighed. Of course there would be no rule Callie would not break if she felt like it. "It was a pike, in fact. Something the boatmen use to catch at the loading cables."

"Mmhmm." She was clearly more interested in stripping his shirt from him than in the finer points of dock work. Ren sat up and pulled his shirt over his head in a swift movement.

Here he was, more naked before her than he'd been for anyone since the last doctor had given him the fateful opinion. Callie sat up upon him, clearly unaware that her hot, damp cunt had his erection trapped and tantalized. "You are a finely made man . . . though you are a bit thin. We need a proper cook."

He reached up to chase down a nipple that insisted on playing hide-and-seek with him. "You may feed me weeds all the days of summer if you like," he said softly.

Callie gazed down at him, so proud of him that she could scarcely speak for the tightness in her throat. So she played the silly gamine, teasing him about being thin when the violence done to his body nearly broke her heart. She wanted to cry over him. She wanted to mother him and she wanted to be his dear companion . . . and she wanted to be his lover.

He wasn't ready to speak of such things yet . . . she could see that it was all he could do to accept tonight for what it was, to accept that she wanted him, that she desired his body and was not repulsed by his dear, damaged face.

He moved beneath her and she found welcome distraction in pondering the size of him.

"Ren?"

"Yes, Callie?"

"Precisely how does it . . . fit?"

She'd meant to distract him from his self-consciousness, but it turned out that she truly needed to know. A faint but distinct trace of worry had crept into her voice.

"Oh, sweet Callie." His big hands came up to sweep the hair from about her face. He gazed into her eyes. "You know I shall try very hard not to hurt you."

She nodded.

"And you know that I . . . well, I have done this before."

She frowned. "Really? How many virgins have you deflowered?"

He laughed. "Oh, thousands," he said airily. "I'm known worldwide." He shook his head. "You are my first, dear little Worthington lass, but I know the general mechanics of it and the working theory . . . so do you trust me?"

She nodded instantly. "Oh, yes. I trust you completely."

He seemed a bit shaken by that. "Good. Ah . . . is there anything you'd like to ask me, other than the fit?"

Callie smiled at him. "No, that is all for now . . . although I'm sure I'll think of something later. Dade says I am made of questions."

"Of that I have no doubt. Oh, and Callie?"

"Yes, Ren?"

"When we are together in bed, would you do me the enormous favor of not talking about your family?"

She bit her lip. "I can see where that might be a bit on the inappropriate side."

"Thank you. I prefer to have only two of us in this bed."

"Consider it done."

He sat up, keeping her astride his lap. "I'm going to remove the rest of my clothing now."

She frowned. "I didn't notice before. Are there any more scars?"

He smiled. "A few. Nothing to concern yourself about. My leg was broken rather badly, but it isn't the outside that is painful."

She allowed him to slide her off his lap, though she stole a kiss on the way and he managed a quick taste of a nipple. All in all it was a most pleasurable slide.

Then he stood. Callie knelt on the bed, not willing to miss a moment. His boots were next. Then his trousers and with them his knee-length drawers. Then he was entirely bare before her, not hiding this time.

Callie gazed at him happily. "I think your form is very fine. And you are standing so much straighter than when I first came."

He smiled. "You have been good for me."

For a moment, her face went pink and her eyes grew very soft and large. "Thank you," she breathed. Then the little clown was back. She pointed at his erection, which, due to the fact that she sat as alert as a kitten but was dressed in a courtesan's gown, had not faded a hint.

"You were going to explain the fit."

He stepped closer to the bed and held out his hand. "Come with me."

He walked her to the chair that sat before the fire and drew her onto his lap. The pink silk caught the glow of the flame and made her look like a rising sun.

"You will be tight around me, like a sheath around a sword," he murmured into her ear. "You will grow wetter and wetter the more I kiss and touch you, until I will slip inside you like coming home."

"Oh, my."

He tipped her chin up and spoke into her wide, wondering eyes. "You will feel pain at first. It is the virgin's wall, a thin barrier of flesh. It will tear when I penetrate you the first time. For some women it hurts a great deal, for others it does not so much. I cannot know until I breach you, so I will be very gentle and slow. But I want you so badly, Callie, that I will be very large, perhaps the largest I have ever been."

She shifted. He noted her squeezing her thighs together tightly. "You know what an orgasm is, my sweet, but I do not think you will feel one this time . . . unless I give you one first."

She swallowed. "First? With your mouth? I should like that, I think."

He smiled. "Yes, and it will help when I pierce you."

She rested her head upon his shoulder and trailed questing fingertips over his chest. "Men are so different," she mused. She stroked his flat nipple. "Does that feel good to you?"

He kissed her ear. "Every part of me delights in your touch, but it is not as sensitive as yours." He reached into her bodice and plucked gently at hers. She gasped and wriggled a bit.

He fought back a groan. "I want to make love to you, Callie. I want to explore every inch of you and I want you to explore me."

She sighed. "I don't mind if I do."

Her touch strayed down to his erection. Ren gasped as cool fingertips trailed a circle of fire about the head of him. He shuddered slightly. She wrapped her hand round him. "I liked sucking on your cock," she murmured. "I liked it when you orgasmed into my mouth. I liked the taste of you."

Ren's head spun. Sweet heaven but she was frank! He fought for a clear thought. "I like the taste of you, as well."

"I didn't know of such a thing and I am rather well read for a lady of standing," she mused. "Did you make it up?"

Ren gasped a laugh. "No, it is a known thing, but most ladies would refuse to do what you did so well."

She seemed surprised. "Why? Would they refuse the other as well?"

Ren was losing his powers of concentration. "Not . . . in my experience."

Before he could catch her, she slid off his lap and knelt between his knees.

Chapter 23

Ren tried to protest. "Callie, I—"

Her hot mouth came down around him. His fingers caught at the arms of the chair as he groaned, so lost in the pleasure he couldn't think.

Callie sucked him deep into her mouth, then rolled her tongue around him as she withdrew him. She mustn't forget the pearl next time.

She wanted him to take her, and she while she found his slow, informative approach adorable and a testament to his character, she wanted her husband. She wanted to be his wife. So she sucked him in long, hard torturous movements, until he bucked deep into her mouth, compelled to enter her somehow.

Yes.

She left him, gasping and shuddering in the chair, and sat back, leaning back on her hands on the carpet before the fire, gazing hotly at him through her falling hair, and let her thighs fall open.

"I want you inside me," she whispered. His blue eyes blazed like afternoon sky but he did not let go his grip on the arms of the chair.

When he still hesitated, she called upon the powers of the magical gown and let one strap drop from her shoulder. The bodice slipped.

He was on her in a single movement, taking her mouth with his, pressing her back down onto the floor, reaching up between her thighs with one hand, pushing her skirts up, spreading her legs with his knees.

She dug her fingers into his hair and fisted them as she kissed him with every ounce of herself offered to him if he would only take it.

It had been always.

It had been never.

His thick cock pressed to her slit; the hard blunt thickness of him gave her pause, but she had driven him too far. He thrust in once, hard, deep.

She squealed in his ear, her fingers tight in his hair. He went still.

"Oh, no. Oh, Callie, I'm sorry. I'll stop—" He began to withdraw from her.

It hurt. Callie captured him with her legs, wrapping them tight about him, keeping him trapped within her.

"No, darling, please, let me go."

She kissed him again, wanting to lose herself in his mouth, wanting to distract herself from the pain of being split like a log!

He wrapped careful arms about her and kissed her, hot and sweet and wild, restoking her passion, reminding her of her need.

The agony became a burn and the burn became a sting. She felt herself becoming wet again, felt herself wrapping tightly around him, but now warm and unresisting.

When her body began to relax, when her fingers began to loosen in his hair, he drew away from her a little, his face tight with restraint. "You are not . . . a patient woman, are you?"

She laughed a small, broken laugh. "No. I am stubborn, which is not quite the same."

He kissed her again, softly, tantalizingly, nipping at her lips, teasing his tongue into her mouth. She felt it, felt the hot, melting sensation deep inside her, felt the hunger, felt the heat . . .

He began to thrust slowly and purposefully. She released her thighs, simply riding his hips with her loosely held knees. He moved above her, within her—her dark lover, her husband, the man she alone had seen. His tongue entered her mouth, even as his cock entered her.

When he slowly penetrated the deepest part of her, she felt a twinge. When the thickest part of him stretched her opening, she felt the burn. But in between, oh yes, she felt the sweet flow of what he did to her, the way he stroked her within, the way he opened her, owned her, gave to her . . .

I love you.

She didn't say it. Now was not the time. Yet she did love him . . . loved the taste of him, the feel of him, the sense of him . . . the mind and heart of him.

He didn't know it. He thought he had her body. He thought he had her senses. He didn't want her heart. Not when he'd just begun to find his own again.

Then the tide of him swept her away, rushing away thought, rocking her in warm salty waves of pleasure, just barely tinged with pain. He kissed her on and on, as if he could never get enough of her mouth.

Then she found it, that golden stair of pleasure, the one that spiraled up and up, leading her high . . .

She needed him to move faster, she wanted him more . . . now . . . He felt it, knew it, he gave her faster, carefully calculated thrusts. He left her mouth so she could gasp for air and moan and wail and then she convulsed around him. Ren managed another thrust, then one more.

Then his own lust overcame him and he groaned deep and low. "Callie." Then he came inside his bride, his wife, his woman. He called her name and he came home.

She fell asleep on the carpet, her limbs wound around him and her head tucked beneath his chin. Ren held her there, the strands of her hair falling over his chest, the remains of her wicked gown draped over his groin.

She was extraordinary.

And someday she would go.

He'd given her half the necklace last night. She'd returned one pearl, to make him remove his hood.

When he'd tried to retract the bargain, she'd deflected him with a jest.

He wanted to keep her.

She wanted to go home. It was quite obvious. Hardly an hour passed that she did not mention her family, with a longing in her voice that she didn't even seem to realize.

There was no one on earth he missed the way she missed them. Although he feared there soon would be.

She stirred against him, slipping her hand around his back. Then she opened her eyes and regarded him drowsily. "You cannot be comfortable on the floor."

He wasn't, but he would not have moved her for the world while she slept draped over him.

"I noticed earlier that there is a perfectly good bed on the other side of the room."

"Hmm." He stole a kiss. Then another. Kissing Callie . . . how could he ever give that up?

She tugged at a bit of shimmering silk that lay beneath him. "This is all your fault," she pointed out grumpily.

He smiled. "Is that so?"

She fought the traitorous skirts for another moment, then lay back in defeat. "Yes. You decided to be all chivalrous and reasonable."

"And you decided to take matters into your own . . . hands."

She regarded him archly even as she wrapped her fingers about his cock. "Reason has no place in the bedchamber, sir."

The blood left his brain, no longer allowing him the powers of speech. In reply, he reached for the bodice of her gown of sin and tore it in half, exposing her bosom for his delectation.

She gasped, then purred. "You are ever a quick study, sir."

He did not enter her, for he knew she would only hide the soreness she must be feeling. Instead, they pleasured each other with their hands and mouths. She came, arching her back in his arms while he fingered her gently. He came in her mouth, her willing plaything.

When his heart once again assumed a normal beat, he picked her up from the nest of her torn and ruined gown and carried her naked to the bed. Exhausted, she allowed him to tuck her in, simply sinking bonelessly into his body when he joined her.

"That dress is . . . what do you call that dress?"

She smiled wearily and came up for one last sleepy kiss. "I believe those in the know call it 'rags on the floor.'"

Ren awoke from the deepest, softest sleep he could remember to find Callie seated tailor-fashion on his bed, wearing her old blue gown and playing with perhaps a hundred pearls in her lap.

To Ren, the pearls represented his shameful bargain and the inevitable loss of her. As she ran her fingers sensuously through the pool of shimmering orbs he felt his heart contract painfully.

He reached out and stopped her fingers with his own. "Please. I cannot look at those without thinking of all the wicked things I meant to do to you."

She looked up at him, her eyes wide. "There's more?"

God, he'd created a monster. "Callie, no. It isn't right for me to use you so. I . . . was lost. I don't wish to bring that darkness back between us."

"Are they pleasurable, these wicked things?"

He shook his head. "Callie, it is a dark and twisted pleasure. I cannot use you thus."

She gazed at him for a long moment. "Say that a man has an ax."

"What?"

"It's a opening argument." She laid a hand upon his covered groin. "Say that a man has an ax."

A man certainly had wood. Ren blinked. "A man has an ax."

She nodded. "Now, say that this man uses his ax to break down his neighbor's door. Would that act be evil or benign?"

Ren blinked. "Evil, certainly."

She narrowed her eyes at him. "What if the neighbor's house was afire and the man wished to save his neighbor's wife and children?"

Ren frowned. "Then the act would be benign. But—"

"It is the very same act. So the difference is one of intent." She tilted her head. "If you were to use your ax, er, *acts* to give me pleasure, would that not be a benign intent?"

He regarded her sourly. "You do this quite often, don't you?"

She blinked innocently at him. "I don't know what you mean."

"Hm." He threw back the covers and swung his legs over the side of the bed. "I can just see it. All the many Worthingtons gathered about the supper table, practicing the art of Socratic debate. I'm right, aren't I?"

She sat up primly. "I refuse to answer that on the grounds that it will compromise my vow to never mention a certain biological grouping whilst in this bed with you."

He tilted his head and contemplated his fiendish bride. "I thought as much." He saw a future of never winning a single argument. That is, if he were very, very lucky. He stood.

"Wait!"

He turned back to her. She gathered up a skirt full of pearls and knee-walked across the mattress to him. "I have something to tell you."

She was leaving him. She had enough pearls and she meant to be on her way.

She took his hand and tugged him to sit back on the bed. Sitting back on her heels, she gazed at him seriously. "I thought about seducing you first, but it felt a little dishonest—"

He drew away from her. "A *little* dishonest?"

She waddled closer, putting her hand on his chest pleadingly. "Ren, please—I know you'll be angry, but that's all right, I deserve a scolding, I know it—"

Ren blinked. Scolding? "Callie, just say it. You're leav—"

"I'm throwing a ball," she blurted, her face squelched up tight. Then she opened one eye. "Leaving? I'm not leaving."

The relief that swept Ren didn't bear measuring, because then he would have to face the fact that he was deeply and irrevocably in the power of his saucy, unpredictable Worthington lass. "Wait . . . a ball?" He leaned away from her, frowning. "At Amberdell Manor?"

She nodded ruefully. "I didn't mean to. It was an accident. I was simply trying to make friends in the village and I sort of . . . went a bit mad."

The hostility she faced in the village was largely his doing. Ren nodded slowly. "I can see the idea has merit. Perhaps in a few months—"

"Tonight."

Perhaps when he agreed to wed a girl he'd found wandering his house in her underthings, he ought to have considered the fact that she may have some trouble containing her impulses.

"No."

"But . . . the invitations went out days ago."

"No."

"But . . . Mr. Button has worked so hard on my gown."

"No."

"But . . . I've already hired staff for the night."

Ren took a deep breath. "No."

"But . . . they're already here. The house is prepared. The musicians are unloading their instruments. Our guests will arrive in a few hours."

Ren stood, casting a glance about his room. His clock was gone from the mantel—and draperies were drawn tight—

In two strides he was at the window, gazing at the early spring sunset in dismay. He turned to glare at his lovely bride. "You are Satan in blue muslin."

She nodded sympathetically. "I know. I'm sorry about that." She brightened. "But I've obtained the most wonderful suit for you tonight!"

Furious, Ren flicked the drapery aside once more to contemplate the wagons unloading before his house.

"Callie, it is rather conveniently too late to cancel your ball. That does not mean I shall have anything to do with it." Riding away in his hood seemed like an excellent idea. He could perhaps find a place to stay the night in one of the other villages.

He was still naked, so he strode to his wardrobe.

Then he closed his eyes on the empty hooks and shelves. "You've taken my clothing."

"Not all of it. There is still the marvelous suit."

Letting his forehead drop to the cool wood of the wardrobe door, he set his jaw. "No. I will stay in this room if I must, but I will not—"

"One pearl, one command. No negotiation."

He went still. "What?"

"I have so many. It only seems fair that I should use some of them, since I am asking you to do something for me . . ."

He could earn his pearls back if he dressed for the ball, if he attended, if he paraded himself before the village, undoubtedly peacocked out in some mad creation of the evil genius Button.

Every pearl earned back meant one more night with Callie.

Priceless.

There was more. This ball would be filled with Amberdell people. People who, if brought round to the right frame of mind, could be made to forgive the madness with the ginger, could help him look out for Callie, could keep sharp suspicious country eyes out for strange giants, could be powerful and numerous allies against his enemies . . .

The last thing, the thing he pushed to the back of his mind, the dangerously seductive thing, was that he wanted so very much to make his sweet, mad Callie happy.

He let out a long breath. "A pearl for dressing in costume."

"Of course."

"A pearl for attending your ball."

"Agreed."

"I shall not dance."

"Two pearls for dancing."

"I thought you said no negotiation."

"I," she said airily, "am more flexible than some."

He hid a smile. "A pearl for each waltz." He could bear those minutes of display if it brought more nights in her warm and willing arms.

"Well, one might say that a gentleman should earn the lady's favors—"

"Those are my terms, Calliope."

She gusted a sigh. "Oh, very well. I accept your terms."

He turned to face her at last. "And I shall wish a kiss to seal our bargain."

She scrambled off the bed, clutching a wad of pearl-toting skirt, and ran into his open arms. The kiss she gave him dizzied his mind and gave rise to difficulties—especially since a hundred people were about to descend upon the manor.

At last she pushed him away and pressed a palm to her face. "My goodness . . . I think I've forgotten my own name!" She shook off the haze of lust and smiled at him brightly. "We should start getting ready."

She ran to the bedchamber door. "I've attached a valet for you for the evening!"

Ren, who was still quite naked and now somewhat aroused, gazed about in panic. "What? *Now?*"

Chapter 24

There were times in a man's life when he must make a choice. Ren's choice in that moment was between hiding in his empty wardrobe or greeting a stranger in his altogether.

The bloody wardrobe was too bloody small.

Ren turned the scarred side of his face away as Callie opened his door. Into his bedchamber walked a dapper little man carrying a very large box. He smiled happily at Ren. "Oh, wonderful!"

Callie stood next to Mr. Button and regarded Ren with satisfaction. "I told you he was delicious underneath."

"An understatement." Mr. Button patted her on the arm. "Scoot now, dear. Mr. Porter and I have much to do."

Callie waved gaily at Ren and then deserted him. Ren kept his gaze averted while Button deposited his burden on the trunk at the end of the bed.

"I—"

"Turn, please. I must get a good look at you."

Ren gave up. The man didn't seem likely to run screaming, at least. He turned, still looking away.

"Hmm. You are thinner than your clothing suggested. I shall have to take a quick tuck in the surcoat, I think." Button walked a circle around him, measuring with his eyes. Ren felt rather like an insect under glass, but somehow it wasn't the slightest bit embarrassing. Mr. Button obviously knew his business as a tailor as well as a dressmaker.

Then Button rounded him and gazed unblinking into Ren's face. Ren fought the habitual urge to flinch away and gazed back. "I know I am hideous."

Button nodded thoughtfully. "The scars are frightful, yes. However, you are not your scars."

Ren blinked at that matter-of-fact assessment. A few weeks ago he might have argued it, but somehow, since Callie had danced into his life he felt like . . .

Like more.

Callie ran lightly down the stairs, reveling in her pain-free ankle. Worthingtons always did heal quickly.

The front hall bustled with men bringing flowers and garlands and chairs and whatnots for the ballroom. Mr. Button had rallied staff all the way from London, for Callie heard more than a few Cockney accents. As much as possible had come from local folk, but Button had thought it best to put on a big show for the people of Amberdell. "They will take pride from a fine house and a fine ball. If you bring down the tone a whit, they will be insulted."

Callie left it up to Mr. Button's judgment, but she hoped Ren was as rich as people seemed to think. Oh, but it was all so much fun!

The ballroom was chaos, and looked as though someone had fought another war of the roses within, but a burly gentleman named Rigg assured her that "It'll be a right spring bower, milady, just you wait'n see." He looked rather more like a brigand than a florist, but Callie knew better than to judge by appearances. Many of the men Mr. Button had hired looked like pirates and thieves, while others looked as refined as lords.

On her way to the kitchens to check on the finishing touches for the "nibblements," as Mr. Button called them, Callie was waylaid by a tall, dark-haired girl in housemaid's attire.

"Excuse me, milady, but will you be needin' many more rooms made up? Only we've just found the linen closet and there've been mice nesting. Gone a bit nasty, I fear."

"You should have seen the windows," Callie murmured. The girl blinked at her. Callie frowned off into space. "Well, the local people will likely go back to their homes . . . but Mr. Button asked to invite a few of his friends, as well."

"Yes, milady. Himself told me he'd need four rooms for them."

Callie smiled. "Oh, that's nice. I'm so looking forward to meeting Mr. Buttons's friends. He's such a wonderful man."

The maid regarded her for a moment. "That he is, milady. I'm right fond of him myself."

"I suppose we ought to get as many rooms ready as we can, just in case . . . have you checked for another linen closet in the west wing? I know it's all closed up, but surely they didn't tote pillowcases all the way across the house!"

The maid nodded. "Oh, yes, I shall check." She curtsied and began to dash off.

"Oh—" Callie paused. "I'm sorry, I don't know your name."

"Rose, milady."

Callie smiled. "That's charming. I adore floral names.

I am Calliope. I and all my siblings were saddled with torturous Greek myths. It's such a burden being named after gods and goddesses. People tend to expect miracles."

The maid snorted a laugh, then looked down. "Sorry, milady. I just didn't expect you to be so funny."

Callie rolled her eyes. "Goodness, if you think I'm odd, just be glad my family shan't be attending."

Rose curtsied again, but this time her eyes were twinkling. "Yes, milady. I'll fetch all the linens I can find from the west wing."

Callie continued on to the kitchens but it seemed she'd just missed the cook. Again. Really, the man had the oddest habit of fleeing the kitchens just when she wished to speak with him. However, she was reassured by the bustle and delicious smells and the impressive array of herbs the man had brought with him. And knives . . . such big, sharp knives.

"When the cook gets back, please send someone to find me. I just want to have a word."

The men helping in the kitchen shot each other glances, but they nodded agreeably enough before bustling on. Callie felt as if she were in the way, so she left after sneaking a taste from one of the simmering pots. Oh, heaven.

Perhaps she could leave off worrying about the food, as well.

Really, Mr. Button was a wonder. Callie found herself with nothing to do but to get ready.

When she returned to her bedchamber, she found herself the recipient of a large stack of mauve and white striped boxes. With childish glee she unpacked her own personal Christmas morning, pulling out gowns and gloves and bonnets and shawls and underthings . . . oh, my, the underthings! She tucked most of them away with a naughty little smile on her face. Goodness, Mr. Button was a thoughtful fellow!

Then she found her gown. "Oh."

She pressed her fingers to her lips, then slowly reached out to lift the incredible creation from the box.

Mr. Button did, indeed, have skill unknown to mortal woman. The gown was a pact with the devil by way of heaven.

Callie held up the pale green mist of silk and pearls and shimmering white satin ribbons. In the box beneath the gown there remained a beaded mask and white satin gloves and pearl-encrusted combs and wispy, lace-edged underthings . . . but all Callie could see was the gown.

Mr. Button had decided she was to be Persephone, Goddess of Spring. It was indeed a gown fit for a goddess.

Someone had caused a bath to be sent up for her. Beside the steaming copper tub was a bowl of soft soap. Callie sniffed it. Rosemary soap. She'd only mentioned it yesterday. How had Mr. Button found it so quickly?

Soon she was going to stop asking that question. Button was a very magical fellow!

Callie stripped and climbed into the steaming tub but she couldn't bear to lie about. She scrubbed down briskly and washed her hair, then sat combing it by the lovely fire in her hearth. Wistfully she wondered if she'd be allowed to keep a few of Mr. Button's excellent servant friends, although she'd perhaps do better to hire from the village, for good feeling.

Mr. Button had tried to provide her with a lady's maid but she'd informed him that Worthington girls could do their own hair, thank you! She did miss Elektra's help, although if Ellie were here she'd be too busy pining over Callie's gown to help much with her hair.

And Attie would be disemboweling some carcass in the kitchen with the cook, trying out his array of fantastic knives.

Callie pinched at her cheeks and dusted a bit of rice powder over her nose. Other women might find face paint appealing, but Worthingtons had good skin and no need to hide it. She smoothed her hair with a bit of sweet almond oil, just enough to tame the tendency to frizz. Then she pulled it back into a thick twist, propped by the shimmering combs. With a few stray tendrils around her face, for Ren's benefit, for he dearly loved to toy with her hair. She felt she looked quite nice.

Then she noticed the case on the vanity.

It was the jewel case from the first night she was in the house.

It could only be Ren's doing. Callie tentatively lifted the lid. Within she saw a folded scrap of paper.

"B said you would be in green."

The antique emerald necklace lay shimmering on top of the peacock-toned shawl she'd found in the library.

Oh, it was a lovely thing, as vivid and shamelessly attention-grabbing as she'd remembered. She stroked it with one finger.

He'd bought it for another woman.

Then again, that woman had been fool enough to let him get away. She didn't deserve the man or the shawl . . . but Callie did!

Callie decided to accept the gift as a thoughtful husbandly thing and forget about the other woman. She smiled and swept the shawl over her bare shoulders. "Your loss, idiot woman." She smirked into the mirror.

Fortunately the distinctive ring was nowhere in sight. When that time came Callie wanted her own bloody ring, thank you very much.

The necklace, now . . . this was clearly a family heirloom of some antiquity. An "important piece," as Ellie would call it. Callie smiled. A necklace fit for the lady of Amberdell Manor.

She fastened it about her neck and sauntered naked to where the gown lay in serene state across the bed.

Callie dressed carefully. First the sheer stockings, gartered above the knee with green ribbons. Then the barely there chemise, a mere wisp of batiste so fine Callie would have little trouble reading through it. She looked into the box for pantalets, but Mr. Button seemed to have forgotten those and Callie had none left after the sword fight.

Ah, the sword fight . . .

The clock in the hall boomed distantly and Callie started. Oh, heavens, she couldn't be late to her own ball!

Donning the gown was a simple affair. All the work was in the details and the fit. Which, astonishingly, was perfection. Callie frowned at the mirror. Mr. Button might have made one thing for one woman in those few days he'd had to prepare, but she knew every woman in the village had ordered a new gown and probably masks and gloves and goodness knows what else . . .

It simply wasn't possible for Button and Cabot to fill all those orders. Not humanly possible, at any rate.

But Callie had no time to contemplate the otherworldly powers of the dressmaker. The gown fastened up the back with minuscule buttons, but Callie had always dressed herself and found it no great difficulty.

When she turned back to the mirror, she caught her breath. First of all, she looked stunning, regal, and mysterious. Secondly, there was a great deal of Worthington bosom on display.

She inhaled experimentally. The gown was well fitted, there was no doubt about it. Her bosom only seemed as though it were about to slip its moorings. In fact, it was battened down quite adequately.

When she tugged the satin gloves high upon her arms and donned the little silk slippers that had come in the box—when had Mr. Button measured her feet?—Callie blinked at her reflection. She had often looked fairly pretty, but she had never before been beautiful, not even in the rose-pink dress from the night before. To be truthful, she suspected that "goddess" suited her better than did "harlot."

Although harlot was bound to be more fun.

With her own toilette done, she was finally free to think about Ren's costume.

Mr. Button had been most secretive. If she was to be the goddess Persephone, then would Mr. Porter be forced to go as Hades? That seemed rather the opposite effect than the "let's meet the village" intent of the evening. Callie bit her lip worriedly. Mr. Button did seem to be a theatrical sort of fellow, didn't he?

Ren frowned at Button. "I think this is a bit much. I'd rather not make such a sideshow of myself."

Button didn't sigh, or twitch, or to his credit, even clench his jaw, though this was the twentieth time Ren had tried to wriggle out of his agreement to wear the "costume."

Button did, however, put down the cravat he was attempting to press again, for one more try. He turned to Ren. "Mr. Porter, I have great sympathy for what you will confront tonight."

Ren glanced at Mr. Button's clear, unmarked face and then glanced away. "I doubt that."

Mr. Button clasped his hands before him. "Mr. Porter, there are more ways to carry scars than on one's face. I know a little something about being an outsider. I am the son of a tailor, but my father was a large man, fond of drinking and wagering on races and arm wrestling to prove to one and all that tailoring was a man's work.

"I was not a usual sort of boy. I knew from a very young age that I was different. I am a person of talent and ambition. I am a brave man, much braver than I ever expected I should be. I am well connected with many friends. Now. Then, I was only a lonely boy who never seemed to walk in step with other boys. Or with anyone, really. In particular my father.

"I hid my differences as well as I could, for many years. I think if there is anything in this material world that will kill one's soul, it is the act of hiding oneself. To be so fearful of rejection that one spends every moment alone, just to keep one's secret . . . is that really so much better than taking the chance on rejection?"

"You're talking about me now."

Button slid him a glance. "I'm talking about all of us. Everyone has something they keep secret. Sometimes good, sometimes bad . . . although I think milady would probably argue that the good or evil—"

"Will be in the intent," Ren finished for him, and they both chuckled.

Ren regarded Button. "You said you have friends now. What did you do differently?"

Button looked him right in the eye. "I stopped bloody hiding." Then he shrugged. "Some people rejected me. Some people simply pretended I didn't exist. A few, the best of them all, I think, accepted me just as I am and, furthermore, found value in me that I never knew I had."

"I will not show my face."

Button waved a hand. "No matter. It is a masque, after all. I meant it figuratively, of course. If you expose yourself to rejection, you are also exposing yourself to acceptance. You'd be surprised at who stays and who goes."

She stayed.

For now.

Ren didn't speak. He only eyed the little man with solemn consideration while his cravat was being tied, again. Then he turned to regard himself in the mirror. His face might still be a horror, but the rest of him had never looked so fine.

"I think, Button, that anyone would be blind not to see the value in you."

Button smiled and spread his hands. "Well, but of course! I am, after all, *me*."

Chapter 25

It was almost time for the guests to begin arriving. Cabot brought a cup of tea on a saucer across the busy ballroom to his master. Button took it with a smile. Everything about the little man was gleeful this evening, from the jaunty diagonal jacquard stripe of his ivory silk waistcoat to the bounce in his toes. He obviously had every confidence that his elaborate planning would bear great fruit.

As happy as he was to see his beloved master so certain, Cabot could only gaze about the bustling preparations with a gloom born of apprehension.

Button was a gregarious man. He would naturally think that the way to boost someone's spirits and self-assurance would be to throw a grand party. Cabot, who was of a more introspective nature, suspected that Sir Lawrence might not be as receptive to the oncoming madness as Button hoped.

"Sir, are you quite sure you ought to have invited them?"

Button's grin faltered slightly, but his nod was firm as his eyes followed a trim housemaid carrying a stack of cushions for the chairs arranged in cunning conversational groupings along the far wall. "Her ladyship urged me to invite my friends. What could be so wrong with that?"

Cabot did not pursue the topic. Friends. Enemies. It was such a fine line, in the end.

So he, as usual, stood at his master's side. However, his habitually neutral gaze grew fond as he looked down at the neat part in his master's thinning hair. Button, as usual, took no notice.

Callie held her mask by the ribbon tie as she left her room. It was a delicate slip of satin and beading, worked in a pattern of leaves around the eyeholes with a cluster of tiny satin blooms of lily of the valley at her temple. The sparkling glass beads did not clash with the emerald necklace, but seemed to make it gleam even more richly in concert.

"Callie."

She looked up from adjusting her gloves to see Ren there awaiting her.

Oh, my.

He stood dressed in a very fine forest-green suit, perfectly cut and fitted, trimmed in just a tiny border of gold thread. It was the sort of thing fancied by princes and dukes . . . but more restrained. It said, "Yes, there are rumors that I have royal blood but don't let's go on about it." By being just a hint ostentatious, it had the effect of arrogant grandeur.

The silk surcoat was just the perfect tone of deep green to set off Callie's gown. The weskit was silk of a green so dark as to be black except when the light hit it just right, and the buttons had the glitter of true gold. His trousers were black and he wore boots, giving him a military edge.

Surprisingly, Button had left Ren's wild auburn hair uncut and had simply tamed it back into a lordly queue. His mask . . . oh, Button had outdone himself on the mask.

It was a mimic of Callie's, beaded as if made of leaves, only his was beaded in black and gold and the shimmering effect was of feathers. It turned his eyes dark, like the gloaming of the day. He was a nighthawk, a mystery.

There was no attempt to hide the scars. Ren's mask covered no more than anyone's would. Yet, with the severe dignity of the suit and the screaming drama of the mask, the scars upon his forehead and his cheek seemed . . . almost fitting. He seemed a warlord, a feudal king of old, a soldier and commander.

He looked gentlemanly yet dangerous. Perfect. Then Callie realized that he wore the medal and a medieval-style gold-cloth sash that denoted knighthood.

Ren watched as delight spread across Callie's face and suddenly he felt ready to face the very legions of hell with her at his side armed only with the gold-knobbed walking stick Button had forced upon him.

"A weapon to defend your dignity," Button had claimed. "Such a great many stairs—and such a regrettable opportunity to fall upon one's knightly arse before all."

Ren hadn't dared admit that he was quite taken by the ebony stick with its gold ball grip engraved with the Porter family crest. Apparently not all of his vanity had leaked out upon those docks long ago.

He stepped forward. "You look . . . you look like spring itself." She looked like life itself to him, like green growing things and fat laughing babies and the rise in a young man's blood, but he hadn't the words to tell her. He wanted to kneel at her feet. He wanted to toss her over his shoulder and lock them in his room for a month. Instead he bowed deeply, his hand over his heart.

She held the mask up over her eyes and dipped a curtsy so deep her nose nearly touched the carpet. "Why, Sir Lawrence, I swoon."

Pleased, Ren straightened and tugged self-consciously at his cuffs. He held out his arm and she slipped her gloved hand onto it. "Our guests will be here soon."

She smiled brilliantly up at him. "You look like a king. I like the medal. It suits you."

He smirked. "If you like this one, I've a drawer full I can try on for you."

She swatted his hand with her folded fan. "Don't be improper. I have to concentrate on our guests." Then she slid him a heated glance. "But you may wear them all for me . . . later." She fluttered her eyelashes. "And bring the sword."

Ren was laughing when he took his first steps into the world he'd left behind all those years ago.

Callie and Button had decided that it would be easier for Ren if they introduced him to the entire village at once. Therefore, the ballroom was already filled with brightly colored gowns and dark coats, all topped by an incredible variety of masks. There were homemade masks, sometimes of startling composition—Callie had never seen such a creative use of cornhusks!—and sometimes finely made creations of beads and feathers, though Callie doubted any were as purely elegant as hers and Ren's. Button had obviously reserved the finest of his wares for the host and hostess.

It all made for a most startling moment when they entered the ballroom, for at once a hush fell upon the crowd and every face—that is, every mask—turned their way in the same instant.

Just as Button instructed them, they held quite still.

"Let them look," the little dressmaker had ordered. "Let them look for as long as they like. They will stare. They will gape. Some of them, silly souls, may even gawk." Button had beamed a benevolent smile. "Yours is not to hide away in shame. Yours is to impress and instruct. 'Here are the master and mistress of Amberdell,' your posture must say. 'See us and know us for who we are.'"

So Callie draped her hand casually over her husband's arm. No one would know by looking at her that her fingers pressed deeply into the muscle there, letting him know that she was with him.

If Callie hadn't been attempting to reach bone with her fingernails, Ren might have forgotten she was there. When all those eyes swept to him, to his face, he had to fight the overwhelming urge to step backward, to duck right back through the double doors of the vast ballroom. As it was, he and Callie stood upon a stage created out of the first landing of the great curving double stairway that arched downward to the dance floor below.

With hazy distance, Ren felt Callie's grip. It was a lifeline, a kite string of touch—well, pain, really—that held him to the earth. He tried to remember Button's instructions through the roaring in his ears.

Impress. Instruct.

See us.

That was when Ren realized that if he could simply hold out for a few more moments, he would never have to hide again—not here, not in his home or on his estate or in the village nearby.

The weight of those years of secrets and shadows ahead of him had once bent him nearly to the ground. Now to realize that he might ride bareheaded about the grounds, that he might stop into the village post office to send a letter, that he might hire staff to ease Callie's days—

Air filled his lungs, cool, fragrant air, not stale and humid from coming through black wool. Ren stood straight and tall, the glimmering sash of his knighthood smooth across his expanded chest.

At some instinctive moment—surely instructed by Button, who had quite the flair for the dramatic—Callie gave his arm a squeeze and began to lower herself into a grand curtsy to their guests. Ren matched her with a deep bow.

As they straightened, spontaneous applause broke out in random areas of the crowd. Soon, everyone, even the crustiest villager, had joined in. The thundering applause threatened to send Ren right back through the door, away from the noise, away from the faces, away from the crystals tinkling in the grand chandeliers above from the vibrations.

Callie's ferocious grip kept him pinned like a butterfly in her collection.

He shot her a glance. *Are you trying to draw blood?*

She met his quick glance with a loving glare. *Do not flee. Do not even think about leaving me here alone.*

That thought, of her standing alone to face this mob, did more to fix him in place than any physical grip. If he could find it in him to protect her from falling off a window ledge, it seemed petty to desert her now.

So he bore the applause and the gazes and the gawks. Button was right about one thing. He'd earned these scars in service to the Crown. Just because his mission had been secret—hell, his very existence had been secret!—did not mean that he had to remain in the dark for the rest of his life.

He could stand here for a little while, and earn the right to walk in the light—in Callie's light.

For she shone on this night. He could see it in the faces gazing up at them. First they fixed on him, on his face, on the visible scars, seeking, searching, wondering about the scars that remained hidden. Then, when the first startling impression of his marred face had sunk in, one by one their gazes turned to the incandescent woman at his side.

Pretty Callie, with her snub nose and dash of freckles, Callie of the countryside tramping and the kerchief-headed cleaning, had become exquisite Callie, goddess of spring and all things new.

A goddess with a bosom fit for a god's delight. *Oh, my God.* Why had he not noticed before? How could he have been so caught up in his own nerves that he'd missed the fact that the riches of Callie's bosom runneth over!

Fury flashed through him. He was going to kill Button!

Then Callie unobtrusively tugged him to the stairs and they descended into the ballroom. The walking stick assured their progress was stately rather than lurching. Henry and Betrice stepped forward from the grinning multitudes to greet them. Henry was distinctive in his rustic squire's garb from an earlier century. As costumes went, it looked a bit more like a rummage through the attic. It suited Henry's old-fashioned blustery charm to perfection.

Betrice looked very pretty in misty gray silk and a cat mask created of ermine fur. Callie exclaimed over the gown, praise which Betrice received with a strange discomfort. "It is an old gown."

Callie blinked. She'd thought every woman in the village had ordered something new from Button's shop. "Well, you look absolutely stunning," she assured Betrice. "By far the prettiest lady here."

Betrice eyed her with a slightly furrowed brow. "Have you no mirror, Callie?" Then her gaze slid to Ren's chest. "Or should I say 'Lady Porter'?"

Henry nodded emphatically. "Oh, yes. Lady Porter, indeed! May I be the first to offer congratulations, Sir Lawrence? When did you receive the honor?"

Ren stiffened slightly. Callie felt the muscles of his arm tighten. "Three years ago . . . and yes, you are the first."

Henry's open features begged for an explanation, but Callie knew none would be forthcoming.

She cleared her throat. "Sir Lawrence, I believe the quartet is awaiting our taking the floor for the opening waltz."

With a curt nod to Henry, Ren handed off his stick to a fellow in livery and swept Callie onto the floor in a manner befitting a prince and princess. Then he bowed deeply to her and she to him. On cue, the music began as he took her hand and she flowed into his arms.

There was a long pause. Callie awaited his lead. Then Ren bowed his head toward hers. "Callie?"

"Yes?"

"You not only forgot to ask me if I wished for a ball, but you forgot to ask me if I could dance."

Oh, hell. Oh, damn. Oh, Great George's Balls!

Then he laughed in her ear and swept her into an effortless waltz, even using his limp in time with the rise and fall of the steps.

Callie threw back her head and laughed out loud. After a moment of stunned attention upon the dark, imposing master and his luminous bride, the rest of the guests joined in the dance.

Ren looked down at her, his evening sky-blue eyes twinkling. "Don't forget you owe me a pearl."

* * *

When Ren found Button after the first waltz, the dapper little man was deep in conversation with a lithe young woman in a housemaid's livery. At first glance Ren dismissed her as a plain sort. When she dipped a quick curtsy and left the two men alone, Ren's attention was caught by her athletic grace. If she were a man, he would think she moved like a fighter, a dangerous one.

Which was ridiculous, of course.

He shook the odd thought from his mind and pinned Button with a sour gaze. "What were you thinking, putting Callie in such a gown?"

Button blinked at him blandly. "You don't care for it? I thought the color most becoming."

Ren narrowed his gaze. "It's lovely—what there is of it. Did you perhaps run short of fabric . . . oh, say, in the bodice area?"

Button made no effort to hide his pleased smirk. "Her ladyship's natural assets make you the envy of all the men here."

Ren crossed his arms and loomed, his gleaming new cane in his fist. One talent he'd not lost, looming. "And if I don't care to have all the men here laying their bloody eyeballs on my—on her ladyship's assets?"

"I brought something along in case of textile failure," Button admitted reluctantly, as he slid his gaze aside. "But it will simply ruin the curve of the neckline."

Ren, whose gut went cold with horror as he imagined Callie in the midst of "textile failure," snatched the length of fine lace that Button pulled from his pocket and went in search of his bride.

He didn't see Button watching him go with great satisfaction on his puckish features.

Callie was, rather unsurprisingly, to be found surrounded by a tight circle of male admirers. Since what he really wanted to do was to snatch Callie off the floor and throw her over his shoulder in a territorial display, he forced himself to bow before his bride. "If her ladyship will excuse the interruption, there is something of pressing importance I must discuss."

Callie, who knew perfectly well that he was never so polite to her, nodded warily and sent her admirers onward with urges to draw their ladies and sisters and mothers into the next dance.

Then she lifted her chin. "What have I done now?"

Ren's reply was to grab her by the hand and tow her off to the side of the ballroom, where a curtained alcove awaited ladies in the midst of a faint, or lovers in the midst of a tryst.

It was luckily unoccupied, although Ren felt fully able to evict any and everyone who stepped in his path. Pulling her within the curtain, he turned and glared at Callie.

"I can't believe you would wear that in public!"

She made no pretense at not understanding him. Instead, she crossed her arms beneath her bosom and glared back. "I can't believe it took you so long to notice!"

"I noticed," he growled. "First I had business with that rag-peddling procurer! How could you allow him to dress you like a high-priced demirep?"

"So you do like it." Callie smiled and inhaled a taunting breath. Ren saw the barest pink edge of areole rise above the neckline and nearly swallowed his tongue. Textile failure!

He yanked the length of lace from his pocket. "Put this on!"

She glanced dismissively at it. "I will not. It will ruin the line of the bodice."

Ren took a step toward her. Then another. He wasn't feeling territorial any longer. Now he wanted to wrest her down onto the fainting couch behind her and kiss that knowing smile from her lips. Or possibly erase the teasing tone of her tongue by filling her mouth with his cock, which was even now straining at the front of his trousers.

Callie didn't back down.

Not until he reached into his weskit pocket and pulled out the pearl she'd given him for the first waltz. "Open your mouth."

Chapter 26

Callie glared into Ren's eyes. "You wouldn't dare."

He put the pearl lightly to her lips. "Open your mouth."

She licked her lips nervously and sent an anxious glance toward the ballroom on the other side of the thin curtain. Ren wondered if he were indeed going too far. She didn't want to—

Then her gaze flicked back up to meet his and he saw the heat smoldering in her eyes. Oh, yes, she did want to. A smile quirked his lips.

She opened her mouth.

He laid the pearl upon her tongue and bent to whisper into her ear. "Do not move, nor make a sound, no matter what. You must not respond in any way."

She closed her lips over the pearl but she did not nod. Instead, her gaze fixed in midair. She might as well have been carved of marble, a perfect statue of the Goddess of Spring.

Perfect. Ren dropped his walking stick to the carpet and pulled the length of lace out long between his fingers and raised it to her bodice. He'd truly only meant to shut her up long enough to make her decent—but her heated compliance made his blood burn, just as it always did.

Slowly, he tucked the lace into the edge of her neckline. It was so sheer and gauzy a pattern that even when neatly arranged, it barely kept her nipples from peeking above the fabric. He tucked those nipples down inside, allowing his fingertips to roll them gently back and forth as he did so.

They tightened at his touch, hardening for him even as he hardened for her. Rebellious little pink tips, pouting outward as if begging for his mouth. It took only the slightest tug to release them wholly into view. Bending, he sucked first one between his lips, tugging and rolling his tongue over it. Then he teased the pert, wet little thing with his fingers while he sucked the other into happy hardness.

Lifting his head, he watched Callie's face while he tugged and tweaked at her nipples. She allowed no expression to cross her features, but she could do nothing about the quickening of her breath. He pinched gently, plucking and twisting the tender bits of lustful flesh.

"There are a hundred people on the other side of that curtain, Lady Porter, all of them wondering where you are. At any moment, one of them could sweep it aside and discover you in this shameless condition." He pinched harder, gazing into her stony face, then harder still. She inhaled sharply, but her gaze never left some point over his left shoulder.

He drew out the length of fine lace from her neckline and dragged it slowly across her rigid, sensitized nipples. Her eyelids shivered slightly and he felt a shudder of lust pass through her. "Put your hands behind your back."

She did nothing. No response, just as he'd commanded. So he moved behind her, drawing her hands back to cross at her wrists. Then he wrapped the lace about them. For a moment, he contemplated a simple playful wrapping, one that could be shaken off in a moment.

Then the dark tide of desire and possession rose within him and he found himself pulling a snug knot about her hands. She was truly bound, helpless and half naked at her own ball. The wickedness turned his desire into a sudden harsh wave of black lust. She was his.

His.

The lonely years, the hiding, the bleak betrayal had turned his normal male desires into something seething and deep. He didn't simply want her—he *required* her. He needed to have her, keep her, own her, and make her know herself owned.

So he tied her up and pulled her breasts entirely free of the snug bodice and pushed her hard against the wall of the alcove while he devoured her nipples. Hard hands squeezed her soft flesh until he heard her breath catch. He sucked her deep into his mouth, grazing the rigid tips with his teeth in his urgency, eating her alive, consuming her.

It wasn't enough. He wanted more, so much more. If he could have drawn her right into his own body and trapped her there forever, it would not have been enough.

And what of her?

He drew back to gaze into her face, still closed and distant—but her cheeks were flushed and her eyes bright and her breath panted quick and broken. She was as aroused as he.

Should he roger her right here, splay her out right on the sofa, to hell with her gown, to hell with the ball, and make her come screaming ten steps away from their guests?

Yes.

Or up against the wall, her thighs wrapped around his

hips, her bound hands behind his neck, her soft bottom squeezed bruisingly hard in his hands while he plunged into her?

Yes.

No.

She was caught up in the moment, she was awash with lust. She would allow it. She would likely even enjoy it—in the moment. But after, when she would have to face the scandalized occupants of the ballroom wearing the evidence of her ravagement?

He dropped his face into her soft, delicious bosom and tried to wrest his lust under control. She wanted him. Her heart pounded in his ear. He could detect the warm, sea-salt scent of her lust rising up through her gown.

The perfume of her drove him to the edge of sanity, calling to mind the taste of her and the hot, soft, wet feel of her.

She stood so still, willing and waiting.

Just one taste . . .

He dropped to his knees before the object of his desire and lifted her skirts.

Callie pressed her bared shoulders into the cool plaster of the wall behind her back and wound her fingers tightly together in secret, but it was all she could do to suppress the shudders of hunger that swept her like waves on a shore. Her exposed nipples throbbed from his rough treatment, crinkling in the chilly air, jutting reddened and naked above the crumpled silk of her bodice.

He was wicked to bind her thus, to take her to this dark plane of temptation and submission—and during her very first ball, too!

Yet the pull she felt to him—more than simply the twisted ropes of domination and submission—and the need she felt emanating from his very skin kept her there, kept her still, kept her at his mercy yet again.

Her eyes were fixed on a speck of light shining through a flaw in the curtain, but she'd become blind to it long before. Her bound wrists were truly quite immovable, for this was no game he played in this dark little room.

No, for all his teasing, there was something that he wanted from her, something that he needed.

He was not the only one. She stood completely still. Her hair was not even mussed! Yet she ached for him, for his touch, for his cock within her. Her thighs were slick with her wanting and when his hot hands slid up her legs to discover this, she nearly wept with relief.

He pushed gently on the inside of her knees to part them, but she did not respond. She made him force her thighs apart with hard hands and shivered inwardly with delight when he spread her feet far apart and knelt between them, exposing her for his delectation.

Her gown he pushed high, tucking the hem into her fallen bodice, keeping the silk far away from his wicked intentions. Then he slid the fingers of one hand between her swollen, slippery labia, seeking and finding.

She didn't make a sound, but she was quite certain her tongue would be sore for days from the biting.

His fingers pushed into her, first one long middle finger, thrusting deep into her slick readiness. Then two long fingers, pressed together, opening her, spreading her. His thumb joined in, rubbing slow circles over her clitoris. She felt his mouth then, his lips kissing down her exposed belly even as his fingers began a rhythmic slow pace, invading deep and then withdrawing, spreading her wetness.

His hot mouth descended upon her then, his tongue taking the place of his hard thumb. Hot, slick circles broken by quick sweeps from side to side, all while his hard, insistent fingers violated her as she stood bound, helpless, and exposed, just seconds from discovery.

It was marvelous. She loved losing herself in the heat and need, that moment of time slowing until she could hear her breath panting in and out, could feel the slight calluses on his fingers. This closed, dark, rich place, here in his hands . . .

If she'd been allowed, she would have driven herself into his hand thrusting and grinding upon it whilst keening like a banshee.

She was not permitted such a release. Instead, she remained his statue, his creation to be sculpted by his hand alone. The teasing was exquisite.

She needed more. She ached for him, ached to be impaled upon him, riding the waves of his lust. She needed her sweet, painful craving filled.

To hell with her dress. Damn the ball! She needed to be taken, right now in the dark, in this secret wicked world he'd drawn her into!

His hand withdrew from inside her and she wanted to scream her frustration aloud—but he'd commanded her silence and she obeyed. Her submission had taken on a life of its own somehow, as if he'd slowly built a vibrating sentient cage about her will, a cage she had no wish to leave.

Not even when the cold, metal knob of his cane pressed against her hot, slippery labia.

Though icy shock flooded her body, she did not so much as flinch. She was not on this journey alone. If he wished to see how far she would go, to know how much her loyalty would accept, to learn when it would be that she would reject him, well, the idiot man had a long row to hoe.

Therefore, she kept as still as stone as he slid the egg-sized knob of gold slowly up and down her slit, wetting it, warming it.

Ren lifted his mouth from her and rolled the ball over and around her swollen clitoris. The gold gleamed in the dimness, wet and slick from her.

She must realize what he meant to do. He wanted to do it, wanted to shock and violate her, wanted to push her to the edge and beyond, to make her understand that she must never leave him—that she *belonged* to him.

He held the cane a few inches below the ball and pressed it to her, slipping the blunt end just barely into her. His family crest disappeared into the sweet, wet heat of her. A warning. A promise.

She did not move. She did not protest.

Darkly enthralled and yet simultaneously disturbed by her seemingly endless obedience, he meant to test every strand of her delicious submission to its breaking point.

Callie waited, her nerves strung like piano wire, her vagina hot and throbbing and aching for satiation. The anticipation of his act—of his alarming, arousing, insanely wicked act!—had her belly trembling and her mouth dry. Her stillness never faltered.

"Mrs. Porter, I believe you are the most unusual creature I have ever known." His breath was hot, tickling the soft curls of her mound. His voice was thick with lust and wonder.

Then he slowly, implacably thrust the head of the walking stick into her. He penetrated her carefully, pressing far inside, yet never too deeply.

Callie struggled not to move, nor even shift her weight, though hot wicked pleasure swept her. The depth of her own wantonness stunned her. She *wanted* this hot and unthinkable invasion. Furthermore, she wished he would get on with it!

Ren paused, yet Callie stayed bound and silent.

A submissive goddess. A whirlwind tamed by his hand.

Mine.

Triumphant, he once again dove his mouth down upon her clitoris. He savored her with his tongue as he pleasured her slowly with the golden ball.

That she allowed him to do such a thing to her shattered him. He felt humbled by her trust even as his cock throbbed at her obedience. He buried the gold ball with the crest deep within her, planting it there, branding her with it as he drove her to new heights with his tongue, teeth, and lips. Did she know that he was her willing slave as well, bound to her by so much more than a length of lace? How could she, when he'd gone to such lengths to hide it?

Yet now having proved his possession, he found he wanted more. He wanted her orgasm. He needed proof that she wanted this, that she was not simply rigid with revulsion and grim determination.

And, to be darkly honest with himself, he knew he wanted to feel the power over her pleasure.

Callie had no more thoughts of the people outside or her dress or even that what he was doing to her should have shocked her senseless. She was not Callie. She was simply sensation. Her stillness had taken over, allowing her to do nothing but feel.

The thick hard ball moved inside her, rubbing and rolling, thrusting slowly and relentlessly while a hot, wet mouth devoured her, driving her on and on until her breath panted from her open mouth and her heart pounded. The point of light caught in her lust-blind gaze became a star and she was on her way to it, rising . . . climbing . . .

When hot, hard fingers came up to torment her throbbing nipples further while he tongued her clitoris and thrust the ball into her, the star blurred in her vision. She could feel the orgasm rising within her, could feel the waves of it sweeping her up dangerously high. In a moment she would come out loud and there was nothing she could do to stop it—

She broke. At the perfect moment, he stood and kissed her deeply, keeping his hands busily driving her higher, swallowing her moans as her entire body shuddered and spasmed. She tasted him, tasted herself, and the wickedness only drove her higher. The dark waves to which only he could drive her crashed together within her, a riot of heat and shadowy, wicked joy. She screamed into his mouth. He leaned into her, pressing her tight against the wall, keeping her upright as he purloined every last shiver of orgasm from her flesh.

Her knees were weak. She could not catch her breath. As she gasped and leaned dizzily upon him, she was only barely aware that he was untying her hands, putting her gown to rights, tucking her swollen nipples gently away into the bodice, using his handkerchief to dry her slippery thighs. He was so strange, so outlandish in demanding this twisted obedience from her.

And yet so kind.

Her own willingness she understood completely. This was her grand adventure. This was her journey of exploration and danger. One could not see the light of a new world without stepping into the shadows.

She was still not sure what her compliance proved to him, but she knew he yet needed to know it. She pressed shaking fingers to her hot cheeks, cooling them. She wondered if their lovemaking would ever truly come out into the light, or would there always remain a shadow of the beast within him?

I lost the pearl. Dimly she hoped she hadn't swallowed it.

Ren could barely look at her. Self-loathing swept him. The things he'd done, the things he'd wanted to do—she was his lady wife, not his plaything—except she was now, a willing one and it was all his doing. She could never recapture her purity, never again see the world through eyes unshadowed by worldly knowledge.

Yet even now his body betrayed him. His erection was like forged iron, strangling within his breeches. He wanted it all still—everything he'd imagined. His black addiction to her submission shamed him. Even as her obedience inflamed him, deep inside he knew he was missing something. He was missing her passion, her desire, free and giving.

That is . . . if he could truly believe that she did give it freely.

Yet how could he know if he never asked?

"Callie—"

She was half turned away from him, fretting over the creases in her bodice. "Do you think anyone will notice? Oh, goodness, do you think Mr. Button will be upset?"

Button, Ren thought sourly, would likely applaud. He handed Callie the length of lace that had somehow become draped over his shoulder. "Use this."

This time she took it gratefully, tucking it carefully over the exposed portion of her bosom, now reddened from his mouth and his stubble. Well, he'd accomplished one thing, anyway. He reached for her hands and folded them within his own. "Callie, stop. You look lovely. They've been dancing for an hour. You won't be the only lady looking flushed and a little wrinkled."

She clapped her hands to her cheeks. "I'm flushed," she wailed quietly. "I look all blotchy, don't I?"

There was no possible response but to kiss her silly worries away. She went statue-still the moment he touched her and he hated himself. "Kiss me back, Callie," he whispered. "Just please . . . just kiss me."

As if released by a spring, she threw herself upon him. Her arms wrapped about his neck and she went up on tiptoe, and her sweet, hot mouth rose to devour his. Ren took the added weight upon his bad leg and stumbled backward, into the wall behind him. He cared not at all, for the deep fount of Callie's passion was unleashed at last—upon *him*.

And all he'd ever needed to do was ask.

Callie poured everything into that kiss—her gratitude, her determination, her need to heal him, her awakened desire—

The taste of him, the feel of him beneath her hands, the softness of his lips as he submitted to her only fed her own need. She wanted so much!

A tiny fraction of her mind retained sanity. Any more and she ought to salt him and serve him properly on a plate! Reining in her zeal, she released her death grip on his neck and stepped back with a small laugh. "Goodness, that's a tap best turned another time, another place!"

He gazed at her, his eyes shadowed by the mask in the dim alcove. What was he thinking?

The sounds of the ball penetrated their privacy. It was past time to get back to their guests, but she hesitated, waiting, hoping for a response from him.

Just as she gave up and reached for the curtain, she felt his hand close gently over her arm. He towed her back to him and enclosed her gently in his arms.

"Callie," he whispered. "Do you think that tonight

we might . . . just this once—that we might put away the pearls?"

Nestled against the warm silk of his waistcoat, Callie smiled. From the shadows into the light.

"I suppose so . . . just this once."

Chapter 27

When Ren reemerged from the alcove with Callie on his arm, as serene and composed as she could manage, it was to find the ball in full parade. The string quartet was pouring its heart into a swinging country dance and the guests were doing the old tune proud. It was familiar to Ren.

In fact, he could even now hear Callie's sweet voice singing the accompanying lyrics as she frolicked in the lane.

> *Go on, fellow, grab your girl.*
> *Take her hand and let her whirl!*
> *If she comes back, then dance you on.*

He looked down. Sure enough, Callie's foot tapped along with the beat. He released her hand and gave her a push. "Go on. Dance."

She blinked at him. "Don't you wish to?"

He looked down at her and smiled slightly. It was growing easier to do so by the day. "I can very nearly fake a waltz. Perhaps even a nice, slow quadrille—but this is quite out of my reach, I fear. Look, here comes Henry."

Henry, bless him, was cordially eager to dance and led Callie off to join in with the galloping couples now kicking up their heels. Ren drifted closer to the group of interweaving dancers, his gaze on Callie's bright eyes and happy smile as she dipped and skipped.

She looked like a child finally let out of doors in the springtime. The music, the crowd, the dancing—she obviously dearly loved a good and proper bash. How could he have ever thought to lock such a luminous and lively creature in this dark, stone cave with him and his shadows?

Except that it wasn't a cave any longer. She'd done that. She'd made it a home, quite against his wishes, just as she'd made him a husband, quite against his will.

He lingered behind a group of village matrons, hardly even looming at all. Enchanted by the sight of Callie dancing, he nearly missed the busy commentary of the old guard.

"She's a pretty thing—and so finely dressed."

"I saw her once in the post office and she didn't look nearly so fine that day."

"Well, we all put our finest feathers on tonight!"

This was accompanied by much waggling of their own elaborately feathered masks. Really, the things people did to perfectly innocent ostrich plumes.

Ren almost moved on, out of range of the cackles now rising toward the chandeliers, but one of the ladies went on.

"It's true, you know! My Adam spoke to Henry Nelson and he said that Henry said that he truly has been knighted!"

"A real knight, at Amberdell Manor!"

"And a real lady, too! With such a spritely sort of manner about her."

"Well, I heard from the vicar's wife that the wedding was a brief affair, if you know what I mean!"

"Is it true she wore an ordinary day dress? To be married in?"

There was much tut-tutting. Ren resolved to buy out Mr. Button's establishment by dawn tomorrow. These old cats wouldn't find another word to say about Callie's wardrobe!

"I think it's romantic," one of them announced stoutly. "So swept up in love that she didn't care a fig what she wore."

"But where did they meet? She lived in London and he never leaves the manor—at least, he never did before . . ."

"Well, I for one don't care what he's been doing up here all these years, not if he's finally going to be a proper master! And he's a fine-looking fellow—well, he's a fine figure of a man, anyway!"

Ren looked around. He needed to escape now.

"Oh, yes! I don't know who started those silly rumors of a hunchback!"

Hunchback? *Hunchback?* Ren forcibly resisted the urge to twist his head to check his posture.

"Really, gossips can be so tiresome."

To Ren's astonishment, all four ladies nodded sagely in agreement.

"Poisonous as snakes in Eden."

On the dance floor, Callie was being handed off to gentleman after gentleman in the steps of the dance. Finally, she found herself back with Henry. His dear suntanned face was aglow with perspiration and good cheer.

"You've done a marvel, you have!" He spun her enthusiastically. "The village is agog!"

"Thank you, but I had a great deal of help. I never could have put it together without Betrice directing me to all the local merchants."

"Well, I for one am glad you're here to take the burden from my Betty." Then he smiled once more and spun her off to another fellow, taking up the interweaving steps once more. Callie smiled at her new partners easily enough, but Henry's words rang in her mind.

I'm glad you're here to take the burden . . .

It was becoming quite clear to her that if she stayed with Ren, stayed here as lady of Amberdell, it would not be all freedom and peaceful afternoons of sketching.

If.

The wife of the master of Amberdell had an important part to play in the community. She would indeed be in the matriarchal role, as lady of the manor.

But for all Callie cherished her newfound time to herself, she had come to see that one was nothing if not the reflections one saw in others' eyes and, in return, they in ours. Her bonds defined her. Daughter, sister, wife . . . lover. Alone might be peaceful but she was beginning to suspect it was also bloody dull. She realized that she was willing to be needed, and moreover, to need, which she had never truly dared to do before.

She needed Ren. And, she hoped, he needed her. And Amberdell needed them both.

Across the ballroom, Betrice watched Callie dance with Henry. He was a bit of a buffoon on the ballroom floor, all swinging arms and galloping feet.

Poor Henry. Affection and warmth warred with a self-conscious knowledge that next to the new and improved Sir Lawrence, Henry looked like a true country bumpkin. Of course, she'd hardly ever laid eyes on Lawrence before his impromptu wedding but he certainly was not the lurking, lurching fellow she remembered.

Nor did he look to be on his deathbed, as Henry had so sadly assured her years before. In fact, he looked like a man in his prime, albeit battered and scarred.

He turned suddenly, his eyes shadowed by the mask as he turned his head as if searching the crowd, as if he felt her gaze on him. Betrice dropped her eyes and fluttered her fan nonchalantly, but she shivered in the warm room.

He was still every bit as dangerous as he'd ever been.

So she smiled and complimented and gossiped and asked after everyone's children, crops and ailments, details that only came from a lifetime in the community. Match that, *Lady* Porter!

Yet for all her ties to the people of Amberdell, she'd never felt so alone among them. When she knew them all so well, how could not a single person there perceive the seething discontent that twisted inside her?

No one but Unwin.

Henry came back with Callie on his arm. Betrice pulled herself together and smiled warmly at them both. "You looked to be having a marvelous time. Henry, you must fetch Lady Porter a cool drink—she's absolutely"— *sweating like a horse, really, she's a scandal!*—"glowing!"

Henry dutifully sprang to milady's rescue, scurrying away to fetch a glass of champagne from one of the ubiquitous staff—Betrice's envy rose to near unbearable proportions at the thought of such a wealth of servants— and Callie smiled joyously at Betrice.

"Henry's such a dear! You're a fortunate woman."

I will not twitch. Ladies do not twitch.

Betrice frowned. "Oh, Callie. Couldn't you convince Lawrence to spare you more than one dance?"

Callie's smile faltered slightly. "I'm sure he'll beg another waltz . . . eventually. His injury . . ."

Betrice put her gloved hand on Callie's. "Of course, of course! And . . . if I may be so bold? It actually appears that matters between the two of you have . . . improved?"

Callie blushed instantly and Betrice knew. The marriage had been consummated. Then Betrice noted the well-kissed plumpness of Callie's lips and the betraying burn of beard upon the exposed portion of her bosom. Factor in the shining eyes and the easy smile and it was clear that Callie was now most completely in thrall to her husband. Betrice wondered if Ren even knew. Men could be quite stupid that way.

Betrice took a deep breath. Then another. She favored Callie with her best future-lady-of-Amberdell smile. "That's wonderful news." She tucked her arm into Callie's and drew her aside. "But, as one married woman to another—there is more to the union than the physical. Have you earned his trust? Has he begun to confide in you?"

Callie blinked. "Well . . . he is not one for words."

Betrice chuckled. "Not like my dear Henry, then. One can hardly stop him!"

Callie nodded and smiled uncertainly. "Henry certainly seems to consider communication to be important."

"Heavens, yes! Why, I'd scarcely known him a week before I knew every single thing about him—and he about me!"

Callie's smile slipped again. "A . . . a week?"

"Why, I thought with the two of you rattling around in the manor by yourselves—What do you two do all day?"

Callie's shrug fell just on this side of miserable. "Not . . . talk."

She was melting like a neglected candle. Silly, lonely child. She'd be better off back in London with her family, truly.

"Marriage can be so difficult," Betrice commiserated. "If only you had your dear mother to discuss it with. She must be missing you terribly right now, as well."

"My mother?" Callie's eyes grew wide. "How odd that you would mention her just now. I . . . I did not think I would miss my family so. But I cannot go now." She shook her head as if shaking off a temptation. "No, now is not the right time. I need . . . Ren and I need to . . ." She trailed off, biting her lip, with a glaze of dampness in her eyes.

"My lady, if I might interrupt?"

It was that insufferable little dressmaker from the village. Betrice had walked out of his establishment when that ridiculously beautiful young man had taken her back behind the curtains—why, he'd wanted her to remove her gown to be "properly" measured! Proper, indeed!

It was that and only that which had spurred her decision to reject the new gown that Henry had assured her they could very nearly afford—not the fact that she'd been wearing an old chemise beneath, the one with the tear in the seam she'd mended with mismatched thread.

Mr. Button had a lady on his arm—and there was not a doubt in Betrice's mind that this was a lady, indeed—whom he introduced to Callie as "Lady Raines."

Betrice looked askance at the little man and he smoothly introduced her, as well. Everyone curtsied, Betrice the lowest, being merely "Mrs. Nelson."

"Welcome to our home, my lady," Callie said easily. "I hope you're dancing—the music is wonderful, is it not?"

Gushing. Appalling.

To Betrice's astonishment, Lady Raines gushed right back. "Blissful! I've danced my slippers to the absolute last strand of silk!" She turned to Betrice with a smile, but there was a definite razor's edge to the glint in her eye. "Mrs. Nelson, you must step out. Your husband is the most delightful dancer."

Betrice blinked. "You . . . you danced with Henry?" Oh, horrors. She was going to make a "kindly" remark about his red-faced, sweaty-handed prancing now. Betrice couldn't bear it, not in front of Callie.

But Lady Raines only smiled. "But of course." Then she turned back to Callie. "Lady Porter, forgive us for forcing ourselves on your conversation, but you looked quite distressed just now. Mr. Button would suffer nothing but to fly to your rescue at once."

Button shot a scythelike smile at Betrice, then warmed it for Callie's benefit. "I hope you are not displeased by any of my little surprises, my dear. I only hoped to further your enjoyment of the evening."

Callie glanced at Betrice, then shook her head. "Certainly not. Your arrangements will be the talk of the village for decades! Everything is absolute perfection—and I am so pleased to make your acquaintance, Lady Raines. Mr. Button has such a marvelous capacity for making friends, does he not? The entire village adores him."

Lady Raines laughed. "It is very easy to like Mr. Button when he has supplied every lady in the village with a one-of-a-kind Lementeur creation!"

Lementeur?

Callie had such a look on her face. Betrice suddenly realized it was precisely the same one as on her own.

"Le—Lementeur?" Callie looked around. "But . . ."

Then Betrice saw what she'd been too distracted to notice before. Every lady in the village did not simply look nice. Every lady in the village, from the butcher's wife to the rough-handed laundress, looked *fabulous*.

Oh, my God. Betrice fought to inhale. *"You?"*

Mr. Button swept her a deep and graceful bow. "At your service, Mrs. Nelson."

I walked away from a Lementeur gown.

Tricked. That young man had known and he had let her stalk out of the shop anyway. The sounds of the ball faded, then swelled.

Callie was distracted from her astonishment by the pale cold marble of Betrice's complexion. She put a comforting hand on her new cousin's arm. "Are you all right, dear?"

Betrice drew a deep breath and favored them all with a glinting smile. "Do excuse me. I find myself with an overwhelming desire to dance with my husband."

Callie frowned as she watched Betrice move gracefully away. "She wasn't one who received a new gown, Mr. Button?"

Button spread his hands. "The lady declined."

Callie looked down at her hands. "She likely thought she could not afford it." Then her gaze rose to meet Button's. "How *did* all the ladies afford them?"

Button beamed pleasantly at her. "I have billed all and sundry to Sir Lawrence. I have it on good authority that he can well afford it."

Callie blinked and stared and then grinned like a child. Gazing around the room at the beaming faces and outrageous masks of the village populace, Callie judged it well done. "Every penny well spent!"

Lady Raines tilted her head at Callie. "Button, occupy yourself elsewhere please."

The great Lementeur bobbed a bow and slipped away in the crowd as if he loved nothing more than serving

Lady Raines. Callie slid her gaze back to the pretty, plump, dark-haired Lady Raines. "Who *are* you?"

The lady waved a ringed hand. "I? I am old news, really. I'm much more interested in *you*, Lady Porter."

Still distracted by her musings, Callie shook her head. " 'Calliope' will do. Or 'Callie' if you like. 'Lady Porter' still sounds like some bosomy matron in widow's silks to me."

Lady Raines snickered. "I know the feeling. I am Agatha." She tucked her arm into Callie's. "Let us take a stroll about the floor, shall we?"

Callie strolled obediently. "Are we headed somewhere in particular, my lady—er, Agatha?"

"Oh, no . . . nowhere at all."

Looking ahead, Callie noticed that their current path would carry them across the view of a small group of very well dressed people who looked nothing like the butcher's wife or the laundress. In fact, they looked almost like royalty. There were three gentlemen and two ladies. The men, two dark and one blond, looked like lords and the ladies, both tall statuesque blondes who resembled sunlight and moonlight respectively, princesses.

"I really must talk to Mr. Button about inviting unknown dignitaries to my balls," Callie murmured. "First there's just one or two, and then suddenly the place is crawling with them."

Agatha laughed, a startled sound. "Just a few old friends of Button's, truly."

"Who I am being paraded before for inspection?" Callie dug in her heels, forcing Agatha to stop, as well. "My lady, it is clear that there is something you wish to know. Ask, I pray you, for I have nothing to hide."

Agatha sighed. "Well, Button wasn't wrong about your mind, that is for certain." She withdrew her arm from Callie's and turned to face her. "It is only that I worried for a dear friend and I wished to reassure myself—that is, we wished to reassure ourselves—that our friend was not being taken advantage of by a pretty face—"

"Masking an evil heart?" Callie shook her head. "My lady, while I am terribly fond of Mr. Button, he doesn't strike me as the sort of man to be swayed by a pretty face—unless that face belongs to young Cabot." Callie gestured to the somber young man holding up a pillar to one side of the dancers.

Both ladies took a moment to appreciate the fellow's astonishing beauty, then resumed their conversation.

"Ah, yes . . . *Button*." Agatha narrowed her eyes at Callie significantly. "Well, anyone who would attempt to interfere with *Button* would quickly discover themselves in a great deal of very hot water."

"Without a doubt!" Callie folded her arms and scowled. "Point me at them. I'll call my brothers and we'll make short work of them. Worse still, I'll set my sisters upon them!"

Agatha blinked at her for long moment, her brow furrowed in confusion. "You would call upon your siblings to defeat anyone who slighted Button?"

"Did someone make jest of him because he is different? Call him a name? Was it here? In *my* house?" Callie swung a sharp gaze about the room, wild for battle. "Who?"

"Hmm." Agatha cast a glance over her shoulder at the group Callie had mentally dubbed the "Royal Handful." Did she shake her head ever so slightly, in some sort of signal? Callie turned to face the room and searched out dear Button, who was quite safely speaking to Ren by one of the potted palms brought in for the occasion. Faithful Cabot lurked nearby.

Callie relaxed. No one would mock Button with Ren and Cabot in his corner.

A gentle hand alighted upon her shoulder. Callie looked down into the wide brown eyes of Lady Raines.

"I'm sorry, my dear. I certainly didn't mean to distress you. No one has attacked our Button, truly. I simply wished to make sure that you were . . . that you were a loyal and stalwart friend."

"Oh." Callie shook her head. "Of course I am. He's done a great deal for me, and for my husband. Just look at Sir Lawrence—standing here, among all these people, as straight and proud as can be!" She sighed proudly, gazing at Ren. "Isn't he magnificent?"

Ren looked up just then and caught Callie's fond gaze. The one he returned to her burned.

Lady Raines gazed across the room at Ren, then let her eyes return to Callie's blushing face. "It seems there is more behind this transformation than merely the admittedly mystical powers of Lementeur," she said quietly. "Another sort of magic entirely, I should think."

Chapter 28

Betrice stalked through the ballroom, every step like walking on broken glass.

"Oh, Mrs. Nelson, did you hear? We're all wearing Lementeur! I can't wait to tell my sister in Locksbury that I'm all the rage, la!"

"Dear Mrs. Nelson, how tragic that you didn't order from that marvelous man! Tragic, simply tragic!"

"Well, dear, I'm sure if Lady Porter puts in a good word for you—"

Betrice could only fix an arch smile on her lips, laugh a meaningless little social laugh, and make her escape, finally diving behind a curtain to hide in a dim alcove to escape the we-love-Lady-Porter barrage.

She pressed her clenched fists against her forehead. Her own skin burned her.

Something small and round rolled beneath the sole of her dancing slipper. Distractedly, she bent to pick it up. The orb was the size of a gooseberry and shimmered in the dim light.

Someone had lost a pearl.

* * *

Callie saw Lady Raines across the ballroom, talking to a statuesque blond beauty—the silvery, moon-goddess one in a mask made in the pointed russet and white features of a fox. The two women shifted their heads slightly the moment Callie spotted them, and Callie knew they had been watching her.

"May I have this waltz?"

She turned to find Ren bowing low, his hand held out. He lifted his head and shot her a steamy glance. Her heart stuttered and she quite lost her breath.

My, what a handsome husband I have.

She lifted her chin and placed her hand in his. It only trembled a little bit, surely. "Why, yes, I do believe I have this dance free—but it is not a waltz."

Ren lifted one hand carelessly and snapped his fingers, his gaze never leaving Callie's. The spritely music segued instantly into the lyrical strains of the waltz. "It is now."

It was a bold lord-of-the-manor gesture—not the action of a man who felt he was a horror, that he needed to apologize for existing. The transformation was indeed miraculous. The power of confidence, to be sure.

Or was it? Lady Raines's voice echoed through Callie's mind. *Another sort of magic entirely.*

Then Ren swept her into his arms. She promptly forgot everything and everyone when he pulled her closer than was entirely proper and whirled her about the floor.

"You look beautiful when you dance," he murmured. "Almost as beautiful as when you . . ." He trailed off, but the look in his eyes said it all.

Callie's heart skidded around in giddy circles in her chest, but she managed a haughty tilt to her head. "Almost? I'll have you know that I am attired in a genuine Lementeur original!"

"I know," he said with a twist to his lips and a glimmer of humor in his beautiful eyes. "I've been informed

I shall be receiving a bill long enough to paper the upstairs gallery."

She bit her lip. "Do you mind? All the women are so happy—it's really so generous and they're truly grateful—"

"Hush, Callie. I do not mind it." He twirled her so fast she was lifted from her feet. He bent his head to whisper in her ear. "Besides, I've decided I shall merely add it to your account. Twenty-five, perhaps thirty gowns? A pearl apiece, yes?"

Thirty pearls.

Thirty more nights in his arms, in his bed, in his life.

Callie turned her head and caught his lips with hers, a quick, hot theft. Then she drew away and smiled. "Oh, I think a Lementeur gown ought to be worth at least two pearls each. But not tonight, if you recall."

He lifted his head and met her gaze. "I recall perfectly," he murmured, his voice a rumble of promise.

With their gazes locked and their hearts pounding in unison, they danced out the waltz he'd commanded, whirling gracefully about the room until the musicians looked at each other, shrugged, and began the tune again from the beginning.

When the waltz ended at last, Ren almost couldn't bear to allow Callie out of his embrace. Dancing with her gave him a sensation of flying. He hardly felt like a monster at all with her in his arms, in the ballroom or the bedroom—or the library! She made him believe he could truly be a man again.

But he'd danced her simply breathless. She hung on his arm, flushed and fanning herself, and quite unmistakably limping.

"Damn. Your ankle. Why did you not remind me?"

"And miss the opportunity to dance with you?"

He led her to one of the ornate little chairs that had

magically appeared in his ballroom. "Sit down, Callie. I'll find some champagne . . . where are all those minions of Button's anyway?"

Callie looked up and caught at his hand. "Oh! That reminds me—we must look after Mr. Button, Ren. This isn't London, after all. Lady Raines said the oddest thing—"

"Callie, every fellow here just found out that Button provided a gown fit for a queen to each of their wives for the price of flour-sacking. Those men have been drinking toasts to Button for the last hour!" He spotted a well turned-out servitor and beckoned urgently. Damned if the fellow didn't spin right about and walk the other way!

"Bloody hell." Ren patted Callie's hand. "Stay here. I'll fetch the damned champagne myself."

He set off to where he was sure he'd seen another servant pouring from magnums of the stuff. It wasn't until the crowd closed behind him that Callie's words registered fully in his hearing.

Lady Raines said the oddest thing.

Raines? Wait—*what*?

He spun on his heel and strode back to the little chair, but Callie was gone.

Raines?

No. It couldn't be.

For the first time, Ren took a good long look at his new staff. There, that bookish-looking fellow in spectacles, carrying champagne flutes arranged upon a tray, reminded him of someone; over to his right, a shorter man bowed two tall, blond ladies past him just as if he were letting them through a door; and that one there, standing at parade rest by the door, almost invisible in the discreet livery of Amberdell Manor.

Ren peered harder at the fellow. Big and thick, with a thuggish air. He'd known a man like that once . . .

A couple danced past, blocking Ren's view. He

stepped to one side and the lady, a curvaceous, dimpled brunette, smiled apologetically at him, her brown eyes alight with curiosity behind her mask adorned with tiny blue silk flowers. The man did not turn his head but Ren found his gaze swinging back to the fellow for another look, only to find the couple had disappeared into the mass of dancers.

Something about the man's stature . . .

Ren's skin prickled. His spine tightened. He longed for eyes in the back of his head.

In his former life he would have interpreted such sensations to mean he was surrounded. But that was nonsense. Those days were over with. This feeling was merely an echo of that past alarm, brought on by being in a crowd for the first time in so long.

Wasn't it?

"Mr. and Mrs. Archimedes Worthington! And . . . er . . . relations!"

Callie, who had decided to wait for her champagne—and perhaps another kiss—in the cooler air of the terrace, turned with a gasp just as her hand touched the latch of the doors leading outside.

Oh, no. Oh, blast. It couldn't be.

It most certainly was.

As Callie's entire family strode en masse into the ballroom, she heard avid murmurs from around her.

"Who is it?" "Is it a parade?" "Is it a circus troupe?"

Well, yes, very nearly. Add a dash of madhouse and you're close.

They were all there, a seeming army outrageously masked and costumed, tall and small, dark and light, all so different and all so much the same—all with the unmistakable Worthington insouciance that Callie had almost allowed herself to lose—

She felt her chin lift and her spine lengthen instantly, immediately imbued with the carefree attitude of resourceful self-assurance that wafted from her family like an exotic perfume.

How could I forget?

On they came, the entire exhilarating, exhausting pack of them, coming at her with smiles and open arms and chaos and mayhem, like a hurricane of love and devastation.

My ball is ruined. I am so happy to see them. This is a disaster. They look so wonderful!

So, appropriately, she greeted them with both laughter and tears, her arms wide.

From across the ballroom, Ren watched as his bride disappeared into the massed madness that was apparently the entire Worthington mob—er, clan.

He couldn't believe it. He'd had no idea there were so many Worthingtons. And by Callie's helplessly astonished expression, they'd not been on her guest list.

Button, I truly am going to kill you.

He must be gracious to her parents, yes, and that arrogant lout, Daedalus. Although Ren had to admit to his own fault on the night they'd met—the night Dade had discovered Callie in Ren's arms.

What must the fellow have thought? That Satan himself had arisen to violate his sister? Perhaps it was time to forgive an older brother's protectiveness. Very well, then, he was willing to tolerate the fellow if Dade behaved himself.

But the others? Ren tried to replay the stories he'd been told. Callie had mentioned the twins, Castor and Pollux—those would be the identical brown-haired fellows in the matching lime-green waistcoats. Awful.

Sisters. There had been a few stories about sisters.

Elektra and Atalanta. Really, those names! Ren saw one rather lovely flaxen-haired sister and one skinny freckled creature with a wild mop of red-gold curls that must be a sister, as well, or perhaps a pet. It sent him a glance full of murderous intent.

More brothers. Names, names ... Ren thought through the classical stories. He remembered hearing about an Orion and a Lysander. One brother was a bespectacled man with lean, dark good looks and a very serious manner. Another one, similar in coloring if not quite so well groomed, lurked in silence that seemed to surround him like a bubble even his own family did not penetrate.

Ren knew enough about burning self-loathing to recognize it when he saw it. Every instinct told him that the silent man was a cannon waiting to fire.

Iris and Archimedes, along with some rawboned elder female relation, held Callie tightly and beamed happily if indiscriminately about the ballroom, indifferent to any stares of avid interest.

But ... was that woman's bodice *moving*?

Still breathless from all the loving compression, Callie was next swept into the embrace of a tall woman in a swirling turban that made her tower over most of the men in the room.

"Er—Aunt Clemmie?"

Something was licking Callie's chin where her face was pressed into the woman's bosom. Yes, definitely Clementine, Iris's eldest sister, furry little bodice-passengers and all.

"There, there, girl. We'll get you out of this mess if it's the last thing we do. Married? Fah! *Men!*"

Callie sighed. *Worthingtons.*

* * *

Ren could not reach Callie, swarmed as she was. Yet, there was an empty space around him, he realized suddenly. Not just in the ballroom, but in the world itself. It was that space that for most was filled with family. He could see it in the way they surrounded her, a circle of loving arms, a fortress of trust and faith and need.

He'd had it as a boy. It had been a small circle, true, but his parents and his elder cousin John had been a family.

That is not the only place you had it.

Yes, he'd thought he'd found it with the Liars, with that motley band of thieves and gentlemen spies.

Of course, in the end he'd been quite mistaken, hadn't he? Watching her now, her face alight with love for her demented clan, something cold went through him.

Was he wrong about finding it with Callie, as well? Would she break his heart now that he had let her hold it in her hand?

He fought the impulse to turn away, to stride from the room and the possibilities. His parents had left him, his mother in an accident and his father quite willingly when he followed her that night, the vial of laudanum standing empty by the bedside, the single-line note scrawled on a crumpled page. *I cannot live without her.*

He'd thought his father a coward then.

And who's been hiding in a cave?

Ren let out a bark of self-deprecating laughter and strode toward the tight knot of Callie's family. If he wanted her he was obviously going to have to fetch her himself. He need not have worried. The Worthingtons parted before him with wide eyes.

Ah, yes. For a moment Ren had forgotten about the exposed portion of his face. *Hello, monster. Welcome to the family.*

Chapter 29

"Ahem."

Never had the mere clearing of a throat implied so much irritation. Callie unwrapped Aunt Clemmie's long arms and turned to smile tentatively at Ren. She saw Betrice and Henry trailing behind him, their eyes alight with curiosity.

"My family came to the ball!" she said brightly. "Isn't that wonderful?"

Ren gazed back at her for a long moment. Callie smiled harder. *Be good. Be a nice hermit and say pretty things to my family.*

His silence continued a beat too long. Whispers began to breed in the ballroom. Callie bared more teeth. The sharp ones. Her toe began to tap.

Her brothers stepped back warily.

Ren, the idiot, held his ground. His shadowed gaze ran over the boys and her sisters, lingered on Aunt Clemmie and the small furry snouts poking out of her neckline, then passed over her parents and came back to meet hers.

Be nice. Please?

Ren deflated before her eyes. He closed his eyes wearily for a moment, then stepped forward and snapped a very formal bow. "Mr. Worthington. Mrs. Worthington. What a pleasant surprise. We are delighted that you traveled so far to join us this evening. Might I beg introduction to the rest of the family?"

His words were very pretty. If his tone was a bit flat, at least it was not harsh.

He continued to behave very well, even prompting some nice manners from Dade, who was ever the competitive sort. The rest of the boys did not embarrass her . . . much . . . and of course Elektra's public etiquette was always pinpoint.

Then Atalanta was presented to Ren. Callie knew she wasn't the only one of the Worthingtons holding her breath. One never knew what Attie would do. *Ought I to worry?*

However, little Attie, clad in a sweet pink gown that used to be Elektra's, topped with a flowered mask cleverly constructed of papier-mâché, curtsied with gangly competence and murmured the usual nonsense with an entire lack of expression. Hmm. The one thing Attie was incapable of was dullness. *I rather think I ought to worry.*

Then Callie noticed that the twins had quietly slipped away. Oh, no. The twins quiet were the twins lethal.

Fortunately, they reemerged almost immediately, coming back into the ballroom through the double doors on the terrace. They moved slowly, bent almost double over wooden yokes, towing something behind them.

Whatever it was sat upon a two-wheeled cart and was draped in canvas. From the ten-foot height Callie surmised that her brothers were not exaggerating the weight of it as they strained at the yokes.

She felt Ren come up behind her. His hand snaked

about her waist. The embrace was ever so slightly too tight.

"Callie . . ."

Closing her eyes and reaching deep for strength, Callie turned into his arm and went on tiptoe. "Please, darling, let me handle them."

She felt the depth of his sigh.

"This is your evening, Callie. You worked so hard. I simply don't wish you to be disappointed."

The worry in his voice made her want to melt into him. *Please fix it for me. Make it better.*

She loved that he would truly try, if she asked him to. Unfortunately, management of the Worthingtons was not for beginners.

So she patted him briskly on the shoulder and smiled up at him. "Everything will be fine!"

He looked as doubtful as she felt, but he nodded. She slipped from his hold with a squeeze of his gloved hand and went to meet the twins as they wheeled the creaking cart across the ballroom to the large inlaid star in the center of the marble floor.

There was no point in playing nice with the twins. She crossed her arms and tapped her toe. "What is that?"

"That, dear sister—"

"is what was formerly known—"

"as the Blasted Contraption!"

The twins had been working on one version or another of the Blasted Contraption since they were fourteen. Attie was sometimes drawn into—and drew on—the creation, as did Iris. All the Worthingtons had contributed over the years. The thing was very nearly a member of the family.

However, it had long been a policy of Callie's to distrust any and all statements from the combined mouths of Cas and Poll. She gazed at the canvas-covered lump with suspicion. "If that's the Blasted Contraption, then where are the articulated tentacles? And what of the spire made of silver hair combs that was supposed to vibrate to the music of the spheres? If you've finally dismantled that bit, I'll be wanting mine back."

"Oh!" Elektra's hand went up. "Mine, as well!"

The twins beamed paternally at them. "All in good time—"

"All in good time!"

Elektra crossed her arms. "You've sold them, haven't you?"

Callie, though she also dearly wished to know the answer to that, waved her sister silent. "You still haven't told me what it is doing here." She glanced around at her guests, now milling in a loose circle, heads bent together as they doubtless discussed the very strangeness of all things Worthington. Callie sighed inwardly. All her hard work to be accepted, now to be at the mercy of her collected oddity of a family.

Someone snickered in the crowd. Callie whirled to see, scowling. She might whinge away in her own head about her strange relations, but no one in Amberdell would get away with a single snide comment about her loved ones!

However, most of the guests seemed intrigued and happily anticipatory. That was nice . . . or, it would be if Cas and Poll had ever invented anything that actually worked—well, other than their marvelous talent for explosives.

Then Orion stepped up. "The articulated tentacles did not support the new theme. The receptor made of combs was simply ludicrous. I made them take it down when I revamped their design."

Callie blinked. If Orion had lent a hand to the twins, then the object "formerly known as the Blasted Contraption" might truly have a chance of operating!

She blinked at her scholarly brother. "But . . ." She tried but she simply couldn't keep the helpless note out of her voice. "What *is* it?"

Mama wafted past on Archie's arm. "A celebration, of course! We're all been slaving over it for days. It is a Grand and Eloquent Expression!" She drifted on, tilting vaguely in the direction of Mr. Button's array of nibblements.

Callie gazed at her blissful mother with fond vexation. Honestly, sometimes Mama made her spine weaken! She rubbed at her temples. "Orion, are you planning to explode my ball?"

Orion blinked seriously at her through his spectacles. "No. Any impending destruction will be entirely unplanned."

There was some comfort to be had in the fact that Orion never lied. He would never bother to shade the truth to make one feel better. He simply didn't see the point in feelings.

Callie turned to find the single voice of reason. "Dade?"

Her eldest brother stepped forward. "I'm sorry, Callie. When I received the invitation, I meant to come alone, but—" He waved a hand helplessly. "The family is getting out of hand without you home to calm matters."

Invitation? Callie swept the room with her eyes, but saw no sign of the traitorous Mr. Button. Well, he'd probably meant well. Honestly, how could he have known?

Henry approached, Betrice on his arm. They greeted her father cordially. Ah, yes. They'd met at the wedding— and still claimed the acquaintance. Callie's estimation of Henry went up another notch.

"We have brought a very special exhibition for this auspicious occasion," Archie said to a rapt Henry. "Such

as never before seen by your village! It is be timed for
the stroke of midnight, concurrent with the moment of
revelation!"

Ren, who stood nearby sourly toeing a grimy mark
on his marble floor from the cart wheel, felt his gut go
cold.

The moment of revelation. The unmasking of everyone in the ballroom.

The unmasking of him.

Betrice left Henry's side and wandered curiously toward
the canvas-covered cart. The two identical young men
were tinkering secretively with something under the tar-
paulin.

"There. Tighten that—"

"Bolt, yes, got it. Now for the—"

"spring. Winding now—"

"And don't forget the—"

A hand emerged, fumbling for something in a wooden
toolbox balanced on the edge of the cart. Curious, Betrice sidled closer.

"Linchpin." The searching hand pulled a gleaming
brass bolt about five inches long from the clutter within
the box.

"There. Wouldn't want to—"

"do without that!"

"Disaster!" The last was said happily, with some
relish.

"Check! Now for champagne!"

"And girls! Country girls and stealing kisses."

"So impressed, we won't have to steal 'em!"

Callie's brothers strode away from the strange thing.
They never noticed Betrice peeking inquisitively beneath the canvas drape.

*   *   *

"It isn't as though I've been gone for months, Zander," Callie said, trying to maintain a reasonable tone. While she spoke, she absently removed a glass of champagne from the grasp of Attie, replacing it with her own lemonade. "Surely you older boys can maintain order for more than a few days at a time!"

Lysander only shot her a dark look.

Callie crossed her arms. "There's no need to get huffy about it. I was bound to get married sooner or later!"

Lysander shrugged sullenly.

Callie rolled her eyes. "No matter what you say, what's done is done. I'm married now!"

Attie scowled at the lemonade and poured it into a potted palm. "You might have thought to marry someone in London," she pointed out. "Someone not *him.*" She gestured across the ballroom toward Ren with her empty glass. Drops of remaining lemonade flew out to land on Callie's lovely new gown. "We'll never see you."

Callie's teeth gritted together as she dabbed her hand-kerchief on the stains. "Less than a fortnight. It's been *less than a fortnight.*"

She needed a bit of water, before the lemon juice dis-colored the silk. She turned away from her brother and sister, tired of arguing with Lysander.

It wasn't actually an argument, of course, since Lysander wasn't one for using actual words. Callie was simply used to filling in the blanks herself.

Where was the blasted water?

It was nothing, really. Merely a snippet of conversa-tion heard between two stout women from the village. One, costumed as Queen Mary with a frilled lacy mask, inclined her head toward a round Queen Elizabeth with a red wig and spoke in hooting tones that carried well.

". . . my Sarah was visiting with her friend Penny,

who is stepping out with the butcher's boy, who told her that Sir Lawrence's new cook is an absolute *giant*!"

Giant.

Callie stopped short, her belly gone cold. Mr. Button's cook, a giant?

Then one of the servants began to beat out the stroke of twelve on a triangle. The chimes rang out over the ballroom. As one, the guests turned to fix their gazes on the mystery cart.

Callie turned with them and held her breath as Archie stepped forward to address them all.

Ren had frozen at the midnight chimes, then began to breathe again when Archie stepped forward, his arms flung wide.

"In days of old," he intoned, "when Daedalus flew and Perseus slayeth the minotaur!"

Ren did not see what Dade had to do with any of it, but the guests were enthralled and even Callie was looking a bit impressed. Additionally, if it kept everyone from remembering the dreaded unmasking, Ren would dance a jig around the thing himself.

Except that Iris was already doing so. Rather, she was wafting and drifting to and fro, waving her arms along with the music. The dance reminded him vaguely of a snake charmer.

He noticed that the pretty sister, Elektra, was near the musicians, her stance cajoling. Sure enough, a new tune had begun. It was eerie and dreamy and entirely inappropriate for any normal sort of dancing.

Archie was just getting started. "There lived a great creature, a magical being, the symbol of birth, renewal, and—" With a great sweeping bow, Archie drew their attention to the covered cart.

At which moment the twins, working as one, whipped

the cover from the large object just as the chimes struck twelve.

Gleaming metal, nearly ten feet high including the cart. It was an egg . . . of sorts. Or possibly a raindrop. Ren peered more closely at the richly embossed sides of the thing, all hammered out in brass and steel. Flames? Ah, it was a flame . . . raindrop . . . egg . . . thing.

The music swelled. Ren glanced over at the quartet and saw that Elektra had managed to inspire the tired musicians to new heights. Well, pretty girls did tend to have their way.

At a creaking sound, he turned back to the display before them all. The flame . . . egg . . . thing was spinning slowly. Ren could hear the resonant clunk-clunk of giant clockworks inside, beneath the music. It was as if the hunk of metal had a heartbeat of its own. That explained the music. Otherwise the thing would be making a severe racket.

Callie clapped her hands in delight. "It's moving!"

Her brother Orion, the arrogant-looking fellow in the spectacles, merely nodded. "Of course."

Ren relaxed. If Callie was happy then it didn't much matter that he found the entire thing foolish and time-wasting. Except that it was rather marvelous, in its mad way. The rotating flame-egg began to part in great triangles, as if the centrifugal force were spreading its shell.

Ren found himself just as captivated as the villagers, holding his breath to see what lay inside.

It was a bird. It was sculpted of brass and iron, each feather cut and applied separately. From where he stood, Ren could see the shining raw edges of the metal feathers.

The beak and claws were crimson and the eyes glowed like green jewels. It was an engineering marvel. Artistically it was hideous. The bird looked like a sort of eagle, except that it also looked a bit like a parrot had mated with an ostrich. The feet were extremely large, but Ren supposed they had to be to hold the entire metallic thing up. He smiled slightly at the pleasurable lunacy of it.

An egg hatching a bird. A lovely ten-foot egg hatching an ugly eight-foot bird.

"Oh, my. I always say, Why do, if you can overdo?"

Ren glanced down to see that Button had joined him. The little man had his hands clasped before him like a delighted child and his eyes were alight with mischief and glee.

Ren drew his brows together. "Was this some notion of yours?"

Button shook his head. "I invited milady's family because she seemed rather lonely for them. I did not ask them to provide entertainment, although perhaps I should have realized. They are quite notorious, you know."

Ren frowned. "Really? Notorious for what?"

"For being entirely mad, of course."

Of course. But then, Ren had already known that.

Button's smile widened as the bird began to shudder. "Oh, it's doing something!"

The great brass-feathered wings were lifting. Ren's brows rose with them, impressed in spite of himself. It really was a sight. The crowd gasped and a few people cheered.

Ren, who was a bit less enamored of the spectacle than most, spotted one of the those insufferable twins down behind the contraption, preparing to pull on some sort of lever behind the base of the egg.

At a signal from the opposite twin, he pulled sharply. There was a loud scrape and a puff and then a great *whoof!*

The bird was aflame.

"Oh, a phoenix." Button sent a sly glance in Ren's direction. "How . . . astute."

Ren watched the flaming bird and thought about his fine house which he had only recently begun to enjoy. Then he thought about it lying in piles of charred timber and rubble. He glanced across the room at Callie, who had drifted closer to where her family stood, watching the show. Another treasure he didn't want to see damaged.

"If you'll excuse me . . ." He didn't wait for Button's pardon, but began to make his way through the crowd to Callie's side.

Just as he was about to reach her, the bird made another creaking, groaning sound . . . and began to spin counter to the spin of the eggshell.

Chapter 30

Except that this new motion of the bird itself was no graceful rotation. The flaming phoenix swayed and lurched and ground around in an uneven spin. The squeal of abused metal rose above the soaring music. Even as Ren watched, he saw the twins glance at each other and then take simultaneous steps backward to disappear into the crowd.

Oh, hell.

Not far from him, he heard the little sister pipe up, her tone critical. "It didn't make that noise when we tested it at home."

The bird began to spin faster, and now the imbalance in its rotation turned it into a lurching pillar of flame. The wings rose higher in response to the speed. The grinding grew louder. The spinning became faster—and so off balance that it began to move the cart in a broken circle with the force of it.

Bloody hell! "Get back! Move away!" Ren shouted to his guests.

The bird began to gyrate wildly. Gobs of whatever the boys had used to make the wings burn began to shear off and fly through the air to splat onto the marble floor, creating a ring of fire around the monstrous shuffling contraption. With gasps of fear, the crowd shrank back, away from the hellish beast.

Ren found himself pinned behind the compressed throng, unable to reach Callie, unable to do anything but watch helplessly as the grinding noise became a hideous groaning and then parts began to fly.

A flaming feather skittered across the floor almost directly at Ren's position. The crowd melted back, finally giving Ren the room to push through. A shove here, a polite lifting and shifting of a stout matron there, a leap onto a potted plant, and then a step on one fellow's broad shoulder.

He landed on his feet onto the ballroom floor with only the circle of burning gobs between himself and the flame-spouting monstrosity.

And I thought my unmasking would be the height of terror this evening.

He began his assault by making a run for the table where sat a great cut-crystal bowl full of lemonade. There was a lump of ice still floating in the center. Ren picked up the entire weight of it and ran at the bird.

He slopped a large splash across the burning gobs, but it did little to dismay the happily burning wads of paraffin. He was forced to dance through them as best he could without catching his shoes afire, blessing the impulse that prompted Button to dress him in boots instead of flimsy dancing slippers like the other men. His ankles felt the heat but then he was through, dodging flying brass feathers like white-hot blades, to fling the giant bowl across the top of the bird's back.

It worked . . . in a way. Unfortunately, the cold liquid on the hot metal did something alarming to the clockworks inside. The spinning slowed, but the bird began to fling itself to and fro. The thing looked to be in a tantrum, groaning and flinging and tottering about. Ren hurriedly stepped back, away from the furiously lurching bird. At least it no longer spat fire, though areas still flickered with flames. Most of the paraffin had flung away to burn fitfully in little piles around the room. He needed something that would jam the gears and stop the motion. The thing was beginning to lose parts at an alarming rate, each missile a potential injury to one of Callie's guests.

His shame had prompted him to leave his walking stick in the shadows of the alcove. The ebony wood stick would likely be turned to sawdust by it anyway.

Something metal and long . . .

There were no sword-bearing military men among the guests tonight, unfortunately. There were swords above the fireplace in the library but that might as well be a mile off in the great house.

Then, through the haze of smoke, Ren spotted a giant fellow in a vast white apron emerging from the crowd across the room. The cook.

With a flick of his wrists, the giant secured two long knives from somewhere on his person and flung them in quick accurate succession.

The knives hit the bird full in the breast, right over its demonic clockwork heart, but even with the great force of the mighty giant's arm they merely dented the metal feathers and fell uselessly to the floor.

Ren rolled beneath a great slicing wing and retrieved one of the blades. Not a sword, but close enough.

But where? The knives had already proven the thing was well armored. Then he saw it. During the creature's gyrations, Ren spotted a hole high on the thing's back where there were no feathers. The clockworks were exposed in a clean square, as if a concealing panel had come off.

Of course. It couldn't be easy. Ren sighed. He was entirely certain that he was going to look ridiculous.

Then he backed away, watching for his opening.

The bird's progress had slowed to a groaning off-center twisting motion. Ren timed his moment . . . not yet . . . now.

He ran forward, ducked the triangle of shell flapping loosely at waist height, grabbed the bottom of the bird's gaping beak and used it to hurtle over a great slicing wing. He took a ringing blow to his bad thigh, but it threw him precisely where he needed to be, astride the great bird's back.

The hot metal hissed beneath his wrist when he laid it down on the bird. Ignoring the searing pain—except for lifting his groin away from the danger—Ren stared down into the alarmingly intricate and large iron gears and prayed that the long knife would stop their turning once and for all.

Raising the knife high with both hands, he plunged it down into the mass of churning metal as hard as he could.

The bird jolted and jerked and flung Ren right off onto the floor. He scrambled backward on his buttocks and hands, unable to tear his gaze from the shining metallic death throes. The phoenix groaned, its gears sprung, and made one last half turn before it rolled gently to a stop, the cart wheel bumping the toe of Ren's boot as if in playful hello. Oh, yes. Every bit as absurd as he'd feared.

The ballroom erupted into cheers.

Ren stood, winced at the pain in his thigh muscle, decided not to bother trying to dust off his smoking singed clothing . . . and then found ready hands there to do it for him.

When they stripped off his surcoat and waistcoat, he realized with a start that he was aflame. Then a hand reached out and yanked off his smoldering mask. He drew back in horror.

"You're on fire, man!"

Ren found himself gazing into eerily familiar blue eyes.

The tall man, dancing with the dark-haired woman, the man who'd kept his face away from Ren . . .

"Simon."

The blue-eyed man removed his mask and extended his hand. "Hello, Ren."

Ren stumbled backward, away from that hand. He hadn't wanted to believe it, even knowing what they were capable of.

"You dare come here? In secret? To my house?"

Simon opened his mouth, probably to explain such hideous betrayal of the privacy that had been promised him—a promise that had been broken, just so they could come and stare at their handiwork—

The rage was so intense, so sudden, Ren felt as though the very air of the ballroom had been poisoned. He was indeed surrounded. The past was all around him. Why was he being tortured with everything he'd lost?

Pain and betrayal, agony and loss—all fighting within him like a pack of wild dogs turning on each other. He couldn't breathe for the crushing weight of the memories, as fresh as yesterday, shimmering and sharp as if to prove to him that he could never outrun them.

His lungs burned, his heart pounded, his gut twisted. He had to get out—

Get out.

* * *

Breathless with alarm, Callie watched from a few feet away. When the first flaming blob of paraffin had sailed through the air, she'd instinctively run to yank Attie away from the fiery chaos and had watched Ren's wild triumph with her arms wrapped protectively around a reluctantly impressed Attie and a romantically swooning Iris.

As soon at the danger had passed, she'd released her charges and run for Ren, seeing the singed and smoldering coat, thinking he would burst into flame before she could reach him, thinking only about his danger now.

The strange man got to Ren first, pulling off the smoldering surcoat, whipping the smoking mask from his face . . .

It was Ren's evident rage that stopped Callie's headlong rush. His damaged face was so twisted with fury that she could barely see the Ren she knew in those livid features.

She saw him turn, then turn again, as his icy-blue gaze swept the crowd around him.

Oh, no.

It was the first time most of the villagers had ever seen his face.

Oh, please, she silently begged the crowd. *Please don't be foolish.*

That was like asking fish not to swim. And could she blame them? Her own reaction the first time had been no better.

Yet she could hear the indrawn breaths, the sounds of revulsion and distress. She could see the automatic flinching, the looking away, the horror and, yes, pity, which for Ren she knew was worse.

She felt each gasp, each gaze, each twitch hit him like

an arrow though the heart. She could feel the blows as if they struck her own flesh.

He turned again and this time his hurt, furious, betrayed gaze fixed upon the clump of Worthingtons standing nearby.

Of course, her father chose this moment to give an uncomfortable laugh and clap her brothers Cas and Poll on their respective shoulders. " 'Why, this is very midsummer madness!' "

Ren fixed Papa with all the fury and hurt and betrayal in his soul burning in his eyes.

Iris opened her mouth. *Oh, Mama, not now.*

"Twelfth Night," Iris announced gleefully. "Act three, scene four!"

"Get out!"

Ren raised his hand and pointed toward the door. "Out. Of. My. House! *Now!*"

"Oh, no!" Callie started forward. "Darling, no! They meant no harm—"

He whirled on her, his gaze too shrouded in dark emotion to even see her clearly, she knew.

"You!" He waved a wild hand at the smoking, scorched, and tattered ballroom. "How can you even stand to look at them after what they've done?"

She went very still. "Because they are my family." She said quietly. *As you are. My family. My heart.*

His eyes narrowed, focusing that brilliant burning gaze upon her and her alone. "Then you should know that they shall never again pass through those doors. Ever!"

"You cannot banish my family."

"I can and I will." He cast his gaze around the room, for some reason focusing on some of the servants as well as the stately couples in the Royal Handful. "I can banish whomever I like."

Callie raised her chin. "Ren, don't—"

His furious, icy gaze shot back to her. "If you prefer your preposterous, insane family, then feel free to join them in their departure."

Oh, no. No, darling, please . . .

She said nothing. What was there to say? He'd forced her hand, publicly and cruelly. One heart could not be torn in two. She turned on her heel and walked back to her mother, taking Iris by the hand and leading her from the ballroom. Worthingtons fell into step all around her, like a wall of love between her and pain.

Unfortunately, even family solidarity did nothing to shield her from the agony in her own heart.

Ren watched Callie's exit with shock and disbelief hammering at him, turning his hot rage into something icy and solid in his belly.

Blinded by it, he turned and strode away, away from the place where his heart lay in mangled pieces on the floor, next to the smoking remains of the great brass phoenix.

Chapter 31

Callie paused in the entrance hall of Amberdell Manor and the Worthingtons gathered in a circle about her. Iris babbled on. "I know I brought the purple cloak, dear, just ask the nice butler who let us in where he put it."

Archie, slightly more aware than his wife, took Callie's hand and patted it a little too hard. "Now, now, dear. We'll be home again by the morrow and you can forget all about this terrible place and that terrible fellow."

Aunt Clemmie wasn't quite so kind. "The man ought to be shot! I've my tiger-hunting musket in the carriage. I'll hang his head on my wall, see if I don't!"

Archie nodded sadly. "'He's a rank weed . . . and we must root him out.'"

Iris waved a hand. "*The Life of King Henry the Eighth,* act five, scene one!"

Elektra, for once with nothing to say, merely wrapped Attie up in a slightly too-large cloak and took her outside. Cas and Poll, silent and shamefaced for perhaps the first time in their lives, followed. Orion and Lysander stayed back, flanking Callie protectively but offering no sort of solace. Not their style, she supposed dully.

Mama carried blissfully on. "But didn't he look dashing, astride that flaming beast? Just like Saint George slaying the dragon!"

Dade leaned down to Callie. "I ought to've shot him when I had the chance," he said. "I'm sorry I ever left you behind."

Still debating Ren's heroism with all the practice of decades of sisterhood, Clemmie and Iris left, having found the purple cloak—which Iris donned inside out.

Papa had not yet let go of Callie's hand. "Let's go home, dear. You'll see. It will be just like you never left."

Callie wasn't sure precisely when she'd decided to stay with Ren forever.

Perhaps it was this moment, right now, even in the face of his fury and fear and desolation.

Perhaps because of it. She could not allow him to be right about her, about the world, about life. She would not.

"Go on, Dade, Papa. I shall be fine where I am."

Dade turned to her, aghast. "You cannot mean that! Stay with that madman? You heard him! He had no regard for you—no family feeling at all! How can you choose him over your own family?"

Callie gazed evenly at her elder brother, whom she had adored all her life. "You don't understand. I am not choosing him over you. I am choosing *me* over you." She kissed Dade on the cheek, then Papa. "Tell Mama I shall write soon." Then she turned away from them and walked quite serenely back into the smoking debacle that was her first ball as Lady Porter of Amberdell Manor.

Button surveyed the empty and echoing ballroom one last time. It was well into the next day and he'd yet to offer any commentary on the events of the evening before.

This worried Cabot. Button without commentary was like Button without air to breathe.

"Sir, the er . . . staff has mostly gone. They did what they could without paint and plaster. There's nothing more we can do here."

Button gazed at the ring of scorched marble in the center of the ballroom. "Have you ever seen a battle-field, Cabot?"

"No, fortunately."

Button sighed. "You have now."

Cabot latched his hands behind his back, carefully not looking at his master, yet entirely aware of him all the same. "May I ask, sir . . . who lost?"

Button looked away from the damage at last, casting a look of rueful weariness over his shoulder at Cabot.

"I suppose we might try to gather a few hours of sleep at the inn."

"Before we set out for London?"

Button said nothing for a long moment. "Do you think he knows that she didn't leave?"

Cabot, who was heartily sick of all things Porter, only snorted.

"Do not mock what you do not understand, young fel-low." Button, his romantic soul yet uncured, waved a hand to dismiss Cabot's scorn. "He was so close . . ."

Cabot tried again. "Shall I pack our things to return to London today?"

Button tilted his head back and gazed at the mostly sputtered-out chandeliers above them with his eyes nar-rowed. "We did."

Cabot frowned. "We did what?"

"We lost the battle." Then he turned to send Cabot a gaze with a glimmer of revived mischief held within it. "But we may yet win the war!"

* * *

If Dade had just finished the job in the first place, none of this would have happened. Callie would be back home where she belonged and all would be right with the world.

Atalanta Worthington had never been much interested in the out-of-doors—except of course in the capture and identification of poisonous creatures and plants that made one itch—but she had become an accomplished rider out of pure survival. One never knew when Cas or Poll might decide to put a burr under one's saddle, or emit a shrill whistle guaranteed to startle the most somnolent mount into a frenzied gallop.

Attie did not believe in going unarmed—hence the array of toxic defenses she kept at hand—but the bundle in her arms was a new and intimidating weight. She raised her chin and quieted the sickening flutter in her belly. Callie needed rescuing and not one of her brothers, not even heroic Dade, was willing to do the job properly.

So, tucked and stuffed and rolled into Lysander's country tweeds, for Zander was still thinner than any of the other boys, Attie made her way into the rickety stable far behind the Wincombes' house. Friends of the family, Papa had called them. They'd all stayed the night there before dressing for the ball . . . yesterday?

Worthingtons didn't bother with excess servants so it was with easy confidence that Attie saddled and bridled Dade's beautiful gelding, Icarus. Not that Dade had ever allowed her to take Icky out by herself before. In fact, it took some grunting and hopping and sprawling—and an overturned water bucket—before Attie found herself upright on Icky's broad back. Just one more quick adjustment to her position—facing the proper direction was imperative to her mission—and Attie was ready to ride the twenty miles back to Amberdell Manor.

Chapter 32

Callie opened her eyes. For a short but happy moment, she thought about nothing at all. She'd had a nice dream but it drifted away, leaving her mind quite empty of anything but thoughts of sleepy warmth and comfort.

Then the faint acrid odor of burned silk teased at her nostrils and the entire awful evening came crashing back down, unrelieved by a night's distance.

It was every bit as horrific and humiliating in memory as it was in the moment. Worse, perhaps, because in memory there was no hope. It had happened. She cast a wary glance at the sumptuous ruin of her gown lying across a chair. It, too, was beyond saving.

It now remained to see if her marriage could be. If her new life could be. If Ren's feelings for her could be.

Those feelings, those poor, newborn, pale sprouts of love . . . at least, she'd hoped they were. It might have been simple friendship . . . and lovemaking.

Yesterday she'd wanted more. Now she would be glad to have back even half of what she'd had.

She'd not dared to seek him out last night after she'd ushered the many guests from the hall with slightly limping dignity. Even Button's stately friends had taken their leave, thankfully. The house had at last gone silent and still once more, as empty as the first night she'd seen it.

She rose and dressed in her old blue muslin. In her excitement over her Persephone gown, she'd forgotten to ask Mr. Button about the rest of her order. It hardly seemed to matter now. Her things might yet come from home anyway, now that she'd thrown her family away.

Mama would understand. Papa would take a little longer. Dade . . . oh, dear, and Attie . . . Callie felt the burn of tears and shook it off fiercely. She was a Porter and Porters never surrendered, not even when bleeding and dying on some filthy dock!

As she searched for her other shoe, she saw the bowl of pearls on her vanity. She picked it up and began to lay out the pearls in a line across the inlaid surface. Then she fetched her small sewing box and began to string the pearls.

As she strung each pearl, it was as though she remembered the very moment she'd received it.

This was the first night together as man and wife.

This was when I took him in my mouth and knew he was mine.

Each pearl was a memory, a moment, a step on the road that had brought her and Ren here . . . wherever here was.

After three quarters of an hour she sat back blinking her eyes to reset her focus. One hundred pearls. There remained a few more pearls rolling about in the bottom of the bowl, but Callie took a dismal enjoyment in the nice round amount of a full hundred. She stroked the long strand with a tender touch, smiling with damp eyes. One hundred perfectly matched pearls.

Some things belonged together.

Today was her tenth day in the Cotswolds.

Ten days . . . a lifetime.

She heard uneven footsteps in the hall outside her room. As she listened, they paused outside her door. She held her breath but the steps moved on after only a moment. If she meant to stay—and she bloody well did!—she was going to have to do something about Ren's tendency to retreat.

He doesn't wish to see me.

Well, that's too bloody bad for him.

Callie ran down the stairs shoving her arms into her spencer.

Outside the day was windy but clear. Ren was nearly out of sight, luckily heading up the hill to the northeast. Callie ran for a bit, but his legs were too long and his stride too furious. Soon Callie had to slow down. She walked, pressing a hand to her side to still the stitch there.

She crested the hill and saw Ren walking down along one of the dry stone walls bordering the fields. Callie called out to him, but the winds caught her voice and carried it away. She trotted down the hill, picking up her skirts again and calling his name.

He turned at last and watched her stumble down the slope toward him.

When Callie came closer, she slowed. He looked quite wild. Without his hood in the daylight, he stood waiting for her with his long hair whipping about his face and his lean form tight with something she'd never seen before.

"I—I wished you had stopped to greet me this morning," she began cautiously. "I heard you go out. I thought that . . ."

"I thought you left."

She frowned at him. "I never had any intention of leaving with them. I simply wanted them to go knowing I was not upset with them."

"Not upset? What ball did you attend last night?"

Callie didn't defend her kin. She was too glad he was speaking to her, though she kept her distance from that feral light in his eyes. "Ren," she said gently. "Come inside. I am cold. I'll make some tea . . ."

She trailed off. He wasn't responding to her at all. "Ren, darling, what is it?"

"You turned your back on me and walked out. I was there, alone, *facing* everyone."

Callie's belly went cold. She pressed her fingertips to her lips. "Oh, Ren. I—"

He half turned away, hiding his scarred face. "I realized something last night. You didn't choose me."

Callie shook her head. "No, Ren, I told you—I stayed! I did choose you."

"You chose to stay . . . this time. But you didn't choose me—I happened to you, like the flash flood on a bridge. The bargain, the marriage, that was you saving your family from the aftermath of that flood." He looked up at the sky and gave a bitter laugh. "I will never be more than the lesser of two evils, will I?" He turned cold eyes upon her. "That is, until the day when I am not. What will your choice be then, Calliope?"

She took a step forward. "No, I—"

She was in motion when the bullet hit her full in the back. At first she thought someone pushed her from behind. She fell forward, and then she rolled down the grassy hillside, coming to rest in Ren's arms.

She looked up at him. "I fell . . ."

She blinked at him; he was shouting at her . . . but she couldn't hear him for the humming in her ears. She lifted a hand to the beloved ruin of his face. "I choose . . ."

Callie went limp in his arms. Ren shook her but her head flopped limply on her neck. Good God, his hands were covered in blood.

He'd thought he'd heard a shot just before she fell, but it had been carried away. He sent a glance around the hills for the rifleman, but he didn't even care about catching the bastard.

God, so much blood.

At the Wincombes' house, Elektra Worthington dropped the bed skirt and climbed to her feet. "She isn't under here," she called out. Across the hall, Castor let out a bellow. "Nor here!"

They met in the hall. Cas's habitually cheerful expression was now grim and tight. "Where else would she be? It's not as though this is our house. She hasn't been here since she was a an infant."

Ellie shook her head. "I barely remember this place! She wouldn't be on the grounds, would she?"

Poll joined them. "I checked the grounds. Dade is canvassing the village. Lysander thinks she's gone back to Amberdell."

Ellie frowned. "But how? I know she's brilliant and bloody-minded, but she is still a twelve-year-old girl! What coachman would take her?"

Cas and Poll exchanged wary glances. Ellie, ever alert to the twins and their mischief, pinned them with equal glares. "Speak."

Cas shrugged. "It was only a game."

Poll nodded. "She didn't come to any harm."

"Although we told her never to try it on her own."

"Still . . ."

Ellie bit back the urge to scream. "What?"

"It was just a ride we cadged."

"On an old freight wagon."

"Just out of the city a bit."

"And then back, of course—"

"It was just a day out—"

"But—"

"You idiots taught her how to stow away on a freight wagon?" Ellie frowned. "Back to see Callie?"

Then she smiled. "Well, that's simple enough. Those things travel much more slowly than our carriage. She'll still be on the road to Amberdell. We can catch up to her easily."

"No we can't." Dade entered the hallway. "She didn't take a freight wagon, she took Icarus."

Impressed, Cas let out a low whistle before Ellie's glare shut him up.

Dade ran frantic fingers through his hair. "It gets worse." He gazed grimly at his siblings. "She took Aunt Clemmie's hunting musket."

Up on the hillside near Amberdell Manor, Attie let the musket drop from her numbed hands. Callie?

Attie had been so focused on aiming downhill against the wind, that she'd never even seen Callie approach. When Porter had finally stopped moving, Attie had rejoiced and closed one eye to gauge the shot better. It wasn't until after she'd pulled the trigger that she'd seen a figure in blue step into her narrowed view.

Then it was too late to call back the bullet. Carried downhill, aimed and fired by a good marksman, it would not have hit her. But Attie had had very little practice with Aunt Clemmie's favorite firearm.

And now Callie lay dead, limp and bloody in that Porter's arms. Attie began to shake. She'd shot Callie.

Callie was dead.

She'd not thought it through, she realized dimly. Everyone said it all the time.

Elektra had told Cas and Poll, "I'm going to kill the both of you."

Dade had cursed Porter's name. "That man needs a good killing."

Aunt Clemmie: "I'll hang his head on my wall!"

It was just what people said.

Somehow, Attie had not realized, not all the way deep inside her, that when one killed someone . . . then they were dead. Dead was forever. Dead was never, ever coming home. Dead was a great eternal hole ripped into a little sister's heart.

Callie was dead.

Attie's knees gave way. She fell to all fours and retched up the buns she'd stolen for her breakfast.

When she was done, she shakily sat up and wiped her mouth with the back of her hand. She couldn't bear to look but she did.

Callie was gone. Porter must have carried her away. Back to his big nasty house. Didn't he know that Callie liked to be outside?

But Callie didn't. Callie was dead and she would never like anything ever again.

Attie crept down the hill, leaving the beastly musket where it lay. She hoped it rusted into dust. It was easy to find the spot. The grass was all trampled and mashed . . . and there was blood, glowing red and hot on the green of the new grass.

At the sight of it, Attie stumbled back, falling down and scrambling backward until she couldn't see the blood anymore.

Callie is dead.

Attie stumbled to her feet and began to run.

But no matter how fast she fled, she couldn't escape it.

I killed Callie.

Chapter 33

Ren lurched and stumbled and pumped his aching legs as fast as they could go through the high grass. Back up the hill and back down again. He ran hard, clutching Callie's limp body to his chest, unmindful of the agony in his shoulder, uncaring about the hot lightning shooting up his once-broken leg with every step. The warmth of Callie's blood soaked through his sleeves. Too much. Too fast.

She's leaving me.

He ran faster.

Yet when he got to the house, he realized his fatal mistake. There was no help there. The manor was deserted—he'd made sure of it. He carried Callie inside and brought her into the first room he thought of, the front parlor, where she and her family had come the first night.

He tenderly placed her on one of the sofas, then stripped off his bloodstained coat and covered her with it.

She lay white and still. He tried to feel for her pulse but his own was pounding too hard. He couldn't feel anything.

No.

"Callie! No!"

"Oh, my God."

Ren jerked his head up to see a miracle. In the open doorway stood a young man in elegant clothing, carting an armload of flat dress boxes.

The fellow tossed the boxes aside, spilling shimmering silks, stockings, and shoes in a fountain over the side of a chair. He knelt next to Ren.

"What happened?"

Ren shook his head. What did it matter? "I think . . . a shot—perhaps a poacher . . . or someone . . . someone . . ." He couldn't speak.

If he'd only stopped and spoken to her this morning, she wouldn't have followed him out. If he'd only stopped the first time he heard her call his name, before he crested the hill. If he'd only kept far, far away from the lilting voice in the dark hallways of his hell.

"I think . . . I think she's gone . . ." His throat closed.

Cabot pushed Sir Lawrence's bloody shaking hands away and felt for Lady Porter's pulse. "She lives." He stood and turned to go.

Sir Lawrence clutched at his wife's hands. "Get help—there's—somewhere in the village, there . . . is there a doctor close by?"

Cabot turned and gazed at the man everyone else wanted to save. Personally he couldn't imagine why. "Help is closer than you think," he said shortly and left.

This would not do. Cabot would not allow Lady Porter to die, for it might upset Button and Cabot couldn't allow that.

Porter didn't deserve her . . . but then again, being deserving didn't always get one what one wanted, either.

She was swimming. Callie moved her arms and legs in perfectly even strokes. She could thank Dade for that, for thinking a girl needed to know how to swim as properly as a man, not simply splash about in the shallows afraid to wet her hair.

The water was warm, as soothing to her skin as bathwater.

Lovely.

Then something happened to her memory. She forgot the stroke, became tangled and fouled in her own limbs. With a frantic gasp she slipped beneath the surface of the water. It boiled about her, scalding her. Then she was under the frozen Serpentine—but this time when she tried to find the hole where she fell in, it was gone. She pounded the thick ice with childish hands. She couldn't get out. She couldn't breathe. She couldn't wake up.

I want to wake up. Dade will be so worried. Mama and Papa and . . .

Ren.

Ren was frantic for her. She couldn't remember why. She only knew that she had to fight this heavy weight of unconsciousness. It was pulling her down, far down beneath the surface. Above her was the icy light, but it only wavered and flowed out of her reach.

Wake up.

Wake up now.

"Calliope? Calliope, you must wake up now."

"Lady Porter. Calliope. Can you hear me?"

Callie could hear him. He was very insistent, this stranger. Annoying fellow. He was disturbing her when she needed to pay attention. She needed to wake up.

Oh. Right. She followed the line of that voice, clinging to it as she was drawn up and up, and the world brightened about her and she was blinking up at a man she'd never seen before.

He smiled approvingly at her. "Excellent. Lady Porter, do you know where you are?"

She looked around the room. *Amberdell.*

"Yes. Very good."

Did I speak? Odd.

"Yes, I know you must feel quite strange. I gave you laudanum whilst I removed the musket ball. It was very important that you kept still during surgery."

Musket ball? I drowned. I don't like this stranger with his nonsense. Where is Ren?

"I'm here, Callie."

Someone squeezed her hand. She rolled her head to see Ren at her bedside, her hand lost in his two big ones. *Oh, good. Ren. I love Ren.*

He ducked his head for a moment.

She looked back at the doctor. *I don't love the doctor.*

The doctor nodded. "No more you should, with all the painful things I've done to you today. You've lost a great deal of blood, my lady. Still, sometimes that can be a blessing, washing potential infection from the wound. Either way, best to lie about for a week or more, build up your strength."

No. I don't like him. He's being much too familiar, standing by my bed. That isn't proper at all. What will Ren think?

"It's all right, Callie." She looked back at Ren. He held her hand pressed to his ruined cheek. "Listen to the doctor, darling."

Well, if Ren said so. She needed to talk to him so she wanted the doctor gone. There was something she'd meant to tell him . . .

"Doctor, if I might speak to you for a moment?"

The room was coming into clearer focus. Ren shouldn't worry so. He knew how she felt about doctors. Idiots, all of them.

But the fear in Ren's voice was real. And the doctor

was talking again, speaking quietly to Ren, saying words like "infection" and "blood loss."

And worst of all, "invalid."

And Callie was suddenly very afraid that her dream foretold that she might never come up for air again.

Ren walked the doctor out politely enough, but he was filled with agonizing worry for Callie, not to mention self-loathing for his own past wallowing about his broken body. He might be scarred, but he was still much more fit than Callie was at the moment.

On their way, they passed Betrice carrying in a bowl of broth to tempt Callie to eat.

The doctor nodded to her. "Mrs. Nelson."

"Doctor." Betrice smiled distantly and hurried on to Callie. Ren was happy that she wouldn't be left alone.

The doctor inclined his head in the direction Betrice had taken. "A wonderful woman, Mrs. Nelson. I don't know what the village will do without her."

Ren was preoccupied with Callie's condition. "Why would they have to?"

The doctor regarded him for a long moment "Sir Lawrence, you have lived here for a number of years, but you know nothing about these people."

Ren almost missed the warning in the man's voice but then old habits kicked in. His attention snapped to. "Meaning?"

The doctor pursed his lips. "The heir to Amberdell was found at last, but people had come to think of Henry Nelson as master of Amberdell. And his wife as lady of the manor." He sighed wearily. "Country people don't care for change. They care even less for change for the worse. This poacher . . . did you see him? Are you sure he was not someone local?"

Ren stared at the doctor for a long moment. This was

something he'd not taken into account. To him, the village was a source of staples and the occasional labor. He'd never thought of it as a source of danger . . . but a village was made of people and people were bloody dangerous.

"The ball was my wife's attempt to remedy just that."

The doctor nodded. "From what I hear it nearly worked." The man drew his greatcoat about him and put on his hat. "Sir Lawrence, you are master of Amberdell. I cannot tell you what to do. But I suggest you investigate the local populace."

Ren frowned. "There have been other attempts . . . but this is the first overt attack." He couldn't put his finger on it, but there was something different about this one. There was true fury powering that musket ball.

The man left, but the thoughts he planted in Ren's mind did not. He ventured thoughtfully back upstairs to Callie's room, not truly noticing Betrice as he passed her on the stair.

Betrice stood in the shadows near the landing. Dr. Snow was an intelligent man. A man who knew every soul in the village. From the man's tone, he knew precisely who was doing these terrible things to Callie. Or thought he did.

Betrice grabbed her wrap from the chair by the door and scurried out into the damp evening.

Ren sat on the edge of Callie's bed. She slept on her side, limp and pale. He reached a tender finger to stroke a twisting coil of hair away from her forehead. She despaired the insistent wave of her hair. Ren loved it, loved the way it clung to his fingers, loved the spring of it, like the spring of Callie herself.

His chest ached as he recalled her bounding about the

countryside and playing the fool with her silly dance in the lane. Would she ever dance again?

Invalid. Forever tied to her bed, forever weak and ill . . .

Whatever the doctor thought, Ren knew that the bullet had been meant for him. Callie had simply been in the way.

She was always in the way. She stood between him and the solitude he'd longed for. She'd stubbornly planted herself, chin raised and arms akimbo, in the way of his dark and bitter decline.

"It's bloody annoying," he whispered to her. "That's what it is."

He bent to kiss her forehead. Closing his eyes, he willed all of his own stubborn desire to cling to life into her.

I love Ren.

Her laudanum-inspired words had gone through him like her silly sword. She couldn't. It was impossible.

"I love you, Callie." He said it because she would never recall it.

From outside the window, Ren heard the clatter of hooves on the drive and the rattling squeaks of a carriage pushed past its limits. He left Callie's side and strode to the window to see.

Below him on the drive, an elderly carriage pulled by elderly horses had pulled to a stop before the manor. Even as he watched, the doors opened to spill the bloody Worthingtons to the ground like a pumpkin spilling seeds.

They were all shouting something. Ren could see Dade and Mr. Worthington helping Callie's mother down from the carriage, even as the woman threw back her head and yodeled a name.

"Attie!"

* * *

Ren had no time for Worthington antics. When he rounded the lot of them into the front parlor, he baldly told them that Callie had been shot and would they please take their exhausting selves back to London as soon as possible?

They gazed at him in horror, then turned to one another.

The hubbub was astonishing. Ren was tempted to lock them into the parlor and shove food under the door once a day. Bloody zoo.

Finally he could bear no more. They were going to wake Callie with their commotion!

"Shut it!"

His roar shocked them all into silence. Dade snarled, but when his mother began to speak again, he put his hand over hers. Then he turned to Ren. "Tell us what happened to Callie."

Ren did so, but he could tell there was something they knew that he didn't. "The doctor left an hour ago. The musket ball was removed, but—" He could scarcely bear to say the words out loud. "There was a great loss of blood, and a terrible risk of infection—"

The sister, Elektra, gasped, her hands to her face. The dark brother, Lysander, said nothing, but his eyes said he knew what it meant, what a musket ball could do to a body. The twins seemed to finally be shaken from their playful attitudes.

The scholarly one, Orion, stepped forward. "I would like to speak to this doctor."

"Rion," Dade warned.

"I want to know, Dade." Orion held Ren's gaze. "I know a great deal about human anatomy. If this fellow is any good, he won't mind running me through his technique."

Ren wouldn't mind a second opinion himself. He

nodded. "He lives in the village, in the house just past the church, with black shutters."

Orion turned and left without another word. Unfortunately, he was the only Worthington who practiced such economy. Dade turned to quiet his family again.

Ren was losing patience. "There is something you aren't telling me."

Dade opened his mouth, but the sister interrupted him. "Sir Lawrence, please, let me take Mama up to see Callie."

Ren could scarcely keep Callie's mother from her side, knowing how Callie loved the silly woman. He nodded shortly and the two women left.

At this rate, he'd be rid of all the Worthingtons soon.

He gazed at Dade. The fellow met his eyes reluctantly.

"It is Attie, our youngest sister. She is missing."

Ren frowned. "That is indeed terrible news."

Dade looked away and ran a hand through his hair. From the way it stood, he'd been doing it for hours . . . but he'd not known of Callie's condition until just a moment ago.

Attie . . . Callie had told him that Attie was an eccentric, fierce child, able beyond her years, a tremendous handful. Of course, the words Callie used were "brilliant" and "creative," but Ren was learning to decipher the Worthington native tongue.

Ren had only seen the girl once, at the ball the night before. She'd glared at him from across the room, intent upon him like a predator on its prey. He'd laughed off the hunted feeling she'd given him, but now—

He swore. "I knew that musket ball was meant for me."

Chapter 34

Attie crept into a small stone hut she found in the middle of a great pasture. It was nothing but four walls and a roof, with rough holes in the walls for ventilation. It smelled of sheep.

There were a few piles of moldy straw on the floor. Attie gathered them into one and snuggled down into it. She wanted a fire, and she knew how to make one with nothing but a willow bow and a shoelace—Lysander had taught her how the soldiers did it when they had no flint and steel—but even if she could hide the light, the smoke would be visible. That was the last thing Attie wanted to be . . . visible.

The spring evening was damp and the shed stank. It was only what she deserved.

Callie is dead.

Maybe she could live here, in this hut. She could kill a sheep when she got hungry. She could even make it look like wolves, so no one would know there was a person living here.

She imagined herself butchering a sheep and shuddered. Red blood on green grass. Tears cut clean paths through the dirt on her cheeks, but she refused to sob. She didn't deserve to cry out her guilt and fear, then to fall into the deep childish sleep of relief.

Callie is dead.

She would sit here, in the cold and stink, and know that her family would never forgive her, just as she could never forgive herself.

She only wished she hadn't thought about wolves.

Ren leaned forward in his saddle and contemplated the small patch of hillside he could see by the light of his lantern.

There was where Callie had fallen. Ren could still see the wild mess he'd made of the area, flinging himself down by her side.

There was the wide trail of crushed grass he'd left, carrying her back to the house with his awkward run.

Too much blood.

He shook off the memory and forced himself to focus. There was little to see in the dark, so he closed his eyes and reconstructed the area from memory. The hill behind him was not much more than a rise between this little vale and the house.

The hill to the north of him was much higher and topped with a flat expanse, like a natural barrow. If he were a sniper, he would choose that hill.

But she's only a little girl.

A Worthington girl. So Ren turned his gelding and headed up the hill to the north.

Callie's brothers had protested mightily his leaving them behind. Ren hadn't bothered to explain the lack of mounts or his own need to ride rather than trust his damaged body to sustain the search on foot. He'd simply walked out to the stables and saddled his horse. The bloody Worthingtons could muddle through on their own.

At the top of the hill he found a place where the grass had been flattened by a small body. The musket and powder sack lay abandoned nearby. Ren picked up the musket and blinked at its antiquity. The little idiot was lucky the thing hadn't blown up in her face.

Callie wasn't.

Ren lay down upon the matted grass and pointed the musket downhill. It was a difficult shot. She'd come bloody close to hitting him, though if Callie hadn't been there the shot would have gone wide by a foot.

With only darkness around him, he could not see down into the vale. He closed his eyes once more and imagined.

He hated the man below. The man had ruined everything, had broken his family, had stolen the closest thing he had to a real mother.

He aimed the musket, opening one eye, seeing before him the green and gold vale in the spring. The man was walking, limping, fleeing the only true happiness he'd ever known—

Ren shook his head and refocused. The man was limping across the vale, his coat flapping open in the wind. The wind had been gusting, he remembered. It had swept Callie's voice away, muting it to the cry of a bird.

A windy day, downhill, at this distance . . .

Ren revised his opinion of the girl's skill. He was bloody lucky to be alive.

So was Callie.

But he had not died. The girl had watched from above while he'd lifted Callie into his arms and run for the manor.

She had to know her sister still lived, didn't she?

Ren remembered how much blood there had been. The grass had been dripping in it, burning like fire in his memory. Callie had lain so white and still. He'd thought she was dead himself.

So . . . he closed his eyes. His gift, once upon a time, in the service of the Crown, had been infiltration. He'd been able to play the parts required of him by using his imagination, placing himself into the fabricated life of a man willing to be seduced by the enemy.

Now he placed himself into the mind of a half-wild, brilliant child who believed she'd murdered her own sister.

He opened his eyes and stood, leaning on the musket as he gazed into the black distance outside the circle of lantern light.

He knew where he would go.

Attie lay curled into a hollow in the straw, listening. There was something out there in the dark.

Rip. Rip.

Breathless and terrified, she scowled fiercely at the stone wall in the direction of the sound. She couldn't bear not knowing.

She shifted to a crouch and approached the wall low and small. There was a hole a little more than halfway up. She knew she could just look through it if she stood on her toes.

Rip. Rip.

Standing as tall as she could, she peered through the window, if one wanted to call it that when it was really just a few missing stones. It was entirely dark outside. She stared until she felt as though her eyes were coming out of her head, but—

Then she heard the unmistakable snort of a horse. It was just some old pasture nag, ripping the grass up bite by bite. Attie relaxed down onto her heels. "Go on now," she hissed at the annoying beast. "Or I shall eat you!"

"There's no need to threaten him. He'd like nothing more than to go home to his nice warm stable and eat real oats."

Attie spun around just as a lantern came into view. "Ow!" She held up a hand before her stunned vision and backed rather painfully up against the stone wall.

"My apologies, Miss Worthington." The light fáded somewhat, but Attie's night vision had been spoiled by multicolored blurs that danced across her sight.

She kept the wall to her back. "Who is there?"

"It's Porter."

He'd come to kill her for taking Callie, just as she'd meant to kill him. Attie felt sick and terrified, and deep inside, relieved. When one had nowhere to go, death seemed like as good a destination as any.

Callie is dead.

The time had come to say it out loud. "Callie is—"

"Callie is alive. She is in her bed at the manor. The doctor has come and gone and he says she shall live."

Attie couldn't absorb the words. *Callie is alive.*

Alive meant Callie was still here, still on earth, still breathing and talking and—

Attie clapped her hands over her face. The sobs that she had coldly kept at bay all day tore a path up her throat and spilled out here, in this stinking hut, in front of blasted Porter!

She fought them, but they came over and over, harsh tearing noises. She hated the sound. She couldn't bear the pressure of holding them in any longer. She dropped to her knees and she cried in front of Porter. She never cried. Ever.

After a while, she could breathe again. She dried the tears and mucus from her face with her sleeve. Drawing deep breaths, trying to steady herself, she leaned back against the wall and stuck her chilled, aching legs out before her.

Something landed in her lap. She looked down to spy a large square of white linen. Fine. She would ruin his handkerchief instead. She picked it up and blew her nose with great energy. Then she offered it back.

"Consider it yours," Porter said dryly.

Attie folded her arms and gazed at the man who had ruined her life. He sat opposite her, even to his extended legs and folded arms. The lantern sat just outside the door, casting a glow inside but not lighting either of them directly. Attie was grudgingly grateful for that. He'd heard her sobs, but that was somehow less humiliating than being watched.

She lifted her chin. Might as well get it over with. "You're supposed to be the one with the musket ball in you."

Ren found himself gazing with great sympathy at the little monster. He knew what it was like to fear losing everyone. It broke his heart that she had been pushed to this point. No child should ever have to take life and death into their own hands. It didn't help that when filthy and rumpled, she looked more like Callie than ever, though there were already signs that the child would someday be a vastly more beautiful woman than either of her sisters.

If the rotten little beast lived that long.

He ought to leave her here and send one of her Worthington clan to fetch her. He knew nothing of children. Then again, he was fairly certain that Atalanta Worthington only bore a passing resemblance to a normal child. Good Lord, the names these people pinned on their unsuspecting offspring.

" 'Attie' doesn't suit you. I believe I shall call you 'Rattie.' "

The look of horror on her face was laughable. "You will not!"

Ren gazed contemplatively at the ceiling. "Rattie, you tried to murder me. I believe that gives me the right to call you whatever I wish."

She struggled with that for a long moment. As he suspected, she felt terrible about injuring her sister. On the other hand, she seemed to have no regrets about him, other than that she had missed the shot.

"Your family came to Amberdell looking for you."

She looked away, sullen to the core.

"Your mother is very upset."

Sullen stare. Sniffle.

Ren was very tired. He'd had a long and terrifying day. If he thought he would survive unscathed, he would toss the pint-sized murderess over his shoulder and cart her back to the bosom of her bedlamite kin.

Callie loved this beastly little person. Callie would want her miniature dignity preserved, he was sure. So, although he'd hardly spoken to a soul in years, it was up to him to coax the malicious urchin home.

"I killed a man once. I sent his own pike through his eye."

He found himself impaled by her glinting eyes. Right. Blood and gore got her undivided attention.

"Of course, that was after he'd already killed me."

She sent him a disbelieving sneer.

Ren poked a finger at the shoulder of his surcoat, right above the starburst of the entry-wound scar. "He drove it right through me first. I wrenched it out and turned it about. I sent it right through his thick skull." He still occasionally relived the sickening sound of that blow, but he kept that detail to himself. "Then I died."

"You didn't die."

Ren met her gaze. "I died. Then I was resurrected by some well-meaning bastard doctor."

"Doctors are idiots."

Ren snorted to hear Callie's derisive remark mimicked in such lilting childish tones. "So I hear."

"Then you lived in spite of everything."

"No. I stayed almost dead for many weeks. Months, really. I don't exactly know. I was somewhere else."

Now he had her. "Where were you?"

"I can't describe it." He'd never tried, not to anyone. "It was dark and cold. So cold I was always numb. I liked being numb."

Attie nodded. "Numb is better than . . ."

Better than feeling the pain of killing a beloved sister.

"Then I woke up and I wasn't numb anymore. I was deeply upset about that. Then I found a mirror. There was further upset, as you can imagine."

She nodded again. "You look like a doll I had once. Cas and Poll burned her in the dining room fire and Ellie tried to fix her with wax and paper pulp. She looked like hell."

Ren nodded. It was a fair assessment. "Does my face frighten you?"

The child shot him a contemptuous glare. "Nothing frightens me. You just make me angry."

"Because I took Callie away."

"Calliope. Only family calls her 'Callie.' "

"I'm family now. I'm her husband. That makes me your brother." Dear Lord, was he really admitting that out loud?

She looked as horrified as he felt. "You are not! You're . . . you're nothing—nothing but *Porter*!"

Ren let out a long breath, gazing wearily at his brand-new little sister. "Rattie and Ren, sitting in a pile of sheep shit in the middle of nowhere, in the middle of the night. If I weren't your brother, would I be here now, with you?"

She gaped at him like a fish, but it was obvious she had no proper argument to that.

He went on. "I told you that story so that you would know that you are not the first person to try to kill me. Forget about trying. It doesn't take. But my vast experience has taught me not to take certain things personally. I won't hold it against you—unless you upset Callie further with your self-important tomfoolery."

Ren stood and brushed the malodorous straw from his trousers.

"Rattie, your family is worried about you and I'm bloody sick of this hut. If I can forgive you, it stands to reason that your parents and your siblings can see their way clear to doing so, as well. So get your bony little arse up on that gluttonous gelding and let us go back to the manor. I miss Callie. I want to see that she's well." When she didn't move, he glared menacingly and pointed at the door. *"Go. Now."*

She went, grabbing up the lantern on her way out. Ren was still congratulating himself on his firm hand when she kicked his horse into a trot and left him standing next to the sheep hut, in the dark.

Worthingtons!

Chapter 35

Halfway between sleep and waking, Callie tried to roll over and stretch in her usual manner. First, she felt a nauseating agony shoot through her midriff. Second, nothing happened. She didn't move. She could feel her toes, wiggle them, hear them brush against the linens, but she had not the strength in her body to sit up.

Invalid.

She closed her eyes. "Bloody idiot doctors," she hissed to herself in the dark. "I don't believe a word of it."

She heard a creak, then a step, then the light of a candle flared. She opened her eyes to see Ren leaning over the fire. He straightened, shielding the candle glare with his hand. "Callie?"

She tried to be brave but her body screamed. A sob escaped her. He came closer and set down the candle on a side table. She watched him pick up a bottle and a spoon.

"The laudanum will ease the pain," he murmured.

She didn't like the stuff, but she couldn't bear the agony spiking through her. Opening her mouth, she took a spoonful of the sickly-sweet stuff. Forcing herself to swallow, she dug her fingers into the bedcovers, willing it to work quickly.

"I've had the strangest day," Ren said conversationally.

Callie couldn't hold back a disbelieving snort, though it made her catch her breath with pain. "Do . . . tell."

"It all started when I went for a walk this morning . . ."

As she listened to his deep voice, speaking so calmly, in such ordinary tones about her falling at his feet with a musket ball in her, about the doctor cutting the ball from her back, about his grim prediction—"but, as you and yours always say, doctors are idiots"—then, astonishingly, about her family and Attie's disappearance.

Callie stirred. "Attie's missing?"

Ren stroked her cheek reassuringly. "Attie is downstairs this very moment, ridding us all of the burden of too much cake. I would have insisted she bathe first, but I've completely lost control of my own house."

Callie frowned. The laudanum was beginning to make the world blur about the edges. "But where did she go? How did she get here?"

She listened as Ren told her a ridiculous story about Attie and a musket and a sheep shit—er, no, it was a shed. A sheep shed. She wouldn't have believed it at all—except it sounded precisely like something Attie would do. Furthermore, she'd never known Ren to exaggerate. That, apparently, was strictly a Worthington trait.

"So it was you who found her?"

Ren smoothed her grip on his hand. "It wasn't terribly hard. I just had to imagine where I would go if I were a short, female, homicidal maniac."

But Callie shushed him. "You found her and you made her come back? No one can make Attie do anything. Not without firepower."

Ren kissed her forehead. "Callie, I didn't stuff her in a sack and throw it over the back of my saddle, if that's what you're asking. In fact, I didn't bring her back. She left me there in the pasture without my horse. It would have been a bloody long walk home if Dade hadn't come back for me."

Callie smiled. "You and Dade are getting on, then?"

"Hmm. We've agreed upon a mutually distant détente. I still think he's an obnoxious prig, but having met the twins, I find myself sympathizing."

Callie snuggled her face into his palm. She was feeling deliciously warm. "Cas and Poll are so creative," she said dreamily. "Raising those two fiends was a bloody nightmare."

"You should sleep." He made as if to stand.

"No." She grabbed his hand tightly. "Talk to me. It helps."

"You should rest, Callie."

She glared at him. "One pearl, one command." She cast a glance at the little bowl on the dressing table. Six left.

His expression quizzically amused, he settled back into his seat. "Command?"

"Question," she amended. "Six pearls, six questions."

"Then will you rest?"

"Absolutely." She rather thought she wasn't to have much choice in the matter. The laudanum had seeped into her very bones, rendering them deliciously limp.

"Question number one. Who is that Simon fellow?"

He rubbed a hand over his face. "I cannot say."

"Then I shall begin for you." Callie raised a brow and recited the facts already known to her. "He is Sir Simon Raines. He found you and sent you to Amberdell, wounded and scarred, so obviously he feels some responsibility for that. His wife is Agatha Raines, who is quite concerned about my intentions toward Mr. Button."

Ren's lips twisted. "Button? Hmm."

"Sir Simon brought the Royal Handful along to the ball—"

Ren frowned. "The who?"

"Didn't you notice them? The big man, like a Viking, and those two blond beauties—Sir Simon, of course— and that hawk-faced man."

Ren drew back. "I'd heard stories . . . but—"

"And I'm beginning to think some of the hired staff weren't really servants," Callie went on. "They didn't seem the slightest bit taken aback by a flaming hell-bird in the center of the ballroom. Then again, Mama always says that ex-soldiers make the best butlers. Trial by fire, she claims."

Ren blinked. She'd put all the clues together, clues he'd been too self-involved to notice until it was almost too late.

"And I know I've seen that big cook somewhere before . . . but I fear my mind is fuzzing over . . ."

Ren put his hand over hers. "Callie, stop." What she'd deduced on her own could endanger her life! If she kept on with her questions, if the wrong party overheard—

So he told her. All of it, from the beginning when he'd been recruited at a gaming hell by an old school-mate who knew his family was gone. The training, the missions—not the specifics, of course—the feeling of being part of something larger than himself, something important.

And then, the betrayal. His covert alias had been re-vealed by someone in the club, his life traded for money, along with the lives of many others. He'd been attacked, been left for dead, his life as he knew it gone forever.

She listened with hazel eyes wide and filled with pain for him. "But . . . they could not have all betrayed you? Why do you hate them so?"

He laughed shortly, a rusty, despairing sound. "I don't hate them."

She drew back to stare at him. "Oh, my heavens. You love them! You miss them!"

A shudder went through him. "I loved them once. I cannot trust them now. I miss them. I miss myself. I lost everything that night on the docks. When I see them—" He halted, his voice too tight to continue.

"When you see them, you see young Ren Porter, whole and strong?"

He closed his eyes and bent his forehead to hers. "No, I don't see my former self. I see a hole where my former self used to be. That Ren is long dead."

She was silent for a long while—an event unusual enough to drag his attention from his own thoughts. "What are you thinking?" It was bound to be something interesting, at the very least.

"I'm wondering what that maze behind the house used to look like. Those boxwoods are very old."

Plants again. It must be the laudanum. Ren let out a laughing sigh. "They were kept in perfect precision in my old cousin's day. This park was a showplace, I think. People would come from far away for a tour of the grounds and my cousin was always proud to show it off. To me, it was a playground for a brief summer in my boyhood. I set out to solve the maze the moment I stepped from the coach. It took me weeks to memorize it. I can still remember the way, even now."

"It's a classic design, quite possibly a Batty Langley original from the mid-eighteenth century, for the boxwoods certainly look old enough." She brought her faraway gaze down and met his eyes with a smile. "And your younger self is not dead. You remember that maze as if you'd solved it yesterday."

"I remember everything, Callie." Ren brought her carefully into the circle of his arms. "At first I thought they were just nightmares. Then the shards and splinters of images began to mean something, began to knit themselves up into sense. I've lived here in the dark long enough to dream them again, awake and panicked and fighting for breath as I remember every single agonizing moment of being murdered."

She snuggled closer. "Almost murdered."

"Yes. Almost murdered."

"So tell me. Tell me every single agonizing moment. Say it out loud."

"No."

"It might help." She tilted her head to look up into his face. "I mean it, Ren. You know how it is when you tell an anecdote too many times? The first time you tell it, it is a strong memory and you seem to live it again, but then, after a while, what you remember more is the telling of it. The true memory steps back, further back every time, until you're telling a memory of a memory of a memory. It becomes simply a story."

"No."

"But why?"

"Because it is not a story for a lady's ears. Because it is past midnight. And because you are wounded and need your rest."

"But what of those men? What if they're still there in the village?"

His arms tightened. "I can face them if you stay by my side."

Her hands slid beneath his waistcoat. "I shall stay as

if glued." Then she sighed. "I do like to touch you. Especially your bottom."

She blinked slowly at his low bark of laughter. "Did I just say that out loud?"

"Yes, you did. I shall treasure it forever."

She didn't mind the amusement in his voice. She liked making him laugh.

"I like laughing with you."

She'd like to make him laugh forever. Make him laugh, make him moan, make him roar out his orgasm whilst she sucked his cock—

"Callie, you're talking in your sleep. I'd allow it, but your mother is due to take over my watch."

Mama wouldn't mind talking about orgasms.

"Well, I should mind it, very much. Why don't you think about something else?"

She liked thinking about Ren. Dear, sad, strong Ren. She loved him so.

But Ren didn't love her. He didn't believe in her at all. He thought she would leave him and she wouldn't, not ever. Not for anything or anyone. It broke her heart that he couldn't believe.

She wept softly in her sleep, warm tears dropping into Ren's palm.

She would never be able to make him believe.

A tender kiss upon her brow. *I believe, Callie. I can be a bit thick, but finally, I believe.*

And I vow, you shall never again be harmed because of me.

He'd lived a life of danger once, surviving on instinct and shrewdness. Since Callie had awoken him, he could feel it once more. It was a tickle on the back of his neck. It was a twitch between his shoulder blades.

It was a shattered ladder, a locked cellar door, a maddened horse.

Someone meant them harm.

The next morning, Ren found Dade in the stables, currying the elderly carriage horses and wearing a flowing lacy shirt from another century. Dade glanced at him ruefully. "I found in it one of the bedchambers. We didn't take time to pack when Attie was missing. I haven't anything else."

"Shut up and listen."

Dade drew back in resentment, but Ren had no time for brotherly camaraderie.

"I need you to take Callie away. Tomorrow. I'd have you go today, but I don't think she should be moved again so soon. All of you, tomorrow. Get away from here."

Dade stared at him. "Now, see here, Porter, what are you saying?"

Ren pushed Dade in the chest with both hands. "Listen to me! There have been several attempts on her life."

Dade drew a breath. "Bloody hell."

"The first came only a day after we wed . . ." The swift recounting didn't take long, but as he heard the facts about each incident leave his lips, Ren cursed himself for not believing sooner—and for needing Callie so badly that he kept her, even after he believed.

"I cannot endanger her any further. This place where you stayed the night—"

"Wincombes'. It's about twenty miles southeast on the road to London."

"Twenty miles should be far enough." Ren rubbed his face. Was it? How far-reaching was this vendetta? If it came from Ren's past, there was no place on earth that was secure. He blinked himself back to the conversation. "It will have to do. She shouldn't travel any farther."

Dade frowned. "She shouldn't travel at all! Why didn't you send her home a week ago?"

Ren ignored his question. "Do you agree? Will you take her away tomorrow?"

Dade gazed at him for a long moment. "Yes, I'll take her. If she'll go. I've tried to make her leave you again and again. She's even more stubborn than Attie. She's just quieter with it."

Ren looked down at his hands. The blood was long washed away. He could still feel it, hot and flowing. "Oh, she'll go." He turned his back on Dade and strode away. Every hour that passed was one where the assailant might muster another attack.

It was time to break Callie's heart.

Chapter 36

Ren paused outside the door of Callie's bedchamber, steeling his resolve, using it to make a cage around the pain in his chest.

It wasn't as though she'd ever been meant to stay.

Liar. All you ever wanted was for her to stay. From the first moment that you found her half naked and draped in jewels, you wanted her to haunt your nights forever.

Well, he could certainly consider that mission accomplished.

When he entered her bedchamber with a swift knock, she turned her smile to him. He hadn't expected to find her sitting up in bed, gazing at the open window, breathing deeply of the rich spring air. Though she was pale and he could see the shadows beneath her eyes, she looked much like Callie of old, thrilled beyond measure by the smallest of things.

"Isn't it wonderful?"

He almost smiled. He didn't. "What is wonderful?"

She turned back to the window and closed her eyes, lifting her face into the perfect breeze. "Everything."

You are wonderful. You are everything.

It wouldn't do to confess to her now. Not now when he most needed her to go. He had to hurt her hard. It had always been his special ability, in covert operations, his instinctive understanding of people, his ability to read them.

Now he would use his best weapon on her, to annihilate her love, to save her life.

"I suppose it is."

At his tense tone, she opened her eyes and turned her head to gaze at him quizzically. "Has something angered you?"

I'm angry, all right. I hate the world at the moment, the world and all in it who would act against us, ruining our happiness, risking your life, murdering our future.

He gazed at her calmly "My dear, it is time for you to go."

He could see the shock wash over her face. If it were possible to be paler, she would have gone entirely transparent.

"Calliope, I'll admit that we've had a lovely time together, but now that I'm no longer at death's door, there are many things I need to see to."

She reached blindly, gesturing at the vast dell that lay outside the window. "The estate? True, there is a great deal that we—"

"Not Amberdell. I'm handing stewardship over to Henry," Ren said curtly. "This was a good enough place when I was ill, but now that I'm gaining back my health, I hardly wish to molder away here any longer."

"I suppose I can understand that." She cast a last longing glance at the Cotswold countryside and then swallowed, turning resolutely away. "Very well. Where are we going?"

"Not we, I'm afraid. I. I'm being recalled to duty." He

lifted his chin. "I'm returning to the work I did before I was injured."

She frowned. "Returning . . . to become a spy?"

"Yes." He nodded shortly. "I'd prefer if you keep that little fact to yourself, of course."

She blinked. "But . . . doesn't that mean London?"

Ren shrugged. "I go where I am sent. Perhaps England, or France or Portugal. Perhaps Russia."

She leaned back upon her pillows shakily. "Russia? That's rather far."

Ren allowed a note of eagerness to enter his voice. "The farther the better. I cannot wait to leave this dismal place behind me. I feel as though I've been in prison. Now I am free, thanks to you." Ren took a deep breath and strode restlessly to the window, shutting it with a slam and whisking the curtains across it. "That's enough of that chill. I'll build up the fire for you, shall I?"

She held out a hand. "No. Wait. Ren . . . what of us? What of our . . . marriage?"

He smiled falsely. "Well, it is not as though we can annul it now, so I imagine we'll carry on much as we'd planned to from the start. You'll go back to your family and I'll carry on with my life."

"Your life."

Callie felt sick inside. Even shot, even lying in the bed, alone with her pain and her laudanum haze, even worried about Attie, underneath it all she'd been happy.

Happy in her love for him, happy in the surety that he would someday soon love her back, that he needed her. That he wanted her with him . . . forever.

Yet, she'd only known him ill. She'd only known him broken. This man, this restless, brisk fellow . . . was this the man he truly was? Was this the man he'd been before? The man who had written racy letters to his old cousin? The man who'd won the Prince Regent's regard with his bravery?

The man who had once loved someone else, someone who favored peacock-blue scarves?

Callie pressed her fingertips to her forehead, trying to force back the growing ache there, trying to force her mind to understand.

"So I am to be banished to London, to wait at Worthington House until you return?"

"Callie, I shan't be coming home for a very long while. I think my missions will be even more long-term. I can hardly skip from identity to identity as I used to. On the other hand, my superiors believe this face might come to be an advantage. A man with scars is someone people don't tend to question too closely. I rather suspect they don't want to know any more than is necessary about my past."

It all made a horrible kind of sense. He'd been very good at what he did before. At what he was. Furthermore, he'd obviously loved that life—needed the adventure, needed the danger.

More than he needed her, apparently.

What do you do when you are the one who loves more?

Do you stay, always waiting, always wondering? Always trying to earn that love, always feeling as though you'll never quite measure up? As though you must work for every scrap of attention, every shred of affection?

Would he come to resent her if she stayed, and what would she do, here on the estate? Stay and sit and wait, like an obedient hound hoping for any scrap?

The pain was enormous. It lay upon her, crushing her sweet hopes, squeezing the life from her newborn dreams. Her Worthington pride fought the tears but, weakened by her injuries, it lost the battle against the onslaught of her emotions. Tears leaked silently, spilling into her hands, running down her wrists.

Stop.

It was no use.

"I don't want to go," she whispered. "Please? I want to stay with you."

"But I am not staying. I am on my way I know not where. You can hardly follow at my heels."

Heels, like a good dog.

She didn't care. She had no pride. All that was left was pain. Inside and out, her body and her heart. The words spilled out. "Ren, I love you. Don't . . . don't make me go. Why can we not simply go on, like before?"

"Here? Not a bad place to die, love, but hardly a place to live."

He'd never called her that before, love, lightly, flippantly. Without meaning, like a Cockney grocer, trying to charm her into purchasing more apples.

The very first time he says the word and he wastes it.

The agony knotted inside her, a tangle of hurt and anger and weak, needful desperation.

He gazed at her disapprovingly. "Callie, my work is important. What I do serves England. It saves lives. Surely you don't mean to put your happiness before that?"

It was a low blow, unworthy of a man who had once considered himself fair in a fight. Yet, it didn't matter how low he sank, as long as she left him . . . and lived.

She straightened painfully, reaching for him. "Please! Ren, I cannot bear it. I cannot! *Please* tell me that you don't mean it! Tell me that you want me to stay, that you want to stay with me . . ."

She dashed the tears from her eyes and looked up at him. She'd once thought him terrifying, then she'd found him beautiful.

Now she knew the true meaning of terror, for he only shook his head with a frown. "Calliope, you'll strain yourself. Let me tuck you back in. I'll send your mother in, shall I? You'll need help to pack anyway. I think it's best to send you home with them tomorrow."

So soon. So sudden.

He lifted her back to rest upon her pillows and tucked her in with considerate hands. She clung to them, wrapping her icy fingers tight, but they were not the hands she knew. Not the hands of a lover. Not the touch of a husband. Just . . . not unkind.

"Pack," she said dully.

Ren ached from head to foot to see her thus.

But alive. Away from him, she would live. Away from him, she would regain her vibrant Callie-ness.

Away from him, but alive.

So he made sure of it. He reached into his weskit pocket to offer her his handkerchief. Something dropped from the carefully folded linen, landing on the coverlet nearly in her lap.

When he was sure her gaze had fixed upon the small gold circle, mounted with a sapphire surrounded by emeralds, he made a wild snatch for the ring. Looking away from her, he tucked it back into his pocket with an appearance of studied nonchalance.

He knew she'd found the ring, along with the medal, long ago. He knew the way her mind worked, how she put clues together. He knew she would have imagined the woman who'd been meant to have the ring.

By the devastated depths of her hazel eyes, he knew he'd accomplished another mission. The life had fled her eyes, her sweet face. Even her body seemed slack and dull.

Drive in another blade? *Why do if you can overdo?* He cleared his throat, making his voice persuasive. "I suppose I have enough pull with the government to have the church grant you a divorce, if that makes you happier."

"Divorce." She blinked down at her hands, limp and shaking in her lap. "I don't . . ."

"Well, as you wish. Write to Henry if you change your mind. I'll be checking in with him every six months or so."

"Yes. All right." She looked away then. "I'm tired. I think I'd like to rest now."

"Good idea. You may pack this evening." Finally he weakened. "Would you like for me to open the window again?"

She closed her eyes. "No, thank you," she whispered. "There is nothing out there I wish to see . . . now."

Chapter 37

The next morning, the Worthingtons prepared to depart forever. Callie tolerated her mother's fluttering and Attie's lack of concentration only because Elektra devoted herself to the preservation and packing of Callie's Lementeur collection.

Callie had nothing to do but rest and watch. Then Attie found the folio of botanical drawings in Callie's drawer.

"What is this?" She peered closely at the genus and species penciled below each specimen. "Are any of these poisonous?"

"Attie, don't poke through everything!" Elektra scolded. She took it from Attie and absently handed it to Callie.

Callie gazed at the leather-bound folio. "Don't bother packing this. I won't be needing it." It wasn't likely she would ever have time for such things again . . . even if she could someday bear to open the parcel full of painful memory. She didn't want to take this place with her . . . these hills, these flowers, these beautiful days and wildly exciting nights . . .

Quickly shutting the folio, she slid it away from her across the counterpane. No. When she shut the door of Amberdell behind her, she wanted no reminders packed with her.

Elektra gathered up what she could carry, directed the twins to lug down what she couldn't—for she was taking every stitch of clothing Mr. Button had provided. Elektra was beyond thrilled to have a Lementeur original and what couldn't be made to fit could be sold for enough coin to keep the household going for many months.

She'd earned every bit of it, in the end, Callie thought with weary resignation.

Her hopes of making a swift and private exit were of course foiled by the usual madness involved in getting the Worthington clan on the road. Attie's bonnet could not be found, then Iris wandered away, only to be found speaking cordially to one of the portraits in the gallery. When Callie, leaning weakly on Lysander, her nerves worn to shaking by her need to be far, far away, watched as Dade wedged her mother between her sisters in the family's shabby carriage, she turned around to discover that Ren had decided to see her off after all.

Bloody hell. There he stood, just as she'd longed to see him, bareheaded in the sunlight, the scars on his face visible yet made less important by the new dignity in his bearing. The man before her was no lurking gargoyle. He was a hero, a knight, the true master of his house, not its inmate.

With all her heart, she wished him to remain so. Truly.

Ren knew that he was dooming himself, sending away this last chance at happiness. He approached her, not shying from the devastation in her eyes.

"You've forgotten something." He held up the strand of pearls she'd strung a few days earlier.

She flinched but then bent her head, allowing him to fasten it around her neck. If his fingers lingered slightly, drifting through the curling strands of hair at the back of her neck, it was only because he fought the urge to drag her back into the house and lock out the world forever.

She did not seem to notice the crack in his façade. She scarcely looked at him at all.

Her brothers helped her into the second carriage, supplied by Amberdell, where she would ride behind with Dade whilst tucked into a nest of cushions, free of the strain of her family's antics.

As the carriages pulled out of the drive, the rickety Worthington conveyance first, followed by the better-sprung vehicle, silence once more descended upon Amberdell.

Ren went back into his house, his beautiful, homey, comfortable, empty manor . . . and he could not bear it.

He found himself wandering the halls. He stood in the center of the empty ballroom, which still reeked of smoke and disaster, and listened to the faint tinkling of the crystalline chandeliers swaying above him.

He walked through the dining room, trailing his fingertips along the great table, recalling the bouncing of dozens of pearls on the polished surface.

He stood before the fire in the library, gazing at the crossed swords displayed above it.

And finally, he opened the door to Callie's bedchamber. He closed his eyes and breathed, still able to detect the faint bouquet of rosemary and girl and wildflowers. He walked around her bed, gazing at the pillow that still contained the impression of her head.

His foot struck something. Looking down, he bent to retrieve the leather folio that lay discarded there.

Unwinding the string closure, he opened it upon a riot of Cotswold springtime.

She'd left it. Forgotten? He knew her better than that. Like a creature gnawing off a limb to escape a trap, she had been forced to leave a piece of herself behind.

He closed the folio carefully and rewound the closure. Then he reverently placed the folio upon her dressing table and left the room.

As he descended the stairs, his steps quickened. By the time he'd reached the front entrance, he was running.

Running from the empty spaces where Callie was not.

On the journey, Dade watched Callie, regretting his selfishness now. She lay pale and wan upon her nest of cushions, a shell of her former brisk self.

Callie of the tidying hands and the managing ways. He'd never realized she possessed such a romantic heart, a heart to be so thoroughly broken by a stranger in less than a fortnight.

He wondered if he'd ever really known his sister at all.

They rode in silence broken only by the creaking of the slow-rolling cartwheels and the faint gasps of pain Callie could not suppress when a pothole was found in the road.

The family had long since disappeared in the road ahead, not even a wisp of dust in the air to mark their passing.

The pace was unbearably slow, yet Callie felt panicked, unsteady, as if they raced away . . . away from Ren.

She felt as though an ever-tightening strand of some kind bound her to Amberdell, to him, and with every revolution of the carriage wheels, that strand became more attenuated, until it was no stronger than a thought, no more permanent than a memory. She fought for breath against the ache in her body, against the ever-tightening bands of heartbreak that threatened to cut off her air entirely . . .

Callie became aware that Dade was speaking . . . something about ". . . glad to have you take Ellie's spending in hand."

"I am not your housekeeper, Dade." She said it without rancor . . . as if, in fact, it was something she had just realized herself. She looked at him.

Dade frowned at her. "I know you aren't. You could have a house of your own. You're Mrs. Porter now—"

"Lady Porter, in fact." Good God, was that pride in her tone? Still, in the end, was she proud to be his distant and rejected wife?

"Well." Dade shifted uncomfortably. "According to him—"

She shot him a look that completely lacked patience. "It isn't some tale he made up. I found the documents, the honors, the medals, the letter of knighthood from the Prince Regent." *Signed "Geo."* "He has too many memories bound up in it, that's all."

Dade's gaze widened. "Then the scars—"

"Every one earned in service to the Crown."

Dade pursed his lips and nodded. "The war. I should have realized . . ."

"You didn't want to." Callie looked out the window. "You wanted to paint him a beast for compromising me, for staining *your* honor." Uttering a dark laugh, she shook her head. "I think it's high time you realized that I wasn't precisely fighting him off."

Dade looked away. "You're my sister. I am responsible for you."

"Actually, since he was my eldest male relative on the premises, I think Papa was the one responsible for me."

Dade didn't quite roll his eyes. Quite. "Well, but . . ."

Callie hadn't the will or desire to be patient with Dade's bigotry any longer. "You weren't interested in him at all, other than to wave a pistol at him. You knew nothing at all about the man behind the scars."

"A point I made when you proposed to stay with him."

"You've made of him an enemy, and because of your ridiculous male posturing, I am shot, Attie is devastated, and Ren . . . Ren is gone forever."

Dade looked down. "I didn't know you blamed me so entirely."

Callie let out a breath, fighting against the urge to weep for the deepening void in her chest where her heart once beat. "Dade, you are not my father. You are not anyone's father. You are just a man, hardly older than myself, with too many responsibilities and not enough nerve to throw them back upon the shoulders to which they belong." She gazed ahead at the empty road their parents' carriage had taken before them. "Why should Papa take responsibility, when he doesn't have to? Why should Mama bother to take note of Attie's confusion or Ellie's vanity"—*or my desperation!*—"when I have borne the weight of it for her all these years?"

"It isn't as though they will ever change," Dade said tightly. "Not at their age."

Callie closed her eyes and leaned carefully back onto the tufted cushions. "How will we know . . . unless we step away from the task ourselves?"

"Nevertheless," Dade went on, his tone stubborn. "It is good that you return with us. You belong with your family."

"Until the day I die? Am I to have nothing of my own? And what of you, Dade? Have you sentenced yourself to life without parole, as well, or have you decided that is to be my fate alone?"

He was silent then. Callie lapsed back into her unhappy thoughts, trying very hard not to let the memories wash over her. It was too painful to have thoughts of that girl, too wrenching to remember the passion and the joy—and to know that, for Ren at least, it had not been made of love.

Chapter 38

Ren was not long upon the lane when he saw ahead of him a trim little pony cart lacquered in deep green with shining brasses, pulled by a pair of perfectly matched ebony ponies.

He pulled up his mount and gazed at the driver with loathing. "You."

Button gazed levelly back. "I've been waiting for you. I believe we have matters to discuss."

"I want nothing to do with the lot of you," Ren said with a snarl. "You couldn't allow me to have a single moment of my own. I would be careful if I were you."

"Nonetheless, there is more here than you realize."

Ren fought back the urge to dismember and reassemble. Callie wouldn't want him to harm Button. Then again, Callie was gone. "You joined after my time, so you don't know. I was like you once. I believed. And then I found myself stabbed in the back, quite literally, by the very brotherhood I so cherished. So step carefully, little man. They can be brutal to those who love them best." He kicked his mount onward at a trot.

"It wasn't the Liars who tried to harm her!"

It was a lie, of course. That was what the Liars did best, wasn't it? Still, Ren halted and reined his mount to face the pony cart. "Explain."

"I mean that it was not we who broke the ladder and jammed shut the cellar and shot her mount from beneath her. I came here at the behest of a dear friend. The others came for the ball, and to be sure you were not being hoodwinked by a seductress."

Ren narrowed his eyes. "Kurt was here all along. I spotted him myself."

Button smiled. "Then he wanted you to see him."

"Firstly, there have been three attempts on her life—not to mention other mischief against her." Ren walked his mount back slowly. "Secondly, I have no quarrel with anyone here in Amberdell. Thirdly, the Liars' foremost assassin showed up to cook for my wife's ball. You expect me to believe that the Liars had nothing to do with all this?"

Button lifted his chin and matched Ren's gaze, most definitely damaging Ren's ability to loom. "Believe your own knowledge, then," Button said. "When has anyone ever escaped three attempts at assassination by the Liars Club?"

Oh, God. It was so obvious. Ren felt the fool for not realizing it before. If Kurt had truly been assigned to dispose of Callie, she would not have lived out the day. "But . . . if not the Liars, then who?"

Button regarded him with friendly pity. "Who stands to gain if you die alone?"

Who, indeed? Ren's gut went cold. Without another word, he turned his mount toward Springdell and answers.

Betrice folded her gray silk gown carefully in fresh rice paper and laid it to store in her best trunk. For a moment, she allowed herself to imagine that it was a fine Lementeur gown . . .

Not for her the fine style and exquisite fit of such a gown.

Which was no more than she deserved.

Callie was gone. Henry had told her over breakfast that he'd helped Lawrence fit out a carriage specifically to carry Callie away.

Permanently.

Betrice shut the trunk carefully. She didn't have many fine things, but this pretty enameled dress box had once belonged to the former lady of Amberdell, and had been a gift from her to Betrice's mother.

From Amberdell comes everything worthy.

And from Springdell comes nothing but lies and trickery.

Perhaps it was guilt from ruining the ball, or fear that Lawrence would take the doctor's words to heart and search for the culprit among the local people, but Betrice had decided in the early hours of the morning that she was done.

It was over in any event. Callie, though gone, would be the lady of Amberdell until the day she died. Lawrence meant to run the estate himself, as he'd informed Henry this morning—although Henry was supposed to keep that fact to himself for some reason that Lawrence refused to explain.

There was nothing for Betrice to aim for, no target to shoot, no mischief to do that would change that. Although for her entire life she had played by the rules—the endless, suffocating rules of ladylike behavior—it was a ridiculous quiz of a girl who took the seat out from under her.

In retrospect, Betrice was quite appalled at the lengths she'd gone to in her obsession. Pushing over Callie's ladder and then ducking back around the corner of the house—that had been the impulse of a moment. Shutting the cellar door and wedging the chunk of wood to keep it closed had been no more than a childish prank, the sort of thing village boys did to their friends.

Lending the skittish Lucy had been worse and fiddling the truth about her riderless return yet more so.

Pulling the brass linchpin—that had been truly appalling. Yet how could she have known the thing's death spiral would be truly dangerous? She'd thought it simply wouldn't work, that the guests—who up until that point had thought the new lady of Amberdell was dipped in gold!—would go home remembering the disappointment instead of the triumph.

That Callie's own family was also working against her—that the illness given the village and the shooting on the hillside were caused by a twelve-year-old girl had given Betrice the most pause of all. Was that what she herself had become in her envy? A dangerous child?

Well, no more. No more plotting or scheming. Yet, she did not think she would revert to her old ways, either. Sometimes, just once in a while, mind you, she might actually give in to a natural laugh.

She put away the gown trunk and went to the kitchen to prepare a hearty luncheon for Henry. He could easily eat the same meals as the laborers, but Betrice had always liked to keep up appearances. The master should not rub elbows too consistently with the dependents.

As she reached high up to lift a cheese down from a shelf in the larder, she heard a heavy tread behind her.

"Could you fetch this cheese, dear?"

Thick fingers reached past hers, wrapping around the heavy cheese and lifting it in one hand.

It was not her husband's hand.

Betrice gasped and whirled to find herself cornered in the larder by the massive form of Unwin.

"Oh! What are you doing in my house? Get out—please."

He loomed over her, his wide shoulders clad in rough linen blocking her view of anything else. Betrice swallowed and forced a cool smile. "A gentleman would call properly," she admonished him evenly.

"Like your husband? Like that ugly Sir Lawrence? You might've noticed, I ain't like them."

Betrice tried to sidle around him. "Unwin, this is inappropriate. You cannot invade my house—"

Her progress was halted by his wide hand wrapping about her upper arm. The breath hissed out between her teeth at the tightness of his grip.

"I did it. I got her to leave. I did it for you."

She stared up at him. "You shot her horse out from under her that day by the river, didn't you?"

He smiled. "She fell like a sack of potatoes. I thought she might be dead." He laughed darkly.

Dead. She pushed at him, at his great immovable chest, at his hand like an iron around her arm. "Unwin, stop. It's over. She's gone . . . and anyway, it's too late. He cannot have the marriage annulled. They've consummated their union. She might be carrying his heir even now—"

He went very still. Betrice panicked. What had she said? What—

Oh, no. "No!"

His gaze was thoughtful. "I'm thinkin' you had the right idea, tryin' to rid us of that woman. She made everyone sick, and she took your rightful place—just like Henry took mine."

Betrice blinked. "What? Henry is my husband!"

Unwin moved in closer until Betrice could smell the sweat on him and the scent of horses. His eyes, a cool, pale blue, held a light of something she only now realized was the lunacy of obsession.

She hadn't seen it. She'd only thought of her own injured pride, her own dismay at the arrival of the new lady of Amberdell and the loss of all her secret dreams. She'd basked in Unwin's regard and told herself that she was doing nothing improper, that merely confiding in a friend was not betrayal—

And she'd completely missed the fact that Unwin had fixed his gaze on her—the fact that, apparently, he'd never taken his eyes off her all these years.

A man who did that, a man who continued to dream of a woman so far out of his reach, was a man living in a mad world of his very own.

A man who wished to take her husband's place.

"She's on the road back to where she come from," he said thoughtfully. Betrice could almost hear the mad gears clicking away in his tainted mind. He smiled sweetly at her, insanity alight in his gaze. "There, you see? It's not too late at all."

Ren halted his mount before the wide, welcoming doors of the Springdell farmhouse and leaped easily to the ground. He had questions for Henry, by God—

There, in the soft soil just before his boots, was the hoofprint of a very large horse.

A very large horse with a crack in its right fore.

Something is not right here.

He let himself in, for Springdell had a dearth of staff. Normally, he'd call out, hat in hand like any visitor, but today his business was too pressing for such niceties. He strode into the parlor in search of Henry, and found Betrice instead, standing at the window, twisting her hands into knots.

She started at his entrance, her hands flying to her throat. "L—Lawrence!"

It was all there in her face, quite frankly. She stood pale and shaking, riddled with guilt and self-loathing.

As expert as he was in such things, he knew immediately.

She swallowed and took a step forward, though he knew he frightened her at the best of times.

"L-Lawrence, I think I ought to tell you something . . ."

Chapter 39

Ren had never ridden so hard nor so recklessly in his life. His horse, relatively fresh yet, devoured the road with the long strides of a Thoroughbred.

The carriage had been moving slowly due to Callie's injuries. The mathematics unfolded in his head, a remnant of training he'd not even known he'd retained.

Everything I have gained back, I would happily expend in defense of her.

If Unwin had left when Betrice claimed, he ought to have caught the party somewhere just ahead.

He topped a hill and saw the Amberdell carriage pulled half into the ditch, the horses taking the opportunity to graze in the high spring grass.

One man lay in the middle of the road. Ren dismounted and knelt beside him. The driver was unconscious, but breathing easily. Ren could only find a single lump on his skull.

Downed with one blow. Useless sod. Then again, the man had not been hired as bodyguard.

Rising, Ren cast about for some sign of Dade. He found Callie's brother draped across the traces, just behind the team's hindquarters. He pulled Dade free, half carrying him to the grassy road bank.

Upon swift examination, Ren found that Dade had made somewhat better account of himself than the hapless driver. Dade had numerous bruises on his face and his own knuckles were like raw meat.

Somewhere in the back of his mind, he recalled being struck down by those very fists not so long ago. Dade knew how to hurt a fellow, all right. Good for him.

It took a few precious moments to rouse him, but Ren knew that Callie would want her brother seen to, no matter what, so he gritted his teeth against the panic and slapped Dade back into consciousness with gentle patience.

Dade opened his eyes at last. To his credit, his first thought was of his sister. "Porter, the bastard took her!"

Ren nodded grimly. "I know. Can I leave you here to see to the driver? I need to—"

"Go!" Dade sat up and waved him on urgently, holding his aching head together with his other hand. "I only wish I knew which way he's headed."

Ren looked down at the hoofprints in the soft mud of the road. "I do."

Powerful hoofbeats thundered down the road. A man planting his crops nearly a mile away lifted his head with a frown, wondering where anyone would need to go in such a desperate hurry.

Ren bent low over his mount's neck, the reins easy yet urgent, his heels spurring the horse on whenever its pace began to slow even slightly.

He might not be the man he used to be, but he could still ride with the best of them.

Callie had given him that.

Along with everything else he valued.

Was she frightened? She must be—even she wasn't insane enough to mistake the danger she was in. He couldn't think about what Unwin might do to her. God, even being thrown onto the back of a horse must be agonizing for her!

Ren shoved his fears down deep and urged the horse faster.

Callie tried to keep her balance on the back of the plowhorse. She truly did not wish to clutch at the man riding before her, but the big horse's gait was rough and it was all she could do to keep from being bounced off onto the hard road.

Oh, just fall. It wouldn't be the first time you've taken a spill.

But it was a long way down. Her legs had long ago gone numb. She would not be able to catch herself, land properly. No, she would thud to the earth like a sack of flour. An image of her insides bursting out and coating all and sundry in brick-red dust crossed her mind.

Attie would understand the joke. Callie didn't bother relaying her slightly insane thoughts to her captor.

Then again, it might make him fear her . . . if he weren't quite so big, or quite so angry, or quite so certain that something was all her fault.

Of course, lately it seemed like everything was.

Don't waste time on melancholy! Think!

Well, why shouldn't she be melancholy? She was going to die soon, wasn't she? Another jolting bounce made her injured back spasm with agony, stealing her breath, sending lightning bolts of pain through her entire body.

If she could spare a hand to press to her lower spine, she knew she would find her gown wet with blood. The idiot's rough handling had opened her wound.

That doctor is going to be quite upset when I die despite his fine work.

Dizziness swept her, followed by a wave of fear. Perhaps it was more blood . . . than she'd thought.

No, stay angry.

By God, if he didn't kill her soon she was going to take matters into her own hands!

He was mad, that was all. A strange madman had assaulted the carriage for absolutely no reason, possibly killing the hired driver and most definitely injuring Dade, and had thrown her across the back of his twice-damned horse—well, she supposed it wasn't the blasted horse's fault, but still!—and galloped away across the countryside!

Mad, definitely.

Dade would follow—except that he'd lain limp and still until she could see him no more in her desperate gaze. Papa and Lysander and Orion and the twins—no, they'd not even realize something was wrong until she and Dade failed to arrive at the prearranged stop this evening.

Hours until someone thought to look for them.

Hours until someone saw to Dade's injury.

Hours until anyone realized that she was in the hands of a mad brute who hadn't said a single word to her, hadn't done more than grunt with exertion as he beat Dade to the ground, hadn't even met her terrified gaze when he'd dragged her off to his horse.

That was perhaps the most chilling thing of all.

Whatever his purpose, whatever his motive, it was quite clear to Callie that she was not a person to this man.

She was an . . . an obstacle.

He didn't look like the sort of fellow who would tolerate an obstacle for long.

* * *

Ren felt the chase coming to close. He didn't bother to interpret the signs: the hoofprints still damp in the soil of the road, the freshness of the twig snapped and fallen to the ground, the droppings that had yet to attract a single fly.

These facts were noted and acknowledged and filed away with the practice of years. All Ren knew was that he had finally caught the bastard.

What remained to be seen was whether or not he'd caught up in time.

Callie felt the horse slow, its pace faltering no matter how much her captor dug in his heels. If she were healthy, she could leap off now, slide right off the draft horse's rump and dash away into the hedges.

If she were able, uninjured, her legs not cold and dead, her torso not leaking, her shaking, weak hands not too numb to do more than to knot themselves in her captor's rough coat.

Escape wasn't possible. It was all she could do to keep breathing in and out and keeping at bay the gray fog that threatened to close over her vision.

When the big horse finally stopped, it lowered its head and blew great gusts of weariness, ignoring the man who howled and beat at the thick neck with his fists. His elbow swung back in his tantrum, catching Callie across the jaw.

Well, that did it, she thought distantly as she began to slide.

She was unconscious before she hit the ground. This was possibly a fortunate thing.

Ren could hear the man before he saw him. The fellow's obscene howling curses filled the dell with his rage, masking even Ren's hell-bent approach.

Ren rounded a curve in the road and took in the scene an instant—the blown horse, foaming with sweat, the thick man beating at it . . . and the still, limp form of Callie dropped in the dust of the road like a broken doll.

Ren thought he'd been angry before. He thought he knew rage.

He'd never experienced the black tidal wave of murderous intent that rose in him then. He was off his mount while still at a gallop. The big black horse ran past Unwin and Ren dropped upon the man like an avenging demon. Unwin outweighed him by more than two stone and topped him by nearly a foot.

Within minutes, Ren had beaten the fellow unconscious with nothing but his bare fists and his bottomless fury.

Running to Callie, he dropped to his knees beside her. So still, as limp as death. She lay awkwardly, sprawled painfully as if thrown from a great height.

Ren straightened her limbs gently. "Callie?" he coaxed. He smoothed her gown. He pressed his palm to her wound, holding back the blood. *Callie. Callie.*

He screamed her name. It came out in a whisper. No amount of noise would call her back if she'd gone too far from him.

Callie. She blurred in his vision. He took her hands and pressed her palms to his cheeks. *Callie.*

He didn't realize that Dade was there until he knelt across from him, taking one of his sister's hands from Ren.

"Callie?"

Too loud, Ren wanted to say. *You'll frighten her off.*

His own insanity failed to dismay him. His entire existence as a human man lay in the balance. If she woke, he would remember how to walk and talk and think. If she didn't, then he would let the beast take him and never attempt to rise to the surface again.

He gazed down into her still, pale face. "Wake up, Callie," he whispered.

A part of him was aware of the driver, with a rag wrapped around his bleeding head, poking at the fallen Unwin with a booted toe. "What'd ye hit 'im with?"

Ren didn't respond.

Callie.

"He hit him with his hands." Dade looked up, his voice choked with anger and worry. "I saw it. I rode up just as he finally let him drop. Is he dead?"

The driver grunted. "No. Not so much bein' alive, as not all the way dead."

Dade's hand tightened on Callie's. "Pity. It was a capital beating. I've never seen the like."

The driver grunted. "Well, Sir's an Amberdell man, ain't he?"

Ren reached out and reclaimed that hand. Dade was being too rough, too loud. The ground was too hard, too cold. Ren took Callie into his arms, across his lap, cradling her so gently, so carefully. *Callie.*

Dade took over, pressing his folded handkerchief to stem the blood.

Ren pressed his cheek to her cool one. *Callie.*

He kissed her forehead, her eyes, the tip of her nose. *I cannot lose you. Callie.*

He called her again and again, his voice hardly more than air on her ear. *Callie.*

She warmed in his careful, sheltered hold. Her cheeks changed from chill marble to a softer pale pink. He thought he saw her chest rise higher, her breath deepen.

Callie. I need you.

She stirred at last, just a flutter of her eyelids, a parting of her lips.

Come on. Come closer.

Come back.

I love you.

At last, her eyes opened. She gazed up at him, unfocused and confused.

Ren held his breath. She blinked and scowled slightly. Then she swallowed.

"Did you kill him?" Her voice was just a rasp.

Ren's voice stopped working. Dade answered for him. "No."

Callie closed her eyes. "Pity." She opened them again, gazing up at Ren with some urgency. "The horse—not his fault—"

Ren blinked rapidly. Callie, two steps from death herself, yet worried about the damned horse.

He thought he might perhaps remain a man after all, just to see what she'd say next.

She focused on his face with some effort, then frowned again. "Why did you come after me?"

Because I cannot breathe without you near me. "I learned the culprit at last," he explained awkwardly. "This fellow is obsessed with Henry's wife, Betrice. He felt you took her rightful place as lady of Amberdell. He meant to remove you from that place."

"So . . . you removed me instead?"

"I . . ." In truth, he had. "That isn't . . ." He shook his head quickly. "I wanted you out of harm's way. But it is over. We can go home now."

She drew back slightly. "What of what you said before—your old life?"

"Life?" He dropped his face into her hair. "I never took a true breath until I met you."

"But . . . all those things you said. It would be selfish of me to keep you home."

"I lied. I only wanted you safely away. My old . . .

friends wouldn't allow me back, nor would I go back. I've found something new to believe in, you see."

She gazed at him with shadows of doubt in her eyes. "The ring?"

He nearly wept. "A trick. That girl left me with my scars and my pride in tatters, but I never loved her. I never loved anyone until I loved you." He cursed his own talent for finding weakness, for nurturing uncertainty. How could he convince her now that he'd meant not a word of it?

He wrapped his hands around both of hers and gazed into her eyes, willing her to believe. "Calliope Worthington Porter, I vow to you that I will hire servants, and tend my lands and look after my people and look after you and protect you from flaming birds and madmen and musket balls and rickety ladders—"

"And asps."

"And asps. Most of all from serpents of all kinds." He pressed her hands to his cheek. "If I do all that, will you come home with me?"

She pulled her hands away slowly, her small fingers slipping away from him. He did not tighten his grasp. If she didn't wish to be his lady, he would not force her to be.

His heart shivered in the growing chill. Though it was only early evening, he saw the world darken. The beast stirred, sure of its triumph.

Her hands fell from his. She pulled them away, drawing them up toward her throat.

What a fool I am. She doesn't want me. She shouldn't want me. There is no place in her light for a man of shadows.

Her fingers scrabbled nervously at her neckline. Ren blinked at what she pulled out, twined about her fingers.

"What—"

With a weak but determined yank, Callie broke the strand of pearls that he himself had fastened about her neck that morning. Ren watched without comprehension until she raised her dampened gaze to meet his.

As the pearls spilled down over the two of them, she gave him a bruised, rueful smile. "It seems we shall have to start over," she said softly.

The joy in Ren's heart burst through the last remaining shreds of darkness, burning away the beast forever.

He grinned down at his valiant, irrepressible, unsinkable Callie. "Yes," he breathed. "No rules this time."

She shook her head. "Just one. Say it again. Say it every day. Forever."

He pulled her close, as gently as he would hold an injured bird. "I love you, Calliope Worthington Porter. I shall love you until the day I die."

"And after that?"

He took a deep breath of her hair. "After that I shall simply have to love you forever."

Epilogue

"Darling, have you seen my paintbrush? I've just collected my first specimens of the spring and I cannot find it anywhere!"

Ren looked up from the estate ledgers on his desk and smiled at his lovely bride, who stood in the doorway of his study looking slightly exasperated. A perfect strand of pearls gleamed against her throat. Should he tell her that she'd used the brush as a hairpin again? Yes, he should, but before he did so, he wanted to fill his gaze with her wide, inquiring eyes and his hands with the rich honey fall of her hair when he pulled out the paintbrush.

He moved his chair back. She flowed into his lap without further urging. One of them was well trained. A year into their marriage and he still hadn't figured out which one.

His hands moved over her back, digging gently into the muscles that still pained her when she was weary. They both had their scars. She purred and fitted herself more snugly into him.

Yes. It was time to admit that he did know who was well trained.

"It's our anniversary," she mused aloud. "I think it most unfair of you to survey the estate books on our anniversary."

He smiled. "Our anniversary is tomorrow. As in, tomorrow your family descends upon Amberdell, bringing chaos, mayhem, and disorder." Or, in his mind, Cas, Poll, and Attie, respectively.

Callie kissed his neck. "Today, as in, today is your last chance to roger me on the dining table for our wedding anniversary."

His eyes crossed with lust. He began to kiss down her neck, down to her lush and lovely bosom. Pink nipples for elevenses . . .

Wait. No. There was something he meant to do first . . .

He sat up and pushed her regretfully off his lap. "I'm afraid I'm terribly busy. In fact, if you might assist me, I shall reward you by telling you where your paintbrush is."

Disgruntled by his rejection, Callie folded her arms and tapped her toe.

Ren busied himself with his paperwork. "There is a volume on the mantel over the fire." He gestured vaguely at the hearth. "If you wouldn't mind . . ."

He heard her heave a sigh and stomp across the study. He waited. Calliope Worthington Porter had never met a book she didn't like. He knew she'd not be able to resist reading the title . . .

She gasped.

And the author.

He looked up at last to find her clutching the volume and blinking at the spine. Then she opened the book and flipped to the title page with shaking fingers.

"Wildflowers of the Cotswolds," she read in a whisper. "By Calliope, Lady Porter."

She sank down into one of the fireside chairs without looking, her rapt gaze on the pages and pages of color plates, each gorgeously depicting a Calliope Porter original botanical drawing.

"I believe there's a dedication," Ren said mildly.

She gazed at him with wide eyes, then looked back down to find it.

"'When daisies pied and violets blue,'" she read aloud, "'And lady-smocks all silver-white,

And cuckoo-buds of yellow hue

Do paint the meadows with delight.'"

Ren smiled slightly. *"Love's Labours Lost,"* he announced. "Act five, scene two."

She blinked and shook her head. "How—but you haven't left the estate in months! However did you manage this?"

He leaned back in his chair, well pleased with himself, treasuring her dumbfounded joy. "Button, of course, with a bit of help from your mother. They worked rather brilliantly together, actually. I am much impressed."

Callie blinked, clearly arrested by some errant thought.

"What is it?"

She shook her head. "No . . . it's just a silly notion." She shook her head again. "There is more than one theater in London, after all," she said to herself. "They might never have met in those days . . ."

Ren frowned. "Iris and Button? I suppose they might have—"

He had that feeling, the woozy sensation of being a mere cog in some greater machine. The connection slid into place. "Callie," he said slowly, "on the night the bridge washed out—where were you four going?"

Callie shook her head, the ghost of a smile lingering on her lips. "Mama wouldn't tell me. It was meant to be a surprise."

Just as he'd suspected. Slowly, Ren leaned forward and slid the paintbrush from her hair. As the wealth of silken waves fell into his hands, he smiled. "Happy anniversary . . . to me."

She plucked the paintbrush from his fingers. "Meet you in the dining room." She gave him a sultry look. "Don't forget to bring your sword."